Infinity

A SUSPENSE MAGAZINE ANTHOLOGY

INFINITY

A *SUSPENSE MAGAZINE* ANTHOLOGY

EDITED BY CATHERINE COULTER

KELLEY ARMSTRONG
ALLISON BRENNAN
J.T. ELLISON
JAMIE FREVELETTI
K.J. HOWE
DARYNDA JONES
SHANNON KIRK
TOSCA LEE
SHEILA LOWE
ISABELLA MALDONADO
SUSAN SANTANGELO
SUSAN WINGATE
DARYL WOOD GERBER

SUSPENSE PUBLISHING

INFINITY
COPYRIGHT
© 2023 Suspense Publishing, LLC.

PAPERBACK EDITION
* * * * *

PUBLISHED BY:
Suspense Publishing
Paperback and Digital Copy, March 2023

ISBN: 979-8-218-08368-7

"Introduction" Copyright © 2023 by Catherine Coulter
"The Joy of Wrong Numbers" Copyright © 2023 by Kelley Armstrong
"911" Copyright © 2023 by Allison Brennan
"Louche 49" Copyright © 2023 by J.T. Ellison
"The Disappearing Place" Copyright © 2023 by Jamie Freveletti
"Under Pressure" Copyright © 2023 by K.J. Howe
"Seven Minutes in Heaven" Copyright © 2023 by Darynda Jones
"Eight Years and Seven Secrets at Ten Stacks" Copyright © 2023 by Shannon
Kirk
"The Cancun Game" Copyright © 2023 by Tosca Lee
"Poniatowa" Copyright © 2023 by Sheila Lowe
"I've Got Your Number" Copyright © 2023 by Isabella Maldonado
"Masquerades Can Be Murder" Copyright © 2023 by Susan Santangelo
"Three Minutes Past Midnight" Copyright © 2023 by Susan Wingate
"Justice is Served" Copyright © 2023 by Daryl Wood Gerber

Cover Design: Shannon Raab
Cover Photographer: Phil Lewis /iStock

Library of Congress Cataloging-in-Publication Data

DEDICATION

For Amy Lignor
You are missed.

PRAISE

"*Infinity: A Suspense Magazine Anthology* features a host of notable writers, from Susan Wingate and Tosca Lee to K.J. Howe, and provides an adventure-oriented thriller collection that excels in the unexpected.

"Thriller readers usually don't receive laugh-out-loud moments. Nor does the genre typically embrace a broad spectrum of age ranges in its protagonists, or perspectives laced with the bite of irony and unusually poetic inspections. All these facets and more support a diverse selection that travels time, space, and the suspense genre to pick out those gems that truly stand out from the crowd. Each story is unique. In a genre replete with formula writing and often-predictable results, it's refreshing to find a gem of unpredictability and diversity. Such is *Infinity*.

"Libraries looking for short story thriller collections that stand out from the ordinary with writers who each craft very different visions of suspense, horror, and the intersection of thriller and life endeavors will find much to relish in *Infinity*, which should be held up as an example of truly creative thriller writing."
—D. Donovan, Sr. Reviewer, *Midwest Book Review*

"In *Infinity: A Suspense Magazine Anthology*, legendary author Catherine Coulter has compiled an addictive collection of short stories that will grip you until the last thrilling page."
—Ellen Byron, Agatha Award-Winning and Bestselling Author

"As I read through the tales to be found in *Infinity*, the second short story anthology from Suspense Publishing, I recalled what Forrest Gump's mama told him about life being like a box of chocolates; you never know what you're going to get. Read it from beginning to end, or pick a story at random, and either way you'll get to sample a tasty confection of murder, mayhem, ghosts, sleuths and avengers penned by some of the finest writers in the country and edited by bestselling suspense writer Catherine Coulter. And if your sweet tooth still isn't satisfied, go back and read the equally enjoyable anthology, *Nothing Good Happens After Midnight*."

—Paul Kemprecos, *#1 New York Times* Bestselling Author

"*Suspense Magazine*'s anthology, *Infinity* is a stellar contribution to the growing number of crime anthologies on the market today. Edited by Catherine Coulter, a master of suspense, *Infinity* features a star-studded mix of today's top women suspense and thriller authors, all bringing their A-game. From well-established writers to newer up-and-comers, every single one of these authors delivers. Put this on your *must read* list, and be prepared to be wowed!"

—Chris Goff, Award-Winning Author of *Dark Waters*

"*Infinity*, Suspense Publishing's latest anthology, is a collection of stories authored by some of today's finest female writers. These tales are not just well-written, they challenge the reader to rethink his core beliefs and to wonder if the impossible is not possible after all. This anthology has all the makings of a literary classic. Highly recommended!"

—Joseph Badal, Amazon #1 Bestselling Author and Military Writers Society of America Writer of the Year

"The stories contained within are by turns fun, fantastical and frightening. Each one is utterly unique and utterly impossible to put down."

—Lisa Black, *New York Times* Bestselling Author of the *Locard Institute* Thrillers

"13 mistresses of suspense, 13 stories that'll keep you on the edge of your seat. 13 distinct voices. 13 plot twists. 13 reasons to want to go to *infinity and beyond*. Who said 13 was an unlucky number? Not me. Brava!"
—Tracy Clark, Author of the *Cass Raines* and *Detective Harriet Foster* Series

"I have just spent the most diverting few weeks curled up with the new *Suspense Magazine* anthology, *Infinity*, edited by Catherine Coulter. Not only has Ms. Coulter selected a wonderful array of stories and writers, she has arranged them in a way that kept me engaged and reading far too late into the night. From the ghostly to the mysterious to the police procedural, there is something in this book for every reader. My personal favorites range from "Seven Minutes in Heaven," the kickoff story by Darynda Jones set in a tony boarding school where all is distinctly not well, to "Louche 49" by the masterful J.T. Ellison, who takes us on a wild ride with a hired assassin that leads us from Paris to Tennessee. Prepare to be surprised and delighted by the collection of stories in *Infinity*. I guarantee you won't be able to stop with just one!"
—Deborah Goodrich Royce, Award-Winning Author of *Reef Road*, *Ruby Falls*, and *Finding Mrs. Ford*

"With this lineup of acclaimed authors, I knew I was in for a treat when I settled into this imaginative collection of short stories, and indeed the suspenseful mysteries kept me reading late into the night."
—Gigi Pandian, *USA Today* Bestselling Author

CONTENT

INTRODUCTION

Strap yourself in for a rollercoaster ride—some exhilaration, some terror, sure, but lots of fun wondering what's going to happen next in each story. You'll cheer for a collection of fascinating characters, each with their own special challenges. Super talented authors are going to make you scratch your head, laugh out loud, confound you with these exciting adventures, all here, folks, in one book with a gorgeous cover. Thirteen original stories, each with a different voice, a different style, very different settings and plots and all of them magic gems.

So, sit yourself down in your favorite reading chair, maybe a glass of Chardonnay beside you, and prepare to wallow in pure reading pleasure. Let me tell you a little bit about each short story, not giving too much away, I hope, just the flavor, the mood.

"Seven Minutes in Heaven"
By Darynda Jones

What can this title mean? Here we are in a private school, walking beside Coco on her first day at Havenmore. Why is she here in the middle of the term? Because her beloved cousin died and it was ruled suicide, but Coco doesn't believe it for a minute. She's determined to find out the truth. Are you ready to cheer on a fascinating heroine as she uncovers the truth, layer by layer?

Amazingly rich characters and unexpected motivations. Oh yes, then there's Duff—

"Poniatowa"
By Sheila Lowe

Present-day Eva finds an old photograph that sets her off on a journey to learn about her namesake, Chawa, which means *life* in Polish. Then we're thrown back to a Nazi Labor Camp, Poniatowa, and witness the horrors through the eyes of seventeen-year-old Chawa who refuses to give up and swears to survive. Eva is determined to find out what happened to her great aunt Chawa. A gritty awe-inspiring story of determination to survive against all odds and the enduring connections over time.

"Masquerades *Can Be* Murder"
By Susan Santangelo

Jump into the engaging mind of Carol Andrews, witty, strong, always on the go, an amazing grandmother, and a husband who she many times wants to drop-kick off the planet and loves dearly and prefers out of the house. You'll be grinning as Carol carries on inside her head since she can't say these gems aloud. Then the unexpected strikes: Carol is beset by the flicker of movement from the corner of her eye and odd and strange sounds. Does Carol really want to ask: Is anyone there? Humorous and delightful, you won't want this one to end.

"Louche 49"
By J.T. Ellison

It's 1985 and you're with an assassin—Annalise—in Paris. Then you're thrown into the present with Tempeste. Who is Annalise to Tempeste? There's acceptance, horror, a journey into the unknown, so many questions all whispering through your mind and a conclusion to blow it. Be prepared to put yourself in the hands of a master.

"Justice is Served"
By Daryl Wood Gerber

What is a loving sister to do when her dirtbag brother-in-law gets off after murdering her sister? Corrine is inventive, smart, a special effects maven with a rich internal dialogue and two best friends. You'll be fascinated as you try to figure what will happen next until justice comes out of left field. It's delicious.

"The Disappearing Place"
By Jamie Freveletti

Time to suspend disbelief and walk beside Artemisia into a strange and unique land that shouldn't exist but does, a place not known to Artemisia where people want to kill her "kind," a place where her sister and many others have disappeared. You'll hold your breath as Artemisia tries to survive in this wild new land and understand an insane enemy who doesn't adhere to the Geneva Conventions. An incredibly imaginative story to make you wonder about infinite realities.

"Three Minutes Past Midnight"
By Susan Wingate

Oh my, prepare yourself for the unexpected. You'll guess, wonder, fret, pulled first one way then another. Zainey Walker, tough, strong, relentless, is someone you want in your corner, particularly if it's a question of life or death. Extraordinarily vivid—you're right there rooting for Zainey, chewing your fingernails as you whisper *Holy shit!*

"The Cancun Game"
By Tosca Lee

Piper enjoys posting on a major media site. She's creative and beautiful and lo and behold, she begins to get followers. Up and up with followers until she's an influencer. Her two closest friends are right with her, helping, arranging, and up and up she goes. What is real, what is illusion? Up, up, she goes—an amazing chronicle of a beautiful girl who has no idea what's in store for her. Fasten your seat belts.

"911"
By Allison Brennan

Jump into a harrowing situation. Witness commitment and determination to survive. But who do you want to survive? If the super suspense doesn't make you hyperventilate, you've got really cold blood. Try to keep your heartrate down as you read this perfectly executed story—good luck.

"I've Got Your Number"
By Isabella Maldonado

Meet a gutsy intuitive cop with brains and grit who's willing to disobey direct orders to do what she knows is right. You'll walk beside Nina, see what she sees, cheer the decisions she must make to save a life. A heartwarming story of courage and dedication. And who's got her number?

"Eight Years and Seven Secrets at Ten Stacks"
By Shannon Kirk

What a title! What does it mean? You're told this is a ghost story, but you're really not prepared for what happens. Trust me on this. You'll be seduced into spectral creepiness lyrically done, but suddenly your toes curl and you're searching out the whiskey bottle to calm down. If you're a big believer in revenge, try this amazing story on for size.

"The Joy of Wrong Numbers"
By Kelley Armstrong

Meet Gran and granddaughter, Lily, two engaging women who'll draw you right in. You'll adore them together and separately as you watch them navigate dangerous waters. What is going on with these wrong numbers? Prepare to be surprised as things simply don't add up. Clever with a twist.

"Under Pressure"
By K.J. Howe

You're underwater with Thea in a cave, your assignment to rescue missionary hostages, but it isn't a cake walk. Your heart will go into overdrive, you'll count the minutes as time creeps by and death lurks around every bend. And worry about breathing. A gripping story of dogged determination, where failure is unacceptable. Enjoy the wild dive.

When I finished reading this collection of short stories, I was struck by what I knew intellectually—every author is different from every other author, each one inventing out of whole cloth a smorgasbord of characters as unique and distinctive as their creators. Just tell an author to "Go" and writing brains fly off into myriad different directions to create new worlds, present confounding inner conflicts, give you characters accomplishing extraordinary things, and hurl you into danger.

When you've finished these incredible short stories, in one sitting of course, pick your favorite (if you're able) and visit the author's web site to tell them what pleasure they gave you.

I raise a glass to you remarkably talented authors and thank you for the genuine entertainment. And I toast all of you lucky readers—have a blast.

~Catherine Coulter

SEVEN MINUTES IN HEAVEN

DARYNDA JONES

I got the call on a Monday. My cousin's body had been found at the bottom of a ravine. They said she'd jumped off a cliff. Taken her own life.

No.

Just…no.

I don't remember Tuesday.

On Wednesday, I began my research. The text she supposedly sent to her parents before she died was hardly proof. Anyone could've gotten her phone and sent that message. Then I found something. Another freshman from Havenmore Academy took her life the year before. The exact same spot. The exact same way.

And four years earlier, another girl.

Now I was onto something real. Something concrete.

On Thursday, I spent half the day trying to convince my dad, who was on the other side of the world, of my plan. I argued and cried and haggled and begged. I made promises and swore blood oaths and presented my paper-thin evidence. But it didn't work. He wouldn't cave. I had no choice but to thwart his wishes. Something I rarely did.

On Friday, I called in a favor. A friend of my dad's happened to be the governor of Connecticut. One call and Coco Sillivent—not my real surname—was in.

On Saturday, I cried. All day. I had to miss my younger cousin's—my best friend's—funeral. If this was going to work, no one could know we were related.

I needn't have missed it, however. Not a single student attended. The school had held its own memorial on Friday so the seniors wouldn't have to miss their camping trip that weekend. Heaven forbid.

My bodyguard, for lack of a better term, went to the funeral in my stead and secretly filmed the entire thing. Only five people attended. Five people paid their respects to the sweetest girl ever to walk the face of the earth.

On Sunday, I drove to Connecticut and checked in with the headmistress. I was shown to my room well past lights-out.

On Monday, I donned a white button-down, plaid skirt, Havenmore jacket, and walked into the halls of my new home. For the next few weeks anyway. I was here. I made it. It had been eight days since I got that fateful text from my cousin. It read simply, *Finally! Seven minutes in heaven. Wish me luck!*

I hadn't. We were in a different time zone and I didn't get the text until the next morning. I'd texted her back: *LOL, what does that even mean?* My phone rang seconds after I hit send.

Knowing I'd missed her last text was almost as heart-wrenching as knowing she was gone. Could I have stopped whatever she'd been up to? Could I have done anything? Had someone lured her out to kill her? Whoever it was hadn't sent her a text to do so. We checked. My bodyguard and I. No texts from anyone but me for days, so it had to be someone in her dorm. At least, that was my best guess.

Right now I needed to find my first-period class.

A high-pitched voice shrieked at me from down the hall. "Excuse me? Excuse me, miss?"

I stopped and squeezed my eyes shut. I'd only been at Havenmore for twelve minutes. How much trouble could I be in?

I swiveled on my toes to face the painfully thin teacher charging toward me, her lips pursed so tight they almost matched the navy skirt suit she wore. Steely gray hair pulled into a harsh bun didn't help ease the depth of her wrinkles as she stalked toward me.

I bristled under the gazes of the students in the hall. Everyone stopped to see what was going on. Not that they hadn't been watching me already. While my goal was to get attention as quickly as possible, this was not the way I'd planned to do it.

"Excuse me," the woman said, pulling to a stop barely inches from my face. "What's your name?" Her brows drew a harsh slash behind black-framed glasses.

I tucked a strand of brown hair behind my ear and tried, as nonchalantly as possible, to lean away from her. She had invaded my space bubble. Not that I was going to tell her that. "I'm Coco.

Coco Sillivent."

Most of the kids around us seemed fairly unconcerned. Perhaps the teacher did this sort of thing often. They assessed the situation and kept walking, only half interested in what was going on. But a few kids lingered close by, very interested in either the confrontation or the new kid. It was hard to say which.

Only one, a tall kid with brown hair and lashes longer than a boy had a right to, didn't even look when he walked past. I watched him until the teacher spoke again.

"You're new here," she said, giving me a once-over.

"Yes. I got in last night." I smoothed a palm over the white blouse and down the red and gold plaid skirt I'd be forced to wear for the next few weeks, only feeling a little like I'd recently been sorted into Gryffindor.

I'd never gone to a private school, much less a boarding school. Thanks to a dad in the spy biz and lots and lots of travel, my education had taken a different path. But at least I could order a kebab in Farsi, because that would come in super handy.

"Ah, I see." She leaned in for an even closer look, apparently counting my pores.

Thank God I'd moisturized.

She stepped back just as a bell chimed. Chimed! Not rang. Not clanged. Not cut a blaring path through the silence like a chainsaw, but chimed. A soft, melodic sound to denote the changing of classes. Boarding school rocked.

"Well, here." She took out a black cloth from her leather satchel and started tying it around my upper arm. "One of our beloved students passed away last week. We're wearing these for the rest of the month in her honor."

I'd seen the band in the kit the headmistress had supplied me with but had no idea what it was for or where it went. Not until I watched my new roomie, a freshman with dark blonde hair and a sad smile, put it on. She'd been Mona's roommate as well. I made sure of it. I'd gotten in too late to make small talk, but today was a new day. And I had all the time in the world to get to the truth.

I looked around. Everyone, students and staff, wore an armband as well. Like they cared. Like any of them had gone to her funeral.

Most of these kids probably didn't even know her name before she died, a scholarship case with a genius IQ and zero real-life experience. Mona had wanted nothing more than to be accepted by the very people who'd looked down their noses at her. The very people who'd murdered her.

I turned back to the teacher. Her fingers shook as she tried to tie the band. She seemed genuinely shook by the loss, genuinely saddened, and it hit me who she was. My cousin had described her very differently, her vision tainted by her love for the woman.

"You're Mrs. Stead."

She blinked at me. "I am. How did you know?"

"Oh, I have you for English. I looked up all of my teachers so I'd know them." It was only a small lie. I planned on telling much bigger ones during my stay.

I'd looked up all the teachers, all the administration and board members, even the custodial staff, but only to run background checks on them. The perks of having a dad in the spy business. A dad who taught his daughter everything he knows. A dad who'd been training said daughter her whole life for this day. And a dad who happened to be on a mission in Jakarta at the moment.

"Honey," he'd said during our hours-long phone conversation, "you said it yourself. She'd been acting strange lately."

"Yes. *Happy* strange. Not jump-off-a-cliff strange. I'll take the Glock if it'll make you feel better."

No matter what I said, Dad stuck hard to his no. I had no choice but to go behind his back. Which was, thankfully, on the other side of the planet. I did, however, bring the Glock—my version of a security blanket, only colder and with harder edges.

"How studious," Mrs. Stead said, snapping me back to the present. "Well, welcome to Havenmore, Ms. Sillivent." The harshness of her demeanor vanished, her sharp edges softening as she finished tying the band on my arm. She patted it; her eyes suddenly as sad as my new roommate's smile. "Best get to class." She turned and walked toward her own classroom just as the tardy bell chimed.

I swallowed the lump in my throat and turned a full circle in the now empty hallway, trying to get my bearings. I'd memorized the floorplan, but that didn't always help if one didn't have a starting point. I was in the main hall, however. How difficult could this be?

After finally triangulating my location using the office I'd visited last night and the dining hall I'd just come from as reference, I turned and headed for my first class only to be stopped short by a male student coming out of the classroom beside it.

He closed the thick, wooden door softly, crossed his arms over his chest, and leaned against the doorframe to stare at me. Standing a head taller than me, he had wavy black hair and a nickel-slick smile. He reminded me of a used car salesman who'd spotted his first customer of the day.

I straightened my shoulders and started forward again when another door to my left opened. Another male student stepped out, closed the door softly, crossed his arms over his chest, and leaned against the doorframe to stare at me, repeating his classmate's actions to a tee. This one was stockier than his friend with smooth dark skin and startlingly light eyes. Blue. Or possibly green.

Catching onto their game, I let out an aggravated sigh, but before I could take another step, two more doors opened, one in front of me and one behind. I glanced over my shoulder. Two boys came out of the door at my back. A blond lounged against the lockers, hands in his pockets, smirk on his face. A brunette followed. He crossed his arms over his chest and leaned beside his friend, tilting his head to peer at me from around him, a similar smirk lifting one corner of his mouth.

Just as I turned back to assess the one farther down the hall, three more doors opened. Three more boys stepped out. Three more vultures joined the ranks of their friends in what had to be a concerted effort. But why? To intimidate? To coerce? Or was this simply a hazing? An unpleasant welcome for the new kid.

I whirled around, glancing wild-eyed at each boy, and forced an expression of alarm. Partly because on some level I was alarmed. But mostly because that was kind of their whole point. That was the thrill, after all. The main reason for the show. To alarm me.

As though the following move was choreographed, each boy shoved off his respective support structure and started toward me. Slowly. Methodically. Like a pack of predators stalking a single prey. The straggler of the herd. The one that dillydallied just long enough to get her jugular ripped out so the beasts could feast.

Only these predators wore white button-downs, black slacks, and red and gold jackets. All of them had their shirtsleeves rolled up to the elbows. Probably the only alteration allowed at the school. And all of them wore the black armband, reminding me of my purpose.

They formed a circle around me, so close I couldn't escape without some kind of physical contact. I used a pretense of faux courage to examine them further. To spot the weak link. My best chance at escape. I set my jaw and turned slowly to look each one of them in the eye.

Their leers neither dissuaded nor hindered me. I could've written a book with what I learned. The blond was a scholarship kid being raised by his grandparents. Judging by the strength in his forearms, he'd been accepted by this group because of his looks and athletic ability.

The one with the smooth dark skin and blue-possibly-green eyes was the son of a diplomat. He wore a green and white pin belonging to the Nigerian consulate in DC.

The sable-haired kid came from old money and would probably never have to work a day in his life. Everything about him screamed entitlement, from his perfectly mussed hair to his manicured nails. He pretended to be *just one of the guys* but he was far richer and he never let them forget it. Either that or I was projecting my bias for underdogs.

These were the popular kids. The upperclassmen who ran the school. And here they were, exerting all this effort for little ol' me. I may have enrolled as a freshman so I could take all of the same classes my cousin had been taking when she died—so I could infiltrate her crowd, interrogate her classmates—but I was by no means the naïve school girl they supposed me to be.

Not that I could let them know that. I'd never been more grateful for being vertically challenged in my life. My small stature was working in my favor for once. Twice, if one counted the time, I wriggled into Mr. Crenshaw's basement to hack his computer and delete the photos he'd taken of me through my blinds. The perv. I left all the child porn on there and called the cops. Mr. Crenshaw moved soon after. To a state-run facility.

When the boys inched even closer, closing the gaps in the circle, I ramped up my reaction. I spun around as they hemmed me in, a hunger glistening in their eyes. They said nothing. Gave away nothing. Their only action was to let their gazes rake over me like sandpaper on sunburned skin.

Though I'd spotted the weakest link instantly, I used this time to reassess. To make sure my initial instinct was correct.

One of them was almost as short as I was, but he was tough. Built like a boxer with a blatant disregard for pleasantries glistening in his eyes. He was most definitely not the weakest link. No, that would be the painfully thin one next to him who was only going along with this to be *one of the guys*. To be part of the popular clique. To be accepted, which, wasn't that what we all wanted?

I settled my gaze on him and watched as he realized I'd singled him out. Panic flashed behind his pale irises. If not for the fact that he wanted nothing more than to impress his friends, I wouldn't have given a physical confrontation with him a second thought. But desperation made people dangerous. I could not let my defenses down if I was going to get past him, a tactic I would save as a last resort. If my antagonists started getting rough. After all, I had a part to play as well.

When a boy behind me lifted a strand of hair off my shoulder, I steeled myself for whatever might come next. Surely, they wouldn't assault me in the middle of the hall. Weren't there teachers all around us? Other students? My mind raced with how to handle it should they decide to throw caution to the Havenmore wind. I couldn't give away my tactical advantage so early in the game.

"Hey!" a male voice shouted from down the hall.

The sea of boys, eight in all, parted as one solitary figure walked toward us. No, toward me. And suddenly the game made sense.

Boys threaten girl.

Girl panics.

Outsider swoops in to save the day, thus winning girl's undying gratitude. And her affection. And possibly her virginity. A con as old as…well, cons.

So, he was to be my knight in shining armor. Okay, then.

25

"Cut the shit, guys," he said as he got closer. And taller. And... prettier. For real? Was every kid in this school good-looking? Then I realized it was the boy who strolled past my confrontation with Mrs. Stead moments earlier without so much as a glance our way.

With a dismissive nod, he sent my hazers scurrying off like roaches. All but two, apparently the pluckiest of the group. The four of us stood in the hall, three sets of eyes taking me in. Which was not awkward at all.

Since I was the meek victim in all of this, I crossed my arms over my chest and pulled my shoulders closer to my ears, waiting for the game to play out.

Finally, the one who would be voted most likely to crash his private jet into the side of a mountain while showing off for his friends, executed a quick bro-hug with the knight, spared me one last smirk-filled glance, then headed out, chuckling under his breath.

The other one, the boxer who I imagined fought like a badger having a bad decade, just grinned at the knight, lifted his chin in greeting, and stepped back into his classroom.

And then there were two. Despite my resolve to despise this boy to the very depths of my soul, a spark of interest spiked somewhere deep inside me. And here I'd thought myself above such triviality. Immune to a pretty face. Hadn't my father raised me better?

As I studied my knight in shining Oxfords, I wondered again, why this guy? With thick, coffee-colored hair, rich, tawny eyes, and a mouth so sculpted it could only be described as sensual, he was far too handsome to want for female attention. How'd he draw the knight card? Maybe he'd recently broken up with his girlfriend and needed a diversion, so his friends decided to help him out by setting up the easy, doe-eyed new kid for him. Or maybe he won rock, paper, scissors. Who knew?

"I'm Duff," he said, gazing down at me, and the name struck a chord so hard I blinked in rapid succession to the point of embarrassment. So, this was the infamous Duff Levacy. I should've known. My cousin had described him, of course, but I thought she'd been exaggerating.

I took the hand he held out to me. "I'm Coco."

Before he could reply, my phone chimed, though not as prettily as the school bell. I took it out of my Havenmore-approved satchel.

"I recommend putting that on silent," he said. "They'll confiscate it if they see you use it during school hours."

"Right. I read that. Thanks." I checked the message. It was from the only other person on the planet who knew what I was up to: Stefan Glock, or *The Glock* as everyone called him.

Officially, Stefan was my bodyguard when my dad was away, but in reality, he was more like a nanny who made me do squats every morning and taught me how to assemble an AR-15 in thirty seconds while hacking into a terrorist's cell phone. Somehow managing to be merciless and nurturing at the same time, the German-born former green beret had been my constant companion since my mom died when I was seven. He was also never far from me, so I shouldn't have been surprised when he magically got hired on as a custodian.

What were those dimensions again?

I texted back, *five by five,* to let him know everything was okay before ferreting the phone away.

"Do you know where your class is?" Duff asked, and I really wished I'd done more research on the students. Yes, he was my cousin's biggest crush, but she'd been a horrible judge of character.

In between reading the school material, sprucing up my social media accounts, and running deep backgrounds on all the employees of Havenmore, I never got around to the kids. I figured I'd see who Mona had hung out with first, find out who'd invited her to that party, if that's even what *seven minutes in heaven* meant, before digging too deep into the backgrounds of 258 kids.

My research had paid off. Havenmore didn't vet their teachers as well as their idealistic parents hoped. The biology teacher had been jailed for DUIs before moving to Connecticut. The American history teacher had been investigated for money laundering. And the French teacher was up to her neck in gambling debt.

But the one I was most interested in was the art teacher, a Mr. Davis Endicott. He had no history. No birth certificate. No school records. No driver's license until five years ago. He was a ghost before coming to Havenmore Academy for Impressionable Young People and I wanted to know how he got hired. I needed a look at his personnel file. A peek at where he claimed to have gone to school. But that was a task best left for the cover of night. The fact that he had been the teacher of Mona's last class on the day she died was even more suspect.

"I don't want to offend you," the tall drink of water walking next to me said. We stopped at the door I'd been heading toward and he blocked me from entering by crossing his arms over his chest and leaning against the doorframe. Apparently, that was a thing here. "But you should probably tell me why you're really here."

I stared up at him, needles prickling the back of my neck. "What do you mean?"

"I mean, a new student starting at a boarding school in the middle of the last quarter?" One corner of his mouth rose. "I have to know. What school did you get expelled from and what did you do?"

A breathy laugh escaped me when I realized he wasn't on to me. How could he be? I had to get a grip. I recovered and stated, matter-of-fact, "I didn't do anything. I was framed."

"But you were expelled?"

"Expelled is such a strong word."

"Thrown out on your ass?"

I fought a grin. "Asked nicely to leave."

"Ah."

"Why do we have to wear these armbands?" I ventured, waiting for his reaction. The behavior of the boys here was troubling. The pack mentality disturbing, and though I had my sights set on the art teacher, I had to take any suspicious behavior seriously.

His demeanor changed instantly. He stuffed his hands in his pockets and glanced down the hall, his brows sliding together. "A kid died last week."

"A kid?" I pressed.

He nodded and dropped his gaze. "A girl. A freshman. Mona Blake."

My stomach clenched at her name being said out loud, the wound so fresh and raw that my eyes stung. I blinked back any hint of tears and inched closer. "I'm so sorry. Were you friends?"

He lifted a shoulder. "I thought we were, but..."

"But?"

"Yes." He pushed off the doorframe and straightened. "I guess I didn't know her as well as I thought."

Admittedly, I wasn't sure how to take that. A guy like him would hardly give Mona the time of day. How well could he have known her? "Well, I'm very sorry for your loss."

He nodded, refusing to meet my gaze again. "Thanks. I gotta get to class."

I watched as he strode down the hall, his gait stiffer than it had been. Just as I was about to enter my first class a full ten minutes late, a custodian turned a corner and headed toward me pushing a cleaning cart. I opened my satchel and rummaged through it to give him time to pass me.

Stefan inclined his head and spoke softly as he passed. Five words that would change everything. "The phone was wiped clean."

I stared after him, fully aware that it would look odd if anyone should catch me. The refrigerator-sized blond tossed a warning glare over his shoulder. It was enough to shake me out of my stupor.

I entered the class with only one thing on my mind. I was right. My cousin had most definitely been murdered.

***

After a full morning of classes, I had a pretty good idea which cliques would cripple my social life and which cliques could catapult me into stardom and prestige. I chose the clique that would cripple me the most.

I asked to sit with a group of three kids, two boys and one girl, at the far end of the dining hall. Even in school uniforms, the outcasts were easy to spot. They were my kind of people, but I didn't strike up a conversation. Not just yet. They looked confused when I sat down. Like deer. Timid. Untrusting. Ready to bolt at the first sign of danger. Duff taking the seat beside me like he owned the place didn't help.

The entire room fell silent and more than one jaw fell open when the homecoming king sat at the table of us outcasts. He acknowledged the lot of us with a nod, then bit a huge chunk off his Italian sub.

We ate in relative silence, the nerds more than a little uncomfortable at having their safe space invaded, until Duff took a swig of Gatorade then asked me, "You blew up the science lab, didn't you?"

The three kids stopped eating and focused all of their energy on me.

I tried not to snort. I failed. "I did not blow up the science lab."

"You flooded the gym."

"Not even close."

"You set fire to Principal Panzerschreck's office."

I turned my best look of surprise on him, only partly acting. He'd checked me out. Probably looked me up on Instagram where fake-me posted all kinds of pics of school and the mall and arcades, many with yours truly in various states of cosplay. He probably thought I was a total geek. That should've kept the cool kids off my back, and yet here one sat.

A disturbing thought crept into my brain. Maybe that's how he got off, giving us lesser girls, the girls he felt were beneath him, a shining spark of hope before breaking our hearts. Was that why Mona was so in love with him? Had he done the same to her?

As much as we talked, she never went into great detail about the kids she interacted with daily. I didn't even know who her closest friends were. The only names that rang a bell had been her roommate, Cecily, who sat at the cool kids' table on the other side of the massive hall, and Duff. But surely she'd mentioned a few more to me from time to time.

Cursing myself for not paying closer attention to my one and only cousin, I made a decision. I didn't have time to mess around. I needed to get to the bottom of Mona's death and get the heck out of Dodge. I could take only so much of high school, an institution I'd put in my rearview over four years earlier.

"So," I said, locking onto his rich, tawny gaze, opting for the direct approach. "Is this what you do? This good-guy act?"

His brows slid together. "Act?"

"Is it personal, the thrill? Or is it just another facet of the infamous Havenmore initiation?"

He propped an elbow on the table and leveled a patient smile on me. "Initiation?"

"Yeah, you know, the hazing." I pointed with my chin toward the boys who came dangerously close to assaulting me that morning. "First the pack of wolves in the hall where you miraculously appeared to save the day—"

"You mean when my teacher sent me to the office to pick up a package for him?"

"—and now the charm turned up to eleven."

A dimple appeared in one cheek. "You think I'm charming?"

"And then what?"

"I don't understand."

"What are you hoping to gain from all of this?"

"Well, if you think I'm charming—"

I held up a finger to stop him. "Don't tell me. You invite me to hook up later only to stand me up so you and your friends can get a big laugh?"

"Wow." His lids narrowed as he studied me.

"Or maybe you invite me to a party and tell me to wait for you outside the gym so you and your friends can witness me getting stood up and get an even bigger laugh."

He rubbed the fine layer of stubble on his chin. "You're really cynical."

"I'm realistic."

"Now that you mention it, though, there is a party this weekend."

"As opposed to last?"

He laughed softly. "You got me. There's pretty much a party somewhere every weekend. But this weekend is special."

"Blood sacrifice?"

"Forty-year-old scotch."

"Ah."

"It may or may not have been stolen from the headmistress's office."

I gaped at him. "Mrs. Norwood drinks forty-year-old scotch?"

"Apparently. You in?"

I looked at our three tablemates. "What do you guys think?"

The girl, a curvy Latina with skin I'd rear-end a cop for, nodded.

"I say go for it."

To my surprise, Duff looked askance at the two guys. "Well? Are we partying this weekend or what?"

They exchanged shocked glances then nodded too, not sure what to think.

"I guess we're partying, then." He bumped their fists, including the girl's, then started gathering his things.

I arched a brow, impressed with his ability to blend in with the locals. "You realize if you stand all four of us up, we outnumber you."

He turned and flashed me a nuclear grin. The kind that left girls weak-kneed and breathless.

Not me.

Other girls.

"Remember," he said, eyeing each one of us, "Friday night. You. Me. Seven minutes in heaven." He turned and walked away as I sat stunned.

Mona's last text—*Finally! Seven minutes in heaven. Wish me luck!*—flickered and buzzed in my head like a neon sign on the fritz.

Deciding to try my luck, I turned to my new besties. "What does seven minutes in heaven mean?"

The boys shrugged but the girl dropped her gaze to her half-eaten lasagna.

Right. Too soon. "I'm Coco." I reached out my hand and finally got my cohorts' names. Jai had olive irises hidden behind thick glasses and spoke with a soft Indian accent. Cody, a ginger with a bashful grin, had yet to hit his final growth spurt. And Rosa had round cheeks and bow-shaped lips like a doll. But her skin…it shimmered like russet-colored silk. She only lacked one thing to be the exquisite diva she was meant to be: confidence. We'd have to work on that.

Feeling pastier than usual, I changed the subject. "So, why do we have to wear these armbands?" I pointed to the black band around my arm.

"Oh, those are for Mona," Rosa said. "A girl who died last week."

"That's awful." I poked at my food before continuing. "What happened to her?"

"She…she killed herself."

Jai shot her a scowl.

Rosa bristled under his scrutiny and went back to studying her lasagna. I'd asked several students the same question to gauge their reactions. Everyone was very respectful, sorrowful even, but no one could tell me a thing about my cousin when prompted. They knew she was a freshman, but that was about it. As though she'd been invisible.

These kids, however. They knew her. They felt her loss. The same cavernous pit of despair I did.

I put down my fork and ventured further. "She was your friend?"

"She was super cool," Cody said. "She sat with us sometimes, but mostly she sat by herself so she could read."

Yep. That was my cousin. We'd been close since we were kids and had Zoomed almost every night for the last two years after her parents sent her to boarding school. They had to get on with their lives, after all. They'd given her a solid twelve years. Twelve years they'd never get back. Enough was enough.

The bitterness and resentment I felt toward my aunt and uncle reared its ugly head yet again. I knew there was more to them sending their only daughter to boarding school than indifference. Probably something to do with my dad's career and the history of my mother's tragic death at the hands of the very terrorist he'd dogged for months. But the depths of Mona's despair at being uprooted and sent away had hardened me toward them and the sour taste I got in my mouth every time I thought of them had yet to wane.

"See you outside?" Rosa asked.

I fought my way back to the present and glanced around. The dining hall was almost empty now. "Yes. Absolutely." I stood, cleared my tray, and walked outside with them. The cool breeze would help wake me up. I'd hardly slept since I got the call, and tonight was not looking any better. I had a headmistress's office to break into.

***

I didn't see Duff the rest of the day, choosing to eat chips in my room instead of going to the dining hall for dinner. I still had a lot of research to do. Now, even more so. I had a list of kids to check out, starting with the pack of vultures. And my new admirer.

When I got back to the room after classes, however, I found my new roomie in bed with the covers pulled up to her chin. According to Mona, Cecily only entered the room when she was forced to. All students were supposed to be in their dorms by nine, but lights-out wasn't until ten, and Cecily rarely came in before then. She hung out in the common until forced to leave.

I tiptoed over to check on her. Swollen eyes and red nose. She'd lost her roommate, after all. Though they hadn't seemed particularly close, they were still roomies. Still friends. I needed to remember I wasn't the only one affected by Mona's untimely death.

Setting up camp on my bed, I sat cross-legged with a soda and a bag of cheese puffs, thankful Stefan couldn't randomly walk into my room like he did at home. He'd never approve. One look and I would've been dropping to give him twenty. It was probably a good thing I never went off to school.

I opened my laptop to check my shiny, new social media accounts. Or, well, the recycled ones. Instead of wasting precious time creating brand new accounts from scratch, I used old ones I'd set up with my dad for a side job he did back in the day. Coco Sillivent was my first dip into the world of espionage. I got to play a gamer at an arcade in London so I could strike up a conversation with a suspected money launderer so I could clone his phone. It was all very clandestine and I'd been hooked on the adrenaline rush ever since.

Why I needed an alternate identity for that, I'd never know, but it all worked out in the end. And we'd kept my first name in case someone recognized me and called out to me, which was highly unlikely. I knew, like, three people in London at the time.

But just in case someone stumbled upon my real accounts, I changed my profile pic to a caramel-colored labradoodle and erased every trace of my cousin, my favorite human, from them. I scoured all of my pictures and deleted dozens of Mona and me together, after saving them to my hard drive, of course. Then I went into her accounts and did the same, deleting a handful of pics and videos with me in them. Each picture that vanished tore off a little piece of my soul. Each memory that disappeared created a new hairline fracture in my heart.

What I didn't understand, what I'd never understood, was why she had so few friends at Havenmore. She had fifty-seven followers on one account and none of them were from the elite school.

Everyone had at least one friend, right? One person who was just as weird as they were? But there wasn't a single pic of her with anyone at the school among the dozens of pics of the school itself. She'd been quite the photographer and Havenmore was like a photographer's dream. It had more than its fair share of ivy and fountains and gargoyles.

It wasn't until I started looking closer at her architectural photographs that I realized something. While there were no students in the pics, there were often glimpses of someone in this corner or that. A hand here. A leg there. The laces of a saddle shoe. The pleated hem of a Havenmore skirt. The frayed threads of a hairband wrapped around a wrist. So minuscule and out of focus, I dismissed them the first time I went through the images.

The discovery still wouldn't have piqued my interest had one salient fact not come to light. It was the same person in each picture. I could have cut the images out and pasted them back together and had almost a complete person had there been any of the girl's face. Was this Mona's bestie? If so, why hadn't she told me about her? Why the secrecy? And why weren't they friends on social media?

Admittedly, I'd been worried about her. She'd sworn to me she wasn't being bullied. She just preferred to keep to herself. She liked being alone. But after this morning's performance by the wolf pack, I was beginning to wonder about the kids and the culture at this school.

The girls at Havenmore had all been pleasant enough. I'd mostly gotten curious glances all day, but every so often, someone would introduce themselves. Ask me where I was from. Give me the lowdown on this student or that teacher. Sadly, none of the information I'd gathered got me any closer to finding out what happened to Mona.

After using a spy app to check on my accounts, one that gave me the behind-the-scenes stats the media companies didn't want anyone to have, I was surprised to learn just how popular I'd become. I got a crap ton of unique hits. I even had over thirty new followers, all from Havenmore High. And I got two direct messages.

A guy who introduced himself as the Candy Man sent the first message. He promised to be super sweet should I want to hook up. Awww. One search and I had the kid's full name, date of birth, and complete online search history. The dark-haired hazer from this morning was more messed up than I'd imagined. I'd be diving deeper into his backstory for sure.

A bona fide prince from Dubai who just wanted my help in getting to his inheritance sent the second message. For that help, he'd split his sizable inheritance with me. So tempting.

Despite the gross invitation from the *candy man,* my hopes and dreams of getting to the bottom of my cousin's death still hinged on Davis Endicott, the art teacher with no past. I checked my watch. Twelve after eight. I had hours before I could sneak out and break into the office to check his personnel files.

A soft knock sounded at the door. But not just any knock. *The* knock. I hopped up and opened the door to what constituted my own personal bodyguard. Before he could say anything, I shoved a finger over my mouth, then whispered, "Are you supposed to be in the girl's dorm, Mr. Perv?"

The massive blond grinned down at me. "A senior slipped me her phone number." His ever-so-slight German accent was even less noticeable when he whispered.

"A senior? As in a senior citizen?"

"A classmate of yours. I thought I'd call on her. I feel like we might have a lot in common."

"Like finding a solution to male pattern baldness?"

He scrubbed his head—the non-balding one with very thick hair. "There is that."

"As long as she's worth ten-to-twenty in prison, I say go for it."

"I have a present for you."

"Way to bury the lead. Love the coveralls." I gave him my best once-over, the lingering one I infused with a subtle hint of horror.

"Thanks. Anything new?"

After a quick glance over my shoulder, I slipped out the door and closed it behind me. "Tons, but nothing concrete. I'm breaking into the office tonight to get a look at Mr. Endicott's personnel file."

"Why?"

"Because I need to get a look at Mr. Endicott's personnel file." I added a hefty dose of *duh* to that statement.

"No, I mean why break in when I have a key?" A sinister grin stole across his face as he produced a key from one of several pockets the coveralls boasted. "Told you I had a present for you."

I snatched it away from him and clasped it to my chest with both hands. "You're the best. And I was just kidding about the male-pattern-baldness thing. You have weeks before that begins. Possibly months."

"I know. But you can't break in tonight."

"What?" Disappointment washed over me. "Why? I promise not to steal the stapler this time."

"Too risky. Apparently, every Monday an all-night crew comes in to clean the offices and polish all the floors."

"Isn't that what weekends are for?"

"This is a boarding school. There are kids even on the weekends."

"Right."

"Now, who's the candy man?"

I gaped at him. "How do you already know about that?" When he didn't answer and deadpanned me instead, I caved. "One of the seniors from this morning. Creepy but nothing to worry about."

"Text me his name. Are you sleeping?"

"Not at the moment."

He leaned in and brushed a thumb over my cheek in a rare— very rare—show of affection. "Get some rest, kumquat. You can't do anything tonight anyway." He was genuinely worried about me. He hadn't called me kumquat since I was a kid, before he became an evil drill sergeant.

The door opened behind me and we both straightened.

"I swear I saw one," I said. "It went that way." I pointed down the hall then turned to Cecily. "Have you seen any mice?"

The sleepy-eyed girl carrying a towel and a bright pink shower caddy blinked at me. "Mice?" She looked down and scanned the area. "Here?"

"Maybe it was just a shadow," I added to reassure her. Because she needed that on her mind right now. "I'm sorry, Mr."—I leaned in to look at Stefan's nametag—"Guttenberg." I was so calling him that for the rest of his natural born life. "I didn't mean to disturb you."

"No problem. You girls call the basement if you need anything."

"Thank you," we said in unison.

He inclined his head and left us to our own devices as Cecily stared starry-eyed after him.

I turned to look at her. Dark blonde with a rich summer glow she did not get from the sun, she practically towered over me. She'd fallen asleep in her uniform, the material almost as rumpled as her hair.

"Are you okay?" I asked her.

Tearing her gaze away from the new custodian, she nodded. "I just need a shower to wake up."

A breathy laugh escaped me. "It's almost bedtime."

"Oh, right." She gave me a sheepish grin, but the tears glistening in her eyes spoke volumes. "It'll help me relax either way."

I moved out of her way and watched her for a minute, a little surprised she hadn't recognized me the minute I showed up last night. Then again, Mona was always either at the library or alone in her room. Rarely had Cecily been in the same area when we'd talked via video.

Though any number of people could've seen her screen, it usually takes several exposures to a face to recognize it out in the real world. I could only hope no one saw mine that often. Or heard my name. Thankfully, Mona had called me Cokie since we were kids, hence my concession to use my real one.

After Cecily made it to the bathroom, I reclaimed my campsite and went to work. I had a ton of research to do and, since I couldn't get a look at Mr. Endicott's file tonight, I needed to take advantage of this time. But first...

I clicked on the video Stefan had recorded. The one of Mona's funeral. I never thought I'd find a casket beautiful, but if my cousin was in it, it was gorgeous. Dark wood covered in a huge spray of Easter lilies. Mona's favorite. At least her parents got that part right.

Stefan had gone one step further while there. Seven people had sent flowers to the gravesite and he took all the cards off them. Since I had yet to check them out, I opened up the small envelopes and started reading. They were from the usual suspects: the school, the mayor's office, my dad. But one wasn't signed. It said simply, *We are so sorry.*

A spike of adrenaline raced over my skin and up my spine. Did no one look at this? Did no one read the cards? Who sent these flowers and what were they sorry for?

The writing was feminine, but it had probably been written by the florist. Still, it wouldn't hurt to check. I looked at the business name on the back of the card and typed the number into my phone to have at the ready first thing in the morning. Then I went back to the video.

Five people were there, not counting the preacher. It had been a simple, graveside service. My aunt and uncle were there, naturally. They'd been on a cruise when she died and barely made it back in time for the service. I was surprised they could fit it in, what with their busy schedules and all.

That wasn't entirely fair. I knew they were devastated. Their daughter had died. I couldn't imagine what they must be going through. But they'd go on with their lives like nothing happened while I missed her so much, I could hardly breathe. My world had been turned upside down when I got that call, and they were probably planning their next cruise.

I bit my lip and cursed into a napkin as I blotted it. I had to get over my resentment. Not, like, today, but soon. I had no right to judge them and I knew it, but only because both Stefan and my dad said so.

Another of the adults was a woman I now recognized as Mona's favorite teacher, Mrs. Stead. The older woman harbored a creative soul behind her steely gray hair and thick glasses. She was a dreamer. A romantic. Very much like my little cousin. She sobbed softly into a cloth handkerchief, and my heart went out to her.

I recognized the other couple as friends of my aunt and uncle's. I'd seen them at parties. The four of them traveled the world together, and I couldn't help but blame them a little for Mona being sent to boarding school in the first place.

And that was it. No one else attended my cousin's funeral. No one else cared.

I didn't realize I was crying yet again until I felt a tear drop onto the back of my hand. I looked down and realized I'd cried on my keyboard. Great. I hurried to sop up the tears before they did any damage, accidentally pausing and restarting the video again and again. But it was that distraction that sent my gaze to a far corner of the screen. Someone else was at the funeral. Someone else stood in the background, leaning against a tree.

I paused and zoomed in, and though the image was too grainy to make out any features, thanks to the red and gold jacket, I could tell it was a male student from Havenmore. One of the students had actually gone. A boy. Now to figure out which one. He was tall with dark hair, but that described at least a quarter of the boys here.

Cecily came back, her hair still wet, and crawled into bed.

"I'm so sorry about your roommate," I said to her. Our beds faced each other; the dorm rooms larger than I thought they would be.

She turned to me and snuggled farther under the covers. "Thanks. She was really sweet."

Didn't I know it. "Did you guys hang out a lot?"

She pulled the cover closer to her chin, an involuntary indication of shame. "Not as much as we should have. She just…she was kind of a loner. She liked to read and be by herself. And she talked to her cousin every night for like an hour. It was kind of her special time, you know?"

I couldn't help it. My adrenaline spiked when she mentioned me, but she seemed genuinely oblivious. Though I didn't want to push her, I ventured forward. "Do you think she killed herself?"

Her startled gaze landed on me and she sat up. "What do you mean? I thought the police said she jumped. Did you hear otherwise?"

"What? No. Not at all." I set my laptop aside and leaned toward her. "I'm sorry, it's just…a couple of the kids said they didn't believe it, so I was just wondering what you thought. I didn't mean any disrespect."

"No." A line appeared between her furrowed brows. "No, it's okay. I just thought maybe the police were looking into it or something."

"Not that I know of." I wanted more than anything to ask her how she'd feel if they did, but I didn't press my luck. I was still the new kid. Asking too many questions would raise more of the same. Possibly from the wrong people. If a teacher was involved, I didn't want to put Cecily in danger.

She laid back down and pulled the covers up. "I didn't get a chance to welcome you to Havenmore this morning."

"Oh, thanks. It's an interesting place."

She laughed. "That's one way of putting it. Duff has taken a shine to you, as my parents would say. That'll keep you safe."

"Safe?"

As though realizing she spoke out of turn, she shook her head. "From the other boys. They hit on anything new that walks through those doors."

And I thought I was special. "Right."

"Lights out soon," she said, pointing to her clock. "But they usually don't catch laptops, especially if you dim your screen."

"Wait. How do they even know if our lights are on?"

She pointed to the bottom of the door. "There's just enough of a slit to see any light shining through. One glance and they know exactly who's staying up late."

"What if you have to study late?"

"You don't. But if you absolutely have to, a flashlight under the covers usually works well."

Weird.

"I can't wait to be a senior," she continued. "Their lights-out isn't until midnight."

Caught up in the moment, I found myself anxious to be a senior as well before remembering I'd graduated high school four years earlier, at sixteen, and had just gotten a bachelor's in psychology.

I took her advice and burrowed under the covers to continue my research. Sleep was for the weak. Or the lucky, depending on one's perspective. I found a few interesting tidbits about several of the students, but nothing that would indicate serious criminal behavior like murder.

Unfortunately, I fell asleep in an awkward position and was rewarded with a crick in my neck when I woke up slumped against the wall with a blanket over my head the next morning. Cecily laughed at me and trounced off to breakfast, so I stayed behind to call the florist. I was still new enough to pretend I got lost when I showed up late for the second day in a row, but the woman who took the order wouldn't be in until eight, so I took a shower and hung out in the dorm room until then.

"It was a walk-in," the woman said to me. "I remember her. A Havenmore girl."

"Did she use a credit card?" I asked after I may have indicated I was a detective working on the case.

"She paid cash. Very cute girl. Curvy with huge eyes and long black hair. I know that's not much to go on."

"No, this helps so much," I said, knowing exactly who sent those flowers. Now I just had to find out why without blowing my cover. "Thank you very much for your time."

The morning went pretty much the same as it had the day before. It took every ounce of strength I had not to argue with one of my teachers about the difference between genocide and ethnic cleansing, but I managed to get through it without drawing blood when I curled my hands into fists.

Lunch was about the same as well, only everyone was much more at ease when I sat at their table. I'd come up with a plan to get Rosa, the girl who'd ordered the flowers, to tell me about it.

"Hey," I said between bites just as Duff sat beside me, "I need to order flowers for my parent's anniversary. Do you guys know of a good florist in town?"

"Spearman's," Rosa said instantly. "I just used them. They're really nice."

"Thank you."

"You sent flowers?" Cody asked. "Why didn't you tell us? We could've pitched in."

"No, it's okay." She folded her hands in her lap. "I just, you know, wanted to. After what happened."

"What happened?" I asked, leaning in as though thoroughly

intrigued. Probably because I was. Had they hurt my cousin? Is that why they were sorry?

Jai spoke up first, but not for my benefit. "It wasn't our fault, Rosa. You can't go through life believing that. It'll eat you alive."

"What wasn't your fault?" That question came from Duff, a sharp edge to his voice.

All three sets of eyes—well, four including mine—landed on him.

I spared a quick glance around the table. Surprise and something strangely akin to fear lined their faces.

Rosa chewed on her lower lip before saying, "The day Mona died...we...we got into an argument."

"About what?" he asked, totally hijacking my investigation. Rude.

"It was stupid." Cody slammed his milk carton down. It didn't have quite the same effect as, say...a beer bottle would have, but who was I to judge?

"Cody, shut up," Jai said.

Duff leaned forward, his expression menacing enough to get the job done. Just in case, he added, "No, Cody, keep talking."

But it was Jai who broke first. "Look, I get it, okay." He looked at his two best friends. "The Flash is invulnerable. He has to be. Anyone who runs that fast would have to be practically bulletproof. Hitting a bug at that speed would be like getting shot. All I meant was that Superman is still more impervious. He's invincible."

Duff and I sat in stunned silence.

I snapped out of it first. "Let me get this straight. You guys got into a fight about who was more invincible, Superman or The Flash?"

Rosa nodded. "We did."

"I sided with Mona," Cody said. "The Flash is badass."

"I didn't say he wasn't," Jai said, clearly touchy about the subject. "I just..." He scraped a hand through his hair.

Duff sat back and fought a grin.

I did the opposite. Well, I fought a grin as well, but I leaned toward them. "Do you think Mona would kill herself because of your argument?"

She nodded, her lower lip quivering. "If we'd known—"

"Stop." I took her hand. "There is no way, Rosa. She would never have done that."

"How do you know? You didn't even know her?"

"I know." I motioned for the boys to give me their hands as well. Cody complied. Jai cast me a dubious scowl. "Come on, Jai. Come in for this."

Finally, and with great reluctance, Jai clasped hands with us. "I don't care how that argument went. I don't care how emotional it got. It had nothing to do with Mona's death. I promise you."

Rosa drew in a shuddering breath and I wanted to hug her but I didn't dare push it that far.

It wasn't lost on me that I'd just annihilated one of my best and only leads. When Mona had left for the party that night, she'd been excited. Her text was proof of that. Their argument may have upset her, but it didn't last long.

I caught Stefan giving me a signal from across the hall as he cleaned up a spilled soda. I grabbed my tray. "I'll catch up with you guys in a minute. I need to run to the restroom."

"Need any help?" Duff asked. Our three cohorts grinned.

"No. I've been going to the restroom all by myself since I was three. But thanks."

He took my phone and typed in his number. "In case you change your mind."

Several of Duff's friends came to our table and actually chatted up the outcasts as I headed to the hall. It was cool to see. Two different cultures meeting on common ground. Like when lions and zebras drink from the same watering hole. Which, apparently, never really happens, but who's to say for sure?

I spotted Stefan as he strode around a corner and out of sight and followed him. It was risky. Teachers and students alike were up and down the halls all day. But when I turned the corner, he was gone. I eased forward, looking back over my shoulder. On any other day, this would be a trap. Surely, he wouldn't test my reflexes here.

And yet a hand shot out of a door I passed and pulled me inside. Freaking green berets.

"What the hell?" I asked, slapping his hands away.

"You have to be faster than that."

I raised my chin and smoothed my jacket. "I let you catch me. What's up?"

"The police chief is refusing to reopen the case."

"Even knowing the cell phone was wiped clean?" I couldn't help the astonished expression on my face. "What the hell?"

"He says it's not enough. And your dad is on his way back to the States."

My spine went ramrod straight at the mention of my dad. "He's finished already?"

"Yes."

"Crap." I bit my lip. "Does he know?"

"Of course, he knows."

"You told him?"

He did the deadpan thing again.

"I have to wrap this up. I really think Mr. Endicott had something to do with it. He's...shady. I'll get his prints tonight. They should be on file, right?"

"They should be."

"Okay, I'll go out first. Wait five minutes then come out."

"Coke," he said, using his nickname for me as I peered out the door.

I looked back at him. "Yes?"

"I've been running covert ops since before you entered this world. I think I can sneak out of a closet without instructions."

"Right. Sorry."

The rest of the day was like watching paint dry. All I wanted to do was get into that office. Of course, I also wanted to find out which boy at school went to my cousin's funeral. I would show the pic around, but I couldn't figure out how to do it without tipping someone off.

At dinner that evening our table was suddenly the hip place to be. The entire in-crowd had gravitated our way, and I wasn't sure if I should feel bad about that or not. Maybe the outsiders liked being on the outside. Maybe they were on the outside for a reason, and I'd just invited the entire school to crash their safe haven. Not that I had a thing to do with it. That was all Duff.

But when I caught Rosa flirting with the shortest basketball player I'd ever seen, I felt better about the whole thing.

"The food is much better here than I thought it would be," I said to Cecily as we walked back to our room.

She'd decided to spend the evening in again. Fortunately, she did seem a little more cheerful than the day before. "What did you expect?"

"I don't know. Something akin to prison food."

"Because you've been to so many?"

"No," I said with a snort. She didn't need to know about my last mission with my dad. Prison food sucked. Prison food in Siberia? Even worse.

Cecily did homework while I did more research. I even tried to run facial recognition on the mysterious funeral attendee to no avail. The fact that my dad would be here any second had me on edge. I figured with the debriefs he'd have to give in Washington and the reports he'd have to write up, I had two days to wrap this up. Three tops.

Still, I was old enough to make my own decisions. Yes. When he jumped down my throat, I'd lead with that. Just in case, however, I'd rehearsed about ten other arguments. One of them involved a mental breakdown and a squirrel named Thor. Hopefully it wouldn't come to that.

After an eternity of playing the guessing game about what really happened that night, lights-out had finally arrived. I waited until Cecily's breathing was deep and even, then I snuck out, clutching the key Stefan had made for me.

Being the new girl would once again work to my advantage. If caught in the halls outside our dorm, I could simply say I didn't realize we had to be in our rooms. If caught in the headmistress's office, however…well, that would be a bit trickier.

I used the master key to get into, first, the main office where the receptionist normally sat, and second, Headmistress Norwood's office. After a quick search, I found the personnel files. I pulled out the one on my suspect, Davis Endicott, and was so deep in my reading, I totally missed the male figure towering over me until he spoke and sent me into cardiac arrest.

"Whatcha doin'?" he asked.

At least my training paid off. Already in a crouched position, I swept his feet and sent him crashing to the ground, but I'd gasped when he surprised me. So hard I choked on my own saliva. I spent the next two minutes with my knee on his chest, my knife at his throat, and my free hand pressed to my mouth, trying to muffle the cough.

Oh yeah. I'd make a great spy.

After another few seconds to catch my breath, I glared down at the intruder who was wheezing a little himself. "What the hell, Duff?" I asked as I climbed off him.

"Sorry." He rolled onto his side to face me, still fighting for air. "I was just wondering why you snuck into Norwood's office."

"That is none of your business. How did you get in? I relocked the door." I pointed toward it with my knife.

He grinned up at me. "Like you're the only one with a key."

"I don't even want to know." I sheathed the knife. It involved lifting my skirt to the holster strapped to my thigh, and he watched my every move.

"I figured I could help."

"I don't need your help."

He sat up and rubbed the back of his neck as I reopened the file. "I want to find out what happened as much as you do."

"You don't even know what I'm doing."

The patient smile that widened his full mouth sent an electrical current rippling through to my core. "I know exactly what you're doing." He sat against the file cabinet, raised his knees, and propped his elbows on them before returning his full attention to me. "You're investigating Mona's death and I want to help."

A thousand scenarios ran through my mind. He recognized me from Mona's social media, but that would mean he paid attention to it. He saw us on Zoom, but that would mean he was watching her. He knew what happened to her, but that would mean he was the killer.

"She was my friend," he added when I only stared at him.

I didn't know he was a comedian. "And how often did you sit with *her* at lunch?"

He bristled. "You don't understand. She didn't want me to."

"Right," I said with a breathy scoff. "Duff, she had a major crush on you."

He scoffed and then studied me as though we were in lab, only he was the student and I was the specimen in the petri dish. "How well did you know your cousin?"

"A hell of a lot better than you did."

"You sure about that?"

"Pretty darned."

"Coco, she wasn't… She didn't have a crush on me."

"She talked about you. All. The. Time."

He shifted as though suddenly uncomfortable. "On my behalf."

I slid a hand under my skirt in case I needed to defend myself. "What does that mean?"

He bit down, the muscles in his jaw contracting with the movement before answering. "She spoke about me on my behalf. She didn't have a crush on me. I…I was the one with the crush."

"What are you talking about?"

He scraped a hand through his hair and grabbed a fistful, blocking his gaze as he explained. "On you, Coco. I had a…slight… thing for you."

"Me?" I sat back on my heels. "You had a thing for me?"

"A slight one."

"How could you possibly know me?"

"I was in the gym one night."

"That explains nothing."

He refocused on me with an excellent impersonation of a dead pan. After a tense moment, he asked, "Are you going to let me finish?"

"Please do."

"Okay, I was in the gym one night after lights-out. Mona had snuck in to get away from her roommate. I guess she was sick, barfing into a bucket."

"Oh, yeah, I remember." I thought back to that night early in Mona's first semester. "She'd gotten drunk on cheap whiskey and the smell was making Mona sick, too."

"And probably the sound."

48

"True." I shivered at the thought. "Cecily couldn't go to the nurse, what with the alcohol rushing through her veins, so Mona had to sneak out."

"Exactly. Mona was on her laptop video chatting with you. I'd just finished my workout and heard talking. At first, I thought it might be a teacher, so I went around the bleachers to sneak past her. I wasn't supposed to be there either. This school is Draconian when it comes to lights-out."

"I noticed."

"It was your laugh."

I frowned at him. "My laugh?"

"It was...infectious. Deep and husky. Not like..." He ran his hand through his hair again, a sure sign of discomfort. "And you were so positive and caring toward your cousin. She'd had a bad day and you'd threatened to kill whoever hurt her. With a straight razor. I had no idea at the time you were actually capable of it." He rubbed his neck again. "I might have rethought my affections had I known."

Worry slid up my spine like cold water. "How much did she tell you?"

He shrugged. "Everything, I think."

I slammed my eyes shut. "Why would she do that? Unless..." I stabbed him with an accusatory glare. "You charmed her."

He lifted a shoulder, not even trying to hide it. "It's a gift. I didn't ask for it."

"But, wait. She told me she was in love with you."

"No. She told you she was in love. She didn't say with who."

I shook my head, trying to wrap my head around everything. "Do you know who then?"

"No. Sorry. She didn't tell me either."

Suddenly the pictures made sense. I grabbed my phone and scrolled through Mona's photographs of the school. The ones with bits and pieces of someone with light hair. After jamming it toward him, I demanded, "Do you know who this is?"

He took the phone. Turned it this way and that. Frowned. Zoomed in. Then scrolled to the next picture. "Are you serious?"

"Do you recognize anything in the pics?"

"Besides the gargoyles?"

"Was she… Did she love this girl?"

"She was in love with a girl at school. I just don't know which one. And I don't know who this is." He flipped the phone again, tilting his head for a better angle.

I joined him in leaning against the filing cabinet. My shoulders sagged in defeat. "How could I not know she was in love with someone? Well, someone else. Someone not Duff Levacy."

"I honestly don't think she was out. Maybe she didn't know how to tell you she was gay."

"Bi, and I've known for years. And that doesn't get you off the hook. She could really have had a crush on you."

"Nope. She would've told me."

"Because teenage girls are so forthcoming about these things."

"Fine," he said, getting frustrated. "Wanna know how I know?"

I crossed my arms over my knees. "I would love to know how you know."

"She had her chance to be with me. She didn't take it."

"What do you mean?"

"Seven minutes in heaven."

A jolt of adrenaline straightened my spine. I turned to face him head on. "What is that?"

"It's a game where—"

"I know what seven minutes in heaven is. How does it pertain to the party you're having this weekend?"

His irises glistened with humor when he explained. "Ah, well, our version is a little different. We call it *seven minutes in heaven or six minutes in hell.*"

"Meaning?"

"Meaning, we all sit around a fire getting drunk at the ruins as we draw names. Two, to be exact. The drawees—is that a real word?" He looked up in thought but just as quickly bounced back to his story. "Anyway, the drawees get to choose. Seven minutes in heaven or six minutes in hell."

I stilled. Was this it? Was this why she died? A game gone horribly wrong?

"It was Mona's first time and damned if she didn't get drawn first."

My heartbeats sped up until they were stumbling over one another in anticipation.

"And I was drawn next."

"You? What did you choose?"

"Had it been my call, I would've chosen heaven, of course. Your cousin was a cutie."

Part of me, a tiny piece that I chose to ignore for the moment, fell a little in love with him. With how kind he'd been to Mona.

"But since her name was drawn first, she got to choose, and she wasn't having any of it." He laughed in remembrance, the sound sad and distant. "She chose hell. Straight up. Dissed me in front of all my friends, much to their amusement."

The tips of my fingers tingled with the amount of apprehension coursing through my veins. "Were you upset?"

"Hell, no. It was all good fun." He hit me with a knowing grin. "It wasn't like we set her up, Coco."

"You sure about that?" I asked, turning the tables.

"Positive. No one was patronizing or bullying toward her. This isn't *Mean Girls*."

There went that theory. I chose to believe him for the moment because the alternative was heartbreaking. "So, if she had chosen heaven, you would've had to comply even if you didn't want to?"

"Yep. Those are the rules. Afterward, the second person is up and another name is drawn. And the game begins anew until all of the names have been drawn."

"So, what did she have to do?" I winced at the thought of what my cousin went through. "What is six minutes in hell?"

"It's usually something silly, like stand barefoot in the river for six minutes or do pushups for six minutes. Whatever the group decides."

I drew in a deep breath and braced myself. "And my cousin? What did she have to do?"

He bit down and turned away from me.

"Duff?"

"It's bad."

My heart stilled in my chest. "Duff, what did you make her do?"

"She had to stand on one foot for six minutes."

I stared at him for an eternity before asking, "That's it?"

"That's it." A mischievous corner of his mouth rose. "Do you know how hard it is to stand on one foot when you're heavily buzzed?"

"Right. So, you guys laughed at her."

"Coco, *she* laughed at her. Everyone did. She giggled the whole time. We had a blast. All of us. Including Mona."

I dropped my head into a palm, ignoring the sting in my eyes. "Then why? Why did she die? What happened?"

He reached over and took my free hand. "I'm so sorry, Coco."

A thought hit me and I looked up at him. "Wait, are all the names in the same jar?"

"Box, actually, but yeah. Why?"

"What if two girls' names are drawn? Or two boys'?"

"Happens all the time." He lifted a shoulder in absolute nonchalance. "The girls often opt to make out. Probably because it's sexy as fuck and it drives the guys insane."

I blinked at him in shock. "Wait, the make-out sessions are live and in person?"

"They are. There are no closets at the ruins and it's pretty much the whole point of the evening."

"So the two drawees make out in front of everyone?" That would explain why Mona chose hell when she had a deep crush on Duff. She'd clearly been embarrassed.

"Yep. In front of God and man."

"That's…pervy."

"I didn't say it wasn't."

He had me there. "And the boys? If two guy names are drawn?"

"We opt for hell. Except Brad. That asshole opted for heaven one night when our names were drawn."

I covered my mouth to squelch a snort. It didn't help. "You made out with him?"

"I don't want to talk about it," he said, scrubbing his face.

"But you're still friends?"

"Of course. I'm telling you, Coco. It's all good fun. Everyone who goes to the ruins is there voluntarily. We all understand the rules and the risks. No one is forced to do anything they don't want to. And you know the saying."

I frowned at him. "What saying?"

He leaned closer until our shoulders were touching, then whispered, "What happens in heaven stays in heaven."

A bark of laughter burst out of me before I could stop it. He didn't need to know that I would've paid to see him make out with a boy. He was no pervier than I was. But again, this was getting me no closer to finding out what happened. "So, that night, who drew the names?"

"Your new roomie, Cecily."

"And what time was all of this over?"

He thought back. "'Bout midnight. It got really cold."

He was right. The coroner couldn't pinpoint the exact time of death because of the rapid drop in temperature. He'd narrowed it down to a four-hour window between midnight and four a.m. But now I had a new pool of suspects. They'd all been with Mona hours, if not minutes, before her death. "Can I get a list of everyone who was at that party?"

"Of course. You think one of them had something to do with what happened?"

"I don't know what to think. I just know my cousin did not kill herself." In all honesty, Duff was one of the last people to see Mona alive. And there I sat, telling him all about my investigation. I sucked at espionage.

A beam of light shone through the window. Before I could work up a proper panic attack, Duff tackled me to the ground and rolled until I was on top of him and out of sight of the security guard. I didn't even know there was a security guard at night.

How did these kids sneak out so often? This place was like Ft. Knox. Cleaning crews. Security guards. Yet not a single camera in sight. I could've pieced this together if I had exact times. Did Mona come back to the dorm after the party and then leave again? Did someone drag her out? Or did someone intercept her on the way back?

We were holding our breaths, waiting for the security guard to move on, when the heat of Duff's hand on my back sank into my consciousness. The hardness of his body beneath mine registered as well. The stirring of my hair with his warm breath.

Though I was probably only a couple of years older than the *child* under me, I suddenly felt like a cradle robber. The second the light disappeared, I rolled off him and sat up, smoothing my hair back. He did the same, but this time we didn't sit in clear view of the outer office.

"How often does security come around?" I whispered.

"Every half hour." He plucked a dust bunny out of my hair.

"Okay, so we have thirty minutes. Wait." I refocused on him. "It was you. You went to her funeral."

He dropped his gaze. "I did."

"Thank you."

He shrugged it off as I opened Davis Endicott's file again. I turned the night vision on my phone, and started snapping shots of every page. We had to get out of there, asap.

"Was anyone acting strange that night?" I asked in the interim. "Unusual?"

He pointed to himself. "Tequila."

"Right. Wait, the party this weekend." I looked up at him. "How can you even think of having another party after what happened?"

He sighed heavily. "Release? Therapy? Fuck, I don't know. It's just our way of blowing off steam." He gestured toward the file. "Why are we in here, anyway?"

"You're in here because you are a borderline stalker."

A gorgeous set of dimples creased his cheeks.

"And I'm in here because it's none of your business. Now keep a lookout for that guard."

He saluted and turned toward the window. "You know, there *was* something kind of strange about that night."

"Your disturbing source of pleasure?" I asked, snapping shot after shot.

"My name was drawn twice."

I stopped and looked back at him. "What do you mean?"

"We only put each name in the box once, but mine was drawn twice. I just figured it got put back in on accident. Or maybe written down twice. It's not unprecedented. Especially considering how much tequila had been consumed."

"Oh my God," I said, closing the file. I rubbed my forehead when everything fell into place.

"What?"

I looked at him through tear-blurred vision. "I know what happened."

***

"Do you know why we got called to the office?"

I looked at Cecily as we waited for the headmistress. Her face pale, her hands shaking, Cecily cast me a worried glance. She'd been woken up early and rushed to the office. Her mussed hair reflected that fact. She still wore her hairband around her wrist. Just like the one in the picture.

"I'm not sure," I whispered. "Something about that girl who died, but what I have to do with it, I'll never know."

"The…the girl who died?" She fidgeted with the hairband, the nervous gesture speaking volumes.

"Yeah." I pointed to my armband. "That was before I even got here. I don't know why I got called in." I looked at the headmistress's desk. "We should steal the stapler."

Cecily's breathing sped up. She was on the verge of hyperventilating. Which was exactly where I needed her.

"Cecily, what's wrong?" I glanced around then leaned closer to her. "Are you okay?"

She nodded but kept her head down.

"Look, if you did something…"

Her head snapped up. "I didn't!"

I nodded. "Good girl. It doesn't even matter. Don't admit to anything. If they accuse you of something, keep your mouth shut and insist on calling your parents."

"My parents?" Her fear increased ten-fold and I almost felt sorry for her. Almost.

"Are you afraid of them?" I took her hand. "Cecily, are they abusive?"

She slammed her lids shut. "No. Not really. Not in the sense you mean. It's just...they don't approve of a lot of the things I do. It's why I'm here at Havenmore. A co-ed school."

"What don't they approve of?"

She looked at me, desperation deepening the lines on her face, and shook her head. "You wouldn't understand."

"Please. I got kicked out of the last three schools I was in. If anyone would understand, it's me, hon." I ran my thumb over the back of her hand. To soothe. To calm. To deceive.

She took my hand in both of hers as a stream of tears slipped past her lashes. At least she felt remorse. I tried to be pacified by that fact, but it didn't work. Not for long, anyway.

The door to Headmistress Norwood's office opened. We turned to look over our shoulders. Two uniformed officers stood in the receptionist's office and I thought Cecily was going to pass out. The blood drained from her face.

"We'll be a few more minutes, girls," Mrs. Norwood said before closing the door again.

Cecily covered her mouth with both hands and began rocking in the chair.

I knelt on the ground in front of her. "Cecily, what's wrong?"

"It was an accident." She clutched onto me and glanced around wildly like a cornered animal. "It was an accident. It just...it just happened."

I grasped her shoulders and shook softly to bring her back to me. "What? Did something happen with that girl?"

She clamped her mouth closed and rocked back and forth.

"Good. Cecily, don't tell them. No matter what happened, don't admit to anything."

"But...but it was an accident. She wanted...she wanted everyone to know. She wanted for us to...to come out. But my parents. You don't understand."

I feigned shock and sat back on my heels. "Oh my God, you loved her."

The tears began anew.

I brushed her hair off her blotchy face.

"We had so much fun at the party, but when I drew Duff's name again, she knew."

"She knew what, sweetheart?" I asked, tucking a strand of hair behind an ear.

"She knew I'd actually drawn my own name the first time. I mean, what are the freaking odds? I drew her name first, then mine, so I said Duff because I knew she'd choose heaven and we'd have to make out and then everyone would know and my parents...my parents would never forgive me." She collapsed into my arms.

I wanted to feel something for her. I wanted to feel sorrow, but I had to swallow back the bile sliding up my throat. A part of me hated her. A part of me hated a society that would force a teenage girl, even in today's day and age, to fear telling the world she was gay. A part of me hated her parents to the depths of their souls for not accepting Cecily as she was. Apparently, something like this happened at her previous school. An all-girls school. So, they sent Cecily here. Hoping she'd fall in love with a boy instead? Because surely all she needed was more contact with them.

I pet her hair and rocked her. We weren't quite there. I needed an actual confession. "Cecily, what happened?"

"We were arguing on the way back," she said between hiccups. "She told me to go back without her and went to sit on Devastation Rock."

The overhanging rock Mona had supposedly jumped from.

"Then what?"

"I followed her to give her phone back. I had it in my pocket. We ended up talking for an hour on the stupid rock. She said she just wanted the world to know how much she loved me. But I...I just couldn't." She broke down again. "I wasn't as brave as she was. She told me she was going to write my parents. Explain what we meant to each other." She refocused on me, begging me to understand. "I couldn't let that happen. They...they were going to cut me off. We stood to leave and she looked over the edge of the cliff and it just happened." I fought to keep a grip on her and a grip on my emotions at the same time when she added softly, "I just pushed."

My emotions finally gave way and overwhelmed me. I wrenched out of her hold and scrambled toward the trashcan. I had nothing in my stomach, so I dry-heaved while the headmistress and the police burst through the door.

"Cecily," Mrs. Norwood said, "don't say anything else."

"Else?"

"I'll get your parents here and they'll get you a lawyer."

"I don't understand."

Mrs. Norwood handed me a tissue just as Duff and Stefan came in. Stefan helped me stand and the officers helped Cecily do the same so they could arrest her.

"I don't understand," she cried, panic-stricken. "I don't understand!"

"Please put your hands behind your back, ma'am."

She looked at me, wild-eyed with panic.

I thought about telling her the truth. Who I really was. But if she'd truly loved my cousin, she would've known. She would've known everything about her. She wouldn't have spent her evenings as far away from Mona as she could get. She would've sat with her at lunch. She would've been curious about what she was reading. About what she was interested in. About her family. She would've met me weeks ago.

Also, had she truly loved Mona, she wouldn't have pushed her to her death. So there was that.

She would learn who I was eventually. Just not from me.

Three hours later, I stood in front of the school being pelted with rain. It was over and I could finally mourn my cousin's death properly. Stefan had finished up with the police and was bringing the car around, but we'd had a long talk with Mrs. Norwood.

Mr. Endicott, the teacher with no background, changed his identity to get away from a stalker. She knew all about it and promised he was not a serial killer, despite my reservations. I'd just have to take her word for it.

The girl who'd taken her life by jumping off Devastation Rock the year before really did take her life. She had suffered from depression her whole life and left behind a long note explaining how she just wanted the sadness to stop. My heart went out to her.

The girl who'd died four years ago had been involved in a car accident. She didn't even die at the school like the paper reported but several miles away when a cement truck rammed into her.

A male voice spoke from behind me. "Leaving so soon?"

I turned to Duff as he descended the stairs with an umbrella. "You probably already know this, but I'm not really a freshman. I have a birthday in a couple of weeks. I'll be—"

"Twenty. I know. And I turned eighteen two months ago."

"You're legal now."

"Wouldn't want you getting into trouble."

"Do I have anything to get into trouble for?"

"Not yet, but the day is young."

I laughed and studied my shoes through the rain dripping off my lashes.

"You're going to George Washington University in the fall for your master's in forensic psychology."

I forgot he knew everything about me. "I am."

"That's so weird. I'm going to George Washington University in the fall, too." He glanced heavenward and scratched his chin. "Thinking about majoring in fermentation sciences."

I laughed. "That's a fine career choice."

He slid an arm around my waist and gazed down at me, his thick lashes spiked from the rain. "The question is, what will we do until then?"

"I bet we can come up with a few options."

"Do any of them involve running from your dad? Because I'm pretty sure he can kill me with a staple." Before I could answer, he pressed his mouth to mine and I wondered if he'd ever considered a career in the spy biz.

***

PONIATOWA

SHEILA LOWE

The photograph was at the bottom of a pile of old envelopes in an ancient-looking tin box. I had never seen it until my father died suddenly at the too-young age of sixty-three and the task fell on me to clear out his house. Like a Russian nesting doll, the tin box was stored inside a cigar box and then under a stack of papers in a larger cardboard one, sealed and jammed to the back of his bedroom closet under a pile of discarded clothing.

I stared at the photo, chilled. A long-forgotten memory evoked by the black and white image made its way back to my consciousness.

Once, long ago when I was twelve, my father brought a friend to our house. His name was Ben and he had a foreign accent. Ben was a nice man; a jolly, kind man—quite a lot older than my father, with greying hair and pouchy facial skin that reminded me of Doc in the Disney version of *Snow White*. My mother, who was afraid of strangers, even nice ones, hid out in the bedroom until Ben left. That night, my parents fought louder and longer than usual while my little brother and I strained to make out through the wall what their muffled voices were yelling.

My father was a pretty good yeller, so it wasn't hard to hear that he felt humiliated by his wife's refusal to come out and greet his friend. After that, he didn't bring anyone home again. Instead, he began having affairs, and eventually my parents divorced.

Ben had never entered my mind again until I came across the photo in the tin box. Now, with a sick feeling, I remembered the crude tattoo on his forearm—a series of numbers in washed-out blue ink. A tattoo very similar to the one in the photo. Except that the forearm in the photo appeared to be that of a young woman, and the numbers inked on her skin—15439—appeared dark and fresh.

I was too shy to ask Ben what those numbers meant back then, but he caught me staring. An infinite sadness clouded his light blue eyes as he leaned down to whisper, "Auschwitz," just loud enough for me to hear. I didn't know what that meant, but when my father sent me out of the room with an angry glare that said, "I'll deal with you later," I knew it must be something very bad.

Turning the photo over, I read the two words written in faded pencil on the back: 'Jakob' and 'Poniatowa.' Obviously, the feminine arm did not belong to Jakob, whoever he was. A string of obvious questions popped into my head: Whose arm was it? What was it doing here? Why was a concentration camp tattoo in my father's possession? And who was Jakob?

There were letters in the box, too, written on tissue-thin paper in envelopes postmarked in 1942-43. The language was unfamiliar, but I guessed it was Polish. My grandmother had been born in Poland, but I never knew her or my grandfather well. My father rarely spoke of his family and I had never thought to ask. But now, with this tangible evidence of their existence—I instantly made the leap that the letters belonged to them—it lit a burning desire inside me to know them.

Everything begins with Google, which returned more than a million hits when I searched on "Poniatowa." It was not the surname of this Jakob person, as I had assumed, but a town in Poland where, in the middle of the war, a concentration camp was built, which became part of a network of work camps.

I read with increasing horror the details of a three-day period in November of 1943. Between the Poniatowa Labor Camp and two others in the network, the Nazis murdered forty-three thousand Jewish prisoners.

Chawa

Chawa Feldberg was seventeen years old on the bleak, wintry Tuesday morning she got her first glimpse of the Poniatowa Labor Camp. Until that very moment, she had dreamed she might escape the fate of so many of her neighbors, her cousins, her parents. As she left the train and climbed down onto that desolate platform, hope began to fade.

Chawa's mind twisted away from the terrible thoughts that started to invade it. The will to live was too strong in her to just give up. She knew that she would survive, no matter what. She would survive and marry Max and have lots of children with him. They would move far away and build a house together and live happily ever after, just like in the fairy tales. She could not allow room for any thoughts other than happy ones.

Max was trained as a tailor and had been sent to work in the Walter Többens factory in Warsaw. As distasteful as the task was of sewing army uniforms for the SS, thank God he was not one of the quarter-million sent to Treblinka for extermination. Chawa shuddered at the word. Why didn't they just call it what it was— murder?

The back of her neck tingled and she deliberately kept her eyes cast down, certain that Jakob Banicki, assigned to guard the barracks, was looking at her, trying to get her attention.

He was not much older than she. Strangely blond-haired, with a wispy moustache that made him look like a little boy trying to be a grown up. She had gone to school with his younger sister a lifetime ago. Before his family had become Nazi collaborators to save themselves. Chawa wanted to spit on his shoes. The gun he carried stopped her.

"You're going to Poland?" Great-aunt Ruchla bellowed. She and my father both had the yelling gene, but she had an excuse—she was eighty-five and getting hard of hearing. Of course, I could raise the volume, too, when the occasion called for it. Maybe it ran in the family.

"No, Aunty. I want to know about our family there. Dad never talked about them, and now that I'm sorting through his belongings, I found some things—well, I want to know where I came from; who my family was."

My aunt fell silent for an uncharacteristically long time before she raised her rheumy hazel eyes to stare intently into my face. She spoke slowly, as if she wanted to make an impression. "Listen to me, Eva, my darling. Some things are better left in the past."

"But I—"

"But nothing," she interrupted forcefully. "My nephew, your father, is dead. My sisters are dead. What good can come of digging up what's gone?" The question was rhetorical, but I could see that

65

if I wanted answers I was going to have to be tougher than this tough old lady.

"You are the only person left who can tell me, Aunty Ruchla. Don't I have a right to know my own family history?" When she said nothing, I took the photograph of the woman's tattooed arm from my pocket and handed it to her. "What do you know about this?"

Peering at it through her thick glasses, she gave a sudden loud gasp and thrust it back at me, pushing my hand away with such force that I was stunned. She leaned her head back against her chair, clutching the arms, breathing so hard she was almost hyperventilating. The last thing I wanted to do was to give my great-aunt a heart attack.

I knelt beside her and grabbed her hand. "I'm so sorry, Aunty. I didn't mean to upset you like that. This photo was in Dad's things and I wanted to know why he had it." And when she still didn't answer, "There were some letters, too, but I think maybe they're written in Polish. You were born over there, weren't you?"

"Yes, I was born there. In Lipsko."

"Do you still read the language?"

Having recovered her equilibrium, she shrugged. "It's been a long, long time, sweetheart." With obvious reluctance, Ruchla held out her hand. I gave her the slim bundle of letters and sat back to wait as she picked up her heavy magnifying glass and began to read silently to herself.

When she had finished, she let the letters fall to her lap with a long, sad sigh. When I saw that her papery cheeks were wet with tears, I felt the stinging slap of guilt. But with my curiosity being stronger than my guilt, I stayed quiet and waited.

"I once had two sisters," she said, followed by another deep sigh. "One younger, your grandmother, Sophie. And—" Another long pause. "And one older. Her name was Chawa." She pronounced it 'Hava', and explained, "In Yiddish, it means '*Life*." Her cynical snort said more than words could adequately express. She looked straight at me. "You were named for her."

That gave me a jolt of surprise. "*I* was?"

Great-aunt Ruchla nodded. "In English, it's *Eva*. You know, like my English name is Rose."

I wanted to ask a dozen questions about my namesake but held them all back, afraid to interrupt the flow, which now that it had started, threatened to become a torrent. She touched the letters in her lap, her eyes losing focus as she stared into the past.

"They're love letters. From Chawa to her boyfriend, Max; Max—what was his surname? Let me think. Dubinksi? Maybe. They were in love from the moment they met as children. This was before the war, of course. They were going to get married." Her eyes narrowed. "How did your father come to have these? Max sent the letters to us later; he couldn't bear to keep them, any more than he could bring himself to throw them away. That he survived the Shoah and Chawa did not, it destroyed him."

"The Shoah?"

"The Holocaust," she retorted sharply. "Don't you know *anything* about your history?"

That seemed unfair when I had just told her I knew nothing of it. My father was a non-religious Jew who married a Gentile, which my mother claims caused an uproar in the family. At least I knew what a Gentile was called—*goy*. Except that he used it as a pejorative sometimes, my brother and I grew up learning nothing of his heritage. Or ours.

Ruchla's expression hardened. "The photo you found—the number. It's Chawa's prisoner number. They took away their names, the Nazis. Stole everything they owned. They even shaved all the hair from their bodies. And they tattooed the prisoner number, as painfully as possible of course, with metal stamps—so horrible."

I wanted to tell her stop, but some masochistic part of me wouldn't allow it.

"They would use the stamps to cut into the flesh and then rubbed ink into the wound to make the tattoo. Even the babies." Her voice cracked. "My beautiful, darling big sister. I don't know who took that picture or how your father came to have it. When our parents saw how the war was going, they sent your grandmother Sophie and me here to America with my father's brother and his wife. My father's plan was to sell their jewelry shop and follow us here. They waited too long." Another extended pause allowed her to collect her emotions, which clearly had not diminished over the many decades since the events that provoked them.

"My uncle got word from a friend that they had been gassed at Auschwitz. Those Nazi bastards murdered my sister, too. Not at Auschwitz. Chawa was transferred to Poniatowa Labor Camp."

After that, Ruchla had little more to say, except that after the war was over and peace declared, her aunt and uncle had tried to find out what happened to her older sister. They received news that she had perished in the massacre that killed all but one-hundred prisoners at the camp. The grieving family had said the prayers for the dead, as they had done for their father and mother, and the two young sisters were told firmly that they must now get on with life in America. So that was what they did, carrying in their hearts the memory of their parents and the sister they had lost, never speaking of her again.

So, that was how I learned about my great-aunt Chawa Feldberg who, along with thousands of other Jews, was ripped from her home in early 1943 and taken first to Auschwitz, where she was tattooed, ending up at Poniatowa Labor Camp some twenty miles away. In the months she was there, my great-aunt sewed uniforms for the German army from early morning into late afternoon. At the beginning of November 1943, a group of prisoners staged a revolt that was quickly squashed. Not only were the prisoners who revolted punished, but on November fourth, all but one hundred of the camp's population were wiped out in 'Operation Harvest Festival.' A quaint name for mass murder.

Ruchla's abhorrent tale of inhumanity sent me searching on Jewish genealogy websites. Looking into the past was addictive and I was instantly hooked. So, naturally, I ordered a DNA kit and spat in a tube.

Chawa

For hours she lay as inert as if she, too, were dead; sandwiched between the naked corpses of other men, women, and children—their blood pooling between her neck and shoulder. The loud music the SS blared over the loudspeakers could not drown out the screams of the wounded. The shooting seemed to go on for hours, until at last, silence. The soldiers went away and the minutes kept ticking as Chawa drifted in and out of consciousness, her ears awash with the faint cries of the dying.

In shock, she found herself incapable of forming a coherent thought, let alone any idea of what she should do. Could not even fathom why she was still breathing. Sometime later, it might have been an hour after the last moans had ceased, the soldiers returned to make sure no one was left alive. Stunned as she was, Chawa could not have moved so much as an eyelash if she wanted to. When the rugged combat boot of a soldier stepped on her shoulder, she did not even flinch. And when they spat on the bodies and covered them with fir branches and lime, she lay unmoving, waiting for death to claim her.

The autumn wind howled. Darkness fell. Amazed afresh to find that she was still alive, Chawa suddenly became aware that near the guard shack, a fire was burning. An immense fire, growing fast and moving toward the barracks. Were the monsters planning to burn their bodies? Her brain started to wake up and connect with reality. To be burned alive was an even greater horror than being shot.

Exhausted by fear and shivering in the cold November evening, she forced her cramped muscles to start working. A bullet had penetrated her arm and left a hole, but that was nothing after all she had endured that day. She pushed the branches off, a memory penetrating the fog that blurred her mind: a mile or so from the camp, there was a town. Not allowing herself to think about what she was doing, Chawa clambered over the corpses and reached the edge of the trench. Somehow—she would never know how—she managed to pull herself up and climb out of the mass grave.

The burning barracks were close to the guard shack at the gate. Could she get past without being seen? What were her choices?

Naked, Chawa fled into the woods.

The DNA results were no surprise. 51% European Jewish and 49% a goulash. But I didn't care about any of that. It was the DNA *matches* that interested me. And there, among the thousand or so possible distant cousins, was one the website said was a close match. Just one. Adam Holt.

According to the site, he had been a member for some time, but had not yet built a family tree, so there was no way to know at what family intersection we connected. Hoping for a quick response, I sent him an email regarding the fact that we seemed to be related but I didn't know how and assumed it must be on my mother's side. We all know what they say about assumptions....

Adam must have been online, being that an excited response popped into my inbox almost immediately. *"Hey, cool to hear from you. I'm pretty new to this genealogy stuff. What surnames are you looking for?"*

After establishing that I was new, too, I listed the few family surnames I knew on both sides and hit Send.

Adam: *"OMG, I can't believe this. We're second cousins. Our grandmothers are sisters."*

Me, confused: *"My mother didn't have any sisters, only two brothers."*

Adam: *"No, not your mother. Your father's side. The Feldbergs."*

That didn't make sense. I frowned at the screen, nonplused. Aunty Ruchla never had kids and my father was her younger sister Sophie's only child. In my generation, it was just my brother and me. Before I had a chance to type that out, another email popped up.

Adam: *"My grandmother had two sisters, Ruchla and Sophie. You said your grandmother was Sophie, right? That makes us second cousins!"*

My head was spinning as I pounded out my next question: *"Wait—what is your grandmother's name?"*

"Eva, same as yours. She changed it when she moved to England after the war. In the old country (Poland), it was Chawa, pronounced like 'Hava.' See, cousins!!!"

I was still trying to make sense of what Adam Holt had written when he hit me with yet another question that left my mind reeling.

Adam: *"Do you know anything about the empress' ring?"*

Me: *"Slow down, please. You're saying Chawa survived the war?"*

Adam: *"Yes! She was at the Poniatowa Labor (concentration) Camp when she was 17. Some prisoners set it on fire after the SS massacre on November 4th. Check Wiki. It tells all about it. My grandmother escaped and was rescued by a farmer. His family hid her until VE Day in 1945."*

By then, I was shaking; hot and sweaty all over. I hardly dared to ask: *"Is she still alive?"*

Adam: *"She's 95 and kickin' hard. What about her sisters?"*

I couldn't believe what I was reading. I told him that my grandmother Sophie died eight years ago, and Ruchla, ten years younger than his grandmother, had recently recovered from cancer and was doing well. Then, I returned to his earlier question.

Me: *"What empress' ring'???"*

Adam: *"Catherine the Great. One of our ancestors was her lady's maid. She 'gave' (?) her a ring. How likely is that?! I only heard about it recently. Granny never spoke about it before. She said the ring was handed down through the generations to the eldest daughter, and she was the latest. She had it hidden on her when she was taken to Poniatowa. The prisoners found some crazy ingenious ways to hide their valuables. She hid it in a mug with a false bottom.*

"Six months after she arrived—like I said before—there was an uprising and the SS killed almost everyone in the camp. Get this— before the massacre, the Nazis made the prisoners dig what they claimed were anti-tank trenches. Guess what they were really for? The bodies. It's completely amazing that Chawa/Eva escaped—a miracle. My Gran is one amazing lady. I can't wait for you to meet her."

As I read what had happened to my great-aunt, my stomach knotted with anger. Like any person with a shred of humanity and decency, I had always been sickened by what the Nazis did. Learning that these atrocities had been committed against my own close family members brought it home with avalanche force. I had to step away from the computer and take a few deep breaths to keep from screaming.

When I calmed down, I learned that Adam had searched for his grandmother's sisters from time to time, but without their married names or locations, there wasn't much to go on. The family had moved from where his grandmother remembered they had lived in the US. And then, Adam joined the genealogy site and entered his DNA into the database. If only I had been curious sooner. Now, there was no time to lose.

The last time the two sisters were together, Ruchla had been a child of seven, Chawa a teenager. Now, they were closer to the end of their lives than the beginning, and yet there was a resemblance, not just in their looks but in their mannerisms, in the way they spoke. I felt a pang of regret to have missed a lifetime of this other great-aunt, but happiness that we had found her in time for the sisters to be reunited.

There is no adequate way to describe such a reunion which, due to the distance, was arranged over Zoom. They talked and cried and talked and cried some more until there was nothing left to say. Except for one thing.

"About the ring, Granny," Adam reminded his grandmother.

"Ah, yes. Do you remember the empress' ring?" Chawa asked her sister in the Polish-accented British that had developed over the years.

Ruchla's eyes lit up. "Of course I remember. Who could forget such a ring? There was a ruby in a gold setting with little diamonds around the ruby. I was once allowed to try it on—under close supervision, of course."

Chawa released a long, pained sigh. "These are things I've never talked about. But at my age, I feel that I need to pass my story on to my children's children. The ring is part of my story."

"I guess the Nazi bastards got it." Ruchla made a spitting sound that was pretty convincing.

"Yes and no. There was a boy who had a crush on me. His name was Jakob Banicki—"

Jakob—the name on the back of the photo that had started me on this journey. I listened harder.

"Yes, yes," Ruchla broke in. "I remember. I used to play dolls with the Banicki girls; the ones who were near my age. Weren't you in school with the older one?"

"That's right, darling, I was. You were so young at the time; maybe you didn't know that the Banickis became Nazi collaborators. Jakob was made a camp guard at Poniatowa. The inmates hated him for that. I know he felt terrible guilt for what his family had done, but how could I ever forgive him for doing the Nazis' bidding just to get better treatment?" Her eyes filled with tears from the pain of eons ago. "I was so sure I would marry Max—my boyfriend. When they took me to Poniatowa, he was kept at Auschwitz. We promised to find each other after the war, but—" Chawa closed her eyes and took two deep breaths.

As grateful as we all were for the ability to communicate electronically with our relatives on the other side of the world, Ruchla's strangled sob made me realize just how limited this kind of contact was. She needed to be in the same room with her sister, to hold her close. It was not adequate for me to hold my great-aunt, or for Adam to embrace his grandmother; they needed each other. Still, at their ages and with thousands of miles separating them, it was the best we could do.

Once she had gathered herself, Chawa continued her story. "Jakob used to follow me around everywhere. We were always starving and he would smuggle extra food to me. I wanted nothing to do with him, but I took it anyway. The most we ever got to eat was a little bread at breakfast and some watery vegetable soup at lunch and dinner; a little coffee. When Jakob was able to sneak me a cheese sandwich, it was a bite of heaven. Of course, I shared with the others in my barracks. We would save the sandwich for Saturday night when everyone could have a tiny piece. It was quite a party, I can tell you."

The story broke my heart, and when Adam cut in, I felt only relief.

"Granny," he said. "Sorry to interrupt, but you *were* talking about the empress' ring?"

Chawa paused to give him a stern frown before returning her attention to the webcam. "After the uprising, Jakob Banicki heard about the punishment that was coming and risked his life to warn me. What could I do to escape it? Nothing. So, I gave him the ring and asked him to please send it to my family in America and to let them know what happened to me."

"If he ever did, I never heard about it," said Ruchla. "I have no doubt our aunt and uncle would have passed it along to Sophie and me if they had it. They never had children themselves and they treated us with love."

While the sisters and Adam ruminated over what might have happened to the precious family heirloom, I got busy researching Jakob Banicki on my tablet. There were a handful of profiles with that name, but only one of them was 98 years old. When I saw where he lived, I let out a gasp. He was less than thirty miles from where I was sitting.

Elmhurst Villas was a modest but decent retirement home in Woodland Hills. When I phoned, they refused to put my call through to Jakob; instead, they contacted his granddaughter, Marlene. When she called to find out who I was and what I wanted of her grandfather, she wasn't particularly friendly and it seemed in my best interests not to tell the whole truth. Without doubt, if I told her I wanted to interrogate him, she wasn't going to let me see him. So I simply said he was an old friend of my great-aunt and I would love to meet him and give him a message from her. That worked.

Jakob Banicki was far from the frail old man I had expected. Not doddering or bent over, he wasn't even wearing glasses. There were wrinkles and liver spots—nobody escapes those—but luckily, his mind was clear and he was eager for a visit.

What I noticed most were his eyes. Even when he was looking straight at me, it was as though he was not seeing me, but looking through me. I searched for any expression of emotion and found none as we engaged in polite chit-chat for a few minutes. Jakob told me he had made his way to America after the war and eventually become an insurance salesman, raised a family. I had told him my great aunt's name, but not that she was still alive.

Eventually, I took the photo of her tattooed arm from my purse and held it out to him with a question. "Does this mean anything to you?"

Jakob took a look at it and his head jerked up. Those empty eyes finally focused on me. His voice shook as hard as his hand. "Where did you get this?"

I told him the story of finding my great-aunt Chawa, trying to harden my heart against sympathy when he broke down and wept.

"My people know nothing about that part of my life; about what we had to do to survive. I don't want them to know."

Recognizing that his family had acted in the interests of self-preservation more than seventy years ago, I found I couldn't hate him for it. Even on behalf of my own family. Maybe it was the cheese sandwiches he had smuggled Chawa that allowed forgiveness.

I handed him some tissues. As he was wiping his eyes, an angry voice spoke from the doorway. "What the hell is going on here? Grandpa?"

A stylish woman stormed into the room, glaring at me. "You said you weren't going to upset him."

I did not remember saying that, but I didn't have to defend myself, as Jakob shut her down with a harsh rebuke. "Who asked you to come, Marlene? I may be old, but I don't need a minder. If you want to stay, sit down and be quiet. Otherwise, leave."

"But, Grand—"

Jakob turned to me as if the interruption had not happened. "I sent that photo to Sophie many years ago."

I stared at him. "How did you know where to find Sophie?"

"The first letter I sent to her aunt and uncle came back 'unknown,' so I realized they must have moved. Many years later, I hired a private detective to find Sophie and her sister, Ruchla. He was able to trace Sophie." Jakob's brow scrunched as he thought back. "This must have been forty years ago."

I was aghast. "Why would you send her a picture like that?"

"Didn't you find the letter I sent with it?" he countered. "Just before the massacre, Chawa gave me a ring and asked me to send it to her sisters as a memento of her. I promised I would do my best, but with all that went on during the war, then the end of the war, and then I moved to the States—it wasn't a good time. The ring got lost. That's why it was so many years later that I wrote to her. I finally came across it in a box of old things."

The same way I had found the photo. "So you sent the ring to Sophie?" I asked, wondering why I had never heard anything about it.

Jakob shook his head. "Sophie wanted nothing to do with the ring. She wrote me back a very strong letter saying she wanted no memories of that part of her life and that I was never to contact her again."

Yet another shock in a string of them. All those years, my grandmother had known where the ring was and hadn't told her sister. Had she told my father? I would never know.

"Thank you for telling me this, Jakob," I said. "But—what happened to the ring?" I expected him to say he had lost it or sold it. I nearly fainted at his answer.

"I put it in a box. The ring wasn't mine. I thought maybe someday I would try contacting Sophie again, but I never did."

I didn't tell him the ring was a priceless artifact that had once belonged to Catherine the Great. Assuming the story handed down through the generations was true, though there was apparently no provenance to prove it, and from what I had read of the empress, she wasn't always friendly to the Jews. It seemed farfetched to imagine one working for her in the capacity of a lady's maid. But who knew?

Jakob handed me back the photo of my great-aunt's tattoo. "Her prisoner number is the combination to the box."

"Chawa will be so grateful to know," I said, almost holding my breath. "Where is the box now?" Behind me, I heard his granddaughter rustling around as Jakob closed his eyes and thought for a moment. He opened them and shook his head. "I'm sorry, it's so long ago. Marlene takes care of everything now. She'll figure out where it is. With my bank records. It's a lockbox."

I didn't think he noticed the look she gave him until he snarled at her. "You'll go and find it, and call Eva right away when you do."

I left Jakob with his granddaughter, whose eyes had an avaricious gleam that made me worry she might start pawing through his things and decide to keep the ring if she found it. At my father's house, I went back to the tin box in the cigar box in the cardboard box, looking for the letter Jakob had sent to my grandmother, Sophie.

My father was a packrat, apparently a trait he had inherited from his mother. The repository of invoices and statements and receipts in the boxes went back more years than he had been alive.

The New York addresses were where Sophie had lived. Sorting through the stacks of papers—searching for anything that might be bank information—by the end of an hour, I sat back on my heels, frustrated.

Then I decided to retrace my steps from the moment I found the tattoo photo.

Returning to the tin box and scraps of paper that I had overlooked in favor of the photo and letters, I wondered whether my father had combed through the box when his mother died, the way I was combing through it now. Since Sophie had rejected Jakob's attempt to make contact, it seemed unlikely she had shared the significance of the photo with her son. He certainly had not shared it with me. He had been devastated when his mother died of a sudden heart attack. It was my guess that he never knew anything about Chawa's internment at Poniatowa or the empress' ring.

I closely examined the papers, which mostly bore phone numbers and various notations written in my grandmother's distinctive scrawl. And then, suddenly, there it was. A letter written in Polish that I could not read. But I recognized the name of Jakob Banicki on the return address.

Three days later, Marlene Banicki met us at the storage facility where her grandfather's possessions had been boxed up since she moved him to the retirement home. Ruchla, who had confirmed the contents of his letter, clutched her handbag tight to her chest while in the passenger seat of my car all the way there. Furious with her late sister, she spent most of the journey—which she wouldn't have missed for anything—muttering how she couldn't believe the ring had been so close all this time, and how could Sophie have done such a thing as not tell her? Anyone would think it had been her highest priority in life, rather than something she hadn't spared a thought on since she was a child.

"Must be a pretty valuable ring," Marlene said with no grace whatsoever as she unlocked the big padlock on the roll-up door.

"Sentimental value," I said, nudging Ruchla when she opened her mouth to tell the story.

Complaining about her grandfather's habits, Marlene was forced to move several boxes before she found the one he had described to her. "I never packed this one," she said. "It was in his attic, packed up and sealed a long time ago. He insisted I shouldn't throw any of this stuff away, and I didn't have time to go through it. Stupid to keep paying the fee for this place every month when it's nothing he—"

I had only been half-listening, but when she broke off with a gasp, I turned, thinking she had found a spider or something. In her hands was something far worse. She was holding up a greyish green jacket. The lightning bolt 'SS' on the collar identified it as a World War II Nazi guard uniform. Marlene dropped it back in the box as if it burned her hands. "What the hell?"

The sight of it made me feel sick, but it wasn't my place to tell her that her grandfather's family were Nazi collaborators. "Must be a war souvenir," I suggested, giving her the easy way out.

"Why would he *keep* such a thing?" She pushed the jacket aside with obvious distaste and dug further into the box.

"Is it there?" Ruchla called from the doorway.

Marlene shot her a dirty look and plunged her hands back inside. "This better be it," she said, taking out a metal lockbox with five sets of dials on the front. "I'm not looking any further." Shoving it at me, she pushed past and went to the door, waiting for me to follow. I got the feeling that she had not bought my explanation for her grandfather's uniform and was upset by the find.

We went back to Ruchla's house, where I connected with my new cousin and his grandmother via WhatsApp and propped the phone up so they could share the moment with us.

But there was something I needed to do before entering the combination and opening the box.

"What's taking so long?" Ruchla prodded, practically jumping out of her chair.

"Give over, darling," the Polish-British tones of her older sister's voice came through the phone. "We've waited seventy years for this. Another minute won't make a blind bit of difference."

Pushing Ruchla's *kvetching* to the back of my head, I got the black and white photograph from my purse. Chawa's prisoner number was etched into my brain—15439—but it seemed fitting to have the photo on the table with us as I twisted the rotary dials to the combination that would unlock the box.

The lock clicked and I pushed the box over to Ruchla. With the eldest Feldberg in England watching on the small screen, it was up to her sister to open it.

Along with a small stack of old Deutsche Marks, which I would return to Marlene, was a small manila envelope, the size you might use for a spare key. I could see that Ruchla's hands were trembling as she reached for it; heard her sharp exclamation as she tipped the contents onto her palm.

"The empress' ring," I breathed.

Whether it had actually originated with Catherine the Great or not—and whether she had actually given it to our ancestor or it had been acquired by less honorable means—it was quite beautiful, the stones undimmed by the passage of time. I stared at it. Was it my imagination that the center ruby seemed to pulse with energy, its aura growing stronger and expanding—like a genie imprisoned in a bottle for centuries, freed at last?

"*Barukh Hashem,*" Ruchla murmured, closing her fist around it and holding it against her heart. I knew very little Yiddish, but I recognized the "Thank God" in those words. She held the ring close to the screen so Chawa could see it. My namesake grabbed hold of her grandson's hand and I could tell she was squeezing it hard.

"I'll find a secure way to mail it to you," I promised, hiding my reluctance to part with it now that we had found it. I didn't care whether the ring was intrinsically valuable; it had been touched by my ancestors for over two-hundred years, binding me to them in some mystical way. And having been hidden in a false-bottomed mug to keep it safe from the Nazis, now being returned to us, gave it meaning far beyond its terrible journey from Poniatowa. This ring was a tangible symbol of my great-aunt's will to survive; her courage; her endurance in the face of the worst that humanity had to offer.

Across the miles on the small screen, Chawa's smile was filled with love. "Eva, my darling, from one eldest daughter to the next generation's eldest, the ring is yours now."

It slipped onto my finger as though it had been made for me.

***

MASQUERADES
CAN BE MURDER

A Carol and Jim Andrews
Baby Boomer Mini-Mystery

SUSAN SANTANGELO

Chapter 1

I miss the good old days, when white bread was good for you and nobody knew what kale was.

"What are you doing on July 7th?" Jim bounded into the kitchen, his face ruddy from the cold.

I'll probably still be sitting at the kitchen table, addressing Christmas cards to people I don't even know but you insist we keep on "our list," just like I'm doing now. I hope to be finished by Labor Day. I didn't really say that out loud, of course.

"Carol, I asked you a question. What are you doing on July 7th? Or, better yet, what do you think *I'm* doing on July 7th? Go ahead, guess. You'll never figure it out."

I swear, I hadn't seen my husband this excited since he'd found out that CVS was offering double coupons in a special midnight blowout sale.

"You may be shocked to hear this," I replied, marking the point on my Christmas card list where'd I'd left off addressing envelopes so I could begin again later, "but as of now, I have no plans. What exactly do you have in mind?" I squinted at my list. "And who the heck are Lydia and Joe White? I've never heard of them."

"I have no idea," Jim said. "They must be your friends. Take them off the list. Heck, take everybody off the list. Start a new list. Or don't send out any cards at all." He frowned. "The cost of postage is going up, you know. We need to watch our expenses."

Oh, joy! Hallelujah! It didn't matter what Jim was doing on July 7th if it meant no more handwritten holiday cards. I just hoped he never found out about ecards. Then I'd have to start a whole new list.

I wriggled my right hand to get the circulation up and going and gave my husband my complete attention. "July 7th?" I repeated. "Let me think. Are you going to the beach to work on your tan? Mowing the lawn? Painting the shutters on our house?"

Reality dawned, and I jumped up and gave my husband a big smooch. "Oh, honey, you finally bought that sailboat you've been talking about for so long. What a great present for both of us! When the weather finally warms up, we'll have a christening party for the boat with champagne and invite all our friends to come. It needs a name, though. What should we call it?"

Jim looked at me like I had taken complete leave of my senses—a familiar facial expression. "I haven't bought a boat, Carol. What I'm doing on July 7th is even better." He grinned, then announced, "The Fairport Business Association is organizing the first-ever reenactment of the British attack on Fairport that occurred on July 7, 1779. I'm on the steering committee, and I'm going to be one of the militiamen defending our town. I'll even get to wear a uniform and carry a musket. And you, my dear wife," he said, giving me a kiss on the forehead, "will be getting all spiffed up to go to a fancy masquerade ball at the Porter Mansion as part of the commemoration. What do you think about *that*?"

Without waiting for a response, Jim grabbed an apple from the fruit bowl on the kitchen table. "I didn't have lunch at the Business Association meeting, so I'm hungry. Here's more information about the event if you want to check it out. We decided to call it Celebrate Fairport." He dropped a folder on the kitchen table, causing my carefully arranged pile of Christmas cards to topple to the floor in a heap, and headed toward the bedroom.

Honestly, that Jim. I've often wondered how long it takes before a married couple becomes completely in sync with each other. Whatever that magic number is, my husband of almost forty years and I still had a long way to go.

***

My name is Carol Andrews, and I've lived in the beautiful

Connecticut town of Fairport all my life. Fairport is one of the Nutmeg State's best-kept secrets. Not quite as tony as Greenwich, Darien or some of the other Gold Coast towns, it's a convenient and fast train ride (assuming Metro North is running on time) into Manhattan, making it an ideal location for commuters.

Fairport is also a very historic town, one of the oldest in Connecticut, and was originally called Uncoway. It was founded in 1639 by Puritans and Congregationalists from the Massachusetts Bay Colony, who purchased a large tract of land from the Pequonnock Indians. Truth to tell, the only reason I know all this stuff is because our son, Mike, had to write a paper on the history of Fairport in junior high school. I made it my business to be sure he did a good job.

I also knew that on July 7, 1779, during the American Revolutionary War, British troops attacked Fairport and burned down the vast majority of its buildings. To this day, there are houses in our historic district with floors that still have burn marks from that savage attack. One of the houses that was totally destroyed by the British was the Porter Mansion, home of the wealthy John and Elizabeth Porter, who were known for giving lavish parties there. The attack took place during a masquerade ball at the mansion. Legend has it that our town was re-named Fairport to honor Elizabeth, reputed to be "fair of hair and fair of face." John was particularly outspoken about his anti-Tory views, and was killed by the British during the attack. The mansion was eventually rebuilt, and still stands to this day.

As horrible as the Burning of Fairport must have been, I was surprised that the Fairport Business Association had suddenly decided to make such a big deal about it. But if Jim was getting involved in something that would keep him busy and out of my hair for the next several months, I was all for it.

I, however, would not allow myself to be roped into helping organize it in any way. Period. And I had the perfect excuse. Our daughter, Jenny, and her husband, Fairport Police Detective Mark Anderson, had presented us with our first grandchild, Carlton James, known as CJ. I was named the official Babysitter-in-Chief so the parents could return to their demanding jobs. Yay!

I sent up a silent prayer of thanks to the Good Lord for the unexpected gift of a busy husband in the new year. The Good Lord, as it happened, had other plans.

Chapter 2

It's the start of a brand new year, and I'm off like a herd of turtles.

"I thought seven was supposed to be a lucky number," I said as I folded and stuffed a "Save the Date" flyer into an envelope and sealed it. "We've been at this for hours. This wasn't the way I'd planned to start the new year."

"I don't know what you're complaining about," said my very best and oldest friend, Nancy Green, who'd already announced as soon as she'd arrived a half hour late that she couldn't stay long because she had to meet an important real estate client. "Seven is lucky. Celebrate Fairport is on July 7. That's the seventh day of the seventh month, which is exactly seven months from today. I'm really looking forward to it, especially the masquerade ball at night, when we get a chance to put on fancy clothes for a change. That's a whole lot of luck if you ask me. So, what's your problem?"

Claire McGee, my sometimes friend (and sometimes not, depending on how critical she's being) spoke up. "We've only been working on this mailing for forty-five minutes. You always exaggerate, Carol." Barely taking a breath, she continued, "And as to your question, Nancy, Carol's problem is that once again she's allowed herself to be coerced into volunteering for another local project because she just can't say no. Which has resulted in her coercing the rest of us to get involved, too. And now, she feels guilty about it."

"I don't feel guilty about involving you three," I clarified, itching to take a quick slug at Claire but restraining myself. I abhor violence. "I'm really mad at myself for getting involved in the first place after

I promised myself I wouldn't."

"You needed our help," Mary Alice, always the peacemaker in our group, chimed in, giving my hand a quick squeeze of solidarity. "Ever since grammar school, we've always been there for each other. You know you can count on us."

My eyes misted over for a quick second, especially when Nancy, and then Claire, nodded in agreement. For the next few minutes, we worked in companionable silence—a rare occurrence for us. Someone's always talking (me) and someone else is always interrupting.

"There's another reason why I'm not keen on helping organize the event." I jammed another "Save the Date" flyer into an envelope for emphasis. "I think the whole idea is stupid."

So much for companionable silence. Everyone started talking at once.

"Everyone else in town is excited about it," Mary Alice said. "Including me." She gave me an apologetic look for disagreeing with me.

"Celebrate Fairport is a terrific way to bring new people to town," Nancy added. "When they see how wonderful Fairport is, naturally they'll want to live here, too. Property values will soar."

"And so will your real estate business," I said, giving her a dirty look. "Admit it. You don't really care about the town history at all."

"That's not true," Nancy protested, her cheeks flushed. I continued to stare at her, and she finally said, "Well, maybe it's partly true. But I do care about the town's history. That was a low blow."

Claire clapped her hands and bellowed, "Quiet! You're all giving me a headache. Besides, you're missing the point. Carol thinks Celebrate Fairport is stupid because Jim's now co-chairing it. She has to take orders from him, and she resents it."

I started to protest, but I realized she could be right. Darn. I hate when that happens. Not that I planned to admit it.

"You have no idea what's been going on around here," I said. "And it'll only get worse as we get closer to July. Contrary to what you may think, Claire, I'm thrilled about him now being the co-chair of this reenactment. He's out of the house all the time going to meetings. You wouldn't believe how many committees and subcommittees a tiny local event like this has. It's absolutely ridiculous."

I held up my hand as Claire started to interrupt me. "I'm not finished talking." *So be quiet for once in your life.* I didn't really say that out loud, of course.

I thought I heard someone mutter, "You never are." But I could have been wrong.

"The Fairport Militia volunteers are having all their practices right here. Can you imagine a bunch of old men marching in formation all around my house for hours? Believe me, it's not pleasant."

"They're not using real guns, I hope," Mary Alice said, looking worried.

"Not so far, thank goodness. Everyone brings a yardstick and pretends it's a musket. But they plan to use actual muskets for the reenactment." I rolled my eyes. "Although where they'll find those is anybody's guess. I don't think Amazon carries them."

"Are they really marching inside the house?" Nancy asked, trying hard not to laugh.

"They're outside, thank goodness. Unless it snows. If the weather's bad, Jim wanted to drill inside the house, but I put a stop to that idea right away. Stop by around three this afternoon and you can check them out for yourself. And that's not even the worst part of it. Jim's growing a beard, and he's not getting a haircut before the reenactment. He wants his hair to be long enough by July 7th to tie in a ponytail. I can't imagine how horrible he's going to look."

"I'm sure you're exaggerating just a teeny bit," Claire said. "It can't be *that* bad. Even if it is, at least Jim's keeping busy. That's what you've always wanted."

"You're behaving now the same way you did about our 40th high school reunion, Carol," Nancy added. "You didn't want anything to do with that, either. We finally talked you into it, and look at the great time we all had."

"Finding the dead body of a classmate in my bed the night before the reunion isn't my idea of a great time, Nancy," I shot back. "In case you've forgotten about that part."

"You do seem to have a knack for stumbling over dead bodies

with increasing frequency," Claire said.

"That's totally Jim's fault. When he retired, I needed to find a new hobby."

Chapter 3

People who say they can't complain should just try harder.

Sleep wouldn't come. Maybe it was Jim snoring next to me that was keeping me awake. Or maybe it was because our two English cocker spaniels, Lucy and Ethel, had spread out so much on my side of the bed that I was practically on the floor. I checked my cell phone for the time. Rats. It was already after midnight and I'd been tossing and turning for over an hour.

Get up, check your email or read a book for a while, Carol. When you stop thinking about sleep, it's guaranteed to come.

I took my own good advice and eased myself off the bed as quietly as I could. The dogs stirred, then spread themselves out even more, now completely taking over my spot on the bed. I decided I'd deal with that problem later.

In a jiffy, I was at my computer, checking and deleting my newest emails. The whole process took less than ten minutes, and I was still wide awake.

It suddenly occurred to me that I'd been given a perfect opportunity to check out more of our town's history. I entered "Fairport, Connecticut" into the search engine and prepared to saturate my brain with local knowledge.

The first thing I learned was that "BB" meant "Before Battle," referring to houses in our historic district which were built before 1779. "BB" houses were considered more valuable, especially if the structures had burn marks from the battle on their floors. I wondered if Nancy knew that.

We live in an antique home, so next I decided to research

our own house's history. A preliminary perusing of the Fairport Historical Society web page only told me that it was built in 1795, so it was an "AB," or "After Battle" structure. Oh, well. I still loved it. My curiosity was really piqued now, so I decided to do some digging and find out more.

I was overwhelmed by the amount of additional websites I had to choose from, and had no idea where to begin. I yawned and decided I'd done enough research for one night. It was time to get some shut-eye. As I was logging off, I was surprised to see a drawing of my house pop up on the screen. As I studied the drawing, I sensed someone watching me. Rats. I was busted.

I turned around to apologize to Jim for waking him up. But no one was there.

***

I awoke from a restless sleep, reluctant to face the day. No matter how much I tried, I couldn't forget the feeling that someone had been with me last night. I wanted to tell Jim, even though I could predict his reaction in advance—that my late-night visitor was merely my overactive imagination working overtime. In fact, I was counting on him to convince me that he was right.

I stumbled out of bed and into the bathroom. Ugh. Who was that old woman looking back at me in the mirror?

I made my way to the kitchen, anticipating the first cup of Jim's delicious coffee—one of the few perks of having a retired husband in the house. Jim rustled the newspaper and mumbled a greeting as I sank onto a chair opposite him.

There's an unwritten rule in our house that, if one person is reading a book, newspaper, or magazine, the other person is not allowed to interrupt them except for a real emergency. Recalling how freaked out my late-night experience had made me feel, I was sure the "emergency" criteria had been met.

"Jim, I have to talk to you. It's important. Someone was in our house last night."

"You must have been dreaming, Carol. I didn't hear a thing."

MASQUERADES *CAN BE* MURDER

Big surprise. You wouldn't hear anyone if he was shouting in your ear. I didn't really say that out loud, of course.

"I wasn't sleeping," I insisted. "I was wide awake. And I wasn't in bed. I was in the office on the computer."

"It's obvious that you were only dreaming you were using the computer, so you only dreamed you heard someone. You know what a vivid imagination you have."

Jim was saying exactly what I wanted him to say, and I was trying hard to convince myself that he was right. A teeny part of me kept insisting that someone had really been there, but I forced myself to ignore it. The more I thought about it, the whole idea of an invisible guest seemed ludicrous. "I guess you're right, dear. I must have been dreaming." I took a fortifying gulp of coffee and immediately felt better.

"Attagirl," Jim said, handing me the newspaper. "Maybe this will cheer you up. My story about the reenactment is on the front page. I may not have told you this, but the Historical Society is loaning us all their research on the attack, so we'll be able to recreate every single detail of the march from the beach into town and the attack on the Porter Mansion."

"Every single detail? You're not actually going to burn the place down, are you?"

"Of course not, Carol. What a silly thing to say. We're thinking of simulating the burning with a fireworks display at the mansion." He made a note on his phone. "I'm off to another planning meeting. I'll be gone most of the day." He grabbed his briefcase with all the event files and was out the door before I could say goodbye.

You just got lucky, Carol. You have the whole day to search for information about your house without any interruption. Then you can give Jim a local history lesson for a change!

Chapter 4

When you ask me what I'm doing today and I say, "noth- ing," it doesn't mean that I'm free. It means I'm doing nothing.

After a quick shower and a satisfactory visit to my bedroom closet—meaning I found a pair of pressed khaki pants that actually fit me and a matching blouse—I was ready to spend my day in front of the computer. Lucy and Ethel, always ready to expand their knowledge base, trotted after me into the office and settled themselves under my desk.

The computer sprang to life, and I saw that the desktop wallpaper had been changed from a picture of our grandson to one of our house. Darn that Jim. He'd done it without asking me first. I had no idea how to fix it, so I'd have to wait until he got home.

Muttering under my breath so the dogs wouldn't hear me (they're very sensitive), I pressed the Google icon and ordered the search engine to wake up. Another drawing of our house appeared, but this time there was a huge red *X* scrawled across a widow's walk on the roof.

"We don't have a widow's walk on our roof," I informed Lucy and Ethel. Lucy gave me one of her famous looks, pointing out how stupid I was. I hate it when one of my dogs is smarter than I am, but I realized she was right. The house must have had a widow's walk years ago that was torn down long before we bought it.

"I get it, Lucy. But who marked the drawing with the red *X*?" Even more puzzling, why was the red so bright, when the rest of the drawing was a faded black and white?

Deciding this was one puzzle I didn't need to deal with right now, I put our address in the search engine again and began to read. In no time at all, I was lost in a fascinating history.

"Our house was built sixteen years after the burning of Fairport," I informed the dogs. Knowing what a stickler for details Lucy always was, I clarified. "According to this website, that's when the first owner, Elizabeth Porter, moved into the house, not when construction on the house actually started."

Receiving no rebuke from Her Majesty on my historical accuracy, I went back to my reading, then stopped, realizing what

I'd just discovered. The first occupant of our house was Elizabeth Porter. I had assumed that when the Porter Mansion was rebuilt after the burning, Elizabeth had lived there until her death. But I was wrong. I had no idea she'd ever lived in our house.

I was interrupted from my musings by a text from my daughter, reminding me of today's babysitting gig and wondering where I was. Yikes! It was time to reset my priorities. There was no way I'd be late for a date with my favorite grandson.

***

I made it to Jenny and Mark's condo in only fifteen minutes, thanks to years of carpooling duty that had forced me to learn every back road in town. "I hope you're not mad at me," I said, giving Jenny a big hug. "I got here as quickly as I could. I set my phone alarm for eleven fifteen, but it never rang. When I checked my phone a little while ago, I swear it was only nine-thirty." I glanced at my phone, which now read 11:45. I checked the alarm setting, which showed it had rung at the correct time. *Why didn't I hear it?*

You're not losing your mind, Carol. You didn't have your glasses on before. Or there's something wrong with your phone.

But when I considered the scary feeling I'd had last night, the house drawing that had popped up on the computer, and now losing track of time, maybe there was something wrong with me.

"It's okay, Mom," Jenny said, misinterpreting my worried look. "I'm glad I gave you a gentle reminder, though. I just fed CJ and put him down for a nap. With any luck, he'll probably sleep for a few hours. You can peek in and say hello to him, as long as you don't wake him up. Go ahead and do that, then come back. Let's talk for a minute."

Focus, Carol. And for heaven's sake, stay calm for Jenny's sake. Don't anticipate the worst. CJ doesn't have a life-threatening illness, Jenny and Mark aren't getting a divorce, and you're absolutely fine.

Rather than speed walk down the hallway to gaze at the most perfect grandchild ever born, I plopped my posterior onto the nearest chair. "CJ's sound asleep, and I'm not really late. What's going on?"

"Mark asked me to talk to you." Jenny fidgeted in her chair. "It's about Celebrate Fairport."

I laughed. "Aren't you talking to the wrong parent? Your father is the one who's involved in that event up to his eyebrows. I'm doing my best to stay out of it."

"I know it's Dad's project, not yours. But Mark was hoping you could get Dad to see reason about some of the plans before things get completely out of control."

"Out of control? I don't understand."

"Here's what Mark told me, and this is 'off the record,' okay?"

"Whatever you say," I said, relieved that I'd have something else to think about than my possible lost grip on reality.

"Fairport's population soars in the summer with all the tourists who want to go to the beach. The reenactment celebration is bound to attract even more people and make traffic a nightmare. The department may have to hire extra police, and there's no money in the budget for that.

"His boss also heard a rumor that the committee wants to add a fireworks display at the Porter Mansion to the re-enactment, which is a safety hazard."

"I don't have input on these things," I said. "Mark or the police chief should talk to the First Selectwoman or the Fairport Business Association about these concerns. And wouldn't the committee need a permit for the fireworks?"

"The major problem is the fireworks," Jenny said. "The chief wants to stop it before it gets to the permit phase, but he's reluctant to bring up anything that might damage the department's relationship with our new First Selectwoman. Carla Grimaldi is the first female ever elected to that position, and unofficially, he's heard that she's all for it. He passed the buck to Mark, and Mark passed it on to me. And now, to you. So, will you help? Please?"

"I think Mark's boss is being a little ridiculous."

"I agree with you. But the chief's contract comes up for renewal in a few months, and he's being extra sensitive. He wants to keep his job. So, will you talk to Dad?"

"Okay. But I can't guarantee how he'll respond."

"Thanks so much, Mom. I knew I could count on you and Mark's not expecting a miracle. At least he can tell his boss that he tried." Jenny picked up her backpack and slung it over her shoulder. "I'm proud of you for not getting sucked into this Celebrate Fairport event. Things are getting a little nuts."

"I'm getting more interested in Fairport's history than I expected," I confessed. "Did you know that Elizabeth Porter was the first owner of our house? I wonder what she looked like."

"Mom, you already know," Jenny said. "There are portraits of her and her husband hanging in the Town Hall lobby. Stop by and say hello to her after you leave here. I'll be back by three." She gave me a quick kiss and was on her way.

***

I was able to put all thoughts about Celebrate Fairport out of my head for the next three delightful hours. Spending time with an adorable baby, even if that time is mostly spent sitting beside his crib and watching him sleep, is a foolproof way to bring joy to any grandmother's heart. Jenny arrived home much too soon for me, but she is his mother, so I surrendered my little love back to her and reluctantly headed home.

On impulse, since I had to pass by anyway, I made a sudden turn into the Town Hall lot, earning a loud horn blast from the driver behind me. I gave him a quick wave of apology (using my whole hand, in case you were wondering) and zipped into a convenient parking space right in front of the building.

"Ready or not, here I come, Elizabeth," I said as I walked up the front steps of the white colonial building. "I hope you're easy to find because I have to get home and start dinner."

Once inside, I immediately saw a pair of large oil portraits flanking the front door of the First Selectwoman's office. The brass plaques identified the couple as Elizabeth and John Porter. How stupid I was. I'd never noticed them before, despite passing by them hundreds of times on my way to renew dog licenses or pay our house taxes.

As I stepped closer to get a better look, I heard a woman say, "I never liked that picture."

I turned to see if the person speaking was someone I knew. But there was no one there.

Chapter 5

When someone asks me what I did over the weekend, I squint and ask, "Why? What did you hear?"

"I'm sure the odd things that keep happening have a reasonable explanation," I told myself, running water over the dirty supper dishes before I loaded them into the dishwasher. (And Jim re-loaded them. One of his many post-retirement hobbies that drives me nuts.) "For instance, someone could have been passing by me today at Town Hall, commented on the portrait of Elizabeth Porter, and then disappeared into an office. That's why I didn't see her."

Yeah, sure, Carol. And pigs fly, too.

I hate it when I argue with myself. I never know which side I'm on.

I looked down at Lucy and Ethel, who were reminding me with gentle nudges that their dinner service was running late tonight. "You don't think I'm going crazy, do you?" I asked them as I poured kibble into their bowls.

It suddenly dawned on me that I was talking to two dogs. Not only that, I expected them to answer me. And I'd been doing it for years.

I had a brief moment of panic, picturing the moment when my family finally figured out my declining mental state. Jenny and Mark wouldn't trust me to take care of CJ, Jim would quietly divorce me, and our son Mike would confess that the real reason he'd moved so far away from home was that he wanted to put as much distance between himself and his loony mother as possible.

There was only one thing I could do. I turned off the kitchen lights, trusting Jim to take out the dogs for one last walk. I sent Jim a quick text outlining Mark's concerns about the upcoming reenactment as an FYI, and suggesting he deal with his son-in-law directly, leaving me out of it.

Then, I went to bed.

***

In the sunny morning light of a beautiful spring day, last night's dark thoughts seemed laughable. But just to be sure, after I sent Jim off to still another marching practice—this one re-tracing the actual 1779 route—I decided to give my sanity a little test.

I often walk into a room and then don't remember why I'm there. Or I leave things someplace, then don't remember where they are. As a test, I walked around my house and carefully placed three everyday objects in three different rooms: my cell phone, my reading glasses, and my wallet. My own version of Hide and Seek. Then I forced myself to take a long shower, followed by a romp outside with Lucy and Ethel.

Satisfied that enough time had passed, I sent up a silent prayer to St. Anthony, the patron saint of lost objects (just in case I needed a little extra help), and set off on my quest.

Every object was right where I remembered. What a relief! Maybe there was hope for me after all.

I decided to reward myself with some retail therapy. I needed to find something suitably fancy to wear to the masquerade ball at the Porter Mansion that was capping off Celebrate Fairport. After all, my husband was an important member of the planning committee, and as his wife, I had to look my best.

I had my hand on my cell phone, all set to invite Nancy, Claire and Mary Alice to come with me, when I realized I had to devise a clever strategy to justify the expensive purchase of a dress I'd only wear once. I'd saved a few of the cocktail dresses I wore during those long-ago New York City party days, when Jim and I were invited to black tie events on a regular basis.

I remembered one basic black number that I still had in my

bedroom closet. It was perfect for any occasion—simple enough to wear for a solemn event (*i.e.*, a funeral), but easily jazzed up with sparkly accessories for a night on the town. In the interest of keeping peace in the family, I resolved to try that one on first. If it fit, I promised myself that I'd wear it for the masquerade ball. And for once, my dear husband wouldn't have anything to complain about.

"I know just where that dress is," I said to the dogs as I sifted through the hangers in my closet. "It's way in the back, next to the navy suit that I also never wear." I realized what I'd just done and clapped my hand over my mouth. "I've got to stop doing that."

I found the suit without any problem, but not the dress. Suddenly, I was right back where I'd started this morning, before my successful game of Hide and Seek. AARRGH.

I closed my eyes and ordered myself to think rationally for a change, instead of flipping out like I did yesterday. I searched my mental filing cabinet and—wonder of wonders—a memory popped up, clear as day. I'd taken that black dress to the attic and stored it in the same garment bag I used for my other fancy duds. Phew.

I normally reserve trips to the attic for a time when Jim is home. My attic is spooky, which isn't unusual for a house as old as ours. Being up there creeps me out, and if you were ever up there with me, you'd feel the same way. Knowing Jim is within screaming distance if I need him gives me much needed peace of mind. But that scenario wasn't going to work today.

Be a brave girl, Carol. Go upstairs, grab the garment bag, and scurry back to safety. You can do it. Before I had second thoughts and chickened out, I headed to the second floor, the two dogs close behind me.

"Stay," I ordered. "I'll only be five minutes. And if you're good, I'll give you a biscuit when we go to the kitchen." I saw their two stubby tails wag when they heard me say, "biscuit," so I figured they'd understood what I said.

I made my way up the attic stairs and was relieved to see the garment bag hanging exactly where I remembered. Thank goodness. I lugged the bag down to our bedroom, and placed it carefully on the bed. It was a lot heavier than I remembered, but I was a lot younger and stronger when I'd taken it upstairs.

I was excited to finally have a chance to dress up again. Maybe I'd have fun at the masquerade ball, assuming Jim put away his musket before we started to dance.

After giving Lucy and Ethel the promised dog biscuits, I unzipped the garment bag and took out one dress at a time, pausing to check each one out before placing it on the bed. All of them were black and in sizes I hadn't had on my body and actually zipped up in years. Depressing! And where was the simple black dress I'd been counting on? I prayed that it had fallen off its hanger and was at the bottom of the bag.

I reached in, felt around, and pulled out one more dress. But not the one I was expecting. This one was very old, and although its blue color had faded over the years, I could tell that it must have been beautiful in its day. Was it possible that the dress had been lying at the bottom of the garment bag for years and I'd never noticed?

I picked it up carefully and wondered if it would fit me. That's when I noticed stains on the skirt. They looked like dried blood. Yuck.

"I've never seen this dress before in my life," I said to the dogs, who were sitting at my feet facing me. "I don't know how it got here, but I'm getting rid of it as soon as I can."

I felt a prickle on my neck, then heard a woman say, "It's *my* dress, Carol."

Chapter 6

When I was a kid, I wanted to be older. This is not what I expected.

OMG. Now I was hearing voices.

"You're not imagining this. Please don't be afraid."

In that split second, I didn't want to know if someone was there or not. Both possibilities were equally terrifying.

Holding my breath and sending up a silent prayer to whichever saint might have a little extra time to protect me when I screamed, I turned around and saw a young woman sitting in my favorite chair. On her lap was the simple black dress I hadn't been able to find.

"I borrowed this to see how it would look on me and didn't get a chance to put it back. I'm sorry."

I stood as still as a marble statue, but the dogs didn't. Both canines bounded over and sat at her feet, allowing her to stroke their heads like they were old pals.

"I love your dogs, Carol. Thank you for sharing them with me."

This entire conversation was much too strange for me. And believe me, that's saying a lot.

I snapped my fingers to call the dogs, but they both ignored me, content to focus their attention on my "guest."

"I don't understand," I said. "Who are you? How did you get here? And why do my dogs know you?" I reached out my hand, then stopped. "Are you really here, or am I imagining this?"

The woman stood up, and I was surprised to see how petite she was. Not even five feet tall. "You're not imagining anything. I live here. I've always lived here. And since you finally found my blue dress, it was time for us to get to know each other, face to face." She held out my own dress. "This looks much better on you than it did on me. I shouldn't have taken it."

Our hands touched as I reached out to take the black dress. I was surprised at how warm her hands were. They felt like real, honest-to-goodness, flesh and blood, normal hands.

"I'm sure this is a shock to you. I'm sorry that you've been so upset recently. I was trying to get your attention before I revealed myself so you'd have some idea of what was happening." She frowned. "But you didn't react the way I hoped you would. Fortunately, you found the blue dress. That's the key for me to tell you my secret."

I was speechless. A rare moment, which Jim would be sorry to have missed.

Jim! What if he walked in right now? What would he think?

As if reading my thoughts, my visitor responded. "Jim won't be back for two hours, so don't worry. We won't be interrupted." She gestured for me to sit on the bed, then made herself comfortable on my chair. *My* chair!

"I know you have many questions. I don't blame you. You've heard me speak before, but you didn't realize who it was. The most recent time was at Town Hall yesterday. You were looking at my portrait and I told you I never liked it. Remember?"

"Do you mean to tell me that you're Elizabeth Porter? But you can't be here. You've been dead for over two hundred years!"

"I know. I think I look pretty good for my age, don't you?"

"I have no idea. I've never seen a person this old before," I said without thinking. *Nice going, big mouth. Now she'll probably put a curse on you.*

"I don't mean to get too personal, but I have another question," I said, emboldened by Elizabeth's apparent friendliness. "Are you a ghost?"

"I'm still working on it. That's where you come in."

"*Me?* What do I have to do with it? I hope you don't mean I'm going to die soon and join you. I just became a grandmother for the first time!"

Elizabeth tsked, sounding very much like Sister Rose, my old high school English teacher. "Don't be so dramatic, Carol. I'll come back tomorrow and we'll continue our chat. Meanwhile, you must promise not to say a word to anyone about our conversation. Agreed?"

"Sure." Telling anyone that I was having friendly girlish chats with a long-dead woman was the last thing in the world I'd ever do.

"Excellent, Carol. Thank you. I suggest you get to bed early again tonight. Sweet dreams." And she disappeared.

Chapter 7

We all get heavier as we get older because there's a lot more information in our heads. That's my story and I'm sticking to it.

I woke up the following morning feeling like I'd never slept at all.

I vaguely remembered having terrible dreams, but none of their details. Squinting at the clock on our bedside table, I was shocked to see it was already 9:00. Yikes! I sprinted to the bathroom, then into the kitchen, where a fresh pot of coffee was, thankfully, waiting for me. My two canines barely raised their heads to wish me good morning, so I figured Jim had fed them breakfast before he left for still another meeting or militia drill for Celebrate Fairport.

I'd been completely unresponsive last night as Jim droned on and on about the ever-changing event schedule. I didn't even react when he announced he was thinking of keeping his beard after the reenactment was over, because he thought it made him look distinguished.

If I'd seen Jim this morning, I might have been tempted to spill the beans about yesterday's surprise visitor. Maybe even brag a little that I had inside information about the reenactment that I couldn't tell him about. But I couldn't run the risk of making Elizabeth angry. Lord knows what she'd do if I broke the promise I'd made to her.

Knowing in advance that I was going to have "out of this world" company, I decided after a quick shower to spiff up the house a little. I was just dragging the vacuum out of the front hall closet, where it'd been lying unused for several weeks, when I heard a discreet cough behind me.

"Please don't feel you have to clean the house because of me," I heard Elizabeth say, startling the heck out of me.

"You surprised me," I said. "I thought you'd be here in the afternoon, like you were yesterday."

"Let's just say that I have a flexible schedule," my new pal said with a smile. "This is a conversation I've been waiting to have for over two hundred years. I'm anxious to get started, if that's all right with you."

"Sure," I said. *Talking to a dead person is tops on my to-do list today, too.* I didn't really say that out loud, of course. I didn't have to.

"Great. It's tops on my to-do list, too."

Realizing I'd better be careful of my thoughts, I gestured toward the kitchen and reverted to my tried-and-true hostess role. "Let's sit down and have some coffee. Or would you prefer tea?"

"That was in Boston, not Fairport," Elizabeth said. I guess I looked puzzled, so she clarified. "The Boston Tea Party. I was trying to make a joke. I'm a little nervous."

I put two mugs of steaming coffee on the table, sat down, and waited for her to begin.

"How did you sleep last night?" she asked.

"I slept through the night," I said. "That's very unusual for me. But I woke up exhausted, like I hadn't slept at all." I yawned for emphasis. "Excuse me."

"You're exhausted because you really didn't sleep," she said. "You were wide awake, and you were really there."

"There? Where?"

"Before I answer you, can you remember anything about the night? Did you have any dreams?"

"Yes. Horrible ones. I don't want to remember them."

"I want you to concentrate on your dreams," Elizabeth said. "It's important. Tell me what you saw."

I closed my eyes and everything came back to me. It was like watching a movie inside my head. "There was screaming. People were running for their lives. They were trying to get away from… soldiers. There were so many soldiers. They were dressed in red uniforms, killing everyone they caught. It was complete carnage. Buildings were burning. There was so much blood everywhere. It was horrible." I started to cry uncontrollably.

"I know it was horrible," Elizabeth said gently. "You went back to July 7, 1779 and witnessed the Battle of Fairport. The real one, not the silly one the reenactors are trying to replicate. They have no idea what it was like."

"I was there?" I repeated. "Are you kidding me? How did that happen?"

"I had to bring you there to see how it happened. Now I can tell you the rest of my story. Please, close your eyes again. Do you see a woman running into a garden with soldiers chasing her? She's wearing a beautiful blue gown. Tell me what you see."

"I see a woman in a blue gown, crying," I said. "Men are attacking her. It's too much! I don't want to see any more."

"I know it's hard to watch," Elizabeth said. "That's enough. You can open your eyes now. Take a deep breath, and tell me when you're ready for me to continue."

A few minutes must have passed. I have no idea how many. "I'm better now. Go on."

"The woman you saw being attacked is me," Elizabeth said.

I exhaled the breath I didn't realize I was holding as she continued to speak. "And the blue dress you found is the one I was wearing that night."

"How in the name of heaven did you manage to survive?"

"I fought like crazy to save myself," Elizabeth said. "And I was able to save my two girls before our house burned to the ground."

"I admire you so much. You were incredibly brave."

"I have to tell you the rest," Elizabeth said. "This is the hardest part. During the battle, I murdered my husband."

I was stunned. Here I was, sitting in my own kitchen, having a cup of coffee with a dead person who'd just confessed to a murder she committed over two hundred years ago. I didn't even bother to search my mental filing cabinet for an appropriate response.

"I can see that you're shocked. I don't blame you. Please let me explain what happened."

"Are you sure you want to tell me?"

"Yes, very sure." Elizabeth took a minute to compose herself, then went on. "John and I married when I was only seventeen. He was ten years older, and wanted a young wife who would provide him with an heir to his fortune. A male heir. I became pregnant right away, and we had a beautiful daughter, Anne. I had barely recovered from giving birth when I became pregnant again." She made a face. "Unfortunately for John, I produced another female. That's when things began to deteriorate between us. After a few months, I became pregnant again, and finally birthed a son. John was ecstatic, and insisted the baby be named after him. Then, our son died. He was only two months old."

"How sad for you both to lose a child. I can't imagine how terrible that must have been."

Elizabeth nodded, her eyes glistening with unshed tears. "I knew I had to give him the single thing he married me for, so I tried again. I became pregnant twice more, both boys, who died at birth. I was a complete failure in my husband's eyes. So he punished me."

"Punished you? For something that was completely out of your control? That's unbelievable."

"He locked me in my room and had meals delivered to me. The only person I ever saw was Polly, my maid. She was a godsend."

"What about your children?"

"I was forbidden to see them. He hired a tutor to live in the house, and told my daughters I was dead. It wasn't until the night of the battle, when I ran from the party to their bedroom to save them, that they found out I was actually alive."

I was having trouble taking all of this in. It was horrible to hear of a man treating a woman this badly. I sent up a silent prayer to the Good Lord and thanked Him for sending me Jim.

"John loved to show off his wealth," Elizabeth continued. "At the beginning of our marriage, we used to give lots of parties. He continued to do that, and that saved my sanity. He insisted I continue to be his hostess, so every time there was a party, I was forced to attend. It was the only time I saw people, and I had strict orders how I was to behave or I would be punished even more. July 7, 1779, was our tenth wedding anniversary, and John threw a lavish masquerade ball to commemorate it." She laughed bitterly. "A masquerade was a perfect metaphor for my marriage. I'd been pretending to be someone else for years."

For a few minutes, neither of us spoke. Finally, Elizabeth broke the silence. "I need to tell you about the murder."

If I'm reading a mystery and the details get too gory, I always skip that part. I dreaded hearing how a real murder was committed, but I had no choice.

"Don't worry, Carol," Elizabeth said, correctly reading my thoughts again. "It's important that you hear this, but I promise I won't give too many graphic details."

"Thank you," I whispered.

"When the soldiers broke into our house, my first thought was to protect my children. I grabbed a carving knife from the buffet table, ran upstairs and shook them awake. Poor sweethearts, they had no idea who I was. They were so frightened. I kissed them and then my older daughter, Anne, recognized me. Anne told her little sister much later that she knew it was really me because I smelled like Mommie. Thank goodness I'd put on perfume that night."

Elizabeth stopped speaking and lowered her head. But I could tell that she was crying. "Please give me a minute. This is very hard."

After a few seconds, she continued. "We tiptoed down the back stairway and out the rear door into the garden. John must have spotted us from a window, because he ran out of the house to stop us. Imagine, he was willing to risk the lives of our precious children to prevent me from having them. British soldiers came after him, followed by members of the Fairport militia. There was blood everywhere. I told the children to run. John tackled me and threw me to the ground, calling me horrible names. I knew he was going to kill me. I stabbed him with the carving knife. When the battle was over, and John was dead, everyone assumed that a British soldier had killed him with a bayonet. I never told anyone what really happened. Until now."

My mind was exploding. I had so many questions, but I only asked one. "Why me, Elizabeth? Why are you telling me?"

"When the original mansion was finally rebuilt, I decided I couldn't live in it again. I had this house built, and it became my home.

"At the moment of my death, however, instead of completely passing over to the other side, I was told that—no matter how justified it was—I had committed a murder and had to be punished. I could not be with my loved ones in the afterlife until I confessed my crime. I could only choose one person, and if that person refused to hear my story, I was condemned to be in limbo forever. I've been waiting for someone special to buy this house for over two hundred years. When you and your family moved in, I knew right away you were the one I'd been waiting for."

I guess I'd just received a high compliment, in a weird sort of way.

Elizabeth stood and I knew that she was leaving. I still had so many questions.

"Continue to trust your instincts," she said. "It's true that you can often be impetuous and overly emotional, and your method of reasoning is creative, to say the least. But you have a heart capable of great love and compassion. More than most people have. That's why I chose you." She leaned forward and gave me a kiss on the cheek. "Thank you for listening, Carol. And now, I'll be on my way."

"Wait!" I cried. "Can I tell anyone about this? Jim? My kids?"

"I'm going to leave that up to you," Elizabeth said. "If you're not sure what to do, ask Lucy and Ethel for advice. Dogs will always tell you the truth, and you can trust them with all your secrets."

She smiled. "I left you a gift in the bedroom to be sure you don't forget me. I hope you like it." And she faded from sight.

I don't remember how long I sat at the kitchen table, thinking about Elizabeth's tragic story. It was unbelievable how the Celebrate Fairport event was the catalyst to connect me with a woman who'd died more than two centuries ago. Finally, the dogs nudged me, bringing me back from 18th century Fairport to the present day.

"I get it," I said. "You want to go outside. Give me a minute to get your leashes."

As I stood, both dogs raced to the bedroom door, then stopped and gave me *The Look*. I suddenly remembered there was a gift waiting for me, which shows how preoccupied I must have been with the past.

Hanging on the closet door was Elizabeth's blue gown, along with a handwritten note. "I thought this would be perfect for you to wear to the masquerade ball. The color matches your eyes."

The dress was now in perfect condition. All the bloodstains were gone.

***

LOUCHE 49

J.T. ELLISON

1.

Paris
1985

Annalise scurries down the Rue de Grenelle in the rain, trying to control her breathing, unsure if the mark is dead or alive. She heard the gunshot, yes. But at the sharp retort, she had run, immediately, out the door, down the winding staircase, and onto the street. Faces turn as she bursts from the building, so she forces herself to slow, to walk casually. She has no coat, no umbrella, nothing to keep the rain off her face and hair. Her shoes are quickly ruined, the bright blue suede spotting dark with droplets and turning black along the sole.

The assignment was supposed to be an easy one. And it has gone wrong, so very wrong.

Here she is, running away from the scene as if she was the one to pull the trigger.

She touches the syringe in her pocket. Still there. Not lost in her flight. Nor the note, her assignment. *Louche 49*, written in black, block letters. The building. The flat.

Let there be no evidence of your intrusion.

She drops the paper in the gutter; it slips away through the grate, gone forever.

Two flics stand on the corner ahead, by the entrance to Le Suffren. *Merde.*

There is nothing to be done. She has to enter the restaurant, has to send the signal, even if it means walking past them.

The woman with the blue suede shoes will sit at table ten. If she orders the tartare, the job is done. If she orders the sole, something went wrong.

Do not order the sole.

Those were the final words before the call had been terminated and she was sure she'd never, ever have to debase herself by admitting defeat.

Do not fail.

She has no idea that, were she to order the sole, it will come with a lethal dose of poison in the tender white flesh. The patrons of the restaurant will assume she's choked on a sliver of bone, the waiter who deboned the fish tableside summarily dismissed, and the body taken to a field near the Bois de Boulogne for a discreet burial.

She takes the table by the window that leads to the patio. She accepts a glass of water and drinks it down. There is no room for error in her world.

She barely looks at the menu. "Le tartare, s'il vous plaît," she says shakily.

"Oui, madame." The waiter whisks away, and she breathes a little easier. The lie will buy some time, but not much. She has to go back. She has to see if he is still alive. And if he is…she must fulfill her mission.

What happened? How has it all gone wrong?

Wine arrives, a glass of ruby courage. She takes it in three gulps, then breathes deeply. Allows her heart to slow.

Burning starts, a slick, wet glow inside her stomach, running up her throat. The waiter stares coldly, gray eyes frigid as the sea.

She knew all but the price of her failure.

***

When they carry the new girl's body from the restaurant, Sirene simply shakes her head and goes to recruit another.

There will be more marks, and pretty girls are a dime a dozen on the streets of Paris these days.

2.

Secrets

One has a secret.

If anyone knew who one really was, they would look at them in a very different way. A dangerous way.

So one holds themself back.

One does not trust easily, or well.

One does what one must to survive.

One laughs and loves and dines and works, all while holding the invisible screen in front of one's body, across one's face, in front of one's eyes.

One cannot let anyone in. The truth is too terrible.

How exhausted one is. How bone-weary. How very alone. How very lonely.

3.

Nashville
Now

I sit at the end of the driveway, watching. The house is massive—three stories of harled white stone, matching chimneys, black shutters, a red door with a brass lion's head knocker. Symmetrical, elegant. The lot is thick with trees and landscaped to perfection, even the last grass clipping gathered up and disposed of—quintessential well-heeled suburban Americana.

Darkness has descended; the gas lights on either side of her door dance in their cages. They are mesmerizing, and I enjoy them for a few minutes before exiting my vehicle. I've rehearsed my conversation so many times it's become ingrained on my tongue, but I run through it once again.

My name is Tempeste Ranier. I think you knew my mother.

I'm halfway up to the gate that blocks the drive when the garage door on the side of the house grinds awake with a *boom*, sliding upward to reveal three cars—two Mercedes SUVs and a silver Porsche Cayman. I halt. This is out of character. She never leaves this early in the evening. After bedtime, when most of the houses on the street shut off their lights, that's when she slips out. She's so rarely seen in the daylight anymore.

The reverse lights on the Porsche engage, and the car shoots backward. I jump the hedge and duck. Probably pointless. There are cameras at the gate and I've most likely already been captured on one. But hiding when things go sideways is instinct.

She whips the car onto the street and guns it, squealing the tires.

I wait for the gate to close, then slink back to my car.

Something has happened. But what?

Chances are she's heading to the club, so I put the Accord in gear and follow her path sedately. Drawing attention to myself is never my goal, and I'm certainly not going to go tearing off after her. It might spook her. I need to handle this calmly, gently. I've taken my time so far; another few hours or days won't make a difference.

Driving around Nashville at rush hour isn't nearly as bad as it used to be. Since the pandemic started, most commuters have been working from home, so the roads aren't clogged. It only takes ten minutes to get from her palace in Forest Hills to the club.

My instincts haven't failed me. Her Cayman is parked beside the dumpster, half across the yellow border that signifies the space. Why they've chosen that spot as her designated place is beyond me. It smells. I know. I've stood there examining the interior of her car often enough.

The club is called Cacher. It's private—beyond private, really. An invitation-only society, home to some of the most elegant—and crooked—people in Nashville. These are the business mavens few know about, the money on the edges, the ones who keep society running, drugs pumping, restaurants and sports teams above water. They collect the vig, provide protection to those who comply, and put the ones who won't out on the street.

Sirene Rimbaud is their queen. She rules this hive with a sharp, spiked glove. No velvet here, no quiet strength. She is brutal. She is legendary. She is untouchable.

And I need to talk to her.

You see, thirty-six years ago, my mother died in Paris, and I think Sirene Rimbaud knows why.

***

My parents met on a train hurtling through the French countryside. It was sheer chance, the kind of story you only see in movies and books. She was heading from Paris to Nantes to answer a job posting; he had been backpacking with his buddies and only arrived in Paris a few days prior. It rained heavily that week, and my father felt the call of the sea. His friends chose to stay in Paris, so he parted ways with them, hurried to the Gare Montparnasse, saw a pretty girl board a train heading west. He took the open seat next to the girl with the trim, brown bob and demurely crossed ankles, and that was it. She didn't speak much English, and he had only a smattering of French, but by the time the train stopped in Nantes two hours later, they were in love. He exited with her, abandoning his summer plans and his friends, and they married in a small ceremony a month later at the *mairie*, my mother finding shortcuts to bypass the limitations of marriage to a foreign citizen.

I was already on the way, my dad likes to tell me, though they didn't know it just then. I am my own cautionary tale—don't sleep with boys you meet on trains, or you'll end up with a baby of your own before you've had a real chance to live.

They named me Tempeste for the raging storm that drove my father to the train station that fateful day.

My father worshipped my mother. I'd like to think she felt the same, but I never got to find out. She died when I was only three years old. She'd been out to dinner with friends and ate something she was allergic to. Anaphylactic shock, they told my father, when he came for her body. Too late, it turned out; she'd already been buried in a grave near the Bois de Boulogne.

He and I had been in Nashville, Tennessee, so I could meet my American grandparents for the first time. My mother had gotten ill moments before the trip and had convinced my father to take me anyway. I've never understood why he agreed. Maybe he sensed something was wrong. Maybe he wanted to see his homeland and his family so badly he was willing to leave behind his sick wife and steal away with her toddler. At the time, they didn't have much, and the tickets were too dear to be wasted. They turned hers in for a refund, and off the two of us went on our grand adventure. I remember the plane ride being so exciting. I was fawned over by the flight attendants, given sweet orange juice to drink and a headset to listen to music that came out of the arm of my seat. Magic.

And I recall, vaguely, my grandparents. Nashville was a quiet place then. My grandfather was a doctor, and my grandmother owned an art gallery. They were thrilled to see their son and treated me, their only grandchild, to car rides through the city, walks by their pond, and so many sweets I got sick in the evenings. It was a magnificent trip, one made all the more alluring by my foggy, patchy memories. It was cut short, though, when my father couldn't reach my mother. Calling around to all of their friends, he finally found one who told him the terrible news. The flight back to Paris was not a joyous one.

Our flat was so quiet without my mother. She was always singing, or whistling, or dancing. She was such a happy woman. My father drooped without her. We left Paris and moved to a small town in the Florida panhandle. Close enough to see his family if we wanted, but not close enough that they were around all the time. He grieved; I started school a year early. He drank; I won the spelling bee. He got too high; I drove him, pale and shaking, to the emergency room. He died; I left Florida behind for good.

I went back to Paris.

I went to find my mother again.

***

Thirty-six years is a long time. It took me three weeks to locate my mother's friend Katriane Cartier, the woman who shared the sad news of her death with my father. When I did—heart pounding as I climbed the wide, chipped, marble stairs to the fourth floor, the scent of onions thick in the air, the small tinny buzzer that announced me—she looked at me blankly when I said my mother's name. "You don't remember Annalise Lavigne? You were her friend, yes? You told my father of her death in 1985."

"Non. I know no one by that name."

"But you informed my father when she passed. Surely you remember her."

The silvered head shook again, and she began to close the door. I stuck the toe of my boot in the crack.

"Please, Annalise. You were her friend."

When the name still didn't click, I showed her a photo from my phone of my mother and me when I was a baby. She is holding me in her arms, smile wide and dreamy, her thick, brown bob slightly wild and rocking a red lip—the Tour behind us lit by a pastel sunset. My dad told me he took it; it has the compositions of a budding professional. He was so good…before he wasn't.

The woman stared, her shoulders tense. Finally, she opened the door to me.

"Ah, yes. Annalise. It has been so very long. I should have recognized you; you look just like her. Entrez, entrez."

It was Katriane who first told me of the shadowy, flame-haired woman she and my mother had worked for. I'd brought a bottle of wine and made sure she drank most of it before I slipped in the scopolamine. Just a touch, though; just enough to loosen her tongue.

It worked quickly, and she became malleable. When I asked who my mother worked for in Paris all those years ago, Katriane's vacant eyes closed as she said the name, a whisper, as if even her mouth knew saying the word aloud was a death sentence, that the woman in question would materialize before us and slice open her former employees' pearly white throat.

Sirene Rimbaud.

Once Katriane started to talk, she couldn't stop.

"Sirene was a very important woman in Paris. She knew everyone, knew all their secrets. She would send us on dates with men to learn what they knew about certain subjects. We were not expected to sleep with them, though we often did, because they would take us to the best restaurants, and we would be drunk on excitement and better wine than we could normally afford. All Sirene cared about was the information. We retrieved it, and we were paid well for it. It was fun, most of the time. Though there were times when we were asked to do too much. I won't speak of it, but I'm sure you know what I mean."

Her eyes grew even more distant, the memory soft on her face. "But then your mother died. Something about her death felt... wrong, to me. The whole evening was unusual. She'd been sent to speak with a man named Georges Chalamet. He worked for the Americans. She told me this before she left. We tried to cover each other's backs when we went on assignments. Sirene wouldn't. She treated us as wild things, not bothering to tame us. We were too expendable to her. We had to take care of each other. Your mother and I, we always shared the date and time of our assignations in case something happened. We knew what we were doing was dangerous. We didn't care, or, I should say, we didn't care enough. When she did not reach out to tell me she was safe, I knew something bad had happened. And then Chalamet's body was found. He had been shot in the head."

"Did my mother—"

"I do not know. I don't. It was not our usual way. Guns were too rare, too hard to get. It was not discreet, and we were nothing if not discreet. But every once in a while, they were used. Usually, to send a specific message."

Her phone rang, and she excused herself to answer it. She came back a few minutes later, and something had changed. She looked scared again.

I realized then she had been pretending not to remember my mother. She now spoke in such a hushed, frantic voice, it was clear she was still scared, all these years later.

"You should go."

"One more question."

"Please, you must leave."

"Do you still work for Sirene?"

"Oh, no. She left Paris many years ago. She went to America, to a small town in the South. Nashville. From what I've heard, she set up shop there."

I was so shocked I allowed her to push me out the door.

Sirene Rimbaud went to my father's hometown to run her shadows.

Why?

***

News of the death of Georges Chalamet was not hard to find. When he was killed, he was acting as a translator to one of the Americans in Paris working on the Plaza Accord, so there was a small write-up in the *Financial Times*, easily found in the archives. It was thought that he was killed in a robbery gone wrong. Witnesses saw him leave a small brasserie with a woman he'd picked up. His wallet and money were missing. French authorities concluded he'd been robbed, killed in the process. They arrested a local thug known for such acts against foreigners, and the case was conveniently closed.

The newspapers do not make mention of another death that evening, of a young mother who had an allergic reaction at a restaurant in the 15th arrondissement. She was nobody. She was nothing. She was not important to anyone but my father, and me.

My mother killed Georges Chalamet for Sirene Rimbaud. But why? To what end? And more importantly, why was she killed if she'd fulfilled her duty?

***

Of interest: the many deaths of young men in Paris between the years of 1980 and 1995. Fifteen years of deaths, all somewhat similar, all blamed on thugs, or Gypsies, or immigrants.

All, I believe, done at the behest of Sirene Rimbaud.

Truly, they matter not. An established pattern, yes, but their deaths are not what I'm concerned about. The 'why' behind them, that's what I've been tracking. Why would a woman named Sirene Rimbaud be killing young men visiting Paris? Why would she recruit young women to spy on, sleep with, and eventually murder her targets? Was she the head, or was there another, higher up than her, calling the shots?

Which led me to an even more interesting question. Had she continued her vicious past in America?

I believe the answer is yes. It's all in the papers, should one want to spend the time to analyze a series of seemingly unrelated deaths. There are common elements, though on the surface, the deaths look different.

But even the most diffuse pattern is still a pattern.

***

There is no choice. Not anymore.

Sirene must be confronted.

So now I am going to talk to her. Get the answers I need to put the ghost of my mother to rest, at last.

Because she haunts me. She won't leave me alone. She knows I am searching for answers, and she wants me to find them.

4.

Lies

One's innocence is lost.

One does things in fear of losing one's life.

One does things in pursuit of money and power that creates untenable situations.

One had no choice but to accept their fate.

One realizes when choice is eliminated, and fear is mitigated, living this life becomes…easier.

One even comes to enjoy the trappings.

It is the cries and pleas one can never handle. One is happier when they are dead.

5.

Nashville
Now

The exterior of the club is plain. An anonymous square box perched between two office buildings. There are no windows, only a single steel door under a black awning and another door leading to a dumpster in the back. The parking lot is down a short flight of stairs. It is these stairs that I mount, then take the winding cement path around to the front of the club. I yank open the door and stride inside. It is dark, music thumping, and a brawny man sits on a stool at the door. He holds up a hand.

"Members only."

"I have an appointment with Sirene."

He is unmoved. "Members only."

"Seriously. I have an interview. She's expecting me. Call her and see." This last is said with a defiance I do not feel, but if I'm going to bluff my way in, I have to risk it. If he calls, either her curiosity or ego will want to know who I am. Who dares to butt into her world?

I dare.

The bouncer shrugs and starts to pick up the phone tucked in his jacket pocket. I see the flash of black metal from the gun in its leather holster under his arm. I debated coming armed myself but assumed I wouldn't make it five feet into either the house or the club with a weapon. I'll have to rely on my wits and some fast moves if I have any chance of achieving my goals. I learned the discreet ways by studying my mother's ghost.

A hand lands on my arm. Surprised, I jerk it away and whirl to see a dark-haired man in a grey pinstripe suit. His eyes are pools of black in his lean face, matched by the shadow of his beard; the sides of his hair are shaved short, so he has a modified mohawk.

"I've got it, Barry." His voice holds the hint of an accent. *Brazilian, maybe?* He eyes me carefully. "Come with me."

I hesitate only a moment at the command, then follow. We wind into the club, passing mirrored doors and bar nooks. This place is a rabbit warren of hidden holes. *All the better to do shady business in, my dear.*

The shadow man stops at one of the doors, opens it with the deft flick of a key, then beckons me inside. It's not as dim as the hallway, and I realize it's an office.

He gets me seated in the chair and takes his place next to me. Not behind the desk, which surprises me. He's not trying to intimidate. He doesn't need to. His quiet presence is threat enough. And when he speaks, I feel a small spark of panic in my chest.

"Hello, Tempeste. Why have you been stalking Sirene?"

Well, so much for the element of surprise. His words tell me the truth. They've seen me coming.

I keep my voice level. "I'm not stalking her. I want to talk to her. Big difference."

"You've been hanging around the house and the club for weeks. Why? Who is she to you?"

"Maybe I want a job. Times are hard."

He steeples his fingers and leans forward, pressing his lips against them. "Why don't we dispense with the bullshit, Tempeste. What do you want?"

"What do I want? It's a good question." I pause for a moment. "What's your name?"

"Santiago."

"Have you ever wanted something so badly you're willing to

risk everything, Santiago?"

His features twist momentarily, then smooth into the bland, implacable look he's been fixing me with since we sat down. He reaches for a glass of water on the table, takes a sip.

"What do you want?" he asks again.

"Are you going to let me talk to her or not?"

"Not until I know why you're after her."

"Don't be so dramatic. I'm not after her. I'm only looking to have a conversation. She knew my mother a long time ago, in Paris. I wanted to hear some war stories. That's all."

I lean back in the chair and cross my too-long legs, bumping my foot on the table and nearly upsetting his glass of water. *Slick move, Tempeste.* I've worn black for this meeting, from my leather jacket to shirt to jeans to my boots. It seemed only fitting to meet my mother's killer in mourning.

Santiago watches me, something dark passing through his eyes.

"Your mother?"

"Yes. Annalise Lavigne. She worked for Sirene. I just want to know if she remembers her. I was very young when she died. I have only a few memories, and I miss her."

This sounds plausible enough, for he relaxes, leaning back himself.

"What do you do for Sirene?" I inquire politely.

"Whatever she asks."

"A jack of all trades. I like it. They should have named you Jack instead of Santiago."

"I think it's time for you to go." He rises, grabbing my arm and yanking me to my feet. I protest, but he ignores me. We're back out through the rabbit warren and I am ignominiously pushed out the rear door to the parking lot. It slams behind me. Though the facade is windowless, I feel eyes on me, just the same.

I smile. *That went well.*

✳✳✳

Home.

I've written up my notes, had three fingers of Oban, and soaked in a hot bath, planning my next move. The bed is cold, too big. I am tired of being alone. I listen to a meditation app to fall asleep.

A soft scrape from the hallway, and I jerk awake at the noise. Someone is in my house.

I ease the gun from the holster attached to the side of my wooden sleigh bed. My forefinger rests lightly on the trigger. I ease myself upright, listening hard. The alarm isn't going off. Either I forgot to set it when I came home, or—

"Don't you dare shoot me, Tempeste Ranier."

I relax, but I don't put away the gun. He seems in an unpredictable mood. I flick on the switch, and he blinks against the sudden glare. His eyes are darker than before, the beard on his cheeks and chin thicker.

"Turn off the bloody light."

Gone is the fake Brazilian accent, replaced by his usual clipped British. He's royally pissed off. But I'm mad, too, so I don't listen, just lean back against the pillows and smile becomingly.

"How was your day, dear?"

"What in the hell were you up to, coming into the club like that? You could have blown everything. I told you—"

"It's taking too long. I need to end this."

"Tempeste, you have to give me more time. I'm doing everything I can."

"It's been six months. *Six months*, and we're no closer to answers than we were when you infiltrated the club. For God's sake, Timothy, what do you want from me?"

He runs a hand through his thick hair, eyes closed as if it hurts. Dark hair. Dark eyes. Posh Brit accent. Filthy sense of humor. He was an extra in a *Harry Potter* film as a kid, studied acting, has grown from a gawky boy into a man who can pass for European or South American without batting an eye, who can lie to your face so convincingly, you'd forgive him the world. If you found out. Which you wouldn't. He's that good. You should see him with a weapon. You should see him in my bed.

My dream man. My shadow man. The only man I've ever trusted.

"I want you to be patient," he says roughly. "I want you to play by the rules for once in your life. This operation is bigger than you. It's bigger than me, than all of us. You jeopardized everything and everyone with your little stunt tonight. The heads aren't happy."

"Why did you tell them?"

I swing out of the bed and pull on my jeans, shove my arms into a sweater. There will be no more sleep for me.

"Why did I tell them, Tempeste? Because you're acting erratically. Why would you risk it? Risk me? Risk us, everything we've planned?"

I hate the plaintive note in his voice. He is not a weak man. He is intense and passionate, a voracious reader and skilled sharpshooter. A dedicated agent who is risking his life for this case, day in and day out. A lover, as well as a friend. But he stands before me now, his walls down, unguarded, truly confused, and I hate him a little for making *me* into the bad guy. It's Sirene. She is the one we must be united against.

"We're getting nowhere, Timothy, and you know it. You have to let me in. You have to get me near her. I can do this. I can end this."

"Absolutely not. You're compromised. You're too close to it, and you know it. I can't be held accountable for your actions. Nor do I want to lose you. Tempeste, please. We need another week. There's a shipment on Friday, and that will be enough to take her down once and for all."

We've been having a variation of this conversation for over a year. It's always the next shipment, the next delivery. The drugs and the girls and the money and the guns, the inflow of tangible goods to keep Sirene's empire afloat come in regularly, like a boat rushing to dock on stormy waves. Too regularly.

But I don't care about her business, shady as it may be, and I'm done waiting for him to give the go-ahead. For the people he works for to acquiesce. They don't care about me. Tim is their golden boy. I'm just the crazy bitch who alerted them to Sirene.

"She killed my mother, Tim. I can't sit quietly on the sidelines anymore. I have to know why. I have to."

He approaches the bed, a hand outstretched as if he will caress me, lift my chin and kiss me, use my body to make me forget my pain. It works, probably more than it should.

"What do you want me to do, Tempeste? Beg? I'm begging. Let me handle this. You—"

There is a heavy shuffle outside the door, like a box knocked off a shelf, and we both freeze. Wordlessly, he draws his weapon. I level mine at the door.

They've come for us.

There's only one question. Is it our people or hers?

***

Lights strobe into the room as they break down the door.

The gun jerks in my hand. Operators in thin, black armor go down. I know exactly where to aim—the soft, exposed carotid. Neck shots are hard, but I train relentlessly. There are cries and screams; men go down as quickly as I pull the trigger. But they are serious, and they are numerous. Nothing can prepare you for the blinding lights of a flashbang, and I have no shield. I am blinded. Tim is blinded. Coughing, eyes streaming, we are overcome. We've been caught in my bedroom, and there is nowhere for us to run.

Hoods are slammed over our heads. Zip ties tightened painfully around our wrists. I am choking in the close, hot air of the thick fabric, the gas coming off of my skin and hair burning, burning. I hear Timothy's calls cut off sharply; I assume a punch to his gut by the sudden painful exhalation.

Cacophony, then a Brazilian voice screaming in fury, "It's me, you idiot. Take this hood off."

The rip of fabric followed by mumbled apologies.

"I was interrogating this woman. Who gave you clearance to enter?"

A rough voice. "We had orders from the top."

I feel him turn to me. I lunge.

The bullet slams into my shoulder and I stumble back, going down hard. Hot blood pours from the wound. The pain is nothing, then overwhelming, and I am almost relieved when I feel the sharp prick of a needle in the crook of my elbow. I am swimming, sailing, soaring.

I do not fear death. When you have nothing to live for, death is an old friend. It is only the frustration of not getting the answers I need before I die that keeps me from fighting them, forcing them to give me the oblivion I seek.

6.

Traitors

One is groomed.
One is good at their job. Too good.
One comes to the attention of the head.
One's opportunities expand.
One loses their inhibition.
One acclimates.
One excels.
One exceeds.
One enjoys.
One is damned.
One doesn't care anymore.

7.

Nashville Now

I have no concept of time. It is hours. It is moments. It is freezing cold.

I come to tied to a chair, shivering, my teeth chattering so hard I'm afraid I might bite through my tongue. I am still blind, still hooded. I don't know if I am alone. Has he managed to stay alive?

"Hello?" I say quietly to the empty, frigid air. "Hello?" Nothing. Either they've separated us, or Timothy is dead.

A brief qualm at the idea of losing him, and I force away his anger that I may have compromised us by coming to the club. I had to do something. I couldn't wait anymore. And he had established himself as Santiago before I passed out. Maybe he's gotten lucky.

Me? Not so much.

I assess my surroundings using the only senses I have—hearing and smell. The low purr of a motor. The soft *whiss* of cold air. The sharp scent of chilly blood, meaty and thick.

Ten to one I'm in a walk-in freezer; five to one it's in the kitchen of the club.

This is actually not the worst-case scenario, assuming I don't freeze to death before they come for me.

And they will come for me. I'm only alive because someone wants to know who I really am.

The door to the freezer opens, and I hear a commotion. My heart leaps.

Sirene Rimbaud is storming through the kitchens, scattering sous chefs in her wake. I know her voice as intimately as if she'd sung me lullabies. She is as much a mother to me as the one who gave me life. Annalise carried me in her womb, but Sirene created me. Created a child who dwelled in the uncertain shadows of grief and loss. Created the monster she is about to meet for the very first time.

The hood is yanked from my head, taking strands of hair. The corner is stuck to my shoulder with coagulated blood. Skin rips away. The pain is almost enough to make me faint.

Pain is strength. Pain means you're still alive. Pain means you can still kill her.

Stay alive long enough to take her out. That's all you need to do.

I grit my teeth and blink against the sudden light.

Sirene comes into focus. Even in her mid-sixties, she is lovely. Hard, eyes like flint and deep lines furrowing her lips, the hair dimmed but still burning red and lovely. Frenchwomen have some strange secret, a genetic elixir.

I am a Frenchwoman, too. But I will never know how I will age. I will not live to see my next birthday.

Happily, if I have anything to say about it, neither will Sirene.

"Who is this?" she sneers. Timothy steps to her side. He has the beginnings of a black eye and a rising bruise on his forehead. His beard is dark, and he looks ready for mayhem.

But it is Santiago who replies. "She has been stalking you. I have been keeping tabs since I discovered her interest a few weeks ago. She came here today, and I followed her home. You needn't have sent a team. I had it well in hand."

"You didn't bother to let me know I was in danger?"

"You weren't. Not from her. She is nothing. A kid with a gun, easily overpowered. I was just getting to the truth of things when your stormtroopers burst in."

Sirene gives a ladylike sniff and turns. "Kill her," she says over her shoulder.

I call after her, "Wait. My name is Tempeste Ranier. You knew my mother."

Sirene stops. I can see the line of tension in her shoulders. The name means something to her. She looks back, slowly, eyes narrowed into vicious slits. "Ranier?"

"Yes. My mother worked for you. In Paris, in the 80s. She died, and I need to know why. Tell me what you know, and then you can kill me. I won't fight. I just need to know."

"Let me handle this," Santiago says. "I will get to the bottom of things."

But Sirene is interested. Like a cat who has spied a mouse, her muscles coil in on themselves. She is readying herself for the strike. I can almost feel her licking her lips.

She takes a few steps toward me. *God, it's cold.* I fight not to shiver. But I can't help it. The movement makes my shoulder scream, but this might be my only chance.

"Get out of my way."

A deep, gruff voice bellows across the kitchen. I can sense people scrambling, a tide parting before someone clearly very

129

important. This has to be the elusive head, Sirene Rimbaud's boss. The person Timothy and I need to take down this organization.

"What is going on here?"

The world tilts. It is a voice I know. A familiar one. My brain doesn't allow the connection just yet though. My eyes are the responsible party.

Sirene is pushed aside. Santiago steps out of the way.

And my grandfather's body blocks the light.

8.

Lovers

One finds love a complicated territory.

One does things one swore they would never do.

One has a code.

One's code is useless in the face of such desire.

One knows attachment is dangerous.

One knows depending on another is folly.

One is weakened.

One is weak.

One is vulnerable.

At last, one is vulnerable.

9.

Nashville
Now

The hot bathwater burns my frigid skin.

It is the bathroom I used as a child, en suite to the guest room with the large, four-post, metal canopy bed and the window seat with the blue damask cushion. The clawfoot tub has been recently reglazed and the exterior painted black. The white tile is hexagonal marble and runs up the wall to the ceiling; the towels are a dusky blue. Very stylish, clearly not something my grandfather did himself. Grand-mère, probably. She always did have exquisite taste. She's been gone for years now. I attended the funeral. Slept in this bed. Comforted my grandfather as he cried.

The house is unassuming under the cover of darkness, the lighting subtle and discreet. I look out the window and see black, wrought iron fencing circling the lot. Unlike Sirene's gaudy mansion, this is the home of someone who has had wealth for so long they have no need to try and show it off.

I always knew my father came from money. Grand-père is a doctor, though retired now. Grand-mère's art studio was successful. But this is older money. Generational money. Dirty money.

My brain is as frozen as my flesh. Sirene Rimbaud works for my grandfather. This makes no sense, and yet, everything has come into crystalline focus.

I have the most awful feeling I know why my mother was killed.

He is waiting for me in the bedroom. A white sheet has been laid upon the bed, piled with old towels and sterilized instruments.

"We must remove the bullet," he says, not meeting my eyes. Santiago stands near the head of the bed, his own eyes downcast. I know he can't look at me, look at what he's done. We need to talk, we need to plan, but that isn't going to happen here. It may not happen ever again.

Unspeaking, I sit on the edge of the bed. My grandfather pulls a light closer, puts on a pair of glasses. His eyes are comically magnified beneath the lenses, and I giggle a little to myself. They have given me something, probably for the pain, and I feel loose and unmoored.

The lidocaine burns as it goes in, and it takes only a few minutes of digging to retrieve the fragment. A *plink* of metal echoes in the basin next to my leg, and the surgery is complete. He washes the wound and stitches me quite gently. He'd given me stitches once before, when I was a girl, after I cut my hand on an apple knife. He was just as patient, just as calm, though I was screaming and crying in fear of my own blood, seen for the very first time outside of a scraped knee. I am still prone to excessive anxiety when I see my own blood, but despite the bath my body temperature is very low, and that combined with the medication keeps me calm.

My grandfather is the head.

So much makes sense now.

"Are we going to talk?" I ask, my tongue thick in my mouth.

"There is nothing to talk about." He gathers his things. "Sleep, Tempeste. Tomorrow we will take a walk, and I will answer your questions."

"No. Now. I need to know now."

Santiago gestures to me to shut up, but I can't. The pain and the fear and the fury spill from me in a torrent.

"She killed my mother. Sirene Rimbaud. Did you know?"

Grand-père sighs, takes the chair by the door. He sits slowly, crossing his legs. His pants ride up and I can see a sliver of tender, milk-white skin above the top of his sock.

"Yes."

The word reverberates through me.

"Did you order it done?"

"No."

"Then why? Who did?"

"Do you really not know? He never told you?"

"Who? Tell me what?"

"My son."

"Dad?"

"'*Dad*,'" he scoffs. "Ha. You were not his. She married him, she entrapped him. He had to get free. Once he knew, he couldn't stand to be with her another moment."

"That's impossible. I was their daughter. I look like him. I look like you."

He is silent. Legs crossed, hands folded, lips curled in a semi-smile, he looks like any other elderly grandfather about to read his grandbaby a bedtime story.

"I look like...you," I say again, my heart dropping.

"He couldn't take the betrayal. She was pregnant, and I needed her seen to. I made sure the two would meet. She was under strict instructions to seduce him as quickly as possible. It worked."

"They were in love. They adored each other."

"Your mother was a very good actress."

His cool calmness is infuriating. I can feel the anger bubbling inside of me, finally getting my body back to a proper temperature.

"Did he know?"

"Yes. That's why he took you away. She told him, and he brought you here to find out if it was true. She'd served her purpose at that point, so she was terminated."

"I grew up without a mother," I cried. "You took that from me. How dare you sit here so smug? I hate you. I'm leaving."

I try to get to my feet but collapse onto the bed. The meds are strong, and I'm dizzy.

"Tempeste—"

"I don't believe you," I say. "She loved my father."

"In her way, I'm sure she did. But she was a loose end. She was meeting with an envoy from the British government who was working with the Americans. She was trying to pass a message. She was going to talk. I had to stop her. She was in love, she said. She needed to get out of the game. She wanted to raise her child, and she didn't care about our business anymore. There. Does that make you feel better, child? That she loved you, that your daydreams about your family were true? She sacrificed herself for you. Is that what you need to hear?"

Who is this man? Is anything he says real?

Something deep inside me tells me he is being honest, and I am filled with revulsion.

"She got in the way, so you took her out. The mother of your child, if what you say is true. How did you even meet her?"

"She worked for Sirene. Sirene was—is—very good at finding the kind of woman we need in our business. The kind of woman who can put just the right pressure on a mark. She was a gift, for a

133

while. Until she became a liability."

"Did Grand-mère know?"

"No. I've never brought my business home."

"You killed my father. You broke his heart."

"I am your father."

I shake my head. "You will never be my father."

"That's enough! Get some sleep. I will talk to you tomorrow. I have things to attend to now. Santiago?"

"I'll keep watch, sir."

"Thank you."

He turns back at the door. "This can go one of two ways. Either you come to work for me…." He doesn't need to finish.

"You would kill your own child to keep your secrets?"

His smile is brief and cruel. "I won't have to. You will do nicely. You're well trained, you're smart, and you're mine. You won't throw away your life for no reason. You work for me now. Let's hope you're better at it than your mother. Now, sleep."

The door closes, and Timothy is staring. He gives me a tiny shake of his head, to warn me, obviously. Not that I'm dumb enough to say anything.

Dear God. My grandfather is the head. My grandfather is my father.

He killed both my parents. My mother because her usefulness had ended. My father with his awful truth.

I turn on my good side and face the wall. Santiago takes a chair. We do not speak.

***

The dream is vivid. Strong. I am in Sirene's office at the club. She is shrinking away from me, cowering on the floor. I have brought the great woman to her knees, and I feel nothing.

"Annalise Lavigne," I snarl.

"I do not know who that is."

"You lie!"

I shove the crumpled photograph of my mother under her nose.

"Annalise Lavigne," I repeat.

She glances at the photograph with a sneer, looks away, out of the plate glass windows to the city skyline beyond.

"Never seen her."

"Paris. 1985. You sent her on a job. Louche 49. The mark was killed before she arrived. He was shot. You killed her anyway."

A spark of recognition appears in those flat tiger eyes.

"'Louche 49.' How am I supposed to remember such a thing?"

"It was *your* job. She worked for you. You betrayed her. You killed her."

I swing with all my might, knuckles connecting with soft flesh, and her head snaps back, lips splitting and blood spraying along the front of her blouse. Torture is not an effective means of extracting information. But Sirene is not young. She is pragmatic enough to know she is beaten. She doesn't want another blow like that.

"Hmm. I assume this woman is your mother?"

"Yes."

Her smile is cruel through the blood-red teeth. "I do remember her. She was nothing. She was no one. She—"

I pull the trigger. Blood sprays. I sit down hard, and watch the life leak from her body.

***

I jerk awake. The sun streams in the windows. For a moment I feel warm and complete, safe.

Then I roll over, and pain blooms through my body. Everything comes rushing back.

Timothy, or Santiago, is gone. I am alone, in the room I slept in as a child, with a stitched-up bullet wound and heavy knowledge in my heart.

I swing out of bed. There are clothes waiting on the chair. I struggle into them one-handed. I am useless like this. I can't fight. I can't even put my hair in a ponytail. It hangs lank around my neck.

I am not at all surprised to find the door is locked.

I don't know if Tim is on my side or not. He's such a good actor.

I've seen him at work these past several months. The question is, does he work for my side? Or was he a plant? Is he Santiago after all, my grandfather's creature, and Timothy the spy the one sent by my grandfather—I will never be able to think of him as my father—to keep tabs on me? To infiltrate me, my life?

After everything that's happened the past twenty-four hours, I have no idea which reality I'm living in.

I have only one play here.

I'm going to have to go along with the charade long enough to allow them to trust me, and then I'll reach out to my people and get them to spring me.

And we will take my grandfather and his organization down.

10.

Shrouds

One gets sloppy.
One makes mistakes.
Mistakes that force one to make new choices.
One doesn't remember what choice is like.
One chooses.
One underestimates.
One loses.
One hurts. One hurts so badly. Heart, soul, body, mind.
One has spent their whole lives on borrowed time.
One looks back on a life marked with pain and suffering.
One's death is inevitable.
One finds the end amusing.
One thought they were above bodily desecration.
The damned are immortal, and one has not been forgiven.
One is wrong.
One is relieved.

One is no longer.

11.

Paris
Le Suffren
Two Months Later

It is raining in Paris today, and I have just murdered a man.

I take a table on the patio. I order the tartare, and a carafe of burgundy. The signal of my grand success is sent. After all these years, the patterns have not changed.

I can see the top of the Tour from my seat by the window. The rain streaks the glass, and across the street, a pigeon preens in the shelter of a linden bough.

My mother died here. Was this her last view as well? The row of linden trees, the Tour? I have no way of knowing if it was at this table or across the restaurant, but I feel her spirit, waiting for release.

It has been two months since the events in Nashville. Two months of slow gains. Two months of not knowing whom to believe. Two months of trying to rationalize what my grandfather has done. Two months of learning all I can about how his organization works.

Two months earning his trust.

I feel a breeze at my back. The door has opened. Santiago slips into the seat opposite me. He gestures toward the waiter, and another glass appears. He helps himself to my wine.

I have not seen Timothy in two months, either. He has been subsumed by the Brazilian my grandfather trusts to oversee my inoculation into the organization.

I miss Timothy. Santiago is rougher. Not nearly as fun.

He doesn't love me.

"All is well?" he asks in that low, accented voice.

"Yes. No issues."

"Good. You've been cleared to go home. If you want."

"Alone?"

"Alone."

This is the moment I've been waiting for. I have been under observation for weeks, my phone tapped, my movements tracked. I have not been able to reach out to anyone for help. I haven't even bothered to try. They must think I'm dead anyway.

I should be dead. I'm not sure why my grandfather didn't just end me when he had the chance. I seem to be a dangerous loose end, but perhaps he underestimates me.

One can hope.

"I'd like to stay. Paris is beautiful this time of year."

With an amused glance at the rain-soaked street, he shrugs. "Suit yourself." He downs the wine and slams the glass onto the table. My tartare arrives. He glances at it, then at me. I smile and take a large forkful. Then another.

"Want some? It's delicious?"

He shakes his head. I sip my wine.

"Was it real? Or was I just a mark?"

He doesn't answer.

"I'm betting my grandfather wanted me watched, so he sent you to infiltrate my life. Everything you said, everything you did, it was all a lie, wasn't it?"

More silence. He swallows the last of my wine.

"Will you ever tell me the truth about who you are?"

"Non." He winks and stands. "A bientôt, ma cherie."

He speaks French as flawlessly as English and Spanish. *Who is this man?*

A small piece of paper flutters to my foot. I reach down for it, and when I look up, he's gone, moving sinuously through the tables to the door.

I pocket the paper, finish my meal.

I do not die.

I walk up the Rue de Grenelle slowly, then cut across the wide lawn leading to the Tour. The sun has come out, chasing away the rain, and the paths before me glisten. Five minutes later, I am at the Seine, the slate water meandering, a small fog rising. I walk aimlessly. I do not sense anyone behind me.

I find a bench and finger the paper in my pocket. Children are screaming for joy nearby, running after a red balloon. A man walks a poodle but doesn't give me a second glance. I am alone.

Slowly, I unfold the paper, glance at my hand. An address, in the 11th. Nothing more.

I let the paper blow into the Seine. It floats for a moment, then disappears under the water.

I move with purpose now, slip into the Metro. A man with a violin and a tangled beard plays a rollicking tune, and I toss him a Euro. He bows effusively, moves to the next car.

He is the first person who has smiled at me in weeks.

This is no way to live. I've become as much of a ghost as my mother. But I know no other way. My training has eliminated the simple life. There will be no children, no partner, no long weekends in ski chalets and summers on the water. No home to tend, no garden to grow. Because of a genetic anomaly of which I have no control, my life has been taken from me. I am indentured to violence.

I get off at Père Lachaise. The stairs smell of urine. The building is dirty white stone, with colorful graffiti up to my eyes. I slip into a café and get a coffee, standing at the bar, using the mirrored glass to look for a tail—still, nothing.

Santiago hasn't lied. I am no longer considered a threat. This was the price of a man's life, someone I don't know, someone who did something to upset my grandfather's dirty little world.

I exit the café through the alley, walk two blocks to the address. I knock.

The door is opened by a woman who used to have hair as red as flame. She looks as shocked to see me as I am to see her.

A chance to right a wrong. That's what Santiago has given me.

The blade is in my hand before I take a second breath. By the third, it's been thrust through the layers of her clothes into the soft, vulnerable space below her breastbone.

"For my mother," I say, watching her round eyes glaze in shock, her mouth go slack. The knife is buried deep in her body, anchored in place by the leverage of my hand. She looks me in the eyes, and I swear to God, she smiles.

Sirene dies standing up. I think she would have liked that.

I shove her backward and close the door gently.

The sun shines brightly on the cemetery walls. Tourists take selfies with the sign. A squirrel scolds from an overhanging branch.

I walk with no destination in mind.

***

JUSTICE IS SERVED

DARYL WOOD GERBER

Members of the jury, look at him sitting on the witness stand fingering the lapel of his knock-off Armani suit. So smug. So cool. Corinne fidgeted on the bench in the gallery. Bile rose up her throat. Her jaw locked. She moved it right and left. *Damn you, Jeremy Plunkett.* He knew he was going to get away with it. And that skinny witch of a lawyer, Inga Gustavson, was going to help him. Graduate of the University of Southern California. Former Miss California. Full of herself. *Take a gander at her, folks. Pacing in front of him, grinning like a racehorse pumped with steroids.*

Ever since Corinne had discovered the beauty of words, she'd had a rich inner monologue. Right now, however, she didn't feel like holding it in. She felt like jumping to her feet and yelling, *Killer!* Except she didn't want a clerk to remove her from the proceedings. A bundle of hyped-up nerves, she wriggled her wool skirt to her knees and clutched the hem to keep herself in check.

"Did you ever think that your wife was suicidal?" Gustavson asked.

Cue maniacal horse laugh, folks, followed by a ghostly horse silhouette racing across the screen. In addition to the running monologue, Corinne viewed everything as if it were a movie. She couldn't help herself. She was a special effects master in Hollywood. Computer graphics consumed her. She dreamed about multiple exposures. And don't get her started about cameras. Her favorite was her Nikon Coolpix P1000, a gift to herself when Lucas Films hired her for her first gig.

"No, ma'am," Jeremy said, answering the question. Firmly. With authority.

Corinne snarled. Who would doubt him? Her brother-in-law was Mr. Trustworthy. Mr. Good Guy. *Not.* She toyed with the sleeves of her sweater. She'd snagged one getting out of her VW. She worried that if she pulled a thread, it might unravel on the spot. Like her emotions.

"Tell us…" Gustavson let her words hang. She pursed her lips just so.

Corinne mentally zoomed in, the lens of her P1000 capturing every sun-damaged pore of Gustavson's smug face. She fantasized about posting the photograph on Facebook. To embarrass the lawyer. *Should have used more sunblock, witch.*

"Tell us about your wife's addiction to pills," Gustavson coaxed.

Corinne wanted to shriek. Her sister hadn't been addicted to pills or anything else. She had been a normal twenty-three-year-old woman who had wanted a happy life with the man of her dreams, except the man of her dreams had turned out to be a nightmare. Corinne jammed her hands under her thighs, her mind reeling. What could she do? How could she bring him down?

"My wife wasn't addicted to pills, as far as I know."

"Not even as a teen?" Gustavson asked.

"No." Jeremy sounded practiced. Kind. Heaven forbid degrading words about Sierra should flow easily from his lips. No, Gustavson would have to pull them out of him. Had they discussed this tactic? How to make the jury root for him?

"Did she ever show signs of depression?" Gustavson's honeyed tone sickened Corinne.

"No."

Bullpuckey, Jeremy!

After marrying him, Sierra had shown every sign in the book. She broke into tears if she dropped a cookie. She didn't shower for days. She mumbled to herself. She would call Corinne and hang up without saying a word. Corinne had said as much in her testimony yesterday. Had anyone on the jury listened?

"Was she seeing a therapist?" Gustavson asked.

"She didn't need to."

Corinne bit back a sob. Sierra hadn't started out life as a mouse. She had been a happy-go-lucky girl. After graduating high school, she'd planned to open her own bakery. Before she could make her dreams come true, however, she met him. Jeremy. Eight years older. A well-respected cop. She fell head over heels. Being two years older and much wiser, Corinne had tried to warn Sierra. She hadn't listened.

"Tell me how you two met." Gustavson offered an earnest smile to the jury.

Corinne flashed on that day. She and Sierra were waitressing at the Corner Diner, the restaurant that had been the inspiration for Sierra's future business. The diner was all pink and blue and filled with aromas that warmed the soul. That day—that fateful day—Jeremy sat at the counter and ordered coffee with cream. He said he didn't need extra sugar as long as Sierra touched his cup. She blushed seven shades of red. Corinne had known then that her sister was toast. When Sierra sidled away, Corinne asked Jeremy if he used that line on all the girls. He smirked. Later that night, sitting on their beds, Corinne told Sierra that Jeremy Plunkett was trouble, but Sierra didn't give a rat's behind. She waxed rhapsodic about him. His hair was so thick and sexy, his lips were luscious, and his voice super silky. *Oily* was the adjective Corinne would have chosen.

"Dang it." The woman with the square jaw and intense gaze sitting next to Corinne on the gallery bench leaned in. "Plunkett's going to get off." She was wearing a somber black jumpsuit and well-worn Doc Martens, black hair pulled into a severe knot at the base of her neck. A black pea coat lay folded beside her. The weather was unusually cold for Los Angeles, even in January. "Am I right or am I right?"

Corinne didn't argue. Jeremy Plunkett, or "Plunk the Funk" to his weekend basketball warriors, was wooing the jurors with ease. They were buying every word. Jeremy was the epitome of a loving, desolate husband. Tears pressed at the corners of his eyes. Was he pinching himself to bring them on?

"See the jury forewoman?" The woman jabbed a finger. "See her? She's hot for Plunkett. She'll be all over him like a cheap suit once they turn in a verdict of not guilty."

With her imaginary camera, Corinne focused on the forewoman's face. Indeed, she seemed to be tamping down desire, her chest heaving ever so slightly with sexual exhilaration. *Crap.*

"Who are you?" Corinne asked.

"Giada Rossi. My partner is the district attorney." She pointed to

D.A. Melissa Warner, the attractive blonde facing forward, a former Marine judge advocate who had become a civilian attorney after leaving the service. "She wants me to listen in. It's a major case for her. I'm not a lawyer. I'm a tech person, thanks to my training in the corp. But I pay attention to details."

"I'm Corinne—"

"I know who you are. Melissa told me. Despite our misgivings about the forewoman, I hope this ends the way you want."

Jeremy gestured from the witness stand. "Corinne can confirm what I'm telling you."

"Corinne?" Gustavson turned to the gallery, her eyebrow raised inquisitively.

"Corinne Justice. My sister-in-law. You questioned her yesterday."

"The special effects gal." Gustavson motioned for Corinne to stand.

Gal? How demeaning. Corinne gritted her teeth and stayed put.

Ever since seeing the mind-blowing movie *A Trip to the Moon*, a French short film by Georges Mélièus that led to the birth of special effects, working in the movies was all Corinne had wanted to do. Over the course of the next few years, she'd studied the movie wizardry of special effects masters. A stint at the Magic Castle in high school, working alongside seasoned artists and learning how seamlessly their tricks and holograms operated, had solidified her plan.

Over Gustavson's shoulder, Corinne saw Jeremy wink, but no one else did because they were all staring at her.

＊＊＊

At a break in the trial, Corinne went outside to gather herself. She buttoned the coat she'd thrown on over her outfit to fight off the cold, but memories of the way she'd shivered at Sierra and Jeremy's wedding haunted her. She'd known what was going to come, but she hadn't been able to prevent it.

Twenty-two months after they said, *I do*, Jeremy turned. Like a voracious worm, he ate his way through their idyllic Red Delicious life from the inside out. First devouring the seeds—Sierra couldn't get pregnant, ergo, she was worthless. Followed by consuming the flesh—Sierra couldn't get her business off the ground, ergo, she was as stupid as a sea cow. When the slime penetrated the skin of the fruit, he told Sierra that she was crazy. Beaten down psychologically, she bought his pronouncement. Her phone calls with Corinne, which until then had occurred every two or three days, tapered off. So did her text messages. When the calls became as infrequent as one every two months and all texting ceased, Corinne stopped by Sierra's pristine Sherman Oaks home with her camera at the ready. She needed documentation of what she suspected: Jeremy was not only undermining her sister, he was abusing her.

The first time Corinne visited, Sierra opened the front door but kept the chain in place. She wouldn't let Corinne in. She gave the excuse that it was too cold outside, and she was feeling sick. Corinne took a picture through the two-inch opening. Sierra cursed her.

The next time, Corinne showed up with an ultra-warm down coat for Sierra so they could venture out—take a walk along the boulevard—but Sierra balked. She couldn't go outside because she was reading Tolstoy. *As if.*

The third time, Sierra was too busy watching her favorite talk show, which was a lie. She hated TV.

On the fourth and fifth visits, Corinne still fouled out. No matter what she tried, she couldn't convince her sister to pass beyond the confines of her front door.

On the sixth visit, Corinne slumped against Sierra's door and cried. After a long while, she heard her sister slide down the door, too. Back-to-back with only the wood separating them, they didn't say a word for an hour. And then the truth poured out of Sierra. She was helpless. She didn't know what to do. Corinne tried to convince her to run away with her. But Sierra couldn't. Wouldn't. Corinne begged her sister to open the door. Sierra refused.

"That camera," Sierra cried. "That P-whatever you call it."

"P one thousand."

"It could be the death of me. If Jeremy finds out you've taken pictures…"

***

Corinne returned inside the courtroom and took her place on the gallery bench. Listening to the softball questions Gustavson was pitching Jeremy, she remembered her last conversation with her sister three months ago. Sierra had called her. Crying. Hysterical. Corinne dropped everything and raced to the house, but Sierra didn't answer the door. Corinne pounded. Still no answer.

Frantic, Corinne sped to the precinct where Jeremy worked. She didn't accuse him of anything; she wasn't stupid. Instead, she told him how concerned she was about her sister. She said Sierra hadn't been acting like herself. Corinne staged the conversation in the main squad room so other policemen would hear. She showed Jeremy one of the digital photos she'd taken with her camera. She displayed it to a female cop, too, one of many on the force that had drawn close to listen in. The woman commented on how frail Sierra looked. Corinne pleaded with Jeremy to let Sierra come home with her. For a little R&R. Jeremy declined the offer. He said that Sierra, as fragile as she was, might contract a virus. Of course that was a load of crap, but Corinne couldn't drum up a rebuttal.

That afternoon, Corinne returned to her sister's house and pounded on the door again. She called Sierra's cell phone. She texted. Silence. Exasperated, she stormed outside, prepared to scale the latticework to the second floor and break a window, only to find the latticework had been removed and the beautiful climbing roses uprooted.

Suddenly, Sierra appeared at the window. All in white, her long dark hair, which had at one time been lustrous, straggled around her shoulders. She placed her palms on the upper pane of the window. Corinne mimed for her to open it, but Sierra gestured that she couldn't.

Corinne howled like a wounded animal. Jeremy Plunkett had made her sister a prisoner.

Sierra breathed on the window and wrote a word. The letters were backward, but Corinne could make it out—*HELP.*

Quickly, she snapped a picture with her P1000. Checking the photo, she realized the zoom lens couldn't capture the word as well as she'd hoped. She cursed and looked up. Sierra had disappeared from view.

The next day, determined to break her sister out of her residential cell, Corinne drove to Sierra's house. Seeing a firetruck outside sucker-punched her. She slung the strap of her camera around her neck, hurried out of her VW, and ran up the path to the porch where the housekeeper, a Latina with gray-streaked hair, was slumped on a rattan chair.

"What happened?" Corinne demanded.

The woman didn't have a chance to answer. The front door opened and two EMTs wheeled Sierra's body out on a gurney.

Choking back tears, Corinne strode alongside while identifying herself. She started to ask them what happened, but she didn't need an answer. She knew her sister was dead. The senior EMT said the housekeeper found Sierra in the bathtub, wrists slashed, and called 911.

Despite the EMT's disapproval, Corinne took numerous photos of her sister's face. The visible bruises. The swollen lower lip. When she noticed the EMTs had left the front door ajar, she got an idea.

While they trundled Sierra toward their vehicle, Corinne slipped inside the house. She stole to the second floor and took photos. The master bedroom window had been wiped cleaned, but drawers were askew and clothes piled on the unmade bed. Had Sierra been planning to pack up and leave? Had Jeremy found out and killed her? Corinne spied the white gown Sierra had been wearing and grabbed it. She also took the charm bracelet of enameled pies she'd given her sister on her eighteenth birthday. In the bathroom, she took photographs of the bathtub, the floor, the broken mirror. There were four bottles of pills on the counter. One for Jeremy—Ambien—and three bottles with her name, Corinne Justice, on the labels, which she found baffling. All were for depression or anti-anxiety. Yes, Corinne had taken meds years ago, but not any longer. She hadn't liked the way they'd altered her mood. She'd tossed any remaining pills down the toilet and had crushed the vials.

Loathe to compromise the crime scene more than she had with her presence, Corinne left the bottles where they were. To be on the safe side, she exited through the door at the rear of the house and rounded the yard to the street.

By then, Jeremy had arrived. He was standing beside the gurney sobbing, not believing what he was hearing. Sierra was dead? *Dead?* Corinne didn't think twice. She aimed the camera at her brother-in-law and snapped photographs of his hardened face, his remorseless eyes. He was lying through his teeth. He had done this.

A day later, she took the photos that she'd processed in her darkroom to the precinct and asked for the lead homicide detective. Unfortunately, the guy turned out to be one of Jeremy's basketball buddies. Guess who *he* believed?

"Starving? Ha!" Giada Rossi snorted. "Was your sister starving herself?"

"No," Corinne whispered.

Jeremy used his pinky to wipe a thin line of perspiration off his upper lip. "My wife never felt good about the way she looked. I'm not sure why. Every day I told her how beautiful she was."

Cue a bomb exploding, Corinne thought. *Fire. Smoke. Incessant ruptures. And a horde of thousands yelling, "Liar!"*

"Let's return to who might have given your wife the drugs," Gustavson said.

"They were in a vial with Corinne's name on them," Jeremy replied, "but I know she didn't give them to her sister. She wouldn't have. I'm not sure how my wife got them."

Corinne had learned a few days after Sierra's death that her internist—*Corinne's* doctor—had prescribed the pills. Authorities decided that Sierra had made the call, posing as Corinne. Why her doctor hadn't asked Corinne to verify the need for the pills was beyond her. Her doctor, a wonderful and caring woman who understood Corinne's family history—losing her parents at sixteen, raising her sister on her own for two years—should have set up a teleconference at the very least. The doctor had testified that the person who'd called the front office had sounded panicked. She did what she thought she'd needed to, written the scrip, and set a follow-up appointment. Corinne was certain Jeremy had paid someone, maybe one of his snitches, to pretend to be Corinne. The poser would have needed a fake I.D. at the pharmacy, which was located on the other side of town—not Corinne's usual site—but a cop would have known how to accomplish that.

When Corinne had taken the stand, the jury had been unresponsive to her. Maybe it was the way she looked. She didn't wear makeup. Her curly hair was always a matted mess, no matter what hair products she tried. At the age of twenty, she'd considered shaving it off but hadn't. She'd had no aspirations to be an actress. She liked being out of the public eye. For an SFX person, she looked normal. She worked in the background. No one would ever aim a P1000, or any camera for that matter, at her.

"The day your wife died..." Gustavson folded her hands in a prayerful way. "Can you tell us about that?"

Jeremy stretched his spine, as if working hard to compose himself. He touched the corner of his eye with his middle finger.

What Corinne wouldn't give to be able to snap a closeup and blow it up for all to see. His eyes were stagnant.

"The housekeeper found her. In the bathtub." His voice cracked. "She said the water was deep red with her blood."

"I'm so sorry."

Corinne coughed sarcastically. How many times had Gustavson rehearsed that trite response?

"The EMTs who showed up"—Jeremy swallowed hard—"said she must have gone berserk. Thrown herself around the room. Crashed into things. To end her pain, she slashed her wrists and climbed into a tub of water."

Bullpuckey.

When Corinne had taken the witness stand, Gustavson had grilled her like an adversary, especially after Corinne couldn't account for her whereabouts on the morning of the incident. Corinne hadn't wanted to admit that she'd spent the morning at Family Services Association trying to find someone who could help her get her sister away from her husband. At one point during the questioning, Jeremy had leaped to his feet and begged the lawyer to stop badgering Corinne. The crowd in the courtroom had heaved a collective sigh, as if acknowledging in unison what a standup guy

Jeremy was.

"Ladies and gentlemen of the jury," Gustavson said, giving her closing arguments, "my client is innocent. Though his wife's death is tragic, it was suicide, plain and simple. I ask you to return with a verdict of not guilty. The defense rests, your honor."

Conversations erupted from the gallery. A few said, *Poor man.*

Giada elbowed Corinne in the ribs. "Told you."

The judge slammed his gavel on the podium to quiet the room then advised the jury of its duty and rose to his feet. Everyone in the gallery stood, as well.

District Attorney Warner looked at Corinne dejectedly and placed a hand over her heart. As an apology. Warner had had a personal stake in the case. Like Corinne, her ex-brother-in-law had killed her sister, but she hadn't been able to prove it. The slug had died of a heart attack before she could make his life hell. She'd hoped with all her heart to prove that Jeremy Plunkett had killed his wife so she could bring Corinne a modicum of comfort.

Corinne covered her heart with her hand, too, and mouthed, *Thank you.*

Two hours later, when the jury reconvened with the expected verdict of not guilty, Corinne vowed she would destroy Jeremy Plunkett.

***

A week after the trial, Corinne started receiving visits from her sister. Not real visits, in the form of ghost or spirit. Corinne wasn't crazy. But she could see Sierra in her dreams, dressed in the white nightgown Corinne had stolen from the laundry basket. Sierra smiled a lot, and she looked at peace. In each visit, she sang a different song, tunes Corinne hadn't heard in ages. Many were from musicals or movies. Throughout their teen years, Corinne had made a big deal of introducing Sierra to all kinds of movies. Dark ones. Films with texture. Stories with substance. But after their parents' car crash, Sierra had only wanted to watch movies with happy endings, and she had loved musicals.

Corinne couldn't get this morning's song out of her head. It was from the Disney movie, *Aladdin*. "I can show you the world," her sister had crooned.

At noon, although Corinne wasn't hungry, she took a break from creating the final scene for *Z-Gen*, her latest film project. Standing in line at craft services waiting her turn, she wondered if her sister had been singing the song to convince Corinne that the great beyond existed and they would meet again.

"Are you kidding?" The woman standing in line beside Corinne, a forty-something gaffer, was gawking at her cell phone screen. "Jeremy Plunkett is engaged to Levanna Jones. He proposed to her at a scenic lookout in Malibu. How romantic!" Levanna was a starlet best known for her turn in the latest Marvel movies franchise. "And she's pregnant with his child!" The woman actually knew Jeremy. He played basketball with her husband. "Isn't it wonderful?" She grinned at Corinne.

How Corinne wished she could wipe the idiotic smile off the woman's gaunt face. If only a *Wizard of Oz*-style tornado would suck her into its vortex.

"C'mon." The woman flicked Corinne's arm. "Lighten up. Your sis has been gone a year."

"Eight months."

"Life goes on."

"For you maybe."

The woman blanched, grabbed a yogurt, and hustled out of sight.

Corinne stared at the food table. The sandwiches and chips blurred together as she tried to devise a way she could kill Jeremy and get away with it. She couldn't run him down with her VW. Too bad she didn't own a gun. Whatever she did would require the element of surprise.

"Corinne, make a choice before the next century," a character actor behind her in line joked.

"Yeah, yeah." She selected a ham and cheese, tucked it into the pocket of her photographer's jacket, hoisted her camera, and spent the next half hour taking shots of everyone eating lunch. She planned to give the director a collage of the crew and actors at the wrap party.

An hour later, sitting at her desk, watching take after take of a teen robot ripping the gun from an evil robo authoritarian named X-Ron, Corinne glanced at the movie posters plastered to the walls of her cubicle and a plan formed for how she could kill Jeremy without detection. A plan that she alone could master.

***

Jeremy Plunkett was enjoying himself. Everything was falling into place. He was on his way up the ladder at the precinct. Soon, he would be working homicide like his grandfather had. The one blip that could have derailed him would have been a guilty plea in his wife's murder, but Inga Gustavson had gotten him off. Case closed.

Now, with Levanna Jones in his life, he was a happy man. He'd loved her from the moment he'd set eyes on her. All twenty feet of her on the silver screen. That hair. That body. He'd made it his mission to get an introduction. As luck would have it, one of his basketball buddies had turned out to be her entertainment lawyer. He'd invited Jeremy to a party at his house, and the rest was history. Jeremy wooed Levanna and won. And now she was carrying his child. He hadn't felt this light-hearted since…since forever. He wished his father, a beloved high school teacher, was around so he could loop him in, but he'd passed away two years ago, not long after Jeremy had married Sierra. If Jeremy was honest with himself, losing his father had rattled him more than he cared to admit. After his mother walked out on the family, his father had raised Jeremy with a firm but kind hand. He'd tucked him in every night. He'd attended every basketball game. He'd been there at Jeremy's swearing in. His father had been his rock. When he died, Jeremy had teetered. In low times, he could admit that losing his father was the reason he'd treated Sierra so shabbily. But he did his best not to have low times. He wasn't his mother, who battled manic depression and had died in a ditch because she hadn't taken her meds.

On Friday evening, as the night turned from a grayish dusk to dark blue, Jeremy climbed into his Firebird, revved the engine, and headed to Levanna's. He was taking her out for a celebratory dinner. *No wine*, she'd reminded him. Who needed wine? Whenever he was with her, he was high on love.

Driving along Sunset Boulevard, he squinted at the headlights strobing the windshield and for the second time in a week, he wondered if he needed to see an eye doctor. His father had needed glasses as a young man. Perhaps it ran in his genes. He opened the car window and drew in a gulp of fresh air—as if air in Los Angeles could be considered fresh. By the time he reached Levanna's house in the hills, he felt alert and upbeat.

Dinner at Bacarri's was incredible and, yes, it was going to cost way more than Jeremy usually paid for a meal, but he wanted Levanna to feel like a queen. *His* queen. Over pasta alfredo with lobster, she told him about her day. He listened attentively. For dessert, they shared a decadent chocolate cannoli. When he took her home, they stood on her stoop gazing starry-eyed at each other. He wanted to come inside with her, but she begged off, rubbing her abdomen. The doctor had told her to take it slow for a month, just to be safe. Her mother had had a scare during her first trimester. Jeremy understood and headed home.

Pulling off the 101 freeway at Van Nuys Boulevard, he caught sight of something in his rearview mirror. Under the overpass. It wasn't a homeless person; the mayor had followed through with his promise and had moved the homeless population to a safe environment. He glanced over his shoulder. No one.

Pushing the notion from his mind, he drove north and turned right on Addison, heading to the home left to his father by his grandparents. Neither Jeremy nor his father, on their salaries, could have afforded it, given the rise in property values. Sierra had been so impressed by the house. *Sierra. What a disaster.*

Something glinted in the sideview mirror. A flashlight? Jeremy peered over his left shoulder. Nothing. *No. Wait. Something.* A man. Running toward him. No, not a man. A stick figure? Jeremy snorted. *Get real, Plunkett.* His temples began to throb. He needed sleep.

Later, studying his face in the bathroom mirror, he decided he looked tired. He couldn't accept that. Levanna deserved better. After brushing his teeth, he downed an Ambien. A good night's sleep would do the trick.

***

On Saturday morning, Corinne was sitting at a table for four at Grinders, a coffee house down the hill from Universal Studios. Breezy pop music emanated from a jukebox. Posters like the ones that lined the walls in her cubicle hung on every wall at the diner, too. Hollywood was, after all, fixated with itself.

Since the non-guilty verdict, Corinne and D.A. Melissa Warner and occasionally her partner, Giada Rossi, had been getting together. After the trial, Corinne had mentioned that she was considering joining a bereavement group, but Melissa had warned her off one. She'd had a painful experience in such a group and suggested that she and Giada could be her support system. A text weekly. A phone call monthly. And coffee in person every two or three months.

Corinne idly reviewed the diner's menu even though she knew what she'd be having. Melissa had made it a hard and fast rule that their get-togethers include cinnamon buns. Sugar, according to her grandma, fed the soul. Corinne had joked that it also fed the thighs.

The door opened and Melissa walked in with Giada.

"Cinnamon buns," Melissa said as she set her briefcase on a spare chair, shrugged out of her tailored pin-striped jacket, and sat down, shoulders square, her Marine bearing evident at all times. She tucked a loose hair from her short bob behind her ear and glanced at the daily menu. "Must have cinnamon buns."

Giada, who had dressed in an outfit that rarely varied, jumpsuit and Doc Martens, raised an eyebrow as she sat. "Why are you looking at the menu then, sweetheart?"

"Because I am compelled to read whatever is put in front of me."

"Have you always been a reader?" Corinne asked.

"Yes. I would read the telephone book if it was sitting on the table." Melissa set the menu aside and guffawed with gusto.

The sound reminded Corinne of one of the characters she'd created for *Laugh Track*, a horror movie set in a house of mirrors. The woman got so carried away by laughter that she was sucked into

156

the mirror to live the rest of her days laughing. Corinne signaled their usual waiter and he nodded. He knew that the order for them never varied. Leaning forward on her elbows, she said, "How are you guys doing?"

"Busy," Giada said.

"Work is crazy for me, too." Melissa set two cell phones face down in front of her. One for work, the other for personal calls. "You?"

"Wrapping up a movie." Corinne told them about *Z-Gen*. "I'm so excited. I get to do some out-of-sight special effects for the ending. When Earth blows up, rocket ships are speeding right and left while firing at aliens with demonic laser blasters."

Melissa laughed. "You're having more fun than I am. I'm dealing with a couple of scumbag cases. If only I'd gone to film school."

"You were born in Hollywood. Did you have the dream?"

The waiter set their coffees and sweets on the table and left.

"Never. Whenever I watched television or movies"—Melissa bit into her cinnamon bun and nearly moaned with pleasure—"I always wanted to be the one exacting justice. Military personnel, attorneys."

"What about you, Giada?" Corinne asked.

"Nope. Like I told you, I was destined to become a techie, thanks to my time in the corp. When master gunnery sergeant got hold of me, it was game over. He taught me everything from ball bearings to microchips. He was my hero."

"Atticus Finch was my hero," Melissa added. "But that was the extent of my craving for the limelight. I keep my nose to the grindstone. I don't like surprises."

"Talking about surprises, if you haven't heard the news..." Corinne took a hefty bite of cinnamon bun, washed it down with a gulp of coffee, and then launched into telling them about Jeremy proposing to Levanna Jones at a scenic lookout in Malibu.

"Less than a year after your sister died." Melissa wagged her head. "Crass."

"And to top it off, she's pregnant."

"The gall," Giada sneered.

"But I have set a plan in motion to bring him down. A movie

poster for *Ghostbusters* hanging in my cubicle was my inspiration. Also something you said, Melissa, about your ex-brother-in-law having a heart attack." Corinne outlined her scheme. "What do you think? I've already executed phase one."

Melissa grinned. "If you can pull off the whole shebang, you should win an Academy Award."

***

Early Saturday morning, Jeremy lumbered into the kitchen, his head splitting. Was it a side effect of the Ambien? He hadn't had a bad reaction before, but he had been taking it more frequently. Ever since he'd killed Sierra. "Enough," he muttered as he made a pot of coffee. "No more." Right then and there, he decided to stop all drugs. When Levanna moved in, he'd have to change his habits anyway. A health nut, she would take a dim view of his weakness for carbonated beverages. He could only imagine how she'd feel about him consuming a controlled substance.

Scrambling a couple of eggs, Jeremy's thoughts roamed to Sierra again. He wasn't proud of what he'd done, but to be honest, she had never been his equal. Levanna was. She was better, in fact. He was determined to rise to her level. Except he wouldn't. Rise. People didn't change after the age of eleven, the precinct shrink had told him. Jeremy was what he was. A control freak. No loose ends. That was what made him such a good cop. Also honesty wasn't one of his best qualities. It never had been. He'd lied to Sierra. He'd lied to his superiors. He'd lied in court. Cautiously, leaving out a few minor details, he'd been up front with Levanna about his personality quirks. She said she understood. In fact, she thought he was very much like her father. If Jeremy was okay with her being a star when she was away from him, she would totally let him be the star when she came home.

His cell phone jangled. *Levanna.* He answered. "Hey, babe, I was just thinking about you."

"In a sexy way?"

"Definitely in a sexy way." That was an acceptable lie.

She laughed warmly. "Listen, I got a juicy role in a new movie. I'll be leaving town for a few days. I've got to take all the work I can get before I start, you know, showing."

"Want me to take time off? I could come with you."

"Boundaries," she said. "We talked about this."

Jeremy nodded. She didn't want him on the movie set. That was her moment to shine. "When you get back, let's set a date for you to move in. I can't wait to spend the rest of my life with you."

"Me, too." She blew him a kiss and ended the call.

The day passed without event.

At the end of his shift when he climbed into his Firebird, Jeremy thought about the vision from the night before and convinced himself that he'd seen nothing. He chalked it up to fatigue. Until fifty feet shy of his house. A woman in a white nightgown darted across the street. No, she didn't dart; she flew. Jeremy slammed on the brakes, set the car in park, and scrambled from the car. "Ma'am!" he called. "Are you all right? Ma'am?"

Only the wind answered.

✱✱✱

"Crap!" Corinne slapped the steering wheel of her VW as Jeremy turned into his driveway. No heart attack. No nothing. Oh, sure, he'd stopped, meaning he'd seen the hologram, the same way he'd noticed the stick man chasing him the night before, but it hadn't scared him enough to make his heart seize. Why not? Because the effects weren't big enough. They weren't creepy enough.

Monday morning, Corinne arrived at the studio eager to set the next phase into action. It was big. It was bold. But she needed to break into Jeremy's house to pull it off. He had never installed a security system in the house. Corinne was certain he hadn't because he'd been afraid Sierra would press the panic button and 911 would save the day. But he did have locks on all the doors and windows. She thought of Andy, a special effects guy who had the hots for her. He'd worked for a security firm years before. Maybe he could give her tools or, at the very least, tips as to how to get in and out without detection.

At lunch, she wedged into the craft services line behind Andy and apologized to an actor for the cut. "Hey, bro, got a minute to chat?"

Andy offered a toothy grin. "For you? I've got a lifetime of minutes."

"A lifetime?" she echoed in an attempt to flirt, and felt her cheeks redden. She hadn't chatted up a guy in ages. She was out of practice.

"What's up?" Andy asked as he loaded his plate with a sandwich and chips.

Corinne took a yogurt and an apple. "I was hoping you and I could go out for pizza soon. My treat."

Andy frowned. "What's the catch? You've said no every time I've asked you."

Corinne leaned close and whispered, "I need you to teach me something."

He chuckled. "I knew it. You don't want me for my bod. You want me for my brains."

"And how."

***

Two days later, Corinne took the day off claiming she was under the weather. Her boss, a germaphobe, was more than happy she'd opted to stay home. Dressed in a pest control uniform, her hair tucked beneath a khaki-colored hat, and armed with a bump key Andy had made for her—a key that would fit Jeremy's rear door, filed down to help lift the pins and *bump* the lock—she drove to Jeremy's house and entered. She tiptoed upstairs to the master bathroom and began setting up her special effects. The moment Jeremy opened the door, a woman would howl in pain. Then wet steam, preset with a timer, would flow through the vents. For the finale, the steam would reveal a message from Sierra on the mirror. *I know you killed me.*

Delighted with her setup, Corinne parked near the corner and hoofed it back to the vacant house across the street. She tucked herself into a stand of bushes by the front porch and readied her Nikon Coolpix P1000. From her vantage point, she could see Jeremy's master bedroom. She couldn't get a full view of the bathroom without climbing on the vacant house's roof, but Jeremy, running in terror, would retreat into the bedroom. He had to.

She waited.

Around eight p.m., Jeremy arrived home. Per usual, he parked the Firebird in the garage and moved into the house. Lights went on. In the kitchen. In the hall. At the top of the stairs. He didn't switch on a light in the master bedroom, but Corinne could still see him because of the stairway light. He stopped in front of the bathroom door and placed his hands on his hips.

Snap-click. Corinne took a burst of photographs.

Jeremy pivoted; his face puzzled. Was he trying to remember whether he'd closed the door? Did he suspect Corinne had entered the house? She'd daubed herself with his cologne to mask her scent.

Giving up, he turned back and twisted the bathroom door handle. The light went on. With the windows closed, Corinne couldn't hear the woman howling, but she caught Jeremy's panicked body language.

Snap-click.

He reeled backward, grabbed his head between his hands, and spun around, his face a knot of anger. But he didn't fall. And he didn't have a heart attack. He stormed to the single-hung window, unlocked it, shoved the lower portion up, and leaned out. "I know what you're trying to do, Corinne Justice. Do not think you'll get away with this."

But she did. Because as Jeremy raced down the stairs to call the police, he'd left the window open. A month after Sierra died, he had reconstructed the latticework. It was easy to climb. In a matter of minutes, Corinne was in and out with her special effects equipment. Latex gloves prevented her from leaving fingerprints. Booties kept her from leaving tracks.

When the Van Nuys Police Department patrolman arrived, there was nothing for him to find.

***

On Sunday morning, Corinne met with Melissa and Giada at Grinders. On Sunday night, she was staking out Jeremy's house. She snapped repeated photographs with the P1000 as he pulled into his garage and...

A stunning Japanese woman landed on the hood of the car.

The woman beckoned him with her fingers.

Her fingers turned into tentacles and her face morphed into a spider's.

Disgusting wet fangs appeared.

She opened her mouth and a horde of spiders spewed out.

Jeremy reversed the Firebird. He cranked the wheel too hard. The car bounced over the curb. But he didn't die. He drove away cursing Corinne out the window.

"Dang it!" Corinne checked the digital renderings on her P1000 as she recalled the inspiration for the Jorogumo. Eighteen months ago, she'd brought the Japanese spirit to life in *The Cave*, the American remake of the Japanese hit film, *Dokutso*. According to legend, Jorogumo seduced men and lured them to her lair. In the first scene of the movie, the spirit was as stunning as the creature Corinne had created for Jeremy's torture. And, yes, Jorogumo had morphed into a spider with disgusting fangs. Unfortunately, Corinne hadn't been able to recreate the rest. In the movie, after unveiling her true spidery form, Jorogumo clasped her prey, bound it in her silk, and for the next thirty minutes, she and her litter of spiders feasted on him alive.

Corinne sighed. *If only.* If only Jeremy's heart would have seized at the sight of Jorogumo's frightening transformation. But he was obviously stronger than she'd thought.

***

At five a.m. the next morning, Jeremy's doorbell rang. Prepared to take anything that Corinne Justice might throw at him, he stormed down the stairs with his Smith & Wesson unlocked. If Corinne dared to show her face, he would shoot her and claim that he thought he was being robbed. Self-defense. No debate.

The doorbell rang again. He whipped it open, weapon raised. Levanna reeled backward. "Jeremy, what the hell?"

A husky policeman flanked her. "Sir, lower the gun. Now!"

Jeremy obeyed. "Officer. I thought…I didn't think…at this time of the morning…" He scrubbed a hand through his hair and eyed Levanna. "Why are you here, babe? Is something wrong?" He glanced between her and the officer.

"You!" she shrieked. "You're what's wrong. All these text messages that you sent me last night and the night before. They're crazy. You're acting nuts."

"What are you talking about?"

Levanna flashed her cell phone at Jeremy. He read the messages.

Monday 12:15 a.m. – Jeremy: *I want to die.*

Monday 1:03 a.m. – Jeremy: *I will kill myself.*

Monday 2:14 a.m. – Jeremy: *It's got to stop. All of it.*

Monday 3:27 a.m. – Jeremy: *My head is going to explode.*

"Are you on something?" Levanna demanded.

"No. I didn't write those."

Levanna swiped through other messages and displayed them. "What about these from Sunday night?"

Jeremy read more of the same. "I didn't send them."

"Your name is on them."

"She's mimicking my phone."

"She, who?" Levanna asked.

"Corinne. My ex-sister-in-law. She's been punking me with her SFX crap. Trying to drive me insane. I didn't want to tell you, babe, because of your new gig." Jeremy regarded the officer. "You've heard of mimicking an account, right?"

"I believe you mean cloning, sir."

"Jeremy." Levanna folded her arms. "Until you get help, you and I are finished."

"But babe—"

"Don't *babe* me. Good-bye." She said to the cop, "Thank you,

Officer," then turned on her heel, marched to her BMW, and drove away.

The cop gave Jeremy a warning to cease and desist and left.

Mulling over how he could fix things with his fiancée, Jeremy crawled back in bed. He needed at least another hour if he was going to make it through the day. Just as his eyes were closing, his cell phone *pinged*. He'd received a text message. He rolled onto his side to read it.

Monday 6:01 a.m. – Levana: *I'm so sorry. I don't want to break up. I was rash and insensitive. Meet me in an hour at Malibu. Where you proposed.*

Jeremy sighed with relief. Sleep could wait.

***

Tuesday night, Corinne was drinking wine while processing the photos she'd taken of Jeremy and streaming the news on her cell phone. She'd had a rough day at work. A program went haywire. She'd had to spend the afternoon fixing it.

"Breaking news!" an announcer said, followed by the *dum-dum-dum* jingle that accompanied it. "LAPD Officer Jeremy Plunkett, arrested but not convicted of his wife's death, died earlier today when his car plunged over a cliff in Malibu near Kanan Dume Road."

Corinne's breath caught in her chest. Jeremy was dead?

A blonde reporter held a microphone to a man with red hair and freckles. "I was his best friend for over twenty years," the redhead said. "I never suspected he was suicidal, but his mom was off her rocker, so maybe it was in his genes."

Was it in his DNA? Corinne wondered, or had she literally driven him to the brink after all?

The next clip featured a heavyset officer Corinne recognized from the trial. He was talking to a stoic reporter. "Yeah, Jeremy had been acting weird lately. Edgy and jumpy, I guess you'd say. Whirling around, staring at nothing."

Cut to Levanna Jones talking to a female reporter almost as beautiful as the starlet was. A handkerchief was balled in Levanna's slim hand. "Earlier this morning, I broke it off. He..." She dabbed her eyes. "He wasn't himself. I was worried that he might..."

"Hurt you?" the reporter asked.

"No. Hurt himself. And he did." The floodgates broke. Tears streamed down Levanna's cheeks.

The doorbell to Corinne's townhouse buzzed. Then someone pounded on the door.

"Coming!" She set the picture she was processing to one side, grabbed her cell phone, and hurried to the door. She peered through the sidelight. Two officers were standing on the porch. One was Davidson, the homicide detective who hadn't taken her seriously when confronted with Jeremy's guilt. The other was a younger, taller, and even better-looking colleague. The glow from the setting sun cast an aura around them.

Corinne knew her hair looked like crap, but she didn't care. These guys hadn't come to ask her for a date. She wiped her hands on the black apron she'd thrown over her work clothes, then opened the door. "Hello. How may I help you?"

"Jeremy Plunkett is dead," Detective Davidson said, no preamble, no introduction to his partner. "Tell me your whereabouts for the past six hours."

"Why?" Corinne hadn't meant to sound defensive, but that was exactly how the word had come out.

"Officer Plunkett's brakes were tampered with. He was murdered. That's on the down low."

"The reporter on the news didn't say that."

"The news hasn't gotten wind of it yet." Davidson lifted his rugged chin. "Your whereabouts?"

Corinne's heartbeat kicked up a notch. *No way. No f-in way.* This guy was not going to throw her in jail for something she didn't do. Channeling the lead actress in *Z-Gen*, a woman who acted without facial movement or inflection, she said, "I didn't do it."

Davidson raised an eyebrow. "Jeremy told me you were pranking him, but he couldn't prove any of it. He said you were like a phantom."

"Pranking him?"

"Trying to scare him to death."

"And how was I doing that?"

"Using special effects tricks."

Corinne smiled tightly. "Detective, I only use those effects in movies, not in real life. Jeremy has...*had* a vivid imagination."

"His fiancée received text messages from him, but he swore to her that he didn't send them. A short while later, he received a text message from her to meet him where he plunged to his death."

"Wow. The news didn't mention that either."

"May I see your cell phone?" Davidson extended a hand.

Corinne produced her phone and opened the home screen with her fingerprint. Davidson reviewed her texting activity and handed it back. "FYI, I was at the studio from dawn until now. I got home about a half hour ago. My work is time-stamped."

"Can someone verify that?" the partner asked.

"My boss. He's a tyrant about me putting in the hours." Corinne wasn't lying. However, if Jeremy had provided dates and times of her so-called pranks, and Davidson or his partner dug deeper and figured out she'd time-stamped other projects to beat the system...

"Detective"—she brushed dust off the sleeve of her blouse—"I'm sorry for your loss. I know you and Officer Plunkett were close."

"Thank you."

"Were you friendly with him, too?" she asked the partner.

"No, but he was a good guy."

Corinne offered a supportive smile. "From what I gleaned on the news, they suspect he committed suicide."

"*They* are not always correct." Davidson scrubbed the stubble on his chin. "Like I said, the brakes had been tampered with."

Corinne splayed her hands. "He claimed he was heartbroken when he lost my sister, and then this morning, Levanna broke it off with him. That's a lot for a guy to handle. He could have tinkered with them himself."

Davidson lowered his head. "He didn't deserve to die."

No, he didn't, Corinne thought. *He deserved to suffer.* "If that's all?" she asked.

"Stick around town, in case we have more questions."

"I've got a steady job. I'm not going anywhere."

Davidson nodded. His partner did, too, and they left.

When Corinne closed the door, she inhaled deeply, held it for a long minute, and exhaled. Every fiber of her body ticked with tension as the past two years flashed through her mind like a movie trailer. Failing her sister. Losing the court case. Resorting to trickery to try to get the job done.

Davidson had suggested that someone had rigged Jeremy's brakes. Who? Had a relative of some lowlife Jeremy had put away come after him? Had Levanna believed killing him was the only way out of their arrangement? Had Jeremy cut the brake line himself, hoping the cops would target Corinne as the likeliest suspect? Could he have been *that* twisted?

Pondering the possibilities, Corinne returned to the darkroom and resumed processing photos.

***

An hour later, as Corinne was singing along with Beyoncé and cooking a big batch of celebratory spaghetti in the kitchen, the doorbell rang. She stiffened. *Not the police again. Please.* Had they guessed what she'd done regarding the time-stamping? She wiped her hands on her apron and trudged to the foyer while dredging up her earlier stoic performance.

When she spied Melissa and Giada through the sidelight, she jolted. She hadn't told them where she lived. On the other hand, as a proud new homeowner, she had shared photographs of the front of her place on Facebook the day she'd closed the deal. A quick search on Zillow would have produced the address. And Melissa did work for the D.A.'s office. She probably had access to tax records and more. Had they come to warn Corinne that she was going to be arrested?

She forced a smile and opened the door. "What a surprise. Come in. Want a glass of wine?"

"I would love one." Melissa stepped into the foyer first.

"Not me," Giada demurred. "I'm driving."

Melissa swiveled her head. "Nice place."

"It's got good bones, but it needs some paint. When I can find the time." Corinne led the way to the kitchen and poured Melissa a glass of chianti. "Hope red's okay. It's all I've got. So what brings you to my neck of the woods?"

"We heard about Jeremy Plunkett." Melissa set her purse on the center island, withdrew her work and personal cell phones as she always did, set them on the counter, and perched on a stool. Giada remained standing.

"Yeah," Corinne said. "Big surprise."

"It's a shame his brakes went out," Melissa added.

Corinne balked. "You know about the brakes?" Detective Davidson had said that information was under wraps.

"I assumed." Melissa glanced at Giada. "That happens a lot going down Kanan Dume Road."

"A lot," Giada echoed.

Corinne breathed easier. Her friend hadn't helped Jeremy to his death.

"The news said he'd broken up with Levanna," Melissa added.

"It was the other way around," Corinne said. "Levanna broke up with him because he was acting weird."

"Thanks to you." Melissa raised her glass in a toast.

Corinne nodded, pleased with the way she'd punked him. If only she had been the cause of his demise. "By the way, this is on the down low, apparently he sent her a bunch of crazy text messages."

"I heard she sent him one, too," Giada said.

Corinne cut a look in her direction. "That's not common knowledge."

"No?" Giada tilted her head.

Melissa's mouth pulled down in a frown "What did you do?" she asked her partner.

Giada hitched a shoulder. "Cloning a phone and impersonating someone in a text message is easy to do nowadays." She twirled one of Melissa's cell phones. "Buy a burner phone. Give it a name. Send a text as someone else."

"So I've heard," Melissa said, cautiously.

"A person with the right skillset could really play mind games with a certain someone."

Corinne's mouth dropped open.

Melissa whispered, "And the brakes?"

Giada smirked. "You might recall I did a rotation as a mechanic in the Marines."

"No-o-o," Melissa moaned.

"Sweetheart"—Giada brushed her partner's arm—"your sister didn't get justice. You fought like hell to get it for Corinne's sister and lost. Someone had to do it, and it couldn't be you. But me? I'm just a tech. I blend into the woodwork. I'm not telling if you don't." She eyed Corinne pointedly. "No photos."

Slowly, Corinne raised her glass in a toast. "*Semper fi.*"

***

THE
DISAPPEARING
PLACE

JAMIE FREVELETTI

If one believes in infinity then one must acknowledge that anything is possible.

Artemisia Sloane worked her way toward the Disappearing Place as the sun set over the ocean, creating a blood orange streak across the horizon. The spreading darkness added to the eerie desolation of the location where more than a hundred people had vanished over the last fifty years. The ocean waves surged in and out in a constant rhythm, their sound helping to soothe Sloane's growing uneasiness at being there. She knew more than she cared to about the place because her sister, Teresilla, was fascinated by it and never wasted an opportunity to tell Sloane her latest theory. Now Teresilla had vanished and Sloane headed there to search for signs of her.

She reached the tall and twisted tree that marked the spot. Its roots curved out of the sand where erosion clawed at the beach and graffiti covered every inch of the trunk, etched by teenagers over the decades. Sloane walked around the base, using the flash from her phone to illuminate the sandy ground. Nothing seemed amiss. No footprints, no bits of cloth stuck to branches, no signs of anyone having been there. She crouched down next to a root that rose up four feet and curved back down into the sand, creating an archway. She shuffled closer and reached her arm into the opening, straining to get as far inside as she could. Her fingers touched a smooth piece of wood deep inside the arch.

The sounds of the ocean stopped and an eerie stillness followed. Sloane shuffled backwards, turned around, still in a crouch, and looked across the water. The ocean remained but not a ripple broke the surface and the nearest wave was frozen in a curve upward. In place of the orange horizon there now hung a moon in a brilliant blue color, unlike any Sloane had ever seen.

And then, as if a switch had flipped, the ocean surged again, the curved wave crashed into shore, and a gunshot rang out in the night.

The bullet hit the arched root and bits of old wood flew in every direction. Sloane looked to her right and watched as a large mob of people ran toward her, their faces contorted in rage and their howls so loud that they threatened to drown out even the sounds of the waves. Some carried torches, others rifles, and still others long sticks, like the handles of brooms. Sloane rose and ran, her arms pumping and her feet churning up the beach. The crowd's yells mingled with the sharp report of more gunfire.

She reached a tall rock outcropping that jutted out into the ocean, cutting the crescent beach in half, and in desperation she turned and ran straight into the ocean. A fool's choice for sure, because three steps more and the beach dropped precipitously. She plunged in up to her thighs, the frigid water shocking her into paralysis. The waves slammed into shore and sucked at her on their way back, threatening to rip her out to sea. Another shot rent the air and she shrieked in pain as the bullet hammered into her shoulder. She swayed a moment and then crumpled to her knees. Now the waves reached her neck and the first broke over her. The next pummeled her hard and she rolled onto her back, coughing and hacking as the water filled her nose and mouth and the salt stung the corners of her eyes. The next wave drove her under.

Through the froth above she saw the face of a man leaning over her. He reached down and grabbed her by the arm attached to the injured shoulder and began pulling her up. She shrieked again in pain, sucking yet more water into her mouth. He let her go and another wave crashed over her, sending her back underwater. He tried again, this time pulling her upright by her good arm. She coughed and hacked while she tried to breathe.

He draped her arm around his neck, and dragged her across the sand and beyond the outcropping, blocking them from view of the mob. She still heard them screaming in rage and bloodlust and their screams were getting louder.

The man was taller than her by a few inches—she was nearing six feet—and even though he was slender, he hauled her across the sand with ease. He kept going up a dirt path through the sea grass and brush. She did her best to help take her weight off him as they climbed upward. Far above loomed a lighthouse with windows lit in a soft yellow glow. It looked safe and warm and she wanted nothing more than to reach it without getting shot again, or bleeding out, or falling backward down the steep, rocky trail.

They continued upward and after another ten minutes reached the top. The lighthouse sat back on the flat plateau and rose from behind a rectangular main house made from white clapboard. Large windows ran on each side of a painted red door. The man pushed the door open, pulled her inside and then kicked it shut with his foot.

They crossed the room past a wooden staircase with a white banister, dark brown treads and white risers. Sloane caught a glimpse of a living room to her right with a couch, a rug in a muted red on the wooden floor and at the far wall a crackling fire burned in a large fireplace. He pulled her through an arched opening into a kitchen area, with a white wooden table in front of them, an island to the right with high stools and beyond that the cabinetry and appliances. He lowered her gently into a chair.

"I'm not sure what language you speak but please wait here. I need to throw the bar across the door and check that the mob hasn't followed." He spoke in softly accented English, and before he left she grabbed his wrist.

"Thank you for saving me down there."

He nodded, headed to the stairwell and ran up. She slumped in the chair; her shoulder throbbed.

He returned a few minutes later, carrying a large plastic case that he placed on the table before her. He opened it to reveal a first aid kit.

"I need to look at your shoulder. Would you like me to cut off your shirt? Or do you think you can lift your arm to remove it?"

"Cut," she said.

He nodded, picked up the shears from the case, and sliced the shirt from the crew collar straight to the hem with an impressive efficiency.

Perhaps a military man? she thought.

175

He paused when he saw what was underneath.

"What is this?"

So not a military man.

"A bulletproof vest," Sloane said.

"The material is so thin."

"It's a new design of a densely woven silk fabric mixed with other fibers. I'd ask that you not cut it, as it's expensive. That seam you see down the back opens if you pull on each side." He did as she suggested and Sloane hissed when he pulled the silk away from the clotted blood at the injury.

"Sorry," he said. "The vest worked well, but the bullet penetrated the skin and it's bleeding. I'll need to clean the wound and then put in a few sutures."

"Keep going. I don't wish it to become infected."

She shivered in her white cotton tank top, though the kitchen was warm. He glanced at her, noting her chill, but said nothing. When he was done, he disappeared back down the hall and returned carrying some folded clothes that he placed on the table in front of her.

"You should get out of those wet clothes. If you give me your shoes, I'll place them in front of the fire to dry." He pointed at a small powder room off the hall. "You can change in there."

He'd given her socks, sweatpants, a long sleeve white tee with a graphic of the constellation Cassiopeia on it, and a zip front navy hoodie. It all fit, more or less, and she was grateful for the warmth. She stepped back into the kitchen and found him standing before an open cabinet. He removed a bottle of amber liquid and two delicate, white teacups with a cherry blossom design on the side, all of which he carried to the table. She shook her head.

"I don't often drink spirits."

"Neither do I. This is an herbal concoction made with tamarind, turmeric, and green tea." He filled the cups, and she noticed that he wore a thin leather bracelet tied around his wrist. When he was done pouring the tea he placed one of the cups in front of her and took a seat opposite. For the first time, she got a real look at him.

He was pleasing to look at, with full lips, kind brown eyes and thick, brown hair that hung down to his shoulders. He wore a soft white linen shirt, unbuttoned at the top to reveal his throat.

"I'm Raimond De St. Leger. But most simply call me Raim. I'm the current guardian at this outpost and a civilian member of the military."

"Artemisia Sloane. Most call me Sloane. I'm the General and First Mathematician of the Republic of Hypatia."

He raised an eyebrow. "How did you fall prey to the mob?"

"I'm searching for my sister, Teresilla Sloane. She's a respected physicist and professor. She went missing three weeks ago. She was last seen close to the area known as the 'disappearing place' and so I began my search there. Initially I was alone, but I took a few steps closer to the place and the next thing I knew the crowd appeared and was upon me. I ran. Do you have an idea why this mob chased me?"

He looked down at the table a moment, as if gathering his thoughts.

"Why do they call it the 'disappearing place'?"

"It's based on folklore, really. Over the last fifty years it's been said that nearly a hundred people have disappeared there. Usually individuals, but one group of five teenagers disappeared all at once. That incident was over ten years ago. The latest happened two years ago and involved a major in Hypatia's army who was stationed nearby."

"And now your sister."

Sloane shook her head. "I don't believe in the legend. People don't just vanish into thin air. And now, having seen the mob, perhaps people aren't disappearing so much as being attacked and killed, their bodies thrown out to sea. I worry that she was attacked by them as well."

"They don't allow anyone to enter their side of the divide."

"Divide? What do you mean?"

"The rock outcropping is the marker for the border between this country and theirs. This lighthouse is the farthest outpost that guards the divide."

"I don't understand. I've never heard of this outpost, and as a general in the army I would have been informed if such an outpost existed."

"And I've never heard of a country called the Republic of Hypatia."

She stared back at him, shocked. "Are you serious?"

He gave her a slow nod.

She decided to play along with this crazy charade. "Then what is this country?"

"The Republic of Mulier."

"And on the other side of this so-called divide? What's that country called?"

"It's not a country. It's a section of our country taken over through war. They call themselves 'The United Righteous.'"

"So you're telling me that I'm no longer in Hypatia, but Mulier, and this country has a hostile nation on its border."

"Yes."

"I don't believe you."

He gave a small smile. "And I'm not sure what to make of your claim that you come from a place called Hypatia."

"We're on Earth. Right?"

He nodded.

"And there is no country called the Republic of Hypatia here?"

He sighed and rose.

"I have a globe in the study, let me get it."

"Yes. Please do."

He returned and placed a large globe in front of her, spinning it until he found what he wanted. He pointed. "This is Mulier."

The area he pointed to coincided with the landmass that should have been Hypatia, but on this globe it was delineated as the Republic of Mulier. A bright line ran across the bottom quarter of Mulier and indicated a border below which was "The United Righteous." The Atlantic ocean, Pacific ocean, and the rest of the globe coincided with landmasses, countries and bodies of water Sloane recognized.

"What's going on here?"

"Perhaps you hit your head on the fall into the ocean, causing amnesia?"

"If so, that still doesn't explain why I would make up an entire country and also have a mob chasing me."

"Perhaps you're a defector? Every year about a thousand United Righteous citizens defect. The government of UR is oppressive, backward, and run by the son of the late tyrannical dictator who claimed to have been appointed by God to run the country. This family rules the UR with an iron fist. Science is banned, except for that which researches munitions and weapons of war. Human rights abuses abound and those that criticize the regime are sent to conversion camps where they are first brainwashed and then worked to death. It's a grim country, to be sure."

Sloane stared at the globe and then looked back at Raim. "I think I'll drink some spirits now."

He gave a soft laugh.

"What would you prefer?"

"Brandy. Do you have any?"

Raim smiled. "I happen to have an excellent brandy that I keep for special occasions."

He poured two small snifters and placed one in front of her before holding his up in a toast.

"To your health."

"And yours." She sipped the brandy, which was excellent.

"You're a mathematician?" Raim asked.

She nodded. "It's the highest calling one can have, though if my sister were here, she'd argue and say physics ranks above." Just mentioning Teresilla caused an image of her to flash in Sloane's memory, her black hair pulled into a ponytail and her head thrown back in laughter as she played in their parents' olive grove. Sloane's throat tightened and she drank another sip of the brandy.

"Why was your sister fascinated with the place?"

"She wanted to prove her theory about the missing people."

"And that was?"

"She detected high energy neutrinos, particles, moving *upwards* from that spot, but with no detectable source. She had two theories for this anomaly. Her first was that the eroding sand and decaying plant life at the site interacted with oxygen and hydrogen in a unique manner."

"And the second?"

"That the particles were emanating from a parallel universe."

179

Raim stared at her in disbelief, and Sloane didn't blame him. She sounded delusional even to her own ears. He shook his head.

"I was concerned that you were a UR spy, but now I know you're not."

"Why is that?"

"Because no one in the UR would know anything about neutrinos, physics or mathematics."

"I know it sounds crazy, but no more than you telling me that I'm not in Hypatia. What do you do?"

"I'm a monk in the Order of the Cathar Templars."

"Like the Knights Templar?"

"Yes. Like the Knights. Does your country have this?"

"So you believe I'm actually from another country, not an amnesiac or a defector or from a parallel universe?"

He looked down at his glass, but remained silent.

"Ah, I see. You're being polite. It's okay. But in my world you couldn't possibly be a knight templar or a Cathar. Pope Clement and King Philip IV combined to torture and kill the knights so the King could confiscate their wealth. They were burned alive. As for the Cathars, they venerated the feminine as divine, believed in equality of men and women, the concept of reincarnation, and also condemned the Church's misuse of power and wealth. Pope Innocent III massacred thousands and wiped out entire towns; men, women and children. None exist anymore."

Raim looked appalled and took a quick swallow of his brandy.

"That's horrifying."

"I agree. Not humankind's most shining moment. Do only Knights guard this outpost?"

He shook his head. "I'm currently fulfilling my two-year mandatory military service. I asked to be assigned to this outpost. My orders are to guard it against intrusion and assist any defectors that may cross the divide."

"You welcome defectors?"

He nodded. "We have a strict code that respects human rights and believes in science and equality for all. Our legal code requires us to assist those seeking asylum."

"Perhaps my sister emerged at the same place that I did. Have you seen this woman?" Sloane held up her phone to show him her favorite picture of them both, taken last year at Sloane's birthday celebration.

He shook his head. "I have not. But that doesn't mean much. There's supposedly an underground tunnel nearby that runs from one side of the divide to another, though none has ever been found. If it truly exists and she ran through that tunnel, I wouldn't have seen her."

"How do you monitor the divide?"

He rose, went to a counter near the sink and picked up a laptop that he carried to the table. He tapped some keys and a live image came on screen of the rocky outcropping and the beach on the other side, all lit by the powerful lamp of the lighthouse that circled its beam. The mob was still there, milling around in groups.

"Do you have weapons aimed at your side of the outcropping?"

He shook his head. "None."

"I don't want to be rude, but as a general that seems to be a grave mistake. They far outnumber you. Why don't they simply come round the outcropping, as I did, and storm this house?"

"They fear stepping into this section of Mulier far more than they hate us. 'Mulier' means 'woman' in Latin. We're a nation with a woman president and women are represented in every branch of our government. The UR believes these women are witches risen from Hell, and if they cross the divide at this location the witches will strike them down with lightning."

Sloane gaped at him. "Witches? You've got to be kidding."

He shook his head. "Sadly, I am not."

"And if she didn't make it to the tunnel? If they captured her? What would they do to her?"

He again looked down at his brandy and Sloane braced herself for the answer.

"They'll burn her at the stake."

Oh God, please let her have escaped that mob, Sloane thought.

She glanced back at the laptop. Now the milling crowd formed into a group and began moving toward the rock outcropping. She pointed at the screen.

"Looks like this group didn't get the memo about being struck by lightning. They're headed this way."

Raim turned the screen to view it and frowned.

"I'm going to the lookout."

Sloane rose. "I'm coming with you."

He nodded, and she followed him as he returned to the stairs, taking them two at a time. At the second floor landing a long hallway ran right and left. Another ran straight ahead and at the end of that long hall was a second staircase. Sloane followed him up those stairs to a door. He swung it open and they stepped into the round room at the very top of the lighthouse.

Glass windows rimmed the entire space, allowing for a three-hundred-sixty-degree view of the surroundings. Beyond the glass was a narrow walkway with a parapet wall, which was accessed by another glass door. Inside the room to the right was a built-in desk with a laptop, phone, a massive dashboard with communication equipment, and several monitors. Next to that was a tall cabinet with an electronic keypad lock that Sloane assumed contained either classified documents, guns or both.

The ocean and the rock outcropping was in view to the left of the doorway, and the crescent beach and the mob was in sight ahead. The lighthouse lamp circled somewhere above them. The noise of the pounding surf below and the whirring light above filled the room. Over that came the cries of the mob, chilling to hear.

Raim crossed the room to the desktop and picked up a set of binoculars. He handed those to her and grabbed another set for himself. Sloane watched as the mob ran toward the outcropping. They stopped short of it, screaming up at the lighthouse. The few that had rifles aimed directly at the structure.

"I don't think those rifles can reach us here, but I'm not familiar with the exact weapon they're holding. Are we safe?" Sloane said.

"We're safe. Even if we were in range the glass is bulletproof."

Raim reached for the wall and flipped some switches. Large searchlights sprang to life, their glare illuminating both the crescent beach and the rocky outcropping. The crowd shrieked and shielded their eyes. He next moved to the dashboard and pressed some buttons. There was a loud explosion, the floor vibrated below her feet, and a laser beam shot down to the rocky outcropping, bringing with it a blinding burst of sparks. The crowd screamed and retreated back down the beach.

"What the hell was that?" Sloane asked.

Raim replaced the binoculars and switched off the searchlight. "A laser beam with a flash-bang effect. It's harmless. Well, loud, but harmless. It's frightening to see, though."

Sloane watched the crowd return to the far end of the beach where a second group worked at building something.

"What are they building?" she asked.

"Where?" Raim picked up the binoculars again.

"Look closely. Behind the mob. You see the four fire torches shoved into the sand? In the center of those it looks like they're building a scaffolding."

"They must be preparing."

Sloane lowered her binoculars to look at him. "Preparing to what? Burn someone at the stake?"

"Yes."

"No. Absolutely not. This should not be allowed." Sloane began to pace the length of the room. "What if they caught Teresilla and it's her they intend to burn? We need to stop them. Can you contact your commanding officer and arrange a rescue?"

He shook his head. "If it's one of their own citizens they're executing we can't interfere, though we condemn it. There are constant skirmishes along the long border of the divide and sometimes marauding UR bands kidnap our citizens. In those cases secret teams are dispatched to recover them, with mixed success. But when they fail and the kidnappers demand a ransom, the families take loans to pay them because the Mulier government has a strict no negotiation policy. If what you say is true and you're a citizen of another country, perhaps your government has a different policy and can negotiate a solution."

"But you say that my country doesn't exist."

He tilted his head. "I'm not sure what to make of this situation. You don't seem insane or delusional."

"Well...thank you, I suppose."

"Yet there is no country on Earth named after a famous ancient woman mathematician from Alexandria."

Sloane stilled. That he knew of the history of her country and the most legendary personage in its past was a relief. Not everything she knew to be true was wiped away when she crossed that divide.

"So what *do* you think?"

"My order believes in reincarnation. That after death our energy remains and survives to inhabit another body and live again. I don't think this belief is very far from the idea that other worlds exist in parallel. I have to presume that your renowned physicist sister was correct and the 'disappearing place' is a portal to another world. This one."

More than anything he'd said before, this simple statement made her want to panic, and as a general she wasn't prone to panic in dire circumstances; far from it. But now untangling the mystery of her current location, finding Teresilla and getting back to Hypatia, seemed an overwhelming proposition, and she was alone. She shook off the moment of weakness.

"I need a weapon. A rifle. One with a scope and the range that will allow me to defend from the top of the rock outcropping, and can reach the scaffold."

"And will you shoot the executioner if one presents himself? Or the mob that forms to watch?"

"If necessary."

He shook his head. "I can't allow that. It would be grounds for war and I'd be court-martialed. Besides, most of our weapons are nonlethal."

"Then give me some sort of weapon and a detailed map of the UR. I'll cross the divide and arrange a rescue."

"Alone? They'd tear you apart."

She shook her head. "I'm trained for this."

"You don't understand. It's possible that thousands will come to the burning. It's a gruesome and barbaric spectacle. You'll be far outnumbered."

Sloane resumed pacing, running idea after idea in her head.

"I've reported tonight's incident. One of my superiors will come here tomorrow to take you to the main headquarters for a debriefing. Perhaps you can convince her to act."

"And after the debriefing? What happens?"

"From there you'll be given an identity card, clothing, and temporary quarters for the next few months until you can function on your own. This is offered to all defectors whether from the divide or…elsewhere. I'm sorry, but that's the best I can offer you right now. However, I will do everything in my power to look for your sister."

Sloane pointed to the now dark rock outcropping. "You must know that one day they'll cross that divide and no harmless flash-bang laser will stop them. And you are alone and this outpost is unprepared to repel them."

He sighed. "I know. But we're not willing to be sucked into their cycle of violence. We only fire in self defense and then with the least lethal methods first. I realize that it must appear cowardly."

"Cowardly? Not at all. To acknowledge another's humanity when they refuse to acknowledge yours is absolute bravery. But it can come at a terrible price."

He walked to the door and held it for her. "You must be tired. I'll take you to your room."

Sloane followed him down the stairs, to the end of the hall and into a bedroom with a thick area rug, a large bed and dresser.

"I'll wake you an hour before my superior arrives."

"One last question."

Raim nodded. "Of course."

"You said you chose this posting. Why?"

Now he smiled. "I'm an amateur astronomer. This outpost is quite remote and the lack of light pollution allows me a better view of the stars. I've set up a telescope on the highest part of this bluff to do so. I was there when I saw the mob chasing you. I'm headed back now, because tonight is a seasonal blue moon and it will fade in the next half hour."

"Blue moon?"

"It arrives once every two and half years or so. An extra full moon in a season. I hope you sleep well." He bowed and left, closing the door quietly behind him.

Sloane waited to see if he'd lock the door, but all she heard was his footsteps as he walked away. She had no intention of being taken from this place until she found Teresilla, and it was clear she would have to cross the divide once again to continue her search. He would easily see her from his telescope if she did and she couldn't risk interference. She needed to wait until he returned and slept before she would creep out and away. She set her watch to wake her in two hours and fell into a dark, dreamless sleep.

At five a.m. her watch buzzed her awake. She dressed and stepped into the hallway, taking care to be quiet. Across the hall she saw that Raim's bedroom door was open, though the light was off. She crept toward the stairs, all the while watching to see if he'd appear and stop her. She passed the open door and glanced in. His bed was made and his curtains fluttered in the breeze.

Something was wrong, she could feel it.

She searched the house and ran outside to the highest point of the bluff, where she found the telescope, broken, with pieces littering the ground. She walked to the edge of the cliff, looked down, and saw the metal bar of what looked like a tripod stuck in the branches of a small bush. She scanned the area but saw no indication that Raim had fallen down the cliff or, worse, been thrown there, so whoever had attacked him took him away.

She ran back and up to the lighthouse room and used the binoculars to view the scaffold's progress.

The crowd had swelled to twice its size and the scaffold was complete. Set about five feet above the sand, it had a square platform with a center beam where its first victim was already tied. The burning torches at each corner of the structure threw eerie light and shadows across the victim's face.

It was Raim.

She would cross the divide, but not for Teresilla.

Sloane put the binoculars down and went to the dashboard that controlled the flash-bang laser. The weapon's settings allowed it to be aimed and fired manually, through motion detection, or on a timer. Another group of settings operated something called a "Dormiens Telum." Sloane's Latin was rusty, but anything that appeared to be a weapon was welcome. She altered the coordinates for both, set the timer to fire in thirty minutes, then headed to the cabinet.

The lock contained both a keypad and a swipe pad. She first tried the word 'moon,' pressing the numbers that spelled it out.

Nothing. Then 'stars.' Nothing. She stepped back and inspected the cabinet. The steel construction was designed to withstand blows and fire, so hammering it open or using a blowtorch was not an option. She returned to working the keypad. In the cabinet's reflection she saw her tee shirt with the Cassiopeia constellation. She used her finger to swipe the pad in that figure. The lock whirred and the door popped open.

"Thank you, Raim," she said out loud.

Inside were two rifles of different calibers equipped with some sort of nonlethal bullets that weren't rubber, but more like tranquilizer darts, and a bottle of small white pills that were either aspirin, tranquilizers or pain killers. Two tactical vests, the bulky and old-fashioned ones, a black baseball cap, and on a hanger hung a uniform with the words "United Righteous Army" plastered across the shirt. She assumed the last allowed Raim to blend in as he slipped across the border to search for kidnapped citizens.

She grabbed the pill bottle, one of the rifles, and put the army shirt over her own bulletproof vest and constellation tee. She was almost at the door before she reversed to the kitchen. She grabbed the bottle of brandy by the neck and shook some of the white pills into it.

The wind whipped at her hair and the surf sprayed her as she made her way around the rocky outcropping. The moon hung low and glowed a dimmer blue. The dark fatigues of her army shirt blended in well with the craggy stone and she hugged the edges, keeping to the shadows thrown by an overhang. She kept her head down and the cap pulled low.

When she reached the other side, she straightened, swung the rifle strap over her shoulder and marched toward the increasing crowd around the scaffold. Most were armed with various weapons, mostly guns, and unlike hers all looked lethal. The gathering had a festive air about it. One man poured beers from a keg he kept on his flatbed pickup and a small boom box blared marching band music. In the midst of all this the workers piled old scrub and branches at Raim's feet, while a woman stood on the side of the platform with a microphone and read from a Bible.

Raim's face was swelling and a large gash ran from his temple down to his jaw. A slash on his right bicep bled and his arms were yanked behind him. He wore the plain black tee shirt and loose-fitting gray sweats that she'd last seen him in, but one leg of the sweats was soaked red with blood and his feet were bare. He kept his head down and his eyes closed, but despite that and his stillness, something about him spoke of consciousness.

An older man in ill-fitting jeans, with a large beer belly and wearing a black, hooded sweatshirt, stepped next to Sloane.

"Woman in the UR Army, huh? Thought that was banned."

"It's my husband's shirt."

"He with them?" He pointed to the top of the bluff where a red Humvee—with a United Army logo and outfitted with a fire hose—sat.

"That looks like a fire truck."

Tyler nodded. "It's a combo fire and tank. Last time the blaze was such that we damn near set the entire bluff on fire. Now the army guys come to every burning to keep an eye out for any Mulier terrorists and to be sure the fire's out when it's over."

"Heard about this one and thought I'd come down to watch."

"Yeah. Great night for a burning. Big old moon."

"What did he do?"

"He's a heretic from Mulier. Believes in equal rights for the sexes, reincarnation, all that stuff. You gotta stamp them out whenever you can."

"I see you have a cup there." She held up the brandy. "You want a sip?"

"Don't mind if I do." He held his plastic cup while Sloane poured. Next to him a woman who looked to be in her late fifties stepped close.

"Tyler, you sharing?" The lady gave Sloane a pointed look.

Sloane smiled back. "Of course."

Soon others eyed her and she poured everyone a shot, stopping only when the bottle was nearly empty.

"Guess I'll go up there and say hi. Offer them some and thank them for their service."

Tyler nodded his approval. "Right nice of you."

She found a path and made her way up the hill, glancing at her watch as she did. Ten minutes until the laser fired. When she was even with the scaffold's height, she saw Raim open his eyes a bit and slide a glance her way.

So you are conscious, she thought.

Two soldiers loitered around the Humvee. She offered up her brandy but both shook their heads.

"No drinking on duty." Sloane would have commended them, but in this case she wished they'd have been less disciplined. One of the soldiers pointed at the scaffold. "Here we go."

The crowd roared as the workers used a torch to set the brush around Raim's feet on fire. The fire took hold, spreading slowly but continually, the flames licking out and catching from branch to branch.

"Burn. Burn!" The crowd clapped in unison. Tyler and the group Sloane plied with the brandy stumbled. The woman held Tyler up and the others fell to a sitting position as the drug took hold. Ten of the attackers were down, but at least a hundred remained.

Sloane checked her watch. Seven minutes.

She jogged away from the Humvee and the view of the burning scaffold and placed the brandy bottle at the base of a bush. She raked her hand across the ground, collecting the dried and dead brush underneath, which she shoved into the neck of the bottle. She removed her lighter and lit it, jogging backwards as she waited for the flame to reach the alcohol. Ten seconds later the bottle exploded and the bush caught on fire. She waited to see if the soldiers would spot the bush and drive over to investigate. If they did, she'd shoot them and take the Humvee.

A billowing, black cloud of smoke rose all around Raim, and the flames licked closer. He raised his head and his face shone from the heat of it. She could see him struggling in panic to escape the ropes. She checked her watch. Three minutes. Too long. The flames would engulf him before the weapons fired. Sloane's plan to distract the crowd long enough to find a way to free him was failing. The bush burned brighter and the woman at the side of the platform with the microphone spotted it.

"Behold, the burning bush! God is here and sanctifies this burning!" She dropped to her knees and some in the crowd followed,

189

still chanting.

One of the soldiers jumped in the Humvee. Rather than drive to investigate, he merely aimed the fire hose at the bush while the other started the engine to get the pump working. She was going to have to reveal herself. Sloane shouldered her rifle and shot the first soldier in the back, the second in the neck through the Humvee's open window.

She ran and jumped up to the hose, stepping on the soldier who lay gasping on the truck bed as the drug in the bullet took hold. She rolled him out of the way and onto the dirt, aimed the hose at the platform, and pulled the trigger. The spray hit the flames and the billowing smoke turned blacker as the water drenched the embers. Raim started coughing and choking; within seconds, he disappeared from view as the smoke engulfed him.

The lady with the microphone pointed up at Sloane. "It's a Mulier terrorist!"

Sloane dove off the truck bed and rolled behind the Humvee while the crowd peppered the area with bullets. Her watch buzzed as the countdown clock hit zero.

A roar emanated from the lighthouse and the air seemed to vibrate. The laser beam shot down, this time landing not at the rocky outcropping but ten feet in front of the burning scaffold. The flash-bang sparks flew everywhere and Sloane winced at the tremendous noise. The crowd screamed, and some bolted away from the platform.

But the distraction didn't last for long. Soon the crowd moved in a mass toward Sloane. She worked her way to the driver's side door, pulling out the soldier and throwing her rifle in before she slid behind the wheel. She rolled the window up, swung the Humvee around and drove straight down the side of the bluff, accelerating toward the crowd that clawed its way upwards. The heavy vehicle swayed and shimmied as the tires dug into the shifting, soft ground, spraying dirt and stones everywhere. It finally lost purchase, swung sideways and stayed that way while it slid down the remaining twenty feet to the beach. Three men fired at the windows, but the bullets merely dented the glass. The truck hit a large boulder, teetered in the air as if deciding to fall or not, and then began to roll. Sloane tumbled inside the cabin while the truck pinwheeled.

The lighthouse gave another roar; this time a spray of grenades hammered into the ground around the platform, exploding into their own billowing clouds as they made contact. The Humvee slid its last two feet to the beach, collecting some of the mob with it, and coming to rest upright and back on its wheels.

The mob surrounded the vehicle, pounding and wrenching at the door handle to get at Sloane. Their rage, close up, was frightening to behold, but within seconds they began to drop. One by one their eyes rolled up in their heads and they slid to the dirt, motionless, until the ground was littered with bodies.

Whatever that weapon is, Hypatia's army needs it, Sloane thought.

She burst out of the Humvee, prepared to shoot whoever came at her first, but no one moved. She ran to the platform and plunged through the cloud of smoke that surrounded it. Raim was awake, still trying to work his way out of the ropes. She stepped up, slid a knife between them and sliced them off.

"We need to run. Now," Raim said. "The smoke cloud kept most of the drug from me, but it will act on us with each breath we take. And that crowd is going to wake up. Once inhaled, the stupor only lasts for two minutes."

"Understood," Sloane said. "Is your leg okay?"

He shook his head. "It's not broken, but every step is agony."

She wrapped the rifle around one shoulder and his arm around another and dragged him forward. They jumped off the platform and plunged into the drug filled air. Sloane tried to hold her breath, but dragging him and running across the sand made her pant with exertion. They were only halfway to the divide when the drug began acting on her. Her head swam and a ringing started in her ears. She heard the mob start up behind them, but she refused to look back, instead focusing on the rocky outcrop. Raim slumped against her and his head lolled down. She kept going even as her legs softened and her muscles relaxed. She reached the outcrop and a gunshot rang out. A bullet hammered into her back.

I've come full circle was her last thought as they both fell into the churning waves.

Sloane opened her eyes to see a woman leaning over her in the soft light of dawn.

"General Sloane? Are you okay?"

Sloane struggled to rise and the woman knelt and helped her to a sitting position. She looked relieved.

"I'm Major Lee Kwan."

Sloane's head was still foggy, but she thought she recognized the name.

"Major Lee…who disappeared two years ago?"

Lee nodded. "I work for the Republic of Mulier now. They dispatched me to pick up a defector. Imagine my surprise to find you, General."

Sloane looked around.

"Where's Raim?"

"Right behind you."

Sloane tried to turn and hissed in pain. Lee helped her move and, sure enough, Raim was stretched out next to her on the sand, still unconscious.

"And the mob?"

"On the other side of the divide. Mad as hell but dispersing fast. Did you come through the Disappearing Place?"

Sloane nodded. "I'm looking for my sister Teresilla. I think she came through as well. I'm afraid they may have gotten her."

Lee frowned. "If so, we haven't heard any chatter about it over the intelligence channels. Perhaps she made it to Mulier safely, as you and I did, or is hiding in the UR."

Raim gave a soft moan.

"Does he know who you are?" Lee whispered.

Sloane nodded. "I told him everything."

Lee's mouth dropped open. "That's quite a risk. I've told only one other person since coming to Mulier and that's another refugee. He came through thirty years ago and helped me by giving me papers and fueling my rapid rise in the military."

"Raim believes I'm from a parallel universe."

Lee laughed softly. "So like him to be open-minded. He's

extremely well liked in his unit. The Cathar Templars are renowned for their humility and their fearlessness. Just about every successful rescue mission in the last twenty years was completed by their order, and Raim's already assisted in four."

"I presume that you've explored whether it's possible to go back?"

Lee sighed. "Yes, but so far none of us have been able to reverse the process."

"I'm staying here until I find Teresilla, anyway. She's a physicist and just may be able to work out a solution."

"Maybe you could join the Order of the Cathar Templars. My mentor knows their highest member and she would take his suggestion seriously. You could run rescue missions and search for your sister with none the wiser as to your identity." She rose. "I'm going to get a stretcher so we can carry him up the bluff. Be right back."

She jogged away.

Raim moaned again and opened his eyes. Sloane leaned over him.

"Thank you for saving me," he said.

She nodded. "Of course."

"You didn't kill anyone, did you?"

She shook her head. "Only nonlethal methods were used."

He smiled. "I'm very grateful you came to Mulier, General Sloane of Hypatia."

⁎

THREE MINUTES
PAST MIDNIGHT

SUSAN WINGATE

Boom! Boom! Boom!

And Zainey Walker is up. Out of bed. Her hair pulled back in a tight knot. Gator around her nose and mouth. Balaclava beanie hat complete with ski mask. A flak jacket.

"Come on, Walter. I gotta go." She lifts the old Westie off the bed and brings him outside to pee before heading out to search for perps. She misses Finn. He was a worthy protector, a guard dog of exceptional quality until the cancer got him.

It's cold outside. Early cold. Icy. Winter has opened its door and is dancing in. The dog scoots back inside. He's cold too. She pats his thick dog pad. He'll be warm there while she's gone.

But she needs gear first. She gets ready, her rifle slung to her back, handgun in holster, side knives secured, one on both ankles. Reminds her of the good old days of ops training for bleak lands and bleaker waters. The black art of ops training.

The good old days fighting in the desert, ship-to-shore. But unlike the good old days, the ground on the island where she absconded is compost and moss, not sand and rock, not dry, and certainly not hot. Wet as tears flowing in *Lamentations*.

How she learned the Bible throughout everything, she'll never know. And she knows the Koran as well, reads both in Arabic.

Thank you, Yalda.

Back in the forces, the O-4 always ordered: *Take no prisoners. Don't muddy the water. Make blue water red.* O-4 called her Frog Girl—an endearment of gender in comparison to the rest of the guys. O-4 took good care of his squad. After Afghanistan, the squad switched her handle to Toad Girl.

A December sky meets her close and dark as a monster.

Zainey pulls a pair of night goggles onto the bridge of her nose. She looks like something out of the apocalypse. All she needs is a gas mask and a clean suit to complete the look.

She scans the perimeter. A raccoon clings high on the trunk of a tree. It spots Zainey and shimmies higher. She hears the rustle of dead grass. A fox disappears into a thicket of spiny blackberry bramble. Its tail, a dense broom now for winter. A small doe hunkers behind a downed alder. The tree fell last winter in the big winds.

No one...*freaking no one* hunts on her property.

Her heart thumps then skips into tom-tom mode. She takes three deep breaths, holds for three, then lets out the air on a three-count, making no sound. She repeats the breathing technique.

Tricks of craft return fast. It's as though she never left the killing trade.

She thanks Yalda again. Yalda, the Afghan military scout who taught her the art of silent, deadly desert trickery. Disastrous for those who mistook Yalda as a sweet girl, complete with reading glasses slung around her neck. *Disastrous.* Like mistaking a thresher for a hairbrush.

"Passion," Yalda instructed, "is for to use. Not for to push away. Use passion."

Zainey's passion never left. Even while settling into island life. Even when she notices the slightest shift toward complacency, she continues to keep her passion close. Still, hates bullies, creeps who pick on meek, unsuspecting humans and creatures alike. Like hunters after her deer. Feeding a herd of deer was craziness and a total money suck but, what the hell. Ya gotta spend it somehow, her dad used to say.

By now, protecting the herd is part of her DNA. She protects them at all costs. Why not? She's on the government's penny. They owe her.

So, Zainey protects her land, at any cost, against creeps like the kid with the gun who gets his jollies playing with *Tannerite*, and why? Because he likes to blow things up? The dumbass.

Only once did she have to have the *talk* with him. Once was enough. But with some boys, well, you just never know.

She wonders now: Were this morning's explosions Brandon acting out again? Was he prodding her? He wasn't that stupid, was he?

Maybe he misses her—she jokes to herself—misses the

suddenness of her arm tightening around his neck. Of his leg clutched between Finn's teeth. *Good boy, Finn.*

Her focus returns. A pang hits her, and she longs for her dog.

She misses the old job, too. A job that rages beneath the layers of her skin, itching to get out. Itching to be relevant again.

She still sticks to the dress code, to a daily routine and workout schedule—running three clips morning and night, jig-jagging through the woods, camo-style ala the season, blurring a wake behind her. Paced and steady. Stealthy.

She runs to forget. She runs so she *won't* forget.

Zainey dips, hunches low and creeps deeper into the woods. There's a trespasser out here.

Apparently, he didn't get the memo. And with all the signs posted too! The idiot.

Quiet is key. Difficult, what with the mire of wetland so close to the lake.

She carries her Glock 17 in a lumbar holster cinched over a pair of sweats and a flouncy thermal shirt she was wearing to bed when the blasts went off. She keeps her favorite knife on her right leg, a slim dagger-style Bowie, the one her dad gave her and the one she used earlier to chop vegetables for dinner. One she often uses to bone a quick chicken for cacciatore.

The left knife is a quick-action stiletto. A short knife meant for sneak attacks. Close up and personal.

She scans the understory of trees. Through the goggles, the ground glistens in shades from bright red to black blood.

Zainey shivers.

Ice crystals ache, hoping to pierce the air. Three minutes after midnight, the gauge had fallen below thirty. That's the time she will chart for Sheriff Cal Drake, a squat, heavy-set officer who likes to show off his multilingual skills with her. She'll say, "I was awakened at three minutes past midnight by three loud, what sounded like explosions, close to or on my property." She'll add, "Trespassers. It's posted. YOU WILL BE SHOT. Can't get clearer than that."

Over beers, she and Cal often chat in a dialectical Uzbek Russian, one she learned in Afghanistan. She fascinates Cal. Cal's curious about her.

They swap Uzbek texts. It's silly, but it keeps one of her feet there and she can't ignore how she still misses the desert life.

After she handles this situation, she will text him all the markers: self-defense, violation of property rights. All the legal jargon to make her case. She has rights. As a property owner, Zainey has rights. She also has special entitlements no one else on their small island has. Cal knows. The agency let him in on her secret. He nearly outed her once about that intel when they went shooting with some people. It was a minor slip. She forgave Cal. Either way, if she doesn't kill whoever is out here, she'll drag his butt into the house and make him explain why he felt it was a good idea to trespass onto her property. She has duct tape and a heavy metal chair to do the interrogation. They'll snap.

Forgive those who trespass against us.

She flexes her fists. The shooting gloves she found aren't great for cold weather, but they're something.

A twig snaps some thirty feet off. She freezes. She hears panting.

Someone is chambering a shell into what sounds like a Mossberg 930 shotgun. The chambering is sloppy and slow, not a smooth action. An amateur's chambering into a noisy beast of a weapon. That explains the shaken windows when its bomb of a blast went off. Three times, no less.

She squats.

Through the red gleam of her goggles, she makes out two sets of fresh tracks. One set, human. The other, mammal.

Her head cocks right. She remains frozen. Listens.

A crunch of twigs under a heavy boot. The perp is large, around 200 pounds. He's situated south and east of her, nearer to the lake. The perp sniffs and coughs.

Whoever's out there isn't worried about making noise.

He isn't worried about being on *her* property. Not worried about *his* trespassing.

Can't this moron read? She's posted signs everywhere.

NO TRESPASSING. VIOLATORS WILL BE SHOT ON SIGHT.

He whistles a short sharp note. The panting and scrambling belongs to a dog.

She hates killing dogs but won't hesitate if one attacks or goes after the herd.

He whispers, "Good girl."

She scans out further in front, locates something moving behind the thick trunk of a Douglas fir. She shifts to the left. If she raised her rifle, she could easily get a bead on him.

He's not tall. Wears a khaki anorak and sloppy pants cut below his stomach. He has on heavy hiking boots. And, like she thought, weighs in at about 200 pounds.

She zooms in on his face. It's familiar even under a flapped-eared cap, even wearing a gator around his chin.

He raises a hand. The dog sits. He beckons the dog with another sign and the dog comes to him. The dog looks familiar, too. It has something flaccid in its mouth.

Then Zainey recognizes them both.

It's freaking Cal Drake and his dog Sandy, an ashy Weimaraner, a dog used for retrieving small game. Sandy hasn't tracked Zainey's scent. Sandy's oblivious.

What the hell, Cal? Why are you here?

Cal keeps Sandy close. Zainey sees that the flaccid thing in between her jaws is a duck decoy. Cal's training Sandy to retrieve.

At this hour?

He takes the decoy from her. She lays down at his feet.

Zainey lowers her goggles. She doesn't need to hide from Cal. She and Cal go back to when he got to the island, three years ago in the role as an interim sheriff when the previous one was killed while on duty. They never found the person responsible. But then, it's a small island with limited staff. Zainey was never sure how much effort they put into tracking the killer down. Wasn't sure, but either way, it was none of her business.

Cal whispers, "Good girl, Sandy." He bends to pat her on the head.

This is ridiculous.

She doesn't need to hide from Cal.

She stands. The dog sits up, alert to her movement. Sandy growls. Cal hushes her and readies his rifle.

"Put it down," she says. "It's me, Walker."

"Oh, man. I didn't hear you." He looks at Sandy. "We didn't.

God, Zainey. You scared the *bejeezus* out of me."

She chuckles.

Bejeezus.

"So, what the hell, Cal? What are you doing here at," she checks her cell, "at fifteen after midnight?"

"Training Sandy."

"At this hour?" she asks. "Why? And why didn't you ask me beforehand. What the hell? Did you fire that weapon?"

He turns behind him as though looking for someone else. Zainey follows his gaze.

He shakes his head. "Wasn't me."

Again, he scans the area around him but now higher as if he's trying to spot someone up in the trees.

Again, Zainey following his lead glances up too.

Someone else then? Could they still be out here?

"Think they're still out here?"

"Could be. Maybe. Maybe not." He rubs a hand under his nose.

She approaches, pulls out a high-lumen flashlight and adjusts the beam to the widest setting. Frost ghosts out in front of both Cal's and Sandy's mouths.

Cal puts a hand over his brow.

"Sorry," she says. Zainey flicks the beam lower. The dimmer setting enwraps both Cal and Sandy in a bubble of soft gray light that dies off into blackness some fifty feet back behind where they stand.

Cal drops Sandy's lead. She quails but approaches Zainey. Her tail low, nearly under her rump but wagging.

"Hey girly." Zainey pats the dog on the neck. Zainey smells a hint of GSR. She glances up at Cal. Gunshot residue hangs around for a while, but it mixes in with the smell of woods, with the mildew of sphagnum moss, crisp tarry sap from the firs, and stale lake water leeching its way onto land.

"Heel," Cal says.

Sandy turns away and quails back to him.

The sky is pitch. She can't locate the moon. The woods dense cluster of branches and evergreen leaves make the sky difficult to see out this close to the lake.

"Did you see any cars coming or going?" Zainey asks, trying to redirect the conversation to the blasts.

"I came out to see who fired after dispatch notified me," he says.

"Sure got here quick. You in the area?"

He nods. "Doin' rounds and seein' who still had my election signs up." He lets out an uneasy laugh. "You think you wouldn't care."

"See mine? It's still up at the entrance."

"We did."

"We?" Her throat tightens around the word. Why is she tense?

"Me and this one. My best girl." He pats Sandy's side. She leans her full weight against his thigh.

"How does Beth feel about a dog being your best girl?"

He shrugs. "Don't much care."

"Look, it's cold out here, Cal. I'm going back in. You have your fun, just try to keep the bad guys off my property. Okay?"

"Sorry. I figured, we were out here and all. So, you know, why not train the dog a little by the lake?"

"Check," she says.

On the other side of the lake, an owl hoots twice, then growls out a guttural finish.

"Lore says, 'something's gonna die,'" she says.

Cal's eyes appear trancelike. He's gazing up high, somewhere out where the owl sent its warning. "Or someone," he says.

"Happy thoughts, Cal. Happy thoughts."

He snaps out of his trance and chuckles. "Oh man. What's gotten into me?"

"Owls. They'll do that." She flips off the flashlight. "Want to come in? Want some coffee? I can make a quick pot."

"Why not? Beth doesn't expect me any time before daylight." He smiles but looks away fast. Another owl, probably its mate, copies the call.

"I can leave Sandy in the car." As he's saying it, he calls the dog to follow.

"Nah. She can come inside. I have a treat for her."

When the dog hears the word treat, her ears perk up.

"See?" Zainey says. "Sandy want a treat?" The dog barks once.

"Does that mean yes?"

Cal isn't laughing. "Who knows with dogs."

"You think you should stay out here instead? I mean, I don't want to distract you from finding whoever's causing trouble."

"They most likely tore off when they saw my car."

"Where is your car?"

"I parked out by the main road."

"You walked that far, did ya?"

"Stop," he says. "More people see the car out on the main road, more people slow down or stop whatever bad thing they're doing."

By the time they reach the house, the cell reads 12:33 in the morning. Walter waits by the front door. When Zainey enters, she says, "Hey bud. Miss me?" She dips down to pet him. Sandy falls in behind her and sneaks past, dashing further up the hall. Cal comes in last and shuts the door behind him. Zainey peels off the balaclava, slips it over the tip of the rifle and leans the weapon against the wall inside the front door.

Cal blows into his fist and everyone piles into the house.

"Didn't realize how cold I was out there."

"Poor Sandy. And she's not wearing any protection."

"She's a dog. They don't need stuff like that."

"Well, there are those who disagree. Me being one of them." She approaches the dog and rubs her coat causing friction between her hands and Sandy's fur. "That better?" The dog parts her teeth and wags her tail. "See? She likes that. Don't you like that?"

"She likes you," Cal says.

"Of course she does. She's a good girl."

Walter walks up. "He's jealous. You better pet him now or else Walter will want to come home with me."

"I would never let Walter go. We can have two dogs, Walter. Wouldn't that be nice? A friend?"

And the barking begins.

"Oh crikey," Cal says.

"Shh, shh," Zainey says to the dogs who quiet down. She fetches two dog biscuits and doles them out. "There. Now they're happy."

Zainey feels a tug of sleep pulling at her eyes.

Under the warm red glow that blankets the den of Zainey's

cabin, the fire from earlier in the evening smolders in the wood stove. "Mmm," she says. "Smells like Christmas, doesn't it?"

"My smeller isn't so good."

"Well, trust me. Smells just like Christmas."

Cal cranks open the heavy metal door, taking charge of the fire, and tosses in a couple pieces of kindling onto a heap of red embers. He smiles at her like it's his job.

"Thanks," she says. "I usually let them go out until morning when I get up. But I guess I'm up now, right?"

"Those are the ugliest damn boots," he says, referring to her green waterproof camos.

She looks down. "Now, why d'you go and say that?" Then she poses, toe pointed, showing off the boots as if she were some boot model.

"Bad ugly."

"They're my camo-quiets." Zainey turns to the counter. "*You* sure didn't hear me."

"You're a sneaky one."

"How do you think I got what's his name last year?" She opens the urn where she keeps fresh ground coffee. The pungency of crushed beans permeates the air, and the ambience shifts from Christmastime to lazy mornings. Zainey yawns.

"You tired?"

"Not bad," she says.

Cal stands with his back to the fire, his hands behind him with Sandy near his left leg.

"Coffee sounds nice. Smells great, but whiskey sounds better."

He unzips his jacket. His torso appears thicker than usual covered by his khaki uniform shirt and flak jacket. He wears a shoulder holster complete with a *San Juan County*-standard issue .357 Smith & Wesson—a sexy gun, showy but prone to misfire. It's those testy trigger screws. They're either too tight or too loose.

Now *her* Glock? *That's* a gun. Her Glock ranges one misfire in 10,000 shots. Zainey chuckles.

"What?" Cal asks.

"Why don't they give your people decent weapons? Why the .357s?"

"They work," he says in defense. He pats the gun.

"You were doing rounds tonight, you say?"

"Unofficially."

Not officially?

"We're short-staffed right now."

She starts to respond, but before she can, he clicks on his radio and says, "Nina. I got nothing here. We'll send someone out tomorrow." The dispatcher, Nina, says something to make him laugh. "Right. Today," he says. Then, "G'night, Nina."

He pushes the earpiece deeper into his ear canal and turns the radio to silent. Nina's voice and the crackle of the radio fade and become a low buzz. He plays with a button on the comm piece to keep the radio on ear-comm only.

"That's better," Zainey says. "That crackling is nothing like white noise." She opens a different cupboard, lifts out a twelve-year-old scotch she keeps for company, and pours the tea-colored fluid into two rocks glasses. No ice. Then she realizes the last company she had was Cal a couple months back.

"That old stuff again?" he asks, joking.

"Terrible, isn't it?" She's smiling and walks over, hands Cal his drink. They clink glasses. She watches him to see if he'll down it. He only sips. Strange. He typically drains the glass then wants a second.

"Oh, we're going easy tonight?"

"Nina, and all. I may get another call."

"Sure, I get it." She sips her drink, too. "You think it was someone from *down* the road?" She tips her head toward the Lesserett's property. Her eyes give away the fact that she thinks it's the boy again.

"Maybe. Who knows? We'll figure it out later."

"You mean when they set off another bomb?"

"We have eyes on them."

Her eyes open wide. "You *do*? You can do that?"

"Hey, we ain't no Podunk kinda outfit, here, missy!" He's doing a terrible impression of a southern drawl.

"Of course not. Not with a new sheriff in town."

He chuckles and settles into a corner of the couch. "That's right." With that, he puffs a little. She's one of his first friends on the island.

It can be a lonely place if you don't have someone to confide in.

Zainey makes her way around the couch to sit, then peels off her own flak jacket, revealing the thermal shirt she was wearing for pajamas. Cal turns away.

"What?" She looks down and realizes she didn't put on a bra. A twinge of embarrassment causes her to fold her arms in front of her chest. "I was sleeping. What did you expect? Anyway, it's nothing Beth doesn't have—and doubly so, I might add."

She shakes her head. Still, Cal has lost his cool. He pulls out a pair of silver-plated shades and slips them over his eyes.

"Seriously?" Zainey says. "Those things keep *me* from seeing where *your* eyes are, Cal."

She sinks onto the leather sofa and curls into the other corner.

"Still," he says, and raises his drink in a toast. "To duck hunting."

"Nice segue. And you'll never get me to toast something like that."

"Tell me, Zain." He often shortens her name. "Who d'you off to make it all the way out here?"

"Now that, my dear friend, would be a violation of my terms. If I told you, I'd have to kill you." She smiles and sips her drink. "God, I love scotch."

He chuckles. "You say that every time you drink it."

"Do I?"

She grins. He looks away.

"Take off those stupid glasses. Here." She grabs a pillow from between them and places it over her chest. "Better?"

He nods and lifts the sunglasses onto the crown of his head.

"Did you see any cars out there?" she asks.

"Nothing."

Sandy rises and slurps from Walter's bowl. Cal pats his thigh and points, making Sandy come nearer to lay by him on the rug. Water drains from Sandy's mouth. By now, Walter is fast asleep on his oversized dog bed near the wood stove.

She smiles at Walter, then at Sandy, lifts her drink to point. "They're a blessing, aren't they? He's my sanity. My focal point," she says about Walter.

"Sandy's okay."

"Okay? Just *okay*?"

"I think of dogs in a more utilitarian way than you. Sandy's in training. Scent training."

Zainey chuckles. "She needs work."

Cal nods in agreement. "Sometimes you get a bad one."

"One?"

"Dogs. Sometimes they're not any good."

She can't relate to his opinion but lets him talk.

"Dogs," he repeats, now in Uzbek, "cost money and sometimes they're useless." The precision of his accent is uncanny.

He likes to talk with Zainey in their private language. It's a connection between them no one else has.

She pauses and thinks in the language before posing the question. "Does Beth know any?"

Still in the language, he says, "Uzbek? Are you kidding me? Her English isn't all that great." He laughs. "Nah. She's not a *language* person."

"Where d'you two meet again?" Zainey switches back to English.

He coughs into a fist. Is he choking? She sets her scotch onto the ottoman just in case he needs help.

"You okay?"

But he continues coughing, then points to his throat and scrapes out two words: "Wrong. Pipe."

Zainey feels embarrassed. After the cough subsides, she persists.

"I know literally nothing about you and Beth. Why don't you talk about her?"

He glances down, then to the dogs, then settles and breathes out as if revealing some deep, dark secret, then copies her. "If I tell you, I'd have to kill you." There's little humor in his eyes but Zainey chuckles to herself until the feeling disintegrates and her scalp prickles—a trained reaction—her body sensing perceived danger.

"Come on. You know you can trust me to keep your secrets."

He acquiesces. "Okay. Okay. But only a few people who *need* to know, know."

She pinches her lips and tosses away an imaginary key. "Shoot."

"It was arranged."

"What?" She isn't expecting that answer and yet, the follicles on the nape of her neck are on full alert.

He switches to Uzbek again. "True. And since it's need-to-know, *you* don't need to know how or why." He takes a swig of scotch.

She searches his face. He glances left and changes the subject. "You're lying."

He tries to recover but he's not a good liar. She is but he's not. Now, she changes the subject. She lies to see if he can tell.

"You know, I was once married."

He looks surprised.

"It's true. We were young. I got pregnant. He married me. I miscarried. He left. End of love story."

"That's sad."

He bought it.

"Ah, no sadder than other people's stories. Guess that's why I love dogs. They're true blue."

Cal swirls his drink. The silence of a drink with no ice, with no clinking, makes her feel cheap somehow. Cheap and vulnerable, like some whore at the end of a bar near some guy who has decided to tell her a lie.

She reaches for her drink again and moves forward to the edge of the sofa. She stands, still holding the pillow.

"You know, I ought to get back to sleep. I have a schedule around here tomorrow, *today*, that'll pound me into the dirt if I don't get some rest."

"But we haven't finished our drinks." He says it like a boy who hasn't gotten his turn up at bat. His voice is clear. He speaks now in English. No sign of choking.

She grabs the glass, tips it back and drains the scotch. "I have." She blows out. The alcohol stings her throat.

He only sips at his.

"What's wrong, Cal? Don't like your scotch? You're the one who wanted the nightcap."

"I feel like sipping slow tonight."

"You mean this *morning*. Hey, maybe another time."

His eyes darken. He refuses to move.

She hopes he hasn't noticed the gun in her waist holster. But why wouldn't he? He knows her. Knows she goes nowhere unarmed,

209

definitely not outside at the darkest hour to inspect the source of three explosions. Of course, he knows.

"You're being ridiculous," she says. Her inflection high, the words taut. "You're being ridiculous," she repeats, this time with more ease.

Cal chuckles at her miscue.

She mimics him.

"Sit," he says.

She considers refusing but takes the lip of the sofa.

He stares her down. His muddy eyes flit back and forth searching her face, trying to decide if he can tell what she's thinking, what her next move might be.

"Unholster your weapon," he says.

"What's going on, Cal?" Let him think he has control of the situation. "You're acting silly. Are you and Beth on the outs?"

"Do as I say."

"It's at the front door. You saw me set it there."

He sets down his drink and at the same time pulls his .357 out of his shoulder holster.

"Your *hand*gun," he says. Like she doesn't know.

Zainey doesn't speak for what seems like an hour. Moisture springs onto her palms.

"Now," he says.

"And if I don't?"

He lifts the gun and shoots Sandy in the temple. The dog jerks and dies.

Walter yelps. He darts off his bed and smashes into the leg of the leather armchair.

"That's what," he says in response.

A fissure splits Zainey's composure, but she holds it together. Her eyes lock on Sandy.

She's seen worse in Afghanistan. Much worse. The dog didn't suffer. Not like the girl she saw bludgeoned and raped by three Afghan soldiers who ended her suffering by slitting her throat. Said she was an informer and made Zainey watch everything. Told her that women were *tools*. Afterward, she made *them* watch while she exacted justice for the girl. An eye for an eye. She knows all she needs to know from the Bible.

A familiar fire ignites in Zainey with a heat that turns her veins to ice. She drags her eyes off the dog, then back to Cal Drake, a name she now doubts is real.

"Don't and *he's* next." Drake points his gun at Walter who is cowering near the sliding door, wet, in a pool of his own urine. A pool that has spread out around his back feet. He's whimpering.

"Slow," he says.

Zainey drops the pillow. His eyes flash onto her chest. A distraction point.

Her scalp prickles. He works to regain his focus. She's moving too fast for him.

"Slow, I said!"

Hands wide, she hangs out her arms in a purgatory of action. He flicks his gun for her to continue. She reaches behind her.

"Slow," he warns.

Under her shirt, she unclips the Glock and brings it around, pinched between her index finger and thumb. She sets the gun on the leather ottoman that sits between them.

He snatches it. Stuffs it into the crease of the sofa behind him.

Zainey's eyes shift over to Sandy. The ice in her veins burns hot in her chest. She knows this icy fire. She can't outrun it. No more than she can outrun the bodies she left on the ground after the fire and ice converge.

Use passion.

God bless you, Yalda.

They will kill me now. Know this. It will be brutal. Use passion. This is for you, Yalda. My passion *for those three men.*

"Now then," Drake says. "Let's get right to business."

"You're here to execute me."

"Soon enough, but let's talk about why." He says this in Russian. No more Uzbek. This Russian is straight from Moscow—Kremlin perfect.

And it all becomes clear. Zainey is Drake's mark. Probably for as long as he's been on the island. And she thought she was safe. He's here because of her. He's an operative, a double. A traitor. Most likely Beth's already on a ferry to the mainland. Or dead.

The fiery ice swells, sizzles.

"I prefer to speak English," she says. "And if you're going to kill me, it would be nice to know your real name."

Drake considers her request. His finger shakes near the trigger. A better agent would have killed her by now. His brow glows moist, glistening in the dim light from the wood stove.

"Kobe," he says. "Kobe Alexeyev."

"Tortoise Defender?" Zainey translates his name literally. "That's your name? The defender of tortoises?" She mocks. Wants him off-balance.

"It will take more than your simple prodding to overcome me, Walker."

"So, how do you intend to do this?"

Alexeyev withdraws a silencer from his pocket.

"After all the noise you've made shooting your own dog. Now, the silencer? Brilliant. They sure know how to train 'em at the Kremlin." She won't stop goading.

His hands quiver.

The radio hisses in his ear. He turns up the volume. "Hey Nina… Nah, no backup necessary." His eyes lock on Zainey. "Just Brandon out shooting… Nope… On their property… Sure… I plan on talking to them. No need to wake up anyone else for this. I'll handle it… Okay. Out." He turns off the radio. "You pissed off the Pope, Walker. Took down too many of Putin's star boys. All but me, of course. You didn't know about me." He sneers.

She hears his accent slipping from American to Russian. "But now, he's sent his best."

"*You're* Putin's best? The future of Russia does *not* look bright."

He fakes a smile. She notes the fury behind his eyes.

"Alexeyev, you're out of shape and a drunk. If you're his best, I'd hate to see his worst."

He still fumbles with the silencer. His face flushes red. His eyes tighten. His nose flares.

"Why, you bitch."

Spittle flies from his mouth. Once again, he tries to screw on the silencer, but his hands shake from anger.

"Need help?" Zainey goads him. "Could be the wrong caliber."

"Quiet."

"Just saying. You might have the wrong caliber for the suppressor. It happened to me once. Once."

"Shut up!"

She sits like a scolded child. But she's not done. She looks at her wrist as if there's a watch.

"Well, if you're going to kill me, tick tock. Do it quickly, please, and my dog after me," she's speaking while he fidgets. "God, turtle, they're not that difficult."

"Quiet, I said!"

He's rattled. She smiles and continues to taunt.

"You simply screw it on until it clicks into place and then—"

He fumbles with it again. Takes his eyes off her.

"Here," she says, bending as if to help.

He bats her hand away. Glares at her. Looks at his weapon but tries to keep watch on her.

"Please. I'm rather good with these things. I can help you."

He flusters. The diversion set. With a *humph*, she sits again.

"Seriously, *Kobe Alexeyev*. What a name. Let me."

She leans forward.

In a split second, she snags the Bowie.

Gouges it into his neck. The blade goes deep.

He stuns. Freezes. Gags.

Blood oozes from his trachea. A sure-death hit, if ever. He'll suffocate on blood.

Alexeyev's arms slacken. The gun and silencer slip from his hands and land on the floor. She reaches and picks them up.

"I just wanted to help, Kobe Alexeyev. You made me kill you. Remember that wherever you're headed—heaven or hell."

He grapples for the blade in his neck but Zainey knocks his arms away. Then, she grabs the knife's hasp and presses it in deeper.

His eyes blink slowly, at first, then they lock on something far off, outside in the darkness as if he's searching for something brilliant, something magical. To save him.

"How ya doin' there, bud?" She says this in his Russian tongue. Then she slides the knife out of his throat and wipes it clean, off onto the stomach of her shirt.

Blood burps out of the gash.

"Whoopsie." She shoves the knife back into his throat, deeper. "You shouldn't have killed Sandy. That wasn't nice."

His eyelids flutter. The whites fill each socket. He slumps to his right. He falls onto his side, inadvertently shoving the blade in deeper. And it's over. He stops struggling and face-plants.

Walter whimpers. He wants outside to pee, to get out.

She needs to take care of this mess, of Alexeyev's body, of Sandy's, all the blood, of her shirt. The fire inside her subsides.

***

A bonfire blazes inside the firepit. Sparks have settled after fluids from the bodies have sizzled off. It smells like a barbecue. The smell mixes with fireplaces glowing in houses around the neighborhood. Smells like winter, like the holidays.

Early morning has gone from black to grayish blue as the sun sneaks up on the horizon. A fine golden thread demarcates the hem where the earth meets the sky.

After pulling off her thermal shirt, Zainey's skin prickles in the chilly morning air. The fire feels warm on her bare skin. With everything else, she tosses the shirt onto the blaze, drops two more logs on top, and pulls a fleece robe around her shoulders.

The agency's handlers will muddy the facts, enough to send the authorities in a different direction. Plus, if they ever learned their sheriff was a Russian spy…

They'll never find his body. They'll never find the dog.

She's made a grave of the razor wire used in the guts of the couch. Everything else burns.

She stares long into the raging fire.

She stokes the fire with the tip of a dead branch. It blazes up then settles. She walks back to the house. She'll be scouring the walls, the ceiling, the floor for hours. She'll call the Sheriff's office and ask about the explosions. They'll tell her it was Brandon Lesserett on his property and there's not much they can do. She'll say that's too bad or something about how people like Brandon shouldn't be allowed to have firearms. They'll apologize but explain the laws. She'll hang up and check the perimeter of her property for signs of Drake or Sandy. Later in the morning, she'll add more wood to the fire until nothing remains but ash. Later still, she'll have two girls over she often calls to help her clean, Marcy and Daria. They'll make it over by early afternoon. They like using a chlorine solution to clean. Zainey will help. The three will work together through the house giving special attention to the den, near the fire, near two chairs where the couch used to be. Daria will ask about the couch but will say she likes the chairs where Zainey's placed them. The girls are nice that way, always complimentary.

Everything happens in threes. Two birds plus one stone.

When will the killing ever end?

But Zainey Walker knows the answer to that question.

***

THE CANCUN GAME

TOSCA LEE

Genevieve practically bounces in her seat as she stares out the window of the 737. The clouds have parted on a gloriously blue Pacific as we begin our descent to Maui.

"Oh my God!" she squeals, fumbling for her phone. The coast comes into view fringed with white surf, green mountains in the distance. Genevieve spends the next five minutes taking short video clips—15, 20, and 35 seconds.

No one watches the long ones.

"Look at that bay," Genevieve breathes. Catamarans trail white wakes like comets through water the color of lapis lazuli below. "We're going to the beach. We're going to snorkel and swim with turtles and go parasailing and then find a luau and eat poke and mahi mahi 'til we explode." She reaches across me to rap Zach on the shoulder. "Zach, wake up. Piper, get your makeup on."

I obediently pull the zipper bag of compacts out of my purse, happy for her. For me, too, but I've been to Maui before—used to come to Hawaii with my family growing up. Genevieve only left the country for the first time when we were in college and has dreamed of seeing Hawaii all her life.

The plane lands and taxis to the terminal. Everyone around us pops up, eager for island sun, tropical air, and to get off this metal tube after the nearly eight-hour flight from Denver.

We wait, pretending to search for errant shoes and ear buds as the plane deboards. I text my boyfriend, Kyle, that we've landed and will call him soon. Zach readies his camera with the little balloon that sits on top—a portable softbox he rigged last year that he now brings everywhere.

"Here." Genevieve produces a carefully rolled pink pashmina from the giant tote she calls a purse.

I unfurl and drape it around my shoulders as she pulls out a pair of sunglasses from a new designer in Chicago. She slides them

219

onto my face and then hands me a box of thin gold rings with the prices still on them. I stack them on one finger, hiding the tags against my palm.

The instant the last passengers head onto the sky bridge, we bolt from our seats and hurry to the front of the plane.

"Here," Genevieve says, pointing to the second row of first class. There's a blanket wadded up on the armrest and crumbs on the floor.

I scooch over to the window seat, shove the blanket away, and casually slide the sunglasses down the bridge of my nose. I recline back far enough so that anyone can see this isn't the old toilet-seat-fake-plane-window trick, but the real thing. Never mind that there's a baggage cart on the tarmac outside; Zach will erase that later.

Genevieve lays an advance copy of some bestselling author's upcoming new novel in my lap. Lastly, she unwraps and hands me one of my mom's champagne flutes—real crystal. I cup this in my hand to disguise the fact that it's empty and curl it in toward my shoulder as I look out the window.

Contemplating the future. My fabulous life.

Snap. Snap, snap, snap. Zach leans in toward me, shooting from several angles.

"Don't get the crumbs," I say.

"I'm not." He leans in closer, one foot on the seat beside me.

I tip my head this way and then that. Look up at the camera through my lashes. Anyone seeing the photo will feel as though they've just woken up beside me on the most luxurious plane ride of their lives.

"Got it!" Zach says.

I shove the glass and book toward Genevieve, slide out and follow them off the plane past a patient flight attendant who smiles and says nothing.

The pictures will go up on Echelon, the social media site that has been my lifeline and livelihood for the last three years. Me, Piper Pikalov, looking out on the turquoise water of Kahului Bay in a thousand dollars of accessories I will never wear again.

We spend three days shooting the sunrise above the cloud line from atop Mount Haleakala, perfectly-plated grilled fish, sunset from the prow of a yacht, and our finely-appointed suite at Honu

Farmhouse—the luxury bed and breakfast sponsoring our trip.

I work my way through a sponsored wardrobe of island-wear and designer shoes that comprises three-quarters of our combined airline luggage allowance. Leaving the backs of too-small sample size dresses unzipped. Chip-clipping the waists of others.

Four days and five thousand photos later, we're back in economy headed home to snow-covered Denver. Honu Farmhouse only comped us three days, but at least the suite had two rooms.

The fourth night was on me—a single room for the three of us at a chain resort booked with frequent flier miles. Not because I don't have the miles for two rooms, but for old times' sake.

I don't know how long we can keep this up.

Or how long I want to.

It's a fast trip and we're exhausted, but Genevieve is as deliriously happy as she is sunburned, and Zach is always up for anything.

The weekend after we get back, Kyle and I drive my mom up to visit her sister, who lives in a nursing home in Woodland Park. It's an excuse to spend the afternoon in nearby Manitou Springs eating pizza at Savelli's and playing pinball at the penny arcade.

We take goofy selfies for no one's consumption but our own; as far as Echelon's 500 million ranked (and as many unranked) users know, I'm in Maui for the next three weeks.

The next night, Genevieve calls me, breathless.

"What's wrong?" I ask, alarmed.

"Sign on!"

I log in. And then stare at the notice splashed all over the home page: MARINA TAPLIN, ECHELON #1 INFLUENCER FOUND DEAD AT WEST HOLLYWOOD HOME.

I'm in shock. I've met Marina—not that she would have remembered me.

I craft a sympathy message on her page. Post a picture of the two of us together at an influencer event we attended in Carmel just last month. She called me "Poppy" after Reena Thomas—#5—introduced us. I didn't correct her.

Genevieve, Zach and I spend the next day watching Marina's

feed whirr by with tributes from her followers, condolences from her luxury brand sponsors, pictures of her from school, at parties and location shoots, her page scrolling too fast to read until I slide it back up the screen with a finger.

According to authorities, she overdosed and drowned in her backyard pool.

The Echelon world mourns in a fervor for days.

A week later, her page has grown cold.

By the time we finish posting the rest of the Maui "vacation," Marina's page rank has sunk to #122.

I catch myself scrolling for her content. Have to remind myself there won't be any more from Marina herself.

Avella Somerfield, second on Echelon's top ten now for weeks, slips into Marina's #1 spot.

Three weeks later, Avella disappears.

***

I never planned this life—would have dismissed it as fake and disingenuous just five years ago. After all, I'm college-educated, having graduated from the University of Chicago just in time to return to Denver, join a hospitality startup, and get married.

At least until the startup went bust and Gordy, my photographer husband of thirteen months, decided he'd rather be with an occupational therapist named Kaylyn…and her regular paycheck.

It turned out fine for me in the end; I was home—literally living in my old bedroom—and reunited with Genevieve, who'd attended a local community college while working full-time after high school.

It also meant I was there when my dad was diagnosed with pancreatic cancer, and with him every day until his death five months later. There, too, for my mom in the aftermath of grief and hospital bills and to help with her corporate catering business.

Until Covid-19 came along.

There I was, looking for ways to make a living and protect my diabetic and increasingly depressed sixty-two-year-old mom.

Genevieve, who had become as pragmatic about making money as I had become idealistic, suggested I become a fetish model on a paid content site called Your Eyes Only.

"People will *pay* to see you do stuff with your feet," she said. "Now that you're not doing ballet anymore, you don't have all those gross corns and callouses. So why not?"

"How do you even know about this?" I asked.

Genevieve had grown up with religious parents who sent all their money to Benny Hinn. Until she met me in sixth grade, she'd never listened to pop music, heard of *Twilight*, or seen a rated-PG movie. And while she literally moved on after graduation, leasing a studio apartment she could barely afford so she could date without a parent-approved chaperone and go to parties and get drunk with her friends—I was genuinely shocked.

"How do you *not* know about this?" she said, opening her laptop.

I leaned in to educate myself.

"Are you kidding me?" I said, as she scrolled past a huge list of categories featuring racy models of all types—bored housewives, naughty teachers, nude cooks.

"Oh, stop," she said, clicking on a foot model charging $15 a month to view daily pictures—and the occasional video—of her feet. Who sold her used socks for $150 a pop.

I screwed up my face. "People *buy* those things?"

"Yes!" Genevieve said impatiently. "I'm telling you, you don't even have to show your face. Look, I'll help you. We'll pour champagne and rainbow sprinkles and sparkling body lotion over your toes. Meanwhile, you're getting paid and you can even write off your pedicures as a business expense!"

I briefly considered it. Even if I only managed to snag the interest of a measly and desperate 100 subscribers, I'd bring in over $1000 a month.

Maybe more if I sold some socks.

In the end, I couldn't get past the idea of fixated voyeurs doing God knows what while staring at my glittery toenails.

That week, Mom applied for and received a pandemic relief loan and I filed for unemployment. We would be fine—as in, able to pay utilities and eat—at least for a while.

I turned to Echelon purely as a creative outlet and means of documenting quarantine. I'd opened an account the year before to spy on my ex and "Kaylyn," morbidly curious to know if they were actually happy together. I had uploaded a grand total of nine entries in the months since in order to keep the account active, given Echelon's "play to stay" policy.

Now I posted pictures of the artisan bread I made during lockdown, the reading nook I set up in the front room near the window, complete with a macramé air plant hanger and, yes, my brightly painted toes in a pair of funky shoes I found in the back of Mom's closet.

I recorded the antics of our cat, King, and the full moon shining on the Rockies. Snapped the all-season room decked out with paper streamers on Mom's birthday, and the purple pea blossoms growing in the basket of an old bike a neighbor had put out on the curb that I appropriated for the garden.

I'd modeled briefly during college—nothing big, just costumes in a party shop catalog, and for a discount store featuring twelve-dollar tank tops and mom jeans. So I set up the camera timer and went grand jeté-ing through the yard in a gauzy summer dress I'd botched during my brief stint trying to design clothing in high school.

I never intended anyone but college friends and the occasional curious stranger to see or care about anything I posted. But eventually, comments appeared.

And then one morning, I woke to find I'd gone from one of Echelon's millions of unranked members to #352,458,987.

Overnight, I'd been boosted into the top 500 million users.

I stared, curious to see that number below my name where none had ever been before. It was meaningless, I told myself. Except that now I wondered what it'd take to move the needle again.

I started creating content several times a week: Genevieve and me giggling our way through drawn-on hand puppet hip-hop lip-synchs. Cooking fails. Cute outfits. The ombre dye-job I attempted on Genevieve's hair.

I didn't try to be glamorous; Echelon was already filled with too many duck-lipped models and makeup tutorials. I swore off skin-tight clothing the one and only time I let Genevieve convince me to duct tape my boobs to create cleavage for a strapless dress in some pageant trick she'd seen online. The post had done great, but it'd taken me weeks to grow back the skin that had peeled off with the tape.

No, being myself was what got me ranked in the first place. I was determined to carry on.

But the numbers hovered and then started to slip, no matter what I tried.

A few weeks after Mom got her second Covid vaccination, I answered a "help wanted" sign in the window of the local Interior Mart—a furniture store spanning three city blocks that sold everything from recliners to electronics. Business was thriving, the entire industry cashing in on the home renovation and decoration boom brought about by the pandemic and subsequent quarantine.

Without time to create content at home, I snapped selfies in the seating areas staged around the store: draped atop an elaborate table beneath a dripping chandelier, frosting a Styrofoam cake in a kitchen with no plumbing, posing in a sundress on an island-inspired rattan recliner with a plate of plastic sushi, lounging under a faux fur blanket in the front row of the store's home theater section.

I tagged the store and furniture brands and encouraged viewers to come see me. After all, I worked on commission.

Three weeks into my job, I cracked Echelon's top million.

I broke the top 500,000 six days later.

I'd been spending the weekend happily snowed in at Kyle's— away from work, home, and the phone I had allowed to die. Some time after I finally laid it on the charger, it started pinging like it was about to detonate.

Genevieve: Are you seeing this?
Genevieve: I'm trying to call you.
Genevieve: Pipe, pick up your phone.
Genevieve: ARE YOU ALIVE?

The last text was a screenshot of my Echelon page. It took me a minute to figure out why she'd sent it until I saw the new rank beneath my name. Striding from the kitchen where Kyle was making us dinner, I dialed Genevieve.

"This is crazy!" I said the instant she picked up.

I braced for the rapid-fire barrage of questions: where I was, why I hadn't answered, when we could get together to stage the Scenes From the Interior Mart content she already had planned for tomorrow.

"I want you to try something," she said instead, a strange tone in her voice. "Remember Cancun?"

Of course I did. It was spring break my junior year, and the two of us had scraped together just enough money to fly there and stay at a roach-infested motel. We'd made it a game to see how much luxury we could fake—from the jet skis we posed on but never rented to the pics we shot at the pool of a nearby luxury resort.

"Yeah, what about it?" I asked.

"Post the pool picture with the drink tonight," Genevieve said.

I knew the one: me, floating in a blue infinity pool, tiki-style coconut cup in my hand.

Not only was the drink empty with a dead fly inside it, the straw bore the mark of someone else's lipstick. But we didn't care; I'd floated along with the "cocktail" in one hand, twirling its tiny little umbrella high in the air with my other. It was hilarious to us at the time.

I posted it before bed with a simple caption:

Flashback to the amazing time my bestie and I had in Cancun. Time to go back!

I loved that trip. It was Genevieve's first time out of the country with her brand new passport. I'd been so happy for her, and proud to be able to show her how to go through security at the airport, recline her seat on the plane, check into the hotel, and haggle with locals selling souvenirs on the beach.

But this wasn't about Genevieve and me anymore. Grabbing my phone off the nightstand, I re-opened the post and clicked "edit." Zoomed in so no one would be able to recognize the pool. Changed the caption from "in Cancun" to "on the Riviera Maya."

Hit "Post."

I woke up the next morning in the top 400,000.

That day, Genevieve hurried into the Interior Mart during lunch, a wild look in her eyes.

"It's lifestyle," she said.

"What is?" I said.

"What's moving you up the ranks. It's aspirational lifestyle."

She took me through a series of photos on her phone as though she were in some corporate presentation.

"It's the travel, the furniture, the clothes and jewelry—like the time you snapped that cute enamel ring at Roxy's Boutique in that antique velvet chair they have in the back of the store. This pic here, and this here, and this one," she said, scrolling in rapid succession.

Each one featured a me that wasn't me, in a place I hadn't really been, on furniture that wasn't mine.

I had wanted to be my creative, quirky self. But what I learned is that every voyeur wants the fantasy.

The one they crave and hate you for.

It would have been easier to post foot fetish pictures, and far less time-consuming.

No makeup or wardrobe changes.

But by the time I broke the top 100,000, Interior Mart was paying me $500 a post to feature their line of carpets and curtains.

I dressed up in them like Scarlett O'Hara. Rolled up like Cleopatra. Got Zach, Interior Mart's graphics guy, to shoot the pics and paid him $50 a pop for his time.

The rank moved and hovered. Genevieve pushed me to invest $75 into the purchase of 100 active followers who would each up-vote my posts.

"Is that even *legal*?" I asked.

"Of course it is," she said.

"Seems kind of like cheating."

She gave me a pointed look. "Not any more than pretending you live in a house the size of Interior Mart."

A few days and a bunch of calls later, Genevieve secured two nights at a boutique hotel in Durango, Colorado. The suite would be free of charge—mileage, a bottle of wine, and gourmet breakfast for two included—in exchange for a video post.

Genevieve, Zach, and I loaded up the cooler on a Friday after work, road-tripped six hours south, shot video all day Saturday, hid out in our room and shared the wine over Cheez-Its and homemade ham sandwiches Saturday night, photographed breakfast before splitting it three ways Sunday morning, and were back at work Monday morning.

We didn't get anything else except great content and a good night's sleep on 1200-thread count sheets. And since Zach hooked up with someone he met at the bar, Genevieve and I didn't even have to share a bed.

That week, I posted the video Zach edited down to 59 seconds during the car ride home. Within 24 hours, we set 20,000 pairs of eyeballs on the resort's elegant saloon and overpriced spa.

Genevieve booked us a glamping trip in Utah three weeks later; a luxury RV stay in Taos the week after that. Then came an all-expense paid shopping trip at a new Vegas boutique—as long as the expenses didn't equal more than $1,500.

"Get in here," I said, gesturing Genevieve to join me in front of the camera on the Taos shoot.

She waved me off. "Nope. All you."

She conceded, at least, when I made her choose half the items from the shopping trip for herself. I shot the video with them. She took them home.

I eBayed mine.

The comments poured in. Images of followers modeling the same jewelry or booking spots to the locations we'd just come from sent my ranking skyrocketing into the top 100,000. Top 50,000.

Top 1,000.

We were having a ball for the first time since we'd created the break from reality that was "The Cancun Game." Since my dad died and Mom sank into depression.

Only one problem: I was out of sick days and vacation time. We both were.

So we quit our jobs and convinced Zach to come with us, which didn't take much strong-arming.

It was work—each trip, each shoot, each angle more time-consuming than the one before. Genevieve partnered me with on-site makeup and hair artists who worked for free exposure. Passers-by stopped to photograph our shoots and tag me.

Top 800.

Top 700.

The climb was tougher the higher I got. It took more effort, more creativity, and more brand partnerships. More time away from Kyle, whose house had become a makeup-free safe haven of pizza and pajama pants on my days off. More time split between all of us answering comments and messages. All of us writing, posting, and pretending to function as one person:

Me.

It also required more rules. Namely, that we never tagged my location when we were home. People recognized me now; the last thing I needed was anyone showing up at my mom's suburban house, compromising her safety or the carefully crafted fantasy of the Piper Pikalov brand.

Also, that I would never be seen in anything so mundane as a grocery store or—God forbid—Walmart.

I'd started to pay Genevieve 40% of anything we made in exchange for her booking the gigs, negotiating sponsored products, and lining up the trips. I paid Zach, who lived out of his van, a flat fee.

We scrimped on anything that wasn't sponsored. Sold the products under a fake name online when we were finished with them. Shared meals and perks and hotel rooms.

I'd been hovering at #28 for weeks, and had briefly slipped to #30 for 48 hours, during which Genevieve practically pulled her hair out.

Until Zach came up with the idea to partner with a luxury

ranch in Wyoming.

"You're kidding, right?" I said.

I looked at Genevieve, sitting across from me in the breakfast nook of my kitchen, which we had nicknamed the War Room. But she'd only tilted her head like a dog hearing a whistle too high-pitched for humans to notice.

"Am I the only one who noticed what happened when we went to Marathon Key?" I asked, looking between them. I'd leapt from #112 to #71—my first time ever in the top 100. "People want turquoise water—not *City Slickers*! We should be going to Barbados, not frickin' Wyoming!"

"Hear me out," he said, tucking a strand of dirty blond hair behind his ear. He pulled up a tab on his browser. He'd obviously been researching this already.

"This might not feel glamorous to us," Zach said, scrolling past resort images of trail riding, fly-fishing…

"You're right, it doesn't," I said, wondering if he was high.

"But it clearly is to some people. People living high-powered lives, making high-powered decisions…with high-powered money." He clicked past several images of gourmet food, an infinity edge hot tub steaming in the winter, and hopped over to the rate sheet.

The place was $1,500 a night. Per person.

Genevieve's tone was near-reverent as she whispered, "I'll make some calls."

Something rose up inside me. "No. You won't!"

They both looked at me like I'd just sprouted a second head.

"This is *my* account," I said. "This is *my* brand. And I am *not* the Wild West!"

Genevieve blinked at me. "Excuse me? Hello? This account may have your name on it, but *we* created this brand. The three of us." She gestured from her to Zach, glaring at me. "Unless you're the one coming up with the ideas, setting up the partnerships, making the arrangements, and editing the videos all by yourself. Considering all that goes into the 'Piper Pikalov' brand, you probably have the easiest job out of all three of us!"

Zach just pursed his lips and looked at me.

I briefly considered getting up and walking out. Screw them. I could change the password on the account, lock both of them out. Refuse to post anymore. Let Piper Pikalov sink into obscurity.

But of course I wouldn't. Piper Pikalov was our livelihood. Our obsession. Our way of gaming the system.

Life.

I was just the brand ambassador.

"Okay, fine," I said finally, starting to feel like an ass.

I wasn't even sure where my objection came from. I liked horses, the country, farms. In fact, I had grown up road-tripping to my uncle's farm in Nebraska to ride four wheelers with my cousins and help put up sweet corn every summer for as long as I could remember.

"You're right." I reached out to pull Genevieve against me. "You probably could do this all without me."

"Not all of it," she said, squeezing me back.

Genevieve wasn't able to land the luxury ranch in Zach's browser, but she did book an agreement with one in Montana.

We spent three days shooting photos and video footage throughout the resort's five thousand acres, eating elk steaks and pan-seared trout, and drinking complimentary wine.

And we got paid nearly a thousand dollars each. No more percentage for Genevieve or flat fee for Zach—the day Genevieve announced the Montana deal I announced we'd split everything from here on out, three ways.

I even got her to take a picture with me during a cooking class in the lodge's opulent kitchen. And unlike the other rare times I'd convinced her to pose, she consented to being featured in the post.

The night my page broke the top 25, the four of us were gathered in the War Room around ham sandwiches and cheap champagne.

"C'mon, c'mon," Kyle said, his knee bouncing as Zach chewed a thumbnail beside him.

I told myself the ranking didn't matter. That it never had. But even as I thought it, I also knew it was a lie.

The minute we landed at #24, Zach and Kyle leaped up and

hollered. I laughed, exhaling a breath I didn't remember holding, having never seen Zach so animated in my life.

Kyle poured champagne as the first comments and congratulations hit the page, the feed starting to accelerate like the revving of a giant engine.

But Genevieve had barely moved.

"Gen," I said. "Everything okay?"

God knew she'd worked as hard for this as I had. Harder, actually.

She looked up at me then, her eyes shining. "It's happening."

"What do you mean?" I said. "It's *been* happening. You should know—because *you* made it happen." I hugged her tightly.

"Just wait," she said. "It's coming true."

That was the thing about Genevieve—she'd always had bigger visions of what could be than I ever had. For herself, for our future.

For me.

I barely heard from Genevieve over the next few days, and even though she assured me she was fine whenever I texted, and she reminded me which content to post and to get my ass online and respond to some of the comments, I finally dropped by her place to make sure she was really all right.

"Oh my God…what happened?" I said when she answered the door. Her face was red and swollen, a bandage wrapped beneath her chin and around her head like something from a cartoon.

She rolled her eyes. "I'm fine. It's just a chemical peel."

"Why would you do that?" I said, flummoxed. "And why do you need bandages for a chemical peel?"

She sighed. "And a little double-chin lipo."

"Gen! Why didn't you tell me?"

"I knew you'd freak out, that's why! It's no big deal."

"I'm not freaking out!"

"You've never had acne scars or a double chin either. Look, I can afford it now, thanks to you, so…there. Okay?" She sounded sheepish.

"Okay," I said, still trying to understand why she hadn't felt like she could tell me. "I could've gone with you, or driven you home at least. That's all I'm saying."

"You don't know what it's like to be with someone like you all the time, Pipe."

I leaned back a little, not quite sure how to respond.

"And then you keep asking me to be in pictures," she said. "And now maybe I will. Because I'll feel better. Okay?"

"Sure, I mean...Okay."

"Good."

I hesitated. "I just..."

She looked heavenward and expelled an impatient sigh.

"I will never judge you," I said. "I promise. You should know better than that. C'mon."

"I know," she said, sounding defeated.

All this time, she hadn't invited me in and I knew she was embarrassed—not just about her face or the fact she was still in her pajamas and looked (and kind of smelled) like she hadn't showered in a few days, but that the apartment behind her was a mess as well.

Clothes were strewn over the back of her new Interior Mart sofa, tags dangling toward the floor. Unopened mail and boxes with designers' logos on them lined the wall beneath a poster of Hawaii I'd never seen before.

We'd been traveling and shooting for so many weeks that I hadn't been to her place in months or even offered to help go through the mail that she picked up weekly from a box rented in my name at the UPS Store.

"I'll come over tomorrow and help go through all that," I said.

She waved it off. "It's fine. It's not like I have anything to do anyway. We're herding cows, remember?"

True. As far as anyone on Echelon knew, we were on an overnight cattle drive in Montana, glamping at a permanent tent site and dining on white linens beneath the stars.

"You need anything? Food?" I asked, glancing toward the kitchenette. I noticed a suitcase with an airline tag standing by the table.

She followed my gaze, gestured to the suitcase.

"I got it done in Phoenix. My cousin knows the doctor and got me in last-minute. It's not like it's easy scheduling this stuff between all our trips, you know?"

I shrugged. "Sounds like a good deal."

I promised to come by with soup and started to leave, then turned back before she could close the door.

"Gen," I said.

She paused, looking tired and, for the first time since I could remember, like she just wished I would go.

"What did you mean, when you said it was all coming true?" I asked.

She smiled slightly then—as much as the tight skin around her mouth would allow.

"That it doesn't have to be a game."

She booked us the Hawaii gig three days later.

***

Six weeks after we get back from Maui, Avella Somerfield's body is found snared in some underwater crags beneath a sheer cliff near Big Sur. According to the news, she was shooting a selfie.

The story breaks all over Echelon and, this time, the TV networks. Late-night investigative journalists dub the tragic deaths of influencers Marina Taplin and Avella Somerfield the "Echelon Curse," and "Deadly #1"—the rank Avella posthumously still holds.

"That doesn't even make sense," Zach says.

We're on a plane fresh off three days aboard the luxury yacht *Return to the Sea*—the newest addition to the Vanguard Cruise Lines fleet—headed to a fairy tale-worthy tree house outside Atlanta. Kyle's come with us, booked with my miles.

"It happens a lot. Selfie on a cliff, a wind gust comes up...." Genevieve shrugs.

"When have you *ever* seen Avella Somerfield in a selfie?" Zach says as Kyle scrolls through Avella's page, connected to the inflight Wi-Fi. "It takes two of us, plus a hair and makeup person to do your photos. She's got to have at least five people on her crew."

"Are you saying they're better than us?" Genevieve sniffs.

"No, I'm saying they're far less efficient." Zach shrugs.

"Might have just been for fun, for herself, or for a lover," Kyle says, pronouncing it "lu-vah."

Genevieve rolls her eyes.

Georgia is hot and sultry, but the tree house is a dream. Kyle helps with the shoot, gamely rearranging furniture, lighting, and props as directed.

"We good?" I ask finally. It's late afternoon, and we've been at it all day.

"There's food in the fridge if you're hungry," Genevieve says, scrolling through the images on Zach's camera while he's hunched over his laptop. "I want to go again around sunset, get some of the color through the trees. Shoot you doing some Southern Gothic stuff around dusk."

"Actually, Kyle and I were planning to go into the city for dinner." I lift my hand before she can protest. "Don't worry, we'll pick somewhere on-brand and worthy of the tags if I get recognized."

Casually venturing into a town like Atlanta for a nice meal out is a privilege I lost when I cracked the top 25. We learned that the hard way when a picture of Genevieve, Zach, and me—drinking tequila in cutoffs and sweats at a dive bar a mile away from our luxury Airbnb in Tahoe—showed up on my feed, posted by someone who recognized me.

We still go out—to cute bistros and upscale eateries willing to partner with the Piper Pikalov brand with a guarantee of free food and good lighting. Or trending clubs, if my feed needs a boost.

This is the first time, however, that I've stated my intention to step out publicly with Kyle since my rising popularity turned date night into a spectacle—and then drove it underground. But the fact is, I'm tired of holing up like we're back in lockdown every time we go back home. Staring at screens and living on takeout and grocery delivery, stuck in a new kind of quarantine.

I'm twenty-five, self-sufficient, and I might even be in love. I want to live. Want to be normal just for one night in practice for the day when Echelon has gone the way of MySpace and my kids screw up their faces when I try to even explain what it was to them.

"I made a reservation at Kaya 08—Korean fusion. Trending

235

and private," Kyle says.

Genevieve looks up, seeming less startled than confused.

"If you would've told me, Piper, I'd have arranged something for you," she says, ignoring Kyle. "Made sure you had a table in a quiet corner, or by the window, if you really want to deal with people watching you eat. You do realize that if you wear anything you had on today, I'll have to delete that content and we'll have to reshoot. But that's fine, we can get up early and redo it. I just wish you'd told me so we didn't have to waste everyone's time."

I prickle, not in the mood for a dressing-down. Not from her, and not in front of everyone. But I also understand her point.

Genevieve gets up and goes into the other room. She returns with an outfit and snaps off the tags. "Here. I brought this as a contingency. I'll call them tomorrow. They'll be thrilled and probably send you an entire wardrobe."

That night, I sit across from Kyle at a corner table, my smile—for the first time today—for him alone.

"You know, I've been thinking..." Kyle says, gazing at our intertwined fingers.

"About what a crazy life I lead?" I say wryly.

He's been such a good sport, but I know it's got to get old. If I'm honest, I've been bracing myself—not so much for an ultimatum, which isn't his style, but a request for an idea of how, or when, we'll be able to transition to something more normal. The way things are going, I figure I've got a year—maybe 18 months, tops—left before users get tired of Echelon's bullshit...

Or I do.

"About, that..." He hesitates.

"I know it's crazy," I say, not sure I like the pensive tilt of his head. "But I don't plan to do this forever. I want things—from life. For us."

Something about the way he presses his lips together, as though not sure how to frame what he's about to say next, sparks anxiety. Is it possible he's already fed up? He wouldn't take me out tonight—in public, where I'm most vulnerable—just to break up with me...

Would he?

"Actually, I was thinking that I could work remotely." He glances up at me.

I feel my brow—the same one Gen wants me to get Botox in—furrow. But not in relief.

"What? Why?"

"To be with you. No pressure, of course," he says, leaning toward me. "I understand if you need time apart to do your own thing or have your own space. But if you don't... I want to be with you."

From the corner of my eye, I just catch sight of someone with a raised iPhone, camera angled toward our table. For the first time in weeks, I wish we were back in Denver, sitting in front of the TV eating pizza.

"But Kyle," I say intently. "Your career."

He's been a top medical rep for years. Visiting clients is the lifeblood of his business.

He shrugs. "I can do it from the road. Or...I could leave it. And help you."

"*What?*"

He covers my hand with his other one. "I don't see your business slowing down any time soon. You're going to need people. People you can trust, who care about you."

"What if I stop?" I blurt. "What if I can't keep doing this forever? You'll have left your career for nothing!"

"Then we move on. Together."

But he frowns as he says it.

"Don't worry, I'm not proposing," he says. "Not yet. But I do love you, Piper." He lifts my fingers to his lips and lets me go as the waiter approaches. "Just say you'll think about it."

I lay awake, listening to the sound of Kyle's soft snores. Unable to put my finger on why our conversation has bothered me all night. After all, he said he loved me.

I finally give up and tiptoe out of our tree house bedroom to the kitchen and make some tea.

"Can't sleep?"

I nearly jump out of my skin as Genevieve's voice issues from the darkness of the sofa.

"You scared me," I hiss, setting down the mug to wipe up the hot water that sloshed over my hand.

"Sorry. How was dinner?"

I pad over to the living room area and sit down on the edge of the coffee table with a sigh.

"Kyle asked me to move in with him," I say. I don't add that it was an afterthought as he paid for dinner.

"That's great," Genevieve says. "In fact, I think we should all move."

"Um..."

"Not in *together*," she says, rolling her eyes. She rises from the sofa and moves into the glow of the kitchen's under-cabinet lighting. "To L.A. Or Miami. Somewhere we can work, but the work is *real.*"

"Gen, it's never going to be real," I say gently.

She comes and takes my hands. "Why not? You don't have to get a mansion. Just something upscale, a luxury apartment where it's okay to be recognized. You can even get rid of your dad's old Acura and get a Benz—a convertible, like you've always wanted."

"*You're* the one who's always wanted a Mercedes convertible," I say. "And even if I did, I can't afford it, let alone a 'luxury apartment' in Miami."

I laugh. I make decent money—my cut might be a thousand dollars a week. Which isn't peanuts, but definitely doesn't make me rich. And I like driving my dad's Acura because it makes me feel close to him.

Genevieve squints at me. "Why do you always do that?"

"Do what?"

"Act like you don't want any of this."

Do I want it?

Of course I do. It's my job.

I just don't know how long someone can pretend to live before they forget how to do it for real, without an audience.

"Gen, maybe this is as far as it goes. And if it is, I'm okay with that."

"No," Genevieve says, shaking her head. "I don't think you are.

And you might think you're happy moving in with Kyle to live some regular life. But you'll regret it. You'll resent him. And you'll wonder. Luckily, you won't have to wonder for long." She pulls out her phone and swipes it open.

I turn away, tired of screens, of talking about work.

"Piper."

I throw a doleful look over my shoulder…and then pause. She's holding up my feed.

There's a #17 below my name.

I snatch the phone from her.

"How did this—?"

"Avella," she says, "dropping like a rock."

"That's not funny," I say.

"My bad. I didn't mean it that way."

I stare at it, everything I just said going out the window.

She takes the phone back. "Bring Kyle to Miami if you like. But I need you to want this. Because it will be real. Very soon."

"How do you know? What's real enough to count?"

"There's real money in the top ten. We're talking luxury apartment money. Piper, we're almost there."

I sigh and kiss her forehead, knowing I'm not going to change her mind tonight.

I wake to a commotion in the living room followed by pounding on our bedroom door.

"What the—?" Kyle lifts his head.

"Turn on the news!" Zach says.

I get up as Kyle grabs the remote from the nightstand, clicks on the TV, and starts scrolling through the guide.

I throw on last night's clothes, stride to the door, and yank it open.

There's Genevieve, tapping madly at her phone. Beyond her, Zach paces in front of the window, chewing a fingernail.

"What is going on?" I demand.

Genevieve holds up her phone.

"Yes, I know—"

"Look."

I look.

It's a picture of Jace Kissling, who's probably #1 now.

I shrug. "So?"

She scrolls down the screen enough for me to see this isn't an Echelon feed, but the news.

ECHELON INFLUENCER FOUND DEAD...

Ice pours down my spine.

I take the phone with unsteady fingers but can't make sense of what I'm seeing.

SHOT OUTSIDE NEW YORK CLUB... DIED LATER OF HIS WOUNDS...

I'd met Jace at the Carmel event. He was charming—sweet, even. Real.

More so than anyone else there.

Her phone rings in my hand. Genevieve takes it from me and turns the ringer off.

"Should you—"

"It's been ringing all morning. News stations wanting to interview you. A couple sponsors checking in. One of them wants to offer a bodyguard service."

Kyle appears in the doorway behind me.

"She has three bodyguards already," he says.

"Guys," Zach says from near the window.

Genevieve crosses the floor and looks out as the sound of a car approaches below.

"Who is it?" I ask.

Genevieve turns away. "Local news."

Kyle takes one look out the window and strides into the bedroom to retrieve the suitcases. "We need to get out of here. Piper, hurry."

We grab the clothes, shoes, and accessories strewn around the living room, start shoving them into our bags.

At one point I stop cold. "How do they know where we're staying?"

Genevieve turns to stare at me. "Anyone follow you two back last night?"

"No—not that I noticed." But I'd been too distracted by our conversation to pay close attention.

"I'll find out," Kyle says, heading down to talk to the reporter.

We finish packing and Zach throws the bags out the window to the grassy ground below before hurrying down the stairs.

I take a last look around, but all I see is the image of that news headline.

Who would shoot someone like Jace?

"Come on," Genevieve says, shoving my carry-on toward me. I don't even know if we've closed the door as we take the stairs.

When we get to the SUV, Zach's examining the rear left tire.

"You've got to be kidding me," Genevieve says.

"Call an Uber."

"We can't call—"

"Well, we can't drive this, so if we want to get out of here, we either have to hitch a ride with Channel 6 or call someone to come get us!" Zach mutters and pulls his phone out to order the ride himself.

Kyle sends the news team on its way and walks over, mouth set in a grim line.

"Well?" Genevieve demands.

"They got an anonymous tip with this address."

"How is that even possible?" I ask.

Genevieve turns on me. "Did you tell anyone where you were staying last night? Mention it?"

"No. We didn't talk to anyone."

"There's more," Kyle says, his expression flat. "Whoever called said you'd been involved with Jace."

"That's impossible."

"You sure he knew that?" Kyle asks.

"Jace was gay," I say. He'd been proud to show me pictures—real, pedestrian selfies—of him and his boyfriend in their new home.

A car comes up the drive. I shoulder my bag and start toward

241

it—and then halt. It's a rusty Honda not even big enough for our gear.

The window lowers and someone leans out and snaps a picture.

"Get out of here!" Zach shouts, running toward them. The car skids away, graveling flying, as a black SUV comes ambling up the drive. I slip on a pair of shades I shot in yesterday and get in as Kyle and Zach load the luggage.

Five minutes later, we're speeding toward the airport and Genevieve and Kyle are on their phones trying to see what we can get for flights.

I'm still in shock. I take out my phone and stare at Jace's face on the Echelon home page. The comments roll by like a wheel, only a few words snagging my eye: Murder. Serial killer. I swipe to an article about the "Echelon Curse."

My picture's on it.

#11 below my name.

It's got to be a typo. I tap my image, and my page springs to life, full of activity.

#11.

How is that even possible?

And then I note the thumbnail map on the corner of my feed. The pin dropped inside it.

Moving along a highway toward the Atlanta airport.

I open the map to find some username I don't recognize has updated my location.

"Hey!" I shout at the driver. "Are you updating my route on Echelon?"

Genevieve shoots up in the seat and Kyle lunges forward, grabbing the phone from its cradle on the driver's dash.

"What? What the—?" the driver yells, swerving. Beside me, Kyle starts scrolling through the driver's phone, looking for the Echelon app. But it isn't on there. He pockets the phone.

"You'll get this back when we get to the airport," he says. "Pretty sure you already know the way."

The driver looks disgruntled but doesn't argue.

"You one of those people on that site?" he says, looking at me in the rearview mirror.

My phone blips and then begins to chime—my mom's ringtone. I answer on the first ring.

"Mom."

"Are you safe?" Her voice is shrill. "I just saw the news on my phone—I want you to come home!"

"We are. I am," I say. "Soon as we can find a flight."

The first flight out only has two seats available. Kyle and I claim them. Genevieve and Zach nab seats on later flights.

We send the luggage with Genevieve and Zach and, upon landing in Denver, hurry out to meet my mom in Hourly Parking.

I turn my phone off of flight mode and check my location on Echelon.

Blank, for the moment.

In the back seat of my mom's car, I turn my cheek into Kyle's shoulder, hiding my face as Mom drives. She's nervous, hands shaking on the wheel. Past the airport, she pulls over long enough to switch places with Kyle, who turns us East on I-70 before heading south around the city.

We don't go home; I can see two cars parked along our curb on the house camera app.

We head to the mountains instead.

My aunt is delighted to see me again—Kyle, too. Even more when Genevieve and Zach show up in her nursing home apartment a couple hours later.

I'm just glad to be somewhere with security where I'm known only as "Dorothy's niece."

We stay until the evening news comes on, pretending to socialize as Kyle secures an Airbnb in nearby Florissant—a cabin with a little brook running alongside it, nestled on the hill.

In a former life, I'd have loved its rustic charm. Now, as we retrieve the key from the lockbox and drag our bags inside, I can only fantasize about living somewhere like this, holed up from the rest of the world.

My mom's been crying. Her hands tremor when she holds them to her mouth.

"It's okay, Mom," I say. "We don't even have the same last name. You're safe."

I never changed mine back when I got divorced—meant to, but never got around to it. Now I'm glad.

"I'm not worried about me," she cries. "I'm worried about you. Something is happening to those people at the top of that stupid social media site!"

I pause. In the two months since Marina's death, I've never once worried about my own safety or entertained the possibility that anyone would want to harm me.

"We're safe," I say, taking her to sit down in a living room recliner. "I promise."

"I want you to get off that site. You have to delete it," my mom says.

"It won't delete. It doesn't work that way," I say. "But my location's off, and we're not posting. As far as anyone knows, we could be anywhere right now. I promise, Mom."

She nods, but she's started to cry again. I dig around in her purse for the bottle of Xanax she keeps there and give her one.

Zach makes a run into town to pick up pizza from the local brewery while Kyle and Genevieve set up laptops and charging stations on the kitchen table.

We spend the evening camped out around a propane fireplace in the living room, glued to the TV. The "Echelon Curse" is all over the news featuring interviews with Jace's boyfriend. A cousin of Marina's. A childhood friend of Avella's.

I check the feed obsessively. Not just mine—which is a frenzy of thoughts and prayers and pictures of me from last night's dinner all posted practically on top of one another—but that of Reena Thomas, who currently sits at the #2 spot behind Jace. Like me, she has gone silent even as her followers speculate on her location. I am glad, at least, to find no pin in the thumbnail map of her location.

At some point in the middle of the night, I wake to find a new notice on my phone.

I am now #10.

I get up in a panic, sweat breaking down my back.

I wake Kyle but can't find Genevieve. She comes in through the front door a moment later, closing it behind her with a quiet click.

"Where were you?" I hiss.

She sheepishly shows me the pack of cigarettes in her hand, and now I can smell it on her, too. I haven't known her to smoke except at parties.

I turn my phone toward her.

"I saw," she says.

"What do we do?" I'm having trouble breathing. Feel the fingers of fear like cold spikes between my ribs. She finds my mom's purse, gives me one of her pills.

It helps, and I sink into a recliner. Genevieve pulls a blanket over my legs.

"Nothing's going to happen to you. I won't let it," she says.

I watch the feed on my phone in a growing stupor. Scroll past the content and comments and images of the last year, unable to appreciate the aesthetic we so carefully cultivated. The way Zach has made each of them look like an editorial layout in the highest fashion magazine.

I go back—in the feed, in time—to the days of Interior Mart. Stop at the photo from Cancun, when we first invented The Game.

Flashback to the amazing time my bestie, @GenevievePinkous, and I had on the Riviera Maya. Time to go back!

I blink and read it again. I hadn't tagged her. I'd been careful not to—she was protective of her privacy. But there it is again, later, during the cooking class we took together.

I think I must be losing my mind because I know for a fact I didn't tag her then—did I? I go back, search the edit history on the post. It shows that I modified it a week after Zach posted it.

But I have no recollection of doing so.

I doze at last, and sleep late. Wake to the sound of an ambulance whirring along the highway, headed down the mountain.

"Mom?"

"She's in the shower," Zach says.

"Where's Kyle?" I mumble, looking around.

"Went to pick up breakfast."

I sit up straight. "What? No! Someone might recognize him."

Zach shrugs. "He put on a hat and pair of shades he found in the laundry room. Said he'd only be doing drive-thru. Should be okay."

The "Echelon Curse" is now global news: the drive-by shooting death of Jace Kissling appearing to be a random act of violence. The top ten accounts have practically been abandoned by their users, but they're kept active by fans, some of whom continue to update influencer sightings and locations.

That morning, Echelon announces it has temporarily disabled the location feature. The site spirals out of control with fan speculation. Echelon is the topic of every current events show and 24-hour news network.

I make a pot of coffee, put on my sweater, and carry a steaming mug out to the cabin's chilly all-season room. I can't take any more of the news.

A half hour later Kyle still hasn't returned. I text him, but he doesn't respond. I call. No answer. I go back inside.

"Guys, did he say where he was going?"

"We're in the mountains," Genevieve says, huddled in front of her laptop at the kitchen table that looks more like Command Central now that Zach's set up all his equipment. "There are dead spots all over."

My mom is rummaging through the cupboards in the kitchen, saying she's found some pancake mix and plans to mix up a batch. Zach says Kyle must have gone into Woodland Park for groceries.

I go into the bedroom where we stashed our bags and start rummaging through them, looking for something to wear. Searching for the t-shirt and joggers I packed to lounge in after our tree house shoot in Atlanta.

I pause when I get to the third bag, noting the airline tag with Genevieve's last name. It's labeled MRY. I frown, trying to remember which airport that might have been. Pull out my phone and search it.

Monterey Regional Airport.

But I don't recall her flying there. Even when we attended the Carmel event, we flew into San Jose and caught the Monterey Airbus because it was cheaper.

I straighten slowly, as though moving through cement. Walk back out into the living room to find Zach and Genevieve staring at the TV.

The Breaking News banner scrolls across the bottom of the screen. Echelon's #2 influencer, Reena Thomas, has died in a head-on collision near her Houston home.

Genevieve turns to me, eyes stark as my breath leaves me all at once.

"Piper. Your phone."

It takes me a moment to register that it's ringing. I don't recognize the number and almost decline the call, but noting the Colorado area code I hit "answer."

"Hello?"

"Is this Piper?"

I almost say no, far too distracted to talk. But there's something about the tremor in the woman's voice.

"Yes?"

"This is Kyle's mother. I just got a call from a hospital in Colorado Springs saying he's been in an accident."

I glance up, the room whirling around me. She's saying something else, but I don't hear it, already moving before I even know even where I'm going. I wander into the kitchen, not sure what I'm looking for until my eyes land on the stack of information in the built-in desk nook, the cup of mismatched pens and Ace Hardware notepad.

I tell Kyle's mom I'll call her as soon as I get to the hospital. She gives me the address. I scratch it onto a pad of paper, end the call. Dial the owner's number tacked above the landline phone.

"What is it?" Genevieve says, face pale.

I ignore her as the owner answers, fumbling over my words as I explain there's been an accident, that I need a ride to the hospital.

Genevieve is beside me in an instant. She takes the phone from my hands.

"Yes, hi. If you have a vehicle we can borrow—you can? Oh, great. Thank you. Yes—see you then."

"Where are you going?" Mom demands, batter bowl cradled in

247

her arm, the whisk in her hand going still.

"Kyle's been in an accident."

She sets the bowl down with a cry. "Then I'm coming with you!"

The owner shows up five minutes later in her Ford Bronco. I say nothing as she drives us down the mountain into town. I know she's looking at me in the rearview mirror.

We arrive at the hospital, and I get out of the car without a word as Genevieve thanks her.

At the front desk I learn Kyle's been admitted. That he's gone in for emergency surgery. We take a seat in the main waiting room.

We sit for hours, Mom attempting to make small talk. Checking with reception to see if he's out of surgery.

We eventually find a secluded corner of the cafeteria, where I pretend to eat a plate of cold eggs.

"Mom," I say. "Why don't you go see Aunt Lilly while we're waiting? It might be more comfortable at her place."

Genevieve smiles slightly and agrees. She orders an Uber to take Mom up the mountain.

"It'll be here in two minutes," she says.

"Can you walk her out?" I say, glancing from her to my mom. "I don't think I should show my face."

She gives me a level look and I think she's about to refuse, but then she rises and, taking Mom by the arm, leads her out to the lobby.

The instant she's out of sight, I grab her unlocked phone off the table, click to the Uber app, and add a new stop to Mom's ride. Next, I go to Genevieve's texts and scroll through them. I don't recognize most of the numbers.

I open her e-mail, scan swiftly down the list. Brand correspondence. Product contracts.

I pause on one from a bank—one I don't recognize: A deposit for five thousand dollars from Vanguard Cruise Lines. And then a second one a few days later.

This is far more than I was aware we were getting paid.

I open her Echelon app. But the name at the top isn't hers. Amanda_234708

My first thought is she's working for another influencer, or maybe as a paid follower. I tap her activity log....

And think I might vomit.

Amanda_234708 was last used to update my location in Atlanta, and then on the way to the airport.

With shaking hands, I open the list in the corner, log out, tap the empty login field. Three stored response options come up: Amanda_234708, GenevievePinkous, and me. I tap Genevieve's name and log in with the stored password.

Her activity log is full of responses to well wishers saying they hope I'm safe. That they're praying for me—and her.

And then I notice the number beneath her name:

#289,851.

I glance toward the cafeteria entrance. Seeing no sign of Genevieve, I quickly open her photos and scroll through images of past shoots, brand name handbags, high-end jewelry, and shoes. I go back three weeks. A month. Two. Past the Hawaii trip, to the month before.

I pause on the image of a coastline, the blue ocean in the background. Swipe and then stop on the image of a beautiful redhead in a jogging outfit posing in the sun as though she hasn't got a care in the world, the craggy surf below her.

Avella.

I become aware of a form standing over me.

I slowly lower the phone.

"What did you do?" I whisper, lifting my gaze to Genevieve.

"What I had to," she says, sitting down quietly across from me.

"*What have you done?*"

"I just told you," she says, picking up the phone and dropping it in her purse.

"And Marina? If I go back far enough, will I find another picture—or a plane ticket to LAX?"

She's quiet a moment. When she speaks, her voice is calm, measured. "I went out to talk to them about the prospect of partnering with you. They were interested, just not enough. But they really liked you. I want you to know that."

A hot tear slips down my cheek.

"You should have seen Marina's house. It was amazing."

249

"And Jace?" I ask, hoarse.

"Obviously, I can't be in two places at once. And I'm not the only one who wants to see you succeed."

"Zach?" I whisper, but he was with us when Jace was shot.

"No," she scoffs. "Not Zach. I made a deal with one of our new sponsors. It's what I do."

"*What?*" Someone glances my way, but they don't seem to recognize me. For all they know, I'm the relative of someone who just got a cancer diagnosis.

"They want a new brand ambassador. Marina and Avella's sponsors had a stranglehold on them. Made them sign exclusivity contracts. And apparently Jace and Reena weren't interested in partnering with any cruise line ranked lower than fourth."

I narrow my eyes. "You're talking about Vanguard?"

"They understand what it feels like to be passed over. They have a real affinity for our position. And connections all over the world."

"You're saying they *had Jace shot?*"

"No. Of course not. I have no idea what happened to Jace." She tilts her head. "But accidents do happen."

"Jace didn't die from an *accident*," I say through gritted teeth.

"Accidents can be arranged."

"What are you saying?" I cry.

"Do you think Kyle just fell asleep at the wheel?"

I bolt up from my chair.

"SIT down." Genevieve says, voice steely.

"No. I'm going to the police."

"I wouldn't," she says, and her eyes look like she's genuinely pleading with me. "You have your mom to think about. And Kyle, too, I suppose."

I slowly lower to the chair.

"And Zach? Does he know?"

"Of course he knows. Piper Pikalov is his entire life. He's given everything to it. Remember when you paid him a measly fifty bucks per shoot?" She snorts, but then leans in and reaches for my hand. I pull away.

"We're so close, Piper. All our hard work is about to pay off. For all of us. You, too. Of course. You'll be number one in two weeks.

Three, tops."

"No. I'm done." I decided last night. Echelon doesn't let accounts close—they just fade away without activity. If I starve it long enough for content, the clamor will quiet, and the page will follow Marina, Avella, Jace, and Reena back into the murky depths of digital obscurity. "That's it. I'm finished."

"Piper..." she says, as though she's about to voice something delicate. "There's someone waiting at the bus station you just diverted your mom to. There's also another someone in this hospital who knows which room Kyle's in. And in case it's not patently obvious, both of these someones aren't particularly nice people. I say the word, and the next tragedy won't be you, but it will be one of yours." She pauses, a smile toying about her lips. "Come to think of it, tragedy like that would garner a lot of attention. We could be number one in a week."

"What do you want?" I whisper.

I could take her. I could lunge across this table and wrestle her to the ground, thumbs pressed against her windpipe.

But she's the only link I have to the nameless, faceless others threatening the ones I love—an exceedingly small inner circle that once included her.

"I want you to be as invested in your success as I am—as we all are. Please say you are. And then I think we should go up and see Kyle." She smiles again.

I sit very still. Search her gaze. But the Genevieve I knew is gone.

So I nod. But even as I do, I promise myself I will find a way out—for all of us. Somehow, I will put an end to this.

Until then, I will play along, and do it convincingly.

Genevieve was right.

The Game is finally real.

I pull the expensive sunglasses from my purse and slip them on.

***

911

ALLISON BRENNAN

911

I.

The plan was perfect—until everything went to hell.

"It hurts, Chris!" Charlie cried out. "I gotta go to a hospital."

"No hospitals," Gina said as she drove east on Jackson Highway. Her voice was calm. Too calm, considering the circumstances.

With the cargo in the back of the van it was a tight fit, but Chris squeezed in with his brother Charlie, trying to determine if the gun shot was serious. A graze they could deal with later, when they were far out of Sacramento. Gina was going a steady five miles over the speed limit. But eventually they'd have to ditch the van and grab something else. The whole operation was now screwed, after all, and the police would quickly ID the vehicle they'd stolen earlier.

"You gotta let me look, Charlie," Chris said. "Come on, buddy."

Charlie winced as Chris pulled up his shirt.

Well, shit. This was no flesh wound.

Charlie had been shot in the lower right side, just above his pelvic bone. But there was no exit wound, so the bullet was lodged in his gut, and he was still bleeding.

This wasn't something they could deal with tomorrow.

But Gina was right; they couldn't go to a hospital. If it was just a matter of Charlie being arrested, they'd do it to save his life. But they had more than Charlie's freedom to consider.

They'd all be dead if they were caught. They had stolen from the wrong people.

You should never have listened to Gina.

"How is he?" Gina asked.

"What do you think?" Chris snapped. "He needs a doctor."

Silence as she continued to drive.

255

"He'll die, Gina," Chris said a minute later. "There's no exit wound. I'm putting pressure on it but he's still bleeding. I'm not letting him die." Their options were limited. What if they dropped Charlie off at a hospital in another county? El Dorado, maybe Placer? Would that buy enough time?

Suddenly, she pulled over into a turn out next to a crumbling barn adjacent to the two-lane rural highway that headed away from Sacramento. She turned to look at them. "We can't go to the hospital, Chris. That's just not an option. We have to think of something else."

Chris wished she hadn't stopped the car. They might draw attention, even in the middle of the night. *Especially* in the middle of the night, if a cop passed by.

"Drive, Gina. We can't just sit here."

She didn't move. "We need a plan. If Charlie is serious hurt, we have to help him. What are the options?"

Charlie was trying not to cry, but couldn't stop the tears. He was only twenty-one. He had his entire life ahead of him and Chris felt like shit for getting their little brother involved in the heist. Gina, not so much—she had been with Chris from the beginning. But Charlie had begged to join them, and for the last year things were great, Charlie's computer skills were an asset…until they took this job.

Never steal from thieves.

He should have adhered to his own rules; instead, he'd listened to Gina.

Dammit.

"A vet," he said. "We'll find a veterinarian, get Charlie stable, then head to Utah." Once they were back on their home turf, they had people who would help.

"Nothing's going to be open," Gina said. "It's after midnight."

Chris pulled out his phone and searched the area. "Okay, I found something—there's a twenty-four-hour vet only fifteen minutes from here, in Wilton." He looked at the property on Google Earth. "He has like ten, maybe twenty acres around the place. Remote, no nearby neighbors. A Dr. William Caldwell, specializes in large animals. Looks like he has a house in the same place."

"He'll call the cops," Gina said. "It's a huge risk."

Chris said, "I have a plan."

II.

Sacramento County Deputy Sheriff Brittan Johns pulled up at a warehouse off Sunrise Boulevard. It was 1:30 in the morning, the middle of her shift, and she'd just finished a twenty-minute break eating a sandwich in her cruiser.

The warehouse was located in a jurisdictionally borderline area, where either the sheriff's department or Rancho Cordova PD could respond. Because Britt was the only K-9 unit on duty in the area, RCPD asked for her support.

Three RCPD units were already on-site. Britt left her K-9, Dennis, a four-year-old German Shepherd, in the idling, air-conditioned car, locking it with her fob. Though the middle of the night, the stagnant summer air weighed her down, made worse by the twenty-nine pounds of gear she wore. She loved Sacramento; however, she didn't love Sacramento in August.

"Good to see you, Jones." Carl Bergstrom, a twenty-year senior patrol officer who she'd worked with many times, nodded toward her.

"What are we looking at?"

"We got called out on a possible 10-71, we were eleven minutes out." Average response time, even for a call of shots fired, was increasing unless there were multiple calls to the same location. All departments were spread thin, and a department mandate was that no officer was to respond to calls alone, not after the increase in attacks on uniformed cops. "When we were four minutes out," Carl continued, "we get another call, same location, private alarm. Dispatch is reaching out to the owner of the facility, though we got the alarm company to turn off the noise. My ears are still ringing. But something weird is going on."

He motioned for her to follow him. Another RCPD officer pulled up and two officers got out. Carl's partner went over to talk to them.

The building was a long, cinder block structure with five separate entrances each adjacent to a two-story roll-up door, the kind where trucks can back in and unload. Only the first business was marked—"Swing for the Bleachers." Batting cages and pitching lessons.

They walked down to the last unit in the building. An officer stood there with his flashlight out, last name Reyes. "I called in the crime techs because I think we have a possible injured party. We can't say this is blood, but this is blood." He rolled his eyes and shined his light down on the ground. It did appear that blood had dripped onto the asphalt and the only reason they noticed it was because it made splatters on the white parking lines. The crime scene techs didn't like when cops made forensic statements. *It's not blood until* we *say it's blood!*

"The alarm came from the batting cages," Carl continued. "We checked the facility; it's locked tight and I don't know what might have set it off. But this?"

He gestured to the roll-up door with his light. It was deeply bent, as if someone had driven a car into it. "The entrance was unlocked, and that's when it got weird."

He had on gloves. The unmarked door was propped open, lights already on. "You turn them on?" she gestured.

"Yep. Couldn't see shit around here."

There was a single, empty desk in the long, narrow space. Some filing cabinets. No phone, no computer, though cords were laid across the floor that could be attached to a laptop. To the left was a wide opening covered by a heavy, rubber drape with an opening in the middle, like those she'd seen in large freezers, which led into the large warehouse space.

Carl separated the pieces and they stepped in.

This space was definitely not empty.

Ten narrow rows of eight-foot-high metal shelves were filled with gallon-sized containers. Without touching anything, Britt walked down the closest row. Each bottle was labeled in Chinese characters.

Against the closest wall to the entrance were huge boxes of empty prescription bottles, and along the back wall were stainless steel tables set up for what appeared to be counting and sorting—trays, scales, tongs. A dozen boxes of latex gloves were stacked at one end.

"Wow, this has to be millions of dollars in prescription drugs," she said.

"I've already called the detectives. They're going to have a fun going through this shit. But this isn't all."

Carl led her to the front of the facility. A wall had been erected near the front, leaving about ten feet of space between the shelves and the roll-up door, enough to pull in a vehicle—two, if parked side by side. Even if the door was fully retracted, no one would be able to see anything inside.

A narrow door—with a lock—hung oddly on the frame, the lock cut.

Britt stepped through the doorway. Blood spatter covered the temporary wall. "The door must have been up if someone was shot at that angle," she said.

"Yeah, but I think there were two people injured." He motioned to a trail that ended where the door had come down. "The door isn't secure, but I didn't want to disturb the evidence until the crime scene techs get here."

"Someone came in to rob the place? Or an employee maybe stealing a few bottles?" she guessed. "Or, hell…I don't know, but this can't be legal."

"It's most certainly not legal. There's a huge market for pharmaceuticals. They get them from overseas, no quality control, then re-package to sell them on the streets, ship to Mexico or up to Canada."

The drug problem had become worse year after year for as long as Britt had been on the force. She had no answers, but she'd been called out on far too many overdoses and talked to far too many grieving families to think ignoring the problem was wise.

Carl asked, "How is Dennis doing? He up for a search?"

Dennis had been shot last year when they were clearing a meth house in a rural area of Sacramento. He'd had emergency surgery, went through re-training, and had been re-certified when she came back from her honeymoon last month.

It had been hard for her to put Dennis back in harm's way, but it's what she had trained for, what Dennis had trained for. He was a working dog and that's what he did best. Working dogs who retired too early tended to have reduced lifespans.

"He's great. Passed all his tests with flying colors."

"We need to search the immediate area. The amount of blood on that wall? Someone could have been driven away, or be hiding in the area."

"If he's nearby, Dennis will find him. We should check out the batting cages first, since that's where the alarm went off."

She went out to her vehicle, opened the back door and put Dennis on his leash.

"Time to get to work, buddy," she said and walked him over to the crime scene.

III.

Will groaned when his phone rang. By the ring tone—an obnoxious hard rock beat that he'd chosen because it would always wake him up—the call was his veterinary clinic's emergency line.

He sat up in bed while simultaneously reaching for his work phone. "Caldwell Vet," he answered. His bedside clock read 1:47 am.

He'd been asleep for less than two hours, but it had been a hard sleep and he was having trouble waking up. He'd spent the last ten hours at the Garcia ranch helping deliver two breech foals. One didn't make it, and he thought he might lose the mare, but she pulled through. He really hoped this wasn't John Garcia telling him something went wrong. They'd all be heartbroken.

"Someone hit my dog!" a frantic woman's voice cried through the phone line. "I'm out front, I need help, *please*...he's breathing but he can't move. I think his leg is broken."

"You're outside? Now?"

"Yes, no one is answering the door, please tell me you're close by. *Please*. I'll pay anything to save Charlie."

He got up, rummaged for jeans in his dresser drawer, and pulled them on over his boxers as he tried to get more information from the caller. "I will be right there. Two minutes, okay? What kind of dog is Charlie?"

He sat on his bed, pulled on socks and tennis shoes.

"A lab mix. I don't know how he got out. Why didn't they stop?"

It was a common story, especially out here in the country. Most people didn't have fences, or the fencing wasn't designed to keep dogs penned. Some owners were negligent, some dogs accidentally got out. He'd had to put down far too many pets who'd been hit on the road, and rarely did the driver stop.

But he'd saved just as many, and he would do everything he could.

"How old is Charlie?"

"Three."

"Is he in your vehicle?"

"Yes. I got him in, but I don't want to move him."

"What kind of car?"

"I have a van."

"Drive around to the back of the building. There's a double door, painted red, you can't miss it. It doesn't open from the outside, but I'll get a gurney and come out that way, okay? I'll be right there."

He ended the call and pulled on a T-shirt. He needed coffee and he might have to call in a tech to assist if the dog needed surgery, but he wasn't going to wake up anyone until he knew exactly what he was dealing with—and if he had a chance of saving the dog.

Jack, his twelve-year-old stepson, stepped into the doorway. He yawned, his sandy blond hair falling into his sleepy eyes. He looked so much like his mom before she had coffee that Will smiled.

"I heard the phone," Jack said.

"Dog hit by a car. They're at the clinic; I'm going there now."

"Oh."

"You okay?"

"Calls at night are never good."

It clicked for Will, something he had only recently discovered for himself. Jack was thinking about his mom, a deputy sheriff, who had worked the graveyard shift for most of the kid's life. They'd only moved into his house two months ago, after Will and Britt married.

Will had never thought he'd marry, until he met Britt last year. She'd come into the clinic with her K-9 Dennis after he'd been shot in the line of duty. She was both the strongest woman he'd ever met, and the most compassionate. It seemed the most natural thing in the world to fall in love. Jack was a bonus.

But this wake-up call reminded him that Jack had grown up knowing that his mom could be injured, or worse, every night she went to work. It was only a year ago that he'd learned in the middle of the night that Dennis, who was as much Jack's dog as Britt's, had nearly died.

"I'll let you know how it goes. You should go back to bed, it's two in the morning."

"Yeah," he said. "You want me to make you coffee?"

"Thanks, but I'll brew some at the clinic." He squeezed Jack's shoulder as he passed him. Even in the fifteen months since Will had first met Jack, the kid had grown at least four inches. He was still shorter than Will's six feet, but Will wouldn't be surprised if the kid surpassed him by the time he started high school.

Lucky, Will's senior Golden Retriever, lifted his head, wondering what all the commotion was in the middle of the night. He gave his tail a weak wag, as if to say, *If it's breakfast time, I'll get up, but I don't really want to.*

Will patted Lucky and told him to stay. Lucky put his head down, watching them with sleepy eyes.

"If I'm not back, can you feed Lucky and the cats before you go to school?" Will asked.

"Sure," Jack said. He walked across the great room to his bedroom. Will's house wasn't large, really barely large enough for him and his animals, and certainly not for a wife and pre-teen son. But they'd never complained. One central room that encompassed the kitchen, dining, and living room, then two master bedrooms, one on each side of the house. Will had plans for a remodel, but the contractor he wanted to use was swamped and couldn't start until next month. Will and Britt had talked about having a kid or two together, and they would definitely need the space if and when Britt got pregnant.

Will left the house and walked on a wide brick path. When

he first moved in a decade ago, a storm hit and turned the field between his house and the clinic into a muddy hellhole until he'd put in the footpath.

He owned ten acres in Wilton, a rural community east of Sacramento, where he'd built up his practice. He'd bought the property, converted the main house into his clinic, and lived in the smaller two-bedroom caretakers' house. There was a barn and corral, which helped since he specialized in large animals and almost always had a horse or two in residence. He saw a variety of animals; he'd even had to brush up on his reptile knowledge because the son of one of his clients had a bearded dragon. But half his business was dogs and cats.

In the end, it was being able to save a beloved animal—pet or working—that gave him the most satisfaction. Will loved what he did, and before Britt he didn't think twice about caring for animals seven days a week. But as a cop, Britt's schedule was hectic, too, and the only time they really had together was Sundays, which she had off and his office was closed. She was moving to the day shift at the beginning of the year, which would give them more time together—time he craved.

He saw car lights behind the clinic, and figured it was the dog owner at the rear entrance. He briskly walked to the side door, keys in hand. He unlocked the door, pushed it open, and was about to close it when someone pushed in behind him.

Will immediately thought it was the owner, who might have seen him cross the yard. He was about to speak, when he saw a man with a gun.

The stranger closed the door behind him, locking the deadbolt. "Had to make sure you were alone," he said.

Will put his hands up, not wanting to give this man any reason to shoot him. "There's no dog, is there?"

He shook his head. "My brother's been shot and you're going to save him. Go to the back door, let him in."

The lights in the clinic were off, but the security lighting gave Will enough illumination to see the stranger. He was average in every way except his eyes: they were cold, focused on Will. His steady hands held a .45 semi-auto.

Will glanced at the security panel to the right of the door and knew that if he didn't type in the code within sixty seconds, the alarm would signal the alarm company. If he didn't answer the phone, they would dispatch the sheriff's department.

He walked, silently counting, but then the gunman said. "Stop. Fuck. Disarm that right now."

Will turned and saw the man pointing at the alarm panel.

"I swear, if you try anything—*anything*—I will kill you and then go to your house and kill anyone inside."

Will's thoughts immediately went to Jack.

"I live alone," he said.

"Then I'll wait for your staff and shoot them one-by-one," he said in a low voice. "Do what I said."

Will considered putting in the wrong code, but he didn't. He couldn't risk Jack. But he had some other ideas to get the police here.

He entered the six-digit code and the light went from blinking red to green.

"Good boy," the gunman said. "Now your phone."

Will reached into his back pocket. "Hold it," the man said. He leaned forward and pulled out Will's phone, slid it in his own pocket. He was close enough that Will might have been able to fight him for the gun, but he didn't know if he would win, how many people were outside, or if someone else had a gun and might go after Jack.

So he did nothing while the man quickly pat him down.

"Back door," the man ordered.

Will walked down the hall. "Can I turn on the lights?"

"No sudden moves."

He carefully flipped the switches on the wall. He had to find a way to set off the silent alarm. There were only two ways to do so when the system was on green—the side door main panel, which would be loud, or the panic button under the reception desk, which was silent.

He had to somehow get to the reception desk. That was his best option.

He reached the double doors. They were steel and could be opened only from the inside.

"Slowly," the man told Will as he pushed on the door. "Prop it open."

Will complied.

A woman stood there next to a dark cargo van, the back doors open. "It's about time. I think the bleeding has stopped, but Charlie's in pain."

"This doctor will fix him."

"I'm a vet, not a surgeon," Will said. "You need to take him to a hospital."

"Not an option."

"Leave him then, I'll take him myself, get him help."

"Shut up. Help my sister get him out. Now."

Will looked inside the van. A young man in his early twenties was slumped against the side of the van and the cargo inside. His dark shirt was wet with blood; someone had attempted first aid and a shirt had been folded and used as a compress. It didn't do much good—it, too, was red with blood. Will wasn't certain the man would survive even if they'd driven directly to the hospital.

Will glanced around the interior of the van. There were bloody, unlabeled boxes packed in between the kid and the front seats, three high, touching the ceiling. He couldn't tell what was in the boxes.

"He needs a hospital," Will repeated. "If you want him to live, he needs a real surgeon."

"You're going to do whatever it takes to save my brother, or I will kill you and I'll kill the first person who walks in through the door in the morning. Do you understand what I'm saying?"

Desperate people made poor decisions.

Will said, "I don't have training for this."

"Do you think I don't fucking know that? You know enough. Just get the bullet out and make him safe to travel, then we'll leave and you'll never see us again."

"Chris, Chris—where are we?" the injured man moaned.

Will had seen their faces, and now he knew the ringleaders' name. They wouldn't leave him alive.

"Getting you help, Charlie. You're going to be okay. Just be calm."

Talking to his brother, Chris had lost his violent edge. He

showed care, concern. Love? Maybe Will could use that.

"Come on, Doc," Chris said, "let's move him. Now!"

If he refused to help, he wouldn't have a chance to escape or call for help. Plus, they might search his house and find Jack. Will had to make a decision. He could bide his time until he figured a way out of this situation, and he could only do that if he tried to save this man.

"I need your help getting him out of the back," Will said.

"Gina," Chris said, motioning for her to help.

Gina. Charlie. Chris.

Will noticed Gina, too, had a gun. She handed it to Chris, who put it in his waistband.

"We need to walk him inside," Will said. "I don't have a gurney big enough for a person." He put his arm behind Charlie's back and shifted him so he could slide out of the back of the van. Charlie cried out and Gina stifled a yelp. "Get his other side. We're going to the left, the room at the end of the hall. It's the operating room. But I need you," he gestured to the gunman, "to get the gurney. It's in the storage room to the right of the operating room. The table isn't long enough for a person."

"No tricks," Chris said.

"I swear, no tricks."

"You've done surgery before, right?" Gina asked.

"On animals," he said. "I told you that. I'm a vet, not a surgeon."

"But you've performed surgery on animals?"

"Yes," he said. It was wholly different, but no matter what he said, they weren't going to listen.

As soon as they walked through the double doors, Chris closed them and followed the three to the operating room. He made a detour into the storage room and came back with the gurney.

Will needed to be alert, assess the situation and find an opportunity to run, get to the house and protect Jack, call for help. He didn't have long. His lab tech was a biology grad student at Sac State and worked six a.m. to noon. He had a key and Will wanted these people gone before David arrived.

Will and Gina half-walked, half-carried Charlie down the hall to the operating room.

The overhead light automatically came on when they walked through the door.

Will told Gina, "Put him down on the table. Get the gurney under his feet."

They positioned him, and Will opened a drawer to get scissors to cut off the man's clothes.

Chris slammed the drawer shut, nearly taking off Will's finger. "Do not make a move without telling me!"

Will stared at him. The man was his height—six feet—slender, agitated. "Do you want me to save him or not?"

"You tell Gina what to get and she'll get it."

"This isn't going to work."

"Yes it is!"

"If I have to cut into him to get out the bullet, you want your sister to do that?"

Chris's lip quivered and he swore under his breath. "I'm watching you," he said. "Don't fuck with me, I'm not in the mood."

Will slowly retrieved the scissors. Charlie was pale, he'd lost a lot of blood, and Will feared he'd go into shock or worse, bleed out.

"Can you give him something for the pain?" Gina asked. "I mean, if you're going to cut into him, he needs something! What about anesthesia?"

"I have an animal anesthesiologist who comes in when I have a surgery. It's a very precise practice, and I have no one to monitor him or his vitals. I wouldn't even know the dosage for a grown man. If you don't want to take him to the hospital to do this right, then this is the best I can do."

"What about blood?"

"I don't have human blood here!" He was getting frustrated over and above his concern about what these people would do to him or Jack, if their brother died. He thought about his options, came up with one idea that might work. "I need to prep him. I'll put a saline drip in him for fluids, and I can put some pain killers in there. It'll take the edge off, but it's not going to knock him out. He might pass out though, so don't be surprised if he loses consciousness. And we're going to have to tie him down, because he could fight me."

Will was torn. It was unethical for him to perform surgery on a human, but they weren't going to take Charlie to the hospital, which meant if Will did nothing, he would definitely be dead.

He didn't know if he could save him. The man had lost a lot of blood.

"Do it," Chris said through clenched teeth.

"You need my keys. The room across from the storage room where you found the gurney is locked. The saline is in the small refrigerator. It's temperature controlled, but not cold. Bring a large bag from the bottom shelf."

"Okay."

"And," Will continued, "the smallest key on my keyring goes to the medicine cabinet. On the third shelf from the top are vials of pain relievers. Bring two labeled 'lidocaine.'"

"Is it safe?" Gina asked.

Now Will was getting angry. "It's the strongest pain medication I have here that I can inject into his saline drip. *Safe?* Safer than me doing surgery at all!"

"Don't yell at her."

"You don't want to do the right thing; we'll do the next best thing. I don't want anyone to die."

"Gina," Chris said, "you get the supplies. I don't trust him."

Gina left the room. Will turned back to his patient. Charlie was conscious, but he wasn't talking, just lying on the table, his body tense, trying to be brave but shaking with pain and fear.

Will cut Charlie's shirt off. Charlie's right abdomen was a mess, but the bleeding seemed to have mostly stopped. He cleaned up the wound, sprayed disinfectant around the area. Charlie moaned, his body jerked. He started bleeding again.

"You need to be still, kid," Will said. "I need to X-ray him. I can't cut until I know exactly where the bullet is or whether there are fragments."

"Shit, if it's not one thing, it's another."

"It's computerized. But I don't usually do X-rays, my tech does. I need his folder and passwords."

"Where?"

"The front desk. A green binder. I can get it—"

Gina walked back in with the saline and the vials of lidocaine.

Chris said, "I'll do it."

"I don't know exactly where it is," Will said.

"You're staying here."

Gina put the supplies on a tray and took her gun back from Chris. "Don't think, Dr. Caldwell, that just because I'm a girl I won't shoot you."

Chris left the room. Will's hope of setting off the silent alarm faded away. He prepared the saline drip and inserted the IV into Charlie's arm. The kid barely responded.

Several minutes later Chris returned with the green binder. "This better be it," he said.

"It is."

Will had another idea to alert Britt about what was going on, but he would have to be very careful.

IV.

Dennis found a body fifteen minutes into their search, lying against the wall of a warehouse three blocks over.

"Good boy," Britt said and held the German Shepherd back.

Though the victim wasn't moving, Britt pulled her gun and said to Carl, "Gun in his waistband."

"I see it."

Carl slowly approached the man while Britt kept her eyes on his hands, looking for any movement that he was going for his weapon. Carl extracted the weapon without a response, handed it to his partner Reyes, then checked the man's pulse.

"Dead," Carl said. "At least, I don't feel a heartbeat."

Reyes said, "I called for paramedics." Cops weren't allowed to declare someone dead, even when there was no doubt.

Britt had seen dead bodies before, and this guy was gone. His chest was covered in blood, and he had what appeared to be a gunshot in his arm as well. "I'm surprised he got this far," she said.

Carl called in for the paramedics ETA, informed dispatch that the victim had no pulse, and asked for the status of the crime scene unit, then he and Britt marked off the area with crime scene tape. "I have more patrols coming, I don't want to sit on this guy for the next two hours."

"It pays to have seniority," Britt said.

Five minutes later, an unmarked car sped up and braked. Two detectives exited. "Bergstrom? The body?"

"Good to see you too, Doug."

"I rushed here as soon as I got the call. This is connected to another case I'm investigating. You're sure he's dead?"

"I'm no EMT, but he's dead."

Doug went over to inspect the body. "Well, shit."

"What's going on?" Britt asked him.

Doug glanced at her. "You are?"

"K-9 Officer Brittan Johns. Dennis found the body." She gestured to her K-9 who was sitting at attention.

"Right—I heard about Dennis. Glad he's back. Look—this is huge. That guy is Reggie Chin, runs a major prescription drug ring with his brother and two other low-lifes. The warehouse you saw? That's the biggest operation we've seen and I've been on this case for over a year. It's a multi-million dollar a year business."

"Did one of his partners whack him?" Carl asked.

"I don't know. I just came from the warehouse; it doesn't make a lot of sense. What was he doing there this late at night? We knew they had a place in Rancho Cordova, but we didn't have the location. We were narrowing it down and now this."

"Was anything taken?" Britt asked.

"I can't be positive, but I think yes—based on the other operations we've taken down, there's an entire section missing. Fentanyl. Whoever took it knew exactly what they were looking for, came in and that's all they took—the drug with the price tag."

"They knew what was there," Britt guessed.

"Yep. They knew the exact location, knew exactly what to take. Either someone inside tipped them off, or they've been casing the place. But based on the space? My best guess is they have a minimum of fifty thousand pills. That's a street value of two million dollars."

"How big of a vehicle are we looking for?"

"Each of those large plastic containers contains a thousand pills. They come in boxes of four containers, so a van could easily carry two high, maybe three wide, four back to front—twenty-four boxes, which would be nearly a hundred thousand pills. I don't think they had that volume, but they had at least half that. It's a huge score."

"And easy to sell?"

"God, yes," he said. "They'll be able to move it. And the DEA will see it once it hits the streets—they monitor the flow of drugs in different communities. But by that time, the distributors will be three, four times removed from the process."

"One of them was shot," Carl said.

"Your partner told me. I've already alerted every hospital in a one-hundred-mile radius. Every police department. We're pulling security feeds in the area—we might get lucky."

A patrol pulled up and Carl went over to assign the officer to stay on-site until the coroner arrived. Britt said to Doug, "Let me know what Dennis and I can do. We followed the blood scent here, but Dennis also hit on another trail."

"The second victim?"

"Yes. My guess is the second victim left in a vehicle. Dennis is trained to circle and sit when he loses a scent. He lost a scent right outside the facility, and since you were already there, you know that a vehicle hit the door, likely when they were escaping."

"Rear—they backed into it. I noticed some red plastic, from taillights. I added that to the BOLO, but I need a better description. I couldn't see any external security cameras on the warehouse, but there's only two directions they can go, and with the rear taillight busted, we might be able to find them. Do you want a lift back to your vehicle?"

"No, thanks—Dennis and I will walk."

Now that they had additional uniforms to guard the crime scene, Carl walked back with Britt to their patrol cars. She put Dennis in the rear and sat in the front. She reported in. Dispatch told her there were no holding calls—surprising for a Friday night, but she wasn't going to look a gift horse in the mouth. Instead, she used the time to write up the report on her on-board computer.

Maybe she'd get off-duty on time. Have breakfast with her son

Jack before he went to school. Spend a quality hour with her new husband before she went to bed and he went to work.

She smiled to herself, humming under her breath as she typed. She'd never thought she wanted to get married—she hadn't married Jack's father, they'd been in high school when she found out she was pregnant. For a long time, it had been her and Jack—and her three brothers who took every opportunity to spend time with her son, for which she was extremely grateful. But when she met Will fifteen months ago…she knew. And the rest, as they say, was history.

V.

After Will verified that the IV was functioning, he injected the pain killers into the drip and then took X-rays of the man's abdomen. On the computer he noted that the bullet hadn't fragmented. That was good. The bad? The bullet had nicked his liver.

Chris glanced at his watch. "How long?" he said.

"I don't know."

"Guess."

"An hour, at least. Probably two."

"Faster."

"I don't know exactly what I'm doing, I don't want to make things worse. Look—here—his liver was nicked. That's a problem."

"Just get the bullet out and sew him up. I have someone I can take him to once we're out of here."

"Chris," Gina said, "he'll be here."

What did that mean? Will thought. Who will be here? Another partner? Someone more dangerous? This was getting worse and worse.

"He's probably lost," Chris said. "Call him."

"I already talked to him. He's coming. We're going to swap out vehicles, get the rest of our money, then take Charlie home. Okay? Be calm. This is a set-back, but everything else is fine."

"It's *not* fine, Gina. Look at him. Look at our brother. It's serious, dammit!"

"I didn't want this to happen, but it did, and we'll deal with it." Gina was calm and cold, much calmer than Chris who was clearly worried about their injured brother. Will wondered how he could use that information.

But right now, he was more concerned about who Gina had invited to his property. He didn't like the idea of another criminal this close to Jack. What if he went to the house first? What if they used Jack as leverage? What if there was more than one? Will felt trapped, damned no matter what he did.

Will turned to the computer where the X-rays were displayed. If he could send an SOS email to Britt, she would know something was wrong. But there was no way to access his email without Chris or Gina seeing him.

He turned to Charlie, checked his vitals. The young man wasn't doing all that great, and Will feared that no matter what he did, Charlie was going to die. That angered him, because his brother and sister should care more about his life than getting caught by the police for whatever they'd done wrong.

There was a landline in his office, the break room, the lab, and of course at the main desk. The other phones—including the one in here—were internal only. But if he could get to one of those phones, dial 911 and leave the phone off the hook, someone would come.

He just didn't know how long it would take. Living out in the country, on the far eastern side of Sacramento County, response time could be upwards of fifteen minutes.

Will injected the second vial of lidocaine into the IV, and said, "Okay, it's now or never. The bullet is wedged between the bottom of his liver and his large intestine."

"I'll be watching you with that scalpel. You so much as raise it too fast, you're dead," Chris said. "Gina," he motioned toward her. "Help him. I'll cover you."

Gina scrubbed up in the sink; Will already had washed and now he put on fresh gloves. Not ideal. The room was clean, but not as sterile as a hospital.

Charlie was conscious, but the drugs had made him lethargic. Will told Gina to secure the straps over Charlie's chest and thighs. He didn't have any for his wrists, but he had used the straps with animals before, for their safety and his own.

"You have to make sure he doesn't grab my hands," Will told Chris. "He's going to feel this and I don't know how he'll react."

Chris hesitated a moment, then stepped forward.

Now or never.

Will turned the X-ray so that he could refer to it while he worked. He angled the bright ceiling light so he could clearly see what he was doing. He made an incision, his hands surprisingly steady considering everything going on around him. Charlie groaned, but didn't fight. Will didn't know if that was good, but at least he could get inside the wound and figure out what was going on.

He was worried most about internal bleeding. Even though the bullet was intact, the loss of blood was serious. Surgeons at the hospital had teams of experts who came in to assist, and Will was relying on two criminals.

Will pushed away all thoughts of the gun pointed at him; he tried to push aside his concern about Jack. He focused on the task at hand: retrieve the bullet without causing more damage.

That part turned out to be the easiest. Using a pair of long forceps, he extracted the bullet and dropped it in a stainless-steel pan on the cart next to him.

"That's great, Doc," Chris said. "Sew him up."

"There's internal bleeding," Will said through clenched teeth. He ordered Gina to take the gauze and soak up as much blood as possible. He couldn't see where the bleeding was originating.

Once the area was cleaned, he noted that several blood vessels were damaged. He needed a hemostatic agent to stop the bleeding, and if that didn't work he could suture them, but it would take longer.

He told Chris exactly where to find the membrane sheets. Chris hesitated.

"I need them to stop this bleeding. I don't have drugs to put in his IV that would do the same thing, I don't have any other way other than suturing and that's going to take time. The less time his abdomen is open, the better it is for him. Do it!"

"I got him, Chris." Gina stepped away from Will and pulled her gun, even though she had her brother's blood on her. Will didn't know whether to be angry or sad.

Chris left, and Will said, "Do not touch your brother until you scrub again."

She stared at him, eyes narrowed. He wondered if she even cared about Charlie. Chris did—Will was pretty certain about that. But this woman was callous. Calculating.

"It didn't have to be this way," he said.

"Shut *up*. I'm tired of your self-righteous bullshit."

As soon as Chris returned with the hemostatic membranes, Will tore open the packaging and applied them to the wound, holding it there.

"Are you done?" Chris asked. "Don't you have to sew him up?"

"I need to hold these here for several minutes and make sure that the bleeding stops. Then I'll stitch him up."

Gina looked at her phone. She hadn't scrubbed or relinquished her gun.

"He's here," she said.

Who was this 'he'? Will tensed, thinking of Jack, fearing the worst.

"We can't leave him alone with Charlie," Chris said with a nod toward Will.

"I'll talk to him. Get everything worked out. Just keep an eye on the vet, I don't trust him."

She tore off her gloves, tossed them in the trash, and walked out.

VI.

Jack hadn't slept all that well since Will left at two that morning, and he was just dozing when he heard a car drive down the narrow road that led to the veterinary clinic.

He didn't think much of it, because Will sometimes had emergencies at odd hours. In fact, far more often than Jack would have thought before he and his mom moved into Will's house.

He looked at his clock and moaned, then threw his arm over his eyes. 3:15 in the morning. This year had been full of changes that, after the first week of school, he was still getting used to. Last year, he walked to school. Now he had a carpool. Kevin was his best friend, so it was cool living closer to him now, but Kevin's mom worked downtown so she picked Jack up at 7:15 and dropped them off at the junior high at 7:30, thirty minutes before classes even started. Half the time, Jack didn't even get to see his mom when she got off work, which was weird. They'd had this morning routine. She'd come home and say 'good morning' and he'd tell her 'good night' and then they'd have breakfast together. He'd outgrown the humor of the comment, but he missed the comfort of the routine.

Jack liked Will, and he was glad that his mom was happy, but he was still adjusting to everything changing. A new house, different schedule, living with the smell of manure and farming and the odd quiet of the country…things just felt out of whack, which was probably why he wasn't sleeping all that well.

He didn't want to get up, but he couldn't go back to sleep. His room was stuffy, so he opened his window. It was warm outside, but at least there was a breeze.

He heard a car door close, next to the clinic. Then another.

And another.

Odd.

He looked out his window. The clinic was about a hundred yards from the house. He saw a van in the back, near the rear doors, and in the main parking area there were two SUVs parked at an odd angle. Three men were there. One stayed with the cars and two walked to the back door.

Something very weird was going on. He picked up his cell phone and called Will.

Will didn't answer.

Maybe he was doing surgery. But Jack knew he didn't do surgery without an assistant, and there were no other cars.

Jack called his mom. She almost always answered his calls, and would always call right back if she couldn't pick up, knowing he would worry.

"Jack?" she answered on the third ring. "Everything okay?"

"Will had an emergency at the clinic, a dog hit by a car, but now there are a couple SUVs out front. Three men got out, and it doesn't look right to me. Will didn't answer his phone, either."

"Hold on," she said. Jack heard her on the police radio, but couldn't hear exactly what she was saying. A minute later she came back and said, "I'm on my way. Dispatch is also sending another unit, but ETA is ten minutes. Where are you?"

"My bedroom. I can see the clinic. Two of the men went around to the van."

"What van?"

"The van that I guess the dog came in. It's next to the back door."

"Can you describe it?"

"Black, dark blue maybe. I can't see a license plate or anything, it's too far away. It's like one of those cargo vans, no windows in the back or sides."

"What time did Will go to the clinic?"

"He got the call just before two. Is everything okay, Mom?"

"I don't know. Stay in the house. Don't turn on any lights, okay? Make sure every door and window is locked."

His mom was scaring him, but he didn't say that. He didn't want her to be worried about him, too.

"I will."

"I'm on Sunrise, near the gun range. I'll be there in less than ten minutes. Call me if anything changes, but *stay in the house.*"

VII.

Will had figured out by watching and listening to Chris and Gina over the last hour that they'd stolen whatever was in the van, the boxes Will had seen earlier. Whatever they stole had led to Charlie being shot. Charlie's injury had prevented the timely delivery of the goods. Whoever Gina was meeting outside was picking up the goods, and he evidentially wasn't happy about the change in plans.

Will was angry that his clinic had become the center for these illegal activities, and he hoped that once the exchange was made, everyone would leave.

But it didn't bode well for him, because Will had seen their faces, he knew their first names, and if any of them had a record, the police would find them.

Their DNA was all over the place. Though Chris and Gina had worn gloves, Charlie's blood was on the table, floor, equipment. Didn't they realize that? But even if they did, Will feared they would choose to leave no witness.

He didn't want to die.

He said to Chris, "You brother really does need a doctor. He's stable, but he lost a lot of blood."

"He's young, he's healthy, he's going to be okay. It's not your concern."

"You can leave him here," Will said. "I'll call him an ambulance as soon as you leave."

Chris pulled Will's cell phone from his pocket. "Who's Jack?"

He turned the phone so Will could see the incoming call. The name read Jack Johns and a picture of Jack playing baseball was on the screen.

Will didn't answer right away. He didn't know what to say. The truth? A version of the truth? *I don't know* wasn't a viable answer.

"He works for me part-time, before school." It was hard to see how old Jack was from the picture, but he was clearly a young teen. "Probably telling me he's not coming in today. He does that a lot."

Will didn't know whether Chris believed him.

But more pressing were the strangers that were now here.

Will hoped that Jack didn't come to the clinic to check on him because he didn't answer the phone. He'd walk right into danger. Yet Jack was a smart kid, raised by a single mom who was a cop, so Will knew he had more common sense than most teenagers. Likely, he called Britt, and that meant Britt would call him, or was on her way here.

Will checked under the hemostatic membrane. The bleeding had stopped. Charlie was unconscious, but his vitals were okay. His blood pressure was on the low side, but not dangerously low. He wanted these people gone as soon as possible so he stitched up the incision. Charlie moaned, but his eyes remained closed.

He glued the corners together and applied a fresh bandage on top of it. He found a blanket—a dog blanket, but it was all he had—in the supply cabinet and draped it over Charlie.

As he thought about his next steps, he saw Chris look down at his phone. "Well shit. You're fucking popular at four in the morning, Doc. This your wife?"

He held out the phone and saw the picture of him and Britt on their wedding day. He was wearing a suit, not a tux, and she was wearing a simple white dress, nothing fancy. They were on the beach in Hawaii. A small wedding, just their closest friends and family.

The name read Brittan Caldwell, so he couldn't lie to Chris. Britt hadn't legally changed her name because everyone in the sheriff's department knew her as Brittan Johns and it was a pain in the ass for her to change all her certifications to a new name, but that didn't bother Will. He'd changed it in his phone because he was happy they were married.

"Yes."

"She's at the house, isn't she?"

"She's working."

"This is fucked."

"I need to answer. I texted her earlier that I had an emergency and she'll want to know—"

"No!" Chris glanced at his brother.

Charlie was regaining consciousness, but he was pale and weak. He tried to sit up and cried out.

"Stop," Will said. "You're going to bust the sutures."

Chris helped ease his brother back down. "Charlie, buddy, just lie down for a few minutes while Gina gets everything taken care of. Rest."

His movements had jostled the IV. "I need to take that out," Will said.

"Do it," Chris ordered.

"He's not in a condition to travel." Why had he even said that? He wanted them all out of here.

"Just take out the IV." Chris looked around, grabbed the lab tech's coat off the rack. "Charlie, you okay?"

"Tired. Thirsty." Charlie's voice was a whisper.

"That's the lidocaine," Will said. "He needs sleep, antibiotics, and if he develops a fever you *have* to take him to the hospital immediately. I put antibiotics in his IV, but that's not going to last." It wasn't ideal, but the antibiotics for dogs were almost the same as those for people.

Why was Will even giving them advice? They didn't care. If Chris cared about Charlie, he would have taken him to the emergency room as soon as he was shot. Hell, he could have dropped him off at the emergency room and then disappeared.

Gina was taking a long time outside, Will thought, but he didn't know exactly what she was doing. He took out the IV and bandaged his wrist.

"Lie still until you're ready to leave," Will said.

It had been nearly fifteen minutes since Gina left; why hadn't she returned? Chris kept looking at his watch, his phone, and then the door. Was he worried?

"Charlie, I'm going to check on Gina. Stay put," Chris said. "Doc, come with me." He motioned for Will to walk in front of him. "No sudden moves," he warned.

Will complied. "I don't want to die, I just want you out of here."

They walked down the hall. As they approached the back door, Will heard arguing. A female and a male. He could see lights from the thin opening in the door—Gina had propped it open with a rock, the same rock Will had often used to prop open the door, leaving about three inches of space.

Will didn't focus on the words, only the tone—but Chris had become agitated. Something had gone wrong, and that meant Will and Jack were now in more danger. Will had to get to the house, lock it down, and protect his stepson until the police arrived. Because he was pretty sure, between Jack's call and Brittan's call, that one or both would have called in the troops.

He only had one chance.

As Chris motioned for Will to turn right toward the double doors—into an even more dangerous situation—Will bolted straight down the hall, hitting the wall switch to plunge the area in darkness.

He crouched low, running practically on all fours, as he heard two gun shots. He felt no impact, but a chip from the cinderblock wall hit his cheek. He was temporarily blind from suddenly going from light to dark, but he knew this building. He reached the break room, hit the glowing red panic button on the alarm panel, and opened the side door as the shrill noise filled the night. Loud enough to wake his neighbors several acres away.

Parked right next to the door was an SUV with an armed man standing next to it. The noise and movement startled him and he raised his gun.

Will couldn't risk being shot, especially at close range. He slammed the door and bolted it. Chris was running down the hall swearing, and Will rushed to the door that led to the reception area. He wouldn't be able to get out the front—he needed his keys to unlock those doors, and Chris still had them—but if he could hide, it might bide him time.

The lights came on; Chris had found the switches.

"Dammit, Doc. You fucking idiot!"

Chris was in the break room. Will knew he couldn't see the reception from there, but Chris would quickly figure out there was another door. Will looked for a hiding place; there was no place to go. The first room next to reception was the smallest exam room, and there was a window. There might be a chance for Will to get out before Chris found him.

He had to try.

Will walked around from the reception area to the short hall. He couldn't hear anything over the alarms. He opened the door of the exam room and from the corner of his eye he saw movement. He tried to step back, but the butt of a gun came down on the back of his head and he fell to the floor.

VIII.

The piercing alarm made Lucky, Will's dog, whimper. Jack pet him behind the ears and told him it was going to be okay, but he didn't know.

He'd opened his mom's gun safe and retrieved the 9mm that he had practiced with the most. His mom had told him from a young age that if he was going to be in a house with guns, he had better know how to use them and stay safe. He didn't want to shoot anyone, but if someone tried to hurt him, he would.

So he loaded the gun and squatted next to the kitchen window, where he had the best line of sight to the clinic.

Jack was worried about Will. If the alarm went off, was that good or bad?

Jack called his mom. She answered immediately. "You okay, Jack?"

"The alarm is going off at the clinic. Will's still in there. I'm worried about him."

"Will's smart, he's not going to do anything to get himself hurt."

"But that might not matter."

"You stay in the house, Jack. Doors bolted."

"I have the nine-millimeter. I loaded it."

"Be careful. And if an officer comes to the door, keep the gun down, understand?"

"Yes, Mom."

"I'm less than two minutes out. Six cars are responding with less than five minutes ETA. Stay put," she repeated and ended the call.

IX.

Over the radio, dispatch relayed the status of each officer en route to Will's clinic. Britt was closest. She couldn't be reckless, even though her husband and son were in danger. She wanted them behind bars, all of them. Jack was scared, and she hated that her son was scared. Will was trapped, and she didn't know if he was injured. When Jack first called her, she thought maybe some gangbangers stealing ketamine, but now she wasn't so sure.

Britt informed dispatch that there was a hostage inside the clinic and gave Will's description. Her comments went out wide, and her colleagues all knew that the hostage was her new husband.

Britt sped down Dillard, but had to slow dramatically to make the left-hand turn onto Apple Street. An Elk Grove PD officer turned right behind her, coming from the opposite direction. The different departments worked well together, and she knew most everyone who overlapped her jurisdiction.

There was one long, paved driveway onto Will's property, which went from the road directly to the clinic, which was in the middle of the ten acres. The house was closer to the road. They parked their units at an angle to prevent the suspects from escaping. The two SUVs were moving; they stopped when their access was blocked off.

Britt said into her loudspeaker, "Turn off the ignition. Keep your hands where I can see them."

The vehicles stopped but no one exited. The EGPD vehicle shined a bright spotlight on the area; Britt saw no other people. Was anyone inside the clinic?

She reported her status to dispatch. The SUVs still hadn't moved, and two more police cars parked behind her. Jack had reported he'd seen three men—were they all in the SUV's? Did they have Will with them? What about the driver of the van?

Dennis was more agitated than she'd ever seen him. He must sense that this was his home, and something bad was happening here. "Down, Dennis," she commanded. "Down." If there was gunfire, she didn't want a stray bullet to hit him. He laid down in the back of the Bronco, his head up, ears at attention, fully alert and waiting for her orders.

She got out of her Bronco, gun drawn, but stayed behind her vehicle to protect herself. The Elk Grove officer—Johnny, she remembered, from a call they answered together last year—did the same.

Britt's sergeant, Tommy O'Donnell, was in one of the two patrol cars behind her. He also got out and approached her. "We're blocking off Dillard Road, SWAT is being mobilized. Do we know anymore of what's going on?"

"Just what Jack called in," Britt said. She glanced toward the house; she couldn't help it. It was her son in there. He'd better be keeping himself safe and out of any potential line of fire. "Will's in the clinic, has been since just before two in the morning. He didn't answer Jack's call or mine. I don't know if he's alive."

"Don't think that way, Britt. Let's focus on what we know. Jack said the two SUV's arrived after the van?"

"Yes, about ninety minutes after Will went to the clinic."

The two SUVs still hadn't moved. Two officers who had circled around the far side of the clinic reported that no one was outside the building, but the interior lights were on.

Now that Tommy was here, he was in charge as the highest ranking officer. Two more police cars pulled in, giving them six cars and nine officers total by Britt's count, plus two vehicles blocking the intersection of Dillard Road and Apple.

Tommy took Britt's microphone and said via the loudspeaker, "This is the Sacramento County Sheriff's Department. No one needs to get hurt here. Exit your vehicles with your hands up. I repeat, this is the Sacramento County Sheriff's Department. We have deputies surrounding the property. Slowly exit your vehicles, keep your hands up and visible. I repeat, keep your hands visible."

Surprisingly, or maybe because of the show of manpower, doors opened. Four men total exited the two SUVs. They complied with Tommy's instructions as he told them to kneel and put their hands behind their head, fingers interlocked.

It was still a sensitive situation because they didn't know whether the people inside the clinic were a threat or in the position to fire on them, but at this angle and distance, with the SUVs between the clinic and the police, if there was gunfire they were covered.

Tommy ordered his deputies to take the men into custody.

"How do you want to do this?" Britt asked Tommy. "Dennis is ready."

"Are you?"

"Yes."

She knew what he was asking—was she ready since her husband was likely a hostage? Tommy wouldn't tell her to stand down; they'd worked together for years and trusted each other.

Suddenly, the alarm stopped, the silence cutting through the night. Her ears were ringing; she picked up the sound of barking dogs from neighboring farms and the crow of a rooster.

"What happened?" she asked.

"Dispatch worked with the alarm company. No one will be able to hear us with that blasted thing going off."

They let their hearing adjust to the silence, then Tommy said,

"SWAT is on their way because of the hostage situation, but I don't like that we don't know what's going on here. Any idea who those people are?"

Britt shook her head. "According to Jack, Will had a call before two a.m. of a dog hit by a car. He met the driver at the clinic. But why these goons? They arrived later."

Tommy had no better idea than she did. "We can wait for SWAT, but they're still twenty minutes out, or I can try to get a dialogue going. Your call."

She didn't want that responsibility. If she was wrong—it was Will's life on the line. Yet…delaying for SWAT was the smart move. If they did nothing, whoever originally called Will might get antsy, and she didn't want to further risk her husband. They didn't know how many people were in the clinic, whether Will was injured or even still alive, or why they'd come here in the first place. It wasn't as if this clinic was on a main thoroughfare.

"Talk to them," she said. "Let's keep things calm and get more information for SWAT."

"Agreed," Tommy said. He announced over the loudspeaker. "To the people in Wilton Veterinary Clinic. This is Sergeant Thomas O'Donnell with the Sacramento County Sheriff's Department. I'm going to call into the clinic. Please answer the phone so we can discuss this situation."

Tommy called the direct number of the clinic. It rang multiple times and no one answered. He ended the call, said to Britt, "Get Dennis. We might need him." He waited ten seconds, then called again.

X.

"Answer the phone," Will said.

Chris had forced him to sit in a chair and zip tied his hands and ankles together. His head ached from where he'd been hit, but Will took heart that he was alive, even though his head ached from both the blaring alarm and being coldcocked.

"Shut up," Gina said.

"We're screwed," Chris muttered.

"I have a plan."

"I've had enough of your fucking plans, Gina! We should *never* have agreed to this job. It was fucked from the beginning."

"We have a quarter million dollars in cash." She patted a briefcase she had collected from the men. "They were going to balk about paying, but I got it before the shit hit the fan. If you hadn't panicked, we would have been fine."

"You were arguing with them. How was I to know they weren't going to shoot you, take the drugs, and keep their money?"

"Because I know what I'm doing, and I know Stanley. He always wants to renege or renegotiate terms, but never does. I just have to play the game with him. With this money, we can disappear for a while."

"We're never getting out of here, Gina!"

After a brief silence, the phone started ringing again.

"Listen," she said, "we go to the van. With the vet. Tell the cops to let us go or he's dead."

"That's a bad idea."

"It's a *good* idea. They're not going to stop us if we have a hostage. We drive away, dump him in the middle of nowhere, and disappear."

"They will never agree."

Gina grabbed the phone off the wall. "What?"

Will couldn't hear what the cop said, he only heard a male voice. Then Gina said, "This is the plan, Sergeant O'Donnell. We're leaving. We're taking the vet with us. You don't let us pass; his blood will be on your hands. Understand? This isn't up for negotiation." She hung up. "There, Chris, I took care of it. Let's go."

"This is a stupid ass idea."

"Do you have a better one?"

Chris swore a blue streak, but didn't offer another solution.

"You and the vet get Charlie. Put him in the back of the van, climb in with him. I'll come right behind you, slip into the driver's seat, it's a narrow space between the building and the van. And we'll go."

"What if the road is blocked?"

"We have a hostage!"

"I don't think this is going to work."

"It *will* work. Trust me."

"I trusted you one time too many. We should never have taken this job."

"Screw you, Chris. This is the best job we've had in over a year. Paid a hell of a lot more than any job you've come up with."

"No one has been shot on my jobs!"

Gina ignored her brother and cut the zip ties that held Will's ankles together. "Up. I'm not in the mood to argue with anyone."

The phone started ringing again. Gina ignored it.

"The police aren't going to let you walk away," Will said.

"Shut up," Gina said. "You started this—they're here because you set off the alarm."

"They're here because your brother didn't let me answer the call from my wife."

"Just get Charlie. We're doing this *now*."

Will looked at Chris, but the man avoided meeting his gaze. Chris walked over to Charlie and helped him sit up. Charlie moaned. "Come up, buddy," Chris said. "We're going home."

"Gina," Charlie said, groggy, his voice pained. "Maybe...maybe we just give ourselves up. Trade information—we know stuff. Stuff that would help the police. Reduce our sentence. I mean, it's an idea."

"That's a great idea," Will said.

"Shut the fuck up, Doc," Gina said. "Charlie, you're tired and worried and hurting. I get that. But we just had our biggest score in *years*. We're not turning ourselves in. And don't you remember? The cops are going to figure out what we hit and realize I shot a man. That's not going to get me five years—and I don't want to go to jail again."

Again? That explained a lot, Will thought.

Chris said, "I'll take Charlie myself. Gina, you get the doc, use him as your shield. I don't want you hurt. I don't want anybody hurt."

Gina pulled Will up from the chair and pushed him ahead of

her, down the hall, holding his waistband, her gun at his lower back. His hands were still zip tied. Will knew he would only get one chance to run, and that was when they stepped outside. He couldn't let himself be taken away. He had to get out, get free, give the police time to take them down.

They turned toward the loading doors. "Open the door slowly," Gina told him. "Then open the back of the van. Nothing funny, I will shoot you."

"The police will fire back. You have to know that."

"But you'll be dead."

"So will you. You should listen to your brothers."

She jammed the barrel of the gun into his side so hard he grunted. "Do what I say."

It was still early in the morning. The police were here. He just had to find a way to get out of Gina's line of fire as soon as he opened the door. Chris was helping his brother, he wouldn't be able to quickly get off a shot—and Will didn't think he wanted to risk his brother's life. There was tension and a difference of opinion between the siblings, but could Will count on that?

Maybe going with them was the best way to get out of danger. They'd drop him off by the side of the road somewhere. He'd be able to get help then.

He was tense, on alert for any sign of what the police might do.

"Open the door," Gina said as she poked him. "Slowly. Carefully."

He pushed it open as she instructed. He saw movement on both sides.

As soon as the door was all the way open, bright lights shined on them from every direction.

Gina's grip disappeared and the pressure on his side lessoned as she put her hand up to shield her eyes.

XI.

Britt and Johnny were on the south side of the clinic. She watched as the doors slowly opened. She had Dennis's release in her fingers.

He was at attention, knowing that this was his big moment. This was what he had trained for.

Will came out first, but a woman had a firm hold on him and it appeared that there was a gun in her right hand, aimed at Will's back. Two men were behind them, only partly visible in the opening.

"Now!" her sergeant said on the comm. Simultaneously, the spotlights atop every police car—that they had moved into place after the call—turned on.

Blinded, the woman brought up her hands to shield her eyes at the same time as Britt released Dennis.

Will dropped to the ground as soon as he felt Gina let him go.

"Gun gun gun!" Britt said to her K-9.

Dennis ran directly toward Gina and Will.

Will didn't move, and for a split-second Britt feared he'd been shot even though she hadn't heard anything.

In two seconds, Dennis reached the suspect and latched his strong jaws around the woman's right wrist. She screamed in pain and the gun fell from her grip. She waved her arm around, trying to force Dennis to release his grip, but that only made him hold on tighter.

Through the loudspeaker, her sergeant said, "Hands up! Drop your weapon! Do it do it do it!"

Will stayed down.

"I'm surrendering!" a man shouted from the doorway. "I'm throwing out my gun!"

"Hands up!"

"I'm holding my brother. He's injured. Please—"

"Hands up now! Do it!"

As Britt watched, the man who tossed his gun put the man he was supporting down on the ground, then he put his hands in the air.

Britt rushed over to Dennis, Johnny right behind her. "Dennis, off! Off!" she ordered.

Dennis released the woman's wrist. She was on the ground, screaming in pain, and immediately put her hand to her chest. Johnny cuffed her as she cried while spewing choice curses at all of them; four other officers rushed them to take the other two men into custody.

Britt put Dennis back on his leash and squatted next to Will. "Are you injured? Are you okay?"

"I'm okay," he said as he sat up.

"You're bleeding."

"Just got hit on the head. I'm okay. Really. Good boy, Dennis." Britt hugged her husband as relief flooded through her.

Her sergeant came over to them. "I'll need to get a statement from you, Dr. Caldwell."

"Yeah. Of course. Can you give me a couple minutes?"

"And let's talk at the house?" Britt said. "I want to check on Jack."

"Of course." O'Donnell looked at his watch. "I'll make sure these three are secure, then I'll be up there in ten."

"That man," Will gestured to Charlie who was slumped in the doorway, "needs an ambulance. They forced me to perform surgery on him, gunshot wound to the abdomen. He's stable, but he needs medical attention."

"Ambulance is already on its way," O'Donnell said.

Britt walked with Will and Dennis to the house. The woman behind them was screaming lawsuit, but the men were silent. Britt blocked everything out. Everything except her husband, her dog... and her son, as he opened the door and ran out to hug them all.

"You had us scared," Britt told Will as the three of them—four, including Dennis—walked into the house.

"I was scared, but I was also angry. That got me through." Will squatted and looked at Dennis. "Thanks, Dennis. You're a good boy. A very good boy."

"You spoil him," Britt said, her voice cracking.

"He deserves it. How'd you get here so fast?" Will asked. "I expected at least fifteen minutes after the alarm went off."

"Jack called me when he saw two SUVs drive up. I was on Sunrise investigating a break-in at a warehouse and a homicide—so I got here fast. And my case was a break-in and shooting—a million dollars of illegal prescription drugs stolen from an industrial park off Gold Center Drive. We recovered them here, in the SUVs. Tommy's guess is that the three who came to the clinic were hired to steal them for a dealer named Stanley Boske, who's now in custody."

"Whatever they stole, that guy paid them a quarter million."

"One of them killed a man. He was a dealer, but it's still murder," Britt said.

"Gina. They talked a lot during the last couple of hours."

"Shhh. You'll give your statement, but for now, I'm considering both cases solved."

She kissed Will, then kissed her son. "If anything had happened to either of you…"

"It didn't," Jack said, hugging first his mom, then Will.

Will hugged both of them in a family hug. That was just what she needed. Then Will gave Dennis his favorite treat, from a jar on the kitchen counter. Lucky came up behind Dennis, so Will tossed him a treat, too.

"Thank you for saving my life, Dennis," Will said and scratched him behind the ears.

Britt shivered, grateful that what could have ended in bloodshed had ended without a shot fired. "You saved his life a year ago," Britt told Will. "I'm grateful to both of you." Then she looked at him, trying to frown, but just so happy that the two men she loved—and her dog—were alive and well. "We're going to have to talk about your security procedures, Dr. William Caldwell."

"Tomorrow, okay? Today I'm just going to be grateful for my family. You, Jack, and our dogs."

***

I'VE GOT YOUR NUMBER

ISABELLA MALDONADO

Fairfax County police officer Nina Guerrera had spent the past four years working toward this moment. If her meeting with the sergeant went well, she would leave the McLean District station in a marked patrol car by herself for the very first time.

"Stay here, Guerrera," Sergeant Conrad said to her as the rest of her squad filed out of the roll call room.

Jim Pascal, one of the veteran officers, lingered in the doorway. "I don't know, Sarge," Pascal said over his shoulder. "Maybe Guerrera needs a few more months before you take the training wheels off."

She raised her ticket book to hide her hand from their supervisor and flipped Pascal off. She heard his laugh as the door closed behind him. Pascal, always the jokester, was one of her favorite officers on the squad.

She had decided on a career in law enforcement when she was seventeen years old, earning a bachelor's in criminal justice from George Mason University at twenty-one. She spent the following six months in the police academy and three months after that riding with a field training instructor who scrutinized everything she did. After all that instruction, she felt nervous, but ready to go it alone.

Sergeant Conrad regarded her from behind the roll call desk. In his early fifties, he had a reputation as a curmudgeon. She had been told the captain sometimes moved problem officers to Conrad's squad where they would either up their game or lose their badge.

"Two things I won't tolerate," he began without preamble. "Laziness and stupidity." He paused for emphasis. "In that order."

He eyed her as if trying to determine whether she showed any signs of either unforgivable sin.

She nodded but offered no response. She would have to prove herself over time.

"I'm putting you in area 310 today," Conrad said. "That will be your beat until further notice."

The department's jurisdiction of over a million residents was divided into eight patrol areas, and the McLean district, which served 180,000 residents and covered 44 square miles, was subdivided into five sectors. She wasn't surprised at her assignment. Rookie officers were usually designated to patrol Langley and Great Falls where the elite lived in mega mansions. Low crime but high maintenance.

"Something else you need to know before you hit the street," the sergeant continued. "I'll be watching you closely to see what number you are."

"Number?"

"What kind of cop you're going to be." Conrad held up his hand, index finger extended. "Group number one follows orders. They make my life easier."

She leaned forward, intrigued.

"The second group is the one that gives me heartburn," Conrad said, raising another finger. "They challenge authority at every turn. Don't be part of group number two."

She thought about her squad. Jim Pascal fit into the second category, but he had managed to earn everyone's respect.

"Every officer starts off in group one." Conrad narrowed his eyes. "Which is where you should stay if you want to get ahead. Keep that in mind, Guerrera."

Thirty minutes later, Nina craned her neck to peer at the dead man behind the wheel of a Mercedes Benz convertible. The paramedics who had rushed to the scene were packing up their equipment. Nothing in their bags would do any good. The driver had been shot in the head three times before his car plowed head-on into the trunk of a massive oak tree.

Conrad stood beside her. "DRT."

Nina straightened. "Come again, sir?"

He gestured toward the EMTs, who were climbing into the ambulance. "When someone dies on the way to the hospital, that's a DOA. Dead on arrival." He turned back to the crumpled car. "When they don't even make a transport, it's because he's DRT. Dead right there."

She wasn't familiar with most of the cop slang yet, and had a lot to learn, as her boss apparently wanted to remind her.

Within two minutes of hitting the street, her Mobile Data Terminal screen lit up with a dispatch to a car crash. What the MDT had initially categorized as a single vehicle accident had quickly morphed into a homicide investigation.

After Nina updated the dispatcher, her sergeant had turned up at the scene to ensure his newly minted rookie officer handled things properly.

"Homicide's on the way," he said to her. "There's been an increase in road rage incidents lately. My guess is this one got out of hand."

Nina had given it thought while she strung up the yellow police tape to hold back the looky-loos who had wandered out of their houses in their slippers and bathrobes earlier. "I'm not so sure."

Conrad's dark brows snapped together. "And you've come to this conclusion because?"

"I ran the license plate number," she said. "The car is registered to a Steven Hargrave." She jerked her thumb over her shoulder. "He lives about a quarter of a mile away on Willard Place." The crash had occurred on Woodhurst Boulevard in a residential area filled with sprawling colonial homes, manicured lawns, and long driveways.

"Did you make a comparison with his driver's license photo?" he asked her.

Conrad was taking no chances, making sure she had performed every preliminary step.

"Yes, sir." Fighting a wave of nausea, she had carefully inspected what was left of the driver's face and spotted distinguishing features despite the gore. "It's Hargrave."

An ME would make it official with a death certificate, but an initial ID based on a photograph was sufficient to start an investigation.

"Woodhurst Boulevard is a quiet side street," she continued. "Don't road rage incidents occur on freeways or major roadways?"

"Usually," Conrad allowed. "But someone could have followed him here from the toll road."

No supervisor would expect to hear a different assessment from a slick-sleeve private fresh out of the academy, least of all Conrad.

She tried to think of a way to respectfully disagree.

"Sir, the call came out at oh-seven-hundred hours," she began. "Judging by the files that flew all over the inside of the car from his briefcase, Hargrave is an attorney."

Conrad crossed his arms. "And?"

"Since he lives here in McLean, my guess is he was on his way into court in downtown Fairfax. He wouldn't have come *from* the toll road…he was headed *toward* the toll road."

"I'll give you that," Conrad said, glancing at the car again.

Encouraged, she pointed at a bullet hole in the driver's door. "Look at the trajectory of the rounds that struck the car and the driver."

"It's a downward angle," Sergeant Conrad said. "But the shooter couldn't have fired from a higher vehicle. This is a two-lane road. A truck or SUV could not have pulled up beside the convertible."

She agreed. "Whoever shot the victim was standing beside the car when they pulled the trigger."

Sergeant Conrad gave her an appraising look. She clearly wasn't fitting into the first group of officers, but she didn't think she'd gotten into the second group yet. It seemed her supervisor might have an anomaly on his hands, and she wasn't sure he liked outliers.

Undeterred, she pressed on. "The suspect would have had to flag the convertible down somehow. There is no stop sign or traffic light here where he could lie in wait for an ambush."

"You think this was a targeted and planned execution, and the perpetrator is hiding somewhere nearby?"

"The suspect could have had a car nearby; in fact, he could have pretended to have a disabled vehicle as part of the ruse to—"

"Be sure to include your observations in your report, Guerrera." Conrad seemed to have heard enough from her. "Homicide detectives will be here any minute. I'll pass on your…theory."

She understood herself to be dismissed and walked back to her cruiser. The bizarre circumstances continued to nag at her as she got behind the wheel. Instead of plugging her key into the ignition, she retrieved a digital camera from her equipment bag on the front passenger seat and got out again.

Conrad was standing by the side of the road talking on his cell phone with his back to her when she walked past him. Camera in hand, she stood next to the convertible and leaned forward to photograph the interior. She snapped extra pictures of the black leather briefcase which had popped open and dumped its contents. Next, she focused on a jumbled pile of Hargrave's business cards, which were strewn across the floorboard like confetti.

She caught her supervisor striding toward her from the corner of her eye and hurriedly clicked several photos in rapid succession.

Conrad didn't bother to hide his annoyance as he disconnected from his call. "What are you doing, Guerrera? There's a team of evidence techs on the way. It's their job to process the crime scene and take pictures, not yours."

She angled her camera's view screen to show him a close-up of a business card. "He was definitely an attorney."

"Then I guess he won't make it to court this morning, if that's where he was headed," Conrad said.

"I'll call his law firm," Nina said, sliding the camera into her pocket. "They can contact the courthouse and maybe help put us in touch with Hargrave's next of kin."

Conrad reddened. "That's up to Homicide. Don't interfere with their investigation."

Aware she had gotten on her sergeant's last nerve, she continued to press the issue. "Someone from his law firm will need to notify the court right away." She glanced at her watch. "It's past eight o'clock and court starts at nine."

Sergeant Conrad let out an exasperated sigh. "Go ahead and call." He jabbed a finger at her. "Don't reveal anything about the case and document every word of your conversation in your report."

"Yes, sir." She made her way back to her cruiser before he could change his mind and pulled out her cell phone. She tapped in the phone number from the business card.

A crisp female voice answered after the second ring. "You've reached the law offices of Hargrave and Roth. How may I help you?"

"This is Officer Nina Guerrera with the Fairfax County Police Department. May I speak to the senior partner right away?"

"Mr. Hargrave is in court this morning," the receptionist said smoothly. "Can I take a message for him?"

That answered one question. Nina tried again. "Is the other partner available?"

The receptionist must have sensed the urgency in Nina's tone and spared her further questioning. "I'll put you through to Mr. Roth."

A gravelly male voice came through the line moments later. "This is Clarence Roth, how may I help you, Officer?"

Nina chose her words carefully. She did not want to reveal that this was a homicide investigation yet, but she could not call it an accident either. "I was dispatched to a car crash in McLean. I believe your partner was driving."

"Has something happened to Steve?"

Nina needed verification before delivering the bad news. A death notification was not something to get wrong. "Does Mr. Hargrave drive a 2021 silver Mercedes Benz convertible?"

"Yes." Alarm put an edge to Roth's words. "What the hell is going on?"

"We discovered a man in the Mercedes after it crashed into a tree," she said. "His license and registration indicate he's Steven Hargrave."

Roth gasped. "Is he at the hospital? Is that why you're calling?"

She had been taught at the academy not to use euphemisms or delicate phrases that might leave room for confusion. "He's dead, sir."

After giving him time to recover from the initial shock, Nina patiently answered Roth's questions about the circumstances of his partner's death. She omitted any mention of the shooting, allowing Roth to assume Hargrave had died as a result of colliding with a tree. Homicide would inform him about that later during a formal interview. Conrad had made it clear he did not want her interfering with that process.

She had her notebook out, ready to copy down information. "Do you have the name of his spouse or significant other?"

"Steve lives alone," Roth said. "Got divorced twenty years ago and never remarried."

She wondered if the shooting had anything to do with a love triangle, then recalled the reason her sergeant had allowed her to call in the first place.

"The receptionist said Mr. Hargrave was scheduled to appear in court this morning?"

"That's right," Roth said. "He was due in Juvenile and Domestic Relations court in Fairfax for the final disposition of a child custody case."

"Could you notify the judge that he won't be able to appear?"

"Of course." A keyboard clacked in the background. "I'm pulling up his files on the server now."

While Roth researched the case, she reflected on the volatile emotions involved with family disputes. During her training, Nina had been putting handcuffs on an abusive husband when someone clobbered her on the back. She turned to see the battered wife wielding a pot she'd grabbed from the kitchen sink. After helping Nina put both parties under arrest, her field training instructor had cautioned her about domestic violence cases in which *anyone* could pose a threat.

"I found the documents for this morning's case," Roth said, interrupting her thoughts. "I've got the judge's name right here. I'll go down the witness list and tell each of them we're going to request a continuance."

Before she could respond, a long tone sounded over her radio. She froze. Every officer knew to stop whatever they were doing and listen up after hearing the emergency signal.

"All units, report of shots fired at 5555 Parrell Avenue in area 330," the dispatcher said. "One subject is down. The suspect is described as a white male, average height and build, approximately forty-years-old, wearing dark clothing. Last seen fleeing on foot. No known direction of travel."

"I've got to go," Nina said into the phone and disconnected. Patrol area 330 was not her assigned beat, but all available officers in the McLean district would be expected to respond to the scene of an active shooter. As she wove her way around other vehicles toward Route 123, she flicked a glance at the address on her MDT.

The address sounded familiar, but she couldn't place it. The numbers 5555 were unusual, and she felt certain she had seen them recently. Very recently.

An instant later, recognition dawned. She pulled over to the shoulder to grab her digital camera again. Clicking through the photos she had taken of the papers that had scattered onto the seat and floor of the crumpled convertible, she finally found the one she wanted. Holding her breath, she zoomed in.

"Bingo," she muttered under her breath as she spotted 5555 Parrell Avenue on the witness list. The name, DR. JOSHUA DANNON, was printed above the address. She read that Dr. Dannon was the psychiatrist who examined the seven-year-old child involved in the custody dispute Roth had mentioned to her on the phone.

Hargrave was representing Grace Foley, who was petitioning for full custody of seven-year-old Timothy, without any visitation rights for the father, Kevin Foley. A documented pattern of abuse and violence had been cited as the reason for the filing.

Nina checked her MDT to see that her sergeant had cleared the homicide scene and was on his way to Parrell Avenue. She called his cell phone.

"Sergeant Conrad." Traffic noise in the background indicated he was on his Bluetooth.

"Sarge, I think I know what's going on."

"What are you talking about, Guerrera?" He sounded harried.

"The shooting on Parrell Avenue, it's—"

"That's where I'm headed right now. I don't have time to talk."

She spoke quickly before he could disconnect. "I think I know where the shooter may be going next."

"Guerrera, I'm trying to set up perimeters to contain an armed suspect. If you know something, spit it out now or get off the phone."

"I spoke to Hargrave's partner. He's representing a woman involved in a child custody dispute with her ex. Witness number one on his list for today's hearing is a psychiatrist named Joshua Dannon who works at 5555 Parrell Avenue."

"What is your point, Guerrera?"

She laid it out in no uncertain terms. "I believe the father is the shooter and that if we don't act quickly, his ex-wife will be next."

"We have two separate crimes on opposite sides of the district with zero evidence they're related," Conrad said in clipped tones.

"You can theorize later, right now I need to prioritize the one thing we do know…which is that an active shooter is on the loose."

When she started to object, Conrad cut her off. "We don't even know if the psychiatrist is the victim in Dunn Loring, and even if he is, that doesn't mean the cases are connected."

"But if they are, the only one left on the list is Hargrave's client. It wouldn't hurt to send someone to check on her."

"I have all available resources deployed on a manhunt. Stay in service and catch radio calls in your patrol area while I set up a perimeter."

Conrad didn't even want her to respond to the second shooting. Effectively sidelined, she made one more attempt. "The ex-wife lives in Pimmit Hills in area 320, I can slide by on my way back to 310."

"I am well aware of where Pimmit Hills is," he said. "I'll pass your theory on to Homicide and they can look into it. In the meantime, I'm ordering you to go straight back to—"

She made a crackling sound and disconnected. Technically, he hadn't been able to say the magic words. Disobeying a direct order constituted insubordination, which could cost her the shiny new badge she had worked so hard to get. Cutting off the call was thin cover, but she'd take whatever she could.

Still in the parking lot, she glanced at the witness list again. Grace Foley lived at 2424 Madrigal Court. Hoping her supervisor was too busy running the scene at the psychiatrist's office to check her status, she pulled onto the road and started for Pimmit Hills.

She used her Bluetooth to call the law firm again as she drove. The receptionist, who sounded as if she'd been crying, put her through to Roth again.

"Did you reach Grace Foley?" she asked him after a brief greeting.

"I talked to her after I spoke to the Clerk of the Court," he said. "Told her she could go home, and I'd be in touch with a new court date."

Nina wanted to warn her directly. "Could you give me Ms. Foley's number?"

"Let me call her back on the other line," Roth said. "I can connect you."

She wasn't sure whether Roth was uncomfortable providing privileged client information or if he simply wanted to listen in, but she had no time to debate.

"She's not answering," Roth said a minute later. "Should I leave a message?"

"Tell her to lock her doors and to call me immediately." She rattled off her cell number. "And keep trying to reach her until you get through." She disconnected before he could ask more questions.

She found Madrigal Court within ten minutes and scanned the numbers on the mailboxes. Grace Foley's home would be on the left side of the street near the cul-de-sac. Nina parked her cruiser a few houses down and marked herself out at Foley's address on the MDT. She got out and made her approach using trees and hedges for cover.

The driveway was empty, and the garage had no windows. No way to tell if Grace Foley was home. Or if she had a visitor.

After a quick check of the perimeter and a minute listening for sounds of a disturbance inside, Nina knocked on the front door.

A slender woman inched the door open a crack, peeked out, and sucked in air. "Where is Timmy? Did something happen at school?"

Nina was still getting used to the reaction people had when a uniformed police officer appeared on their doorstep. More often than not, they immediately assumed someone dear to them had been hurt or died.

"I'm Officer Guerrera with the Fairfax County police. Are you Grace Foley?"

The color drained from the woman's face as she nodded.

Nina did her best to put the woman's fears to rest. "I'm not here about Timmy. I'm here about your ex-husband."

The woman's pale face registered shock. "Kevin? What's he done now?"

"I'd rather not discuss this outside, Ms. Foley." She didn't add that they were exposed to potential gunfire.

"Call me Grace." She stepped aside and opened the door wider. "We can talk inside. Can I get you some coffee?"

Nina followed her into a freshly remodeled kitchen. "No, thank you."

Morning sun splashed in through a picture window in the breakfast nook occupied by a circular maple table.

"Have you heard about your attorney?" Nina asked gently.

"Yes, his partner told me," Grace said. "So horrible what happened. I can't imagine…wait…do you think Kevin had something to do with it?" Her eyes widened. "Is that why you asked about him?"

Nina dodged the question by posing one of her own. "How was Dr. Joshua Dannon involved in your case?"

"He interviewed Timmy," Grace said, distracted. "His assessment was crucial in my getting full custody."

Nina wondered whether a deranged father might see this as grounds for revenge. "Has Kevin ever been violent?"

Grace nodded vigorously. "That's why I left him." A red scald crept up her neck and into her cheeks. "He used to beat me. One time Timmy tried to get in the way, and Kevin hit him. That was the last straw. That's also why I got custody."

"Does your ex-husband own a firearm?"

Another nod from Grace. "He has five or six guns. He turned one of them in after the judge ordered him to after the trial last year…but he kept the others even though he wasn't supposed to."

People convicted of domestic assault were not allowed to keep guns. Nina wondered why Grace hadn't turned him in for that violation but decided to focus on what was going on today.

"Do you have any reason to believe he would harm—" Nina's words were cut off by the sound of a gunshot followed by the shattering of glass.

She grabbed Grace and threw her to the tile floor. Ducking down beside her, Nina yanked her Sig Sauer from its holster as another round punched a second hole through the window, slamming into the cabinet directly behind the space where her head had just been.

Nina pulled the kitchen table over onto its side, providing cover as she shouted over the cacophony of noise to order Grace to crawl out of the line of fire. Grateful she had taken the time to mark out on an investigation at Grace's address, she tapped the transmit button on her portable radio. "Three ten baker, signal thirteen."

Following her distress call, the dispatcher proceeded to broadcast the long emergency tone for the second time that morning. "Channel is ten-three. All available units respond to 2424 Madrigal Court. Three ten baker, what is your situation?"

Nina peered over the edge of the table but could not see the shooter. "I'm with the homeowner inside the house. Unknown subject is shooting at us through the kitchen window."

The dispatcher rattled off more questions as her fellow officers responded to her location. She tuned out the noise and concentrated on the immediate threat. When a round splintered the wooden table, she scrambled backward to join Grace, who had retreated to the family room where she crouched behind a sofa. Aware that upholstered furniture offered no real protection, Nina did a quick scan to locate proper cover.

Most Pimmit Hills homes were built after WWII to answer the need for housing for returning GI's who wanted to raise families in close proximity to the nation's capital. They were one-story bungalows on concrete slabs with no basements. This house had been remodeled and now had a second floor, but a basement was still unlikely.

Nina spotted a door at the back of the room. "Where does that lead?"

Grace followed her gaze. "To the mud room that's connected to the garage."

"Is the door into the garage solid?"

"Y-yes."

"Go into the mud room and lock the door," Nina told her. "I'll come for you when it's safe."

Grace bit her lip. "What are you going to do?"

"I'm going to draw his fire and keep him busy in the front of the house."

If this was indeed Kevin Foley, he was mentally unstable, fueled by rage, and on a mission. Nina didn't want to tell Grace to make a run for it in case he decided to try to get inside through the garage. Kevin would know the layout of the house, including all entry and exit points.

Nina relayed this information over the radio while she watched Grace disappear into the mud room. She also mentioned that Grace's ex could be the suspect and provided his description.

The sound of splintering wood drew her eyes to the front door. The shooter had moved away from the kitchen window and was trying to get into the house through the main entrance. The doorjamb began to fissure as cracks formed in the drywall surrounding the frame.

Nina took up a position behind a corner in the hallway, aimed her sights at the front door, and waited.

Time stretched as she became aware of radio traffic again. She heard members of her squad announce their approach. The closest was still one minute out. Might as well be an hour.

The front door crashed in, slamming against the wall.

She eased the slack out of the trigger and trained her sights on the burly figure bursting into the foyer. "Police, don't move!"

He darted behind the door and bellowed, "Where is she? Where is Grace?"

Nina's hand was rock steady. "Drop your weapon and lie face down on the ground."

"I'm not stopping until she's dead. If you want to join her, that's fine with me."

Wanting his attention on her, she went with her assumption and called him by name. "Kevin, no one else needs to get hurt—including you. Lay down your gun and—"

A barrage of wild shots interrupted her, demolishing the sofa, two paintings, and a floor lamp. Nina had made a rough count of how many times he'd fired and realized he must have reloaded with a fresh magazine. How much ammo did he have?

"Let's do this." Kevin advanced into the room, moving forward as he pulled the trigger in rapid-fire succession.

Bullets flew everywhere. A round hit the mud room door and Grace screamed.

Nina cursed under her breath as he changed course and made a beeline for the source of the noise. Seeking to divert him again, she called out from behind cover. "Drop your weapon, Kevin." She repeated her previous command with more force. "Do it now."

He halted and turned toward her; his bulbous eyes traveled up and down her petite frame. He pivoted to take aim at her.

The crack of a pistol split the air, followed by the thud of a body hitting the floor. Nina lowered her Sig Sauer and rushed forward to kick the gun from Kevin's limp hand. An instant later, a flurry of boots pounded into the house amid shouts from her fellow officers.

As the others fanned out to secure the house, she dropped to her knees to check his vitals.

Nothing.

Giving chest compressions to someone who had a gaping hole in the center of his sternum would not help without direct pressure on the wound, but before she aided Kevin, there was a more urgent concern.

She stood and walked to the mud room. One round had penetrated the door. No sound had come from behind it after Grace's scream. Had Kevin's bullet found its mark?

"Grace?" Nina leaned close to the door. "It's Officer Guerrera, let me in."

The knob twisted and Grace peered out through the cracked door.

"Are you hurt?" Nina asked her.

Grace lurched forward and flung her arms around Nina's neck. "I'm okay." She pulled back. "What about Kevin? Is he…is he… dead?"

Nina glanced over her shoulder to see paramedics taking over from the officers who were administering first aid. "I don't know, but he's not in a position to hurt you now."

"He's insane," Grace whispered. "But I never thought he would go this far."

Sergeant Conrad stepped past the broken door to survey the scene. He zeroed in on her and made his way through the living room.

"A word," he said to her without inflection.

"Can you wait here a minute?" Nina disengaged from Grace's grip. "I'll be back to take care of you."

Grace leaned past her to speak to Conrad. "Sir, this officer saved my life. I would be dead right now if…." Her hand flew to her mouth and her shoulders shook with silent sobs.

"It's okay, Grace," Nina said to her. "I'll be right in the kitchen if you need me."

Nina followed her supervisor through the family room and into the kitchen, making sure to block the grisly scene from Grace's view as she closed the door behind her.

Conrad dropped his voice. "First, are you okay, Guerrera?"

"I'm fine."

He straightened. "Second, what the hell was that stunt with the dropped phone call?"

She arranged her features into a look of confusion. "Stunt, sir?"

His responding glare told her he didn't buy her act. "You knew I was about to give you a direct order to get back to your patrol area just before the line mysteriously disconnected."

She kept her expression blank. "I have no idea what you're talking about."

She sensed she was about to find out what group of officers her sergeant had slotted her into. Clearly, she did not belong in group one, where officers followed orders without question. She was not the type who would make his life easy.

"Right, Guerrera," Conrad finally said, the ghost of a smile playing on his lips. "I've got your number."

***

EIGHT YEARS AND SEVEN SECRETS AT TEN STACKS

A Ghost Story

SHANNON KIRK

It is ironic that the most banal of secrets often prove most dangerous. This trick of irony, the oldest joke of dead souls to play on the living, is possible due to the fact that secrets are relative to the holder. In the collective, however, could a cluster of banal secrets prove fatal? And just how many banal secrets would weigh enough to tip banality to fatality? Siritas Wretch is about to find out.

Siritas, who goes by Siritas in his mind and Sir to others, stands on the grand, gray porch of Ten Stacks Inn. Established in 1790, and remodeled with wings added over the centuries, it is the greatest in size and most gothic in setting of all the New England antiquarian inns with complex halls and hidden passages. New Hampshire, Lakes Region, high on a hill, taking up the entire eight hundred feet of frontage on the good end of Suncook Lake.

A loon cry cuts Siritas' concentration on a giant oak to the side of Ten Stacks' covered porch. Wind pushes all thirty of the porch's empty, white rocking chairs, which creak on the gray planks. Siritas stalls, questioning how he hears the wind, for he swears words are coiled within, whispering in his ear as a gust moves his hair, "So glad you came; so glad you listened." He shakes away the illogical perception of wind talking to him, welcoming him to this old inn.

The loon flies off the surface of the lake, and Siritas returns his concentration on the oak to the side of the porch, where his gaze lingers and his mind wanders. The trunk is as wide as a tire on the *Le Torneau* front-end loader, the largest loader in the construction industry. Meditating on how the drafts of wind move seven wooden swings, he follows his eyes up the swings' ropes to their anchors around fat branches, the seven swings surrounding the circumference of the tree. The vision as a whole, of the oak with seven swings, is like a static version of DaVinci's Dream, the adult swing ride at Canobie Lake Park. Siritas recalls being whipped round-and-round a lights-flashing center column in a hanging

313

bucket-seat, flying over the park for half of the revolution and, frighteningly, over the lake for the other half of the revolution—then round-and-round again. The nausea of DaVinci's Dream returns to Siritas, as he considers the seven wooden swings around the oak. Thinking back to riding Canobie Lake's DaVinci's Dream eight years ago, he sees the faces of the people he sought to avoid by jumping in one of the ride's bucket seats: six classmates who were also attending Suffolk Law School's post-graduation outing.

It's not just the sight of seven swings at Ten Stacks that calls DaVinci's Dream to mind. It is also the wild alchemy of the moment, the blending of the oak swings with the unexpected arrival of inn guests in the pebbled, circular drive: the very same people Siritas sought to avoid at that Suffolk Law School outing. These six fellow alumni spill out of an SUV and toss bags to valets, who are old-timey dressed in green hats and tails. Perhaps, if Siritas could blink, if he could close his mouth, form words; perhaps, if the shock of this sight dissipated, he would agree that the people exiting the SUV are the reason he's thinking on the law school outing. Edit, on *why* he's thinking of law school. It has been, afterall, and after all he learned there and knows of this particular group, eight years. Eight years.

How on Earth is it that they are here, now, when he is too? How could such coincidence collide so fantastically? Even Siritas didn't know he was coming to Ten Stacks until yesterday, when the random idea bloomed in his mind upon reading a *Union Leader* review of New Hampshire's grand inns. He thought he could complete his appellate brief here, in silence, away from his wife and kids and all their friends jumping in the pool, beneath his office window. The brief (trying to undo a jury verdict against a construction company client) is level twelve on a difficulty scale of ten. Siritas needs quiet. No interruptions. And, certainly, no law school drama.

Maybe if he hurries off the gray porch, weaves between the wind-rocked, white rockers and into the granite-lined lobby with the hooked rug—the inn's infamous ten chimneys being the rug's design—maybe if he's swift and hidden within the bustle of bags and green-tuxedo valets, they won't see him. Maybe he can scoot up to his third-floor room, collect his unpacked clothes, and sneak out. Transfer to another inn, less grand, but not here, with them.

"Well, well, well, if it isn't Sir Wretch in the flesh! My man, how long has it been?"

Busted.

Record scratch on that mid-air step, poor Siritas. *Stop, turn, and act surprised to hear your name from a voice of the past.*

"Jim Graves, no way. Wow. What a coincidence! And is that? It is. The Seven Perpetuities." *Dammit. Oh shit,* Siritas catches himself. *Maybe they won't catch the gaffe.*

"It's six now, Sir. The Six Perpetuities. Unfortunately," Jim says, certainly catching Siritas' gaffe and having made up the space between the circular drive and Siritas on the porch. In correcting Siritas that they are not The Seven Perpetuities any longer, and their group only comprised of six, Jim's affect has switched from boisterous to morose.

"Of course. Sorry, sorry. Anyway, good to see you. Are you all up here for a get-together or special event? I don't see any of your significant others, so must be a get-together? You all were so tight in law school."

Susan Red joins them on the porch. "Oh my God, Sir Wretch in the flesh. You're staying here too?"

"Is that Sir Wretch in the flesh?" Others, now coming up the porch steps, say as a valet drives their SUV to a hidden lot in the woods.

All six of them, Jim Graves, Maggie O'Deal, Susan Red, Peter, Paul, and Pike (the last three the Longs, triplets who attended law school together), stand around Siritas on the porch. Maggie O'Deal, ever the caustic one, plumps down in one of the rockers, and says, "Son of a fucker if this ain't all of Suffolk Law up in this joint."

"We're here, yes, for a get-together, of sorts," Jim says, answering Siritas' question after being interrupted by the others. "Somewhat reliving our study group days. Maggie knows the owner. Join us for dinner tonight, Sir, would ya? We've got reservations in the inn's restaurant. We'd love to catch up. Right guys?"

"Absofuckinglutely," Maggie says, rocking back harder so as to launch herself to a standing position. "I'll go add you to the reservation," she says, disappearing into the granite lobby.

Shit, Siritas thinks. *Came here to hide, and now I'm roped into a damn dinner of memories I'd rather forget and small talk. The worst possible scenario.*

It's interesting to Siritas that Maggie and Jim are here without their spouses, that they were permitted to do so. And Siritas knows they're each married and where they work and Jim's various birth announcements over the years, for he follows along with classmates' updates in the monthly Suffolk Law alumni newsletter. Maybe their spouses don't know Maggie and Jim were a thing? How would you define them back then? Maybe nobody knows, like Siritas knows, which he shouldn't know, for *Maggie and Jim, a thing*, was a secret in law school. The two had cheated on their then boyfriend and girlfriend and, yes, indeed, perhaps after all these years, it is still only Siritas who knows, for he's picking up on Jim's glare, a warning to not say anything to tip anyone off, as Siritas follows Maggie's path over the hooked rug with ten chimney stacks and back to Jim, and back and forth along the invisible thread between Maggie and Jim. The thread, Siritas senses, is stronger—maybe a titanium chain, and no longer a simple, invisible thread. *So why not be together if you're so into each other? Why all the years of deception?*

Once Maggie is good and gone and squawking at the front desk clerk, Siritas notes Jim's wedding ring. "Who was it you married? Wasn't Kayla, the nurse, you were with in law school, right? Someone else?" Siritas asks.

"Such a great memory, Sir!" Susan Red says, clapping him on the shoulder. "Jim sure didn't marry Kayla. Ooo boy, she's long gone. Jim married himself a regular-old, perfect-little Kate. She's nice. Home with their four kids, the trooper." Susan Red moves her way into the granite lobby. "See you at dinner, Sir!"

"Hey man, good to see you. Look forward to dinner," Pike Long says. His two identical brothers nod hello, and each say in turn, "Hey, Sir." The three move into the inn, following Susan Red, and Maggie O'Deal before her.

Which leaves Siritas with Jim Graves.

Jim studies Siritas, roves his eyes over Siritas' face, and Siritas' skin burns. Jim has not acknowledged Siritas' memory about Kayla. Jim is not smiling. For it must be that things have remained the same, and it is only Siritas who knows of Jim's past, and apparently present, with Maggie O'Deal, their secret—something Siritas should not have stumbled upon in law school, when Jim was most definitely with Kayla. *But who cares at this point about back then?* Siritas wonders. *And why marry others if you've kept this thing between you alive?*

"See you at dinner, Sir Wretch," Jim says, with no smile. No warmth.

It was so simple, such a common theme amongst horny law students, stressed for second year exams. A quick bang in a dark corner of the library stacks, or in one or another's over-expensive Beacon Hill apartment, and then back to the books. The banality of twenty-something's hooking up. Why was this still such a big deal?

Back then, Siritas had arrived at the fourth floor of the law school at the crack of dawn, hurrying to clinch one of the good desks in the library for Day Three of the week before finals. He assumed nobody but the early-morning cleaning staff was in the building. The elevator doors opened on the library floor, and there stood Jim and Maggie in an embrace. And when Jim moved his mouth to Maggie's and the elevator alarm buzzed, for Siritas stalled too long in the doors, Jim jumped away from Maggie. Siritas tried to disappear back into the elevator, but couldn't, for the doors banged his arms, ratcheting the awkwardness to level ten. Finding himself face to face with Jim and Maggie, they could not deny what he'd stumbled upon.

"Sir, dude, hey. So, look, um, you can't say anything to anyone about this, please. It would really hurt some people, okay?" Jim said. "We're not even a thing. This is nothing. And it's over."

"You can't say anything, Sir," Maggie said, much more abrupt than Jim.

"I don't know what you guys are talking about. I saw nothing and nothing is my business," Sir had said.

"Cool, dude, that's cool. Thanks, man," Jim said, his hands shaking.

"You're right, Sir. Nothing is your business. That's right, good," Maggie said, seemingly less concerned than Jim, but also stern that Sir know nothing.

Thereafter, a couple of one-on-one reminders from Jim and three from Maggie told Siritas to never tell a soul. And Sir never did, except once, to one who is long gone.

Standing on the porch alone, Ten Stacks having absorbed The Six Perpetuities into its winding halls and wings and antique-laden rooms, Siritas stares at the white rockers, now frozen with no wind and no people. He considers the seven swings around the fat oak. He resolves to race up to his room, pack, and flee. But that voice returns, a definite voice outside his body, a whisper delivered on wind that pushes the closest rocker to tilt back and hit the inn.

"Stay, Sir. Stay," the wind voice says. This time Siritas does not pass it off as an imagined perception. This time cold shock freezes his blood. For it wasn't just the definiteness of the words, it was the voice. *Her* voice. The one long gone.

Siritas looks around; nobody is there. The gray boards creak.

"Stay, Sir, truly, you must," the voice says again when a gust blows his hair.

He runs into the lobby, pops in the two-man elevator, manned by a green tuxedoed valet, and rises to the third floor. In his room, he sits on his bed, shaking. Shaking from the wind-voice, from the encounter with The Six Perpetuities, from Jim Graves' glare, Maggie's abruptness, Susan Red seizing on the question to Jim about Kayla and focusing nothing on herself, no questions to Sir, no updates, and her moving so quickly into the inn. And then the Long triplets and their brevity in saying hi and passing by— probably faster than would be customary when running into an old classmate, come to think of it.

"Come to think of it," the wind voice says, repeating Siritas' thoughts, as soon as he opens a window by his room's mahogany desk. He slams the window shut. And, for sure, once again, it was *her* voice.

Siritas knows he should leave, stat. The legal brief he should be focused on is due in two days, but now his brain is all but fried. Still, instead of shoving his pants and T's in his duffel and running, the thought of that wind voice, *her* voice, suspends him in a somewhat atmospheric glue. He resolves to take a shower, calm down, and then decide what to do.

The shower does calm Siritas, some; the fogged mirror, its obscuring blankness, hides his facial concern from his own self. And in following the calming steps he'd been taught to use before court hearings, he breathes deep three times and smiles, the smile to trick his brain away from dumping cortisol and forging a deeper PTSD highway between amygdala, hippocampus, and pre-frontal cortex. He dresses and sits on the end of the bed, watching out the window where her voice invaded, watching as wind toys with the hanging ropes of the seven swings.

As the day progresses and shadows lengthen, he notes the shadows of the ten chimney stacks, drawing their mirror image on the front lawn, rivering over the bumps of the granite benches and curves of the circular drive. One of the shadows leans and appears bulky and misshapen compared to the other chimney shadows, which are straight and lengthened rectangles. Siritas recalls that upon his arrival, he saw that same leaning chimney, not in shadow, but in the reality of its end placement on the high roof. He'd noted how unlike the others it was, wrapped in ropes and scaffolding and tarps. And just as he was questioning the sight of a pile of replacement bricks bungee-corded together and left on a rickety platform of the scaffolding, along with a trowel, circular saw, and a bucket of mortar, the valet holding his duffel had said, "Sorry about the construction on the tenth stack up there. It's an eyesore, for sure. They should be done in a month. Was leaning too much." *What's not safe*, Siritas thought then, and thinks now as he studies the chimney contraption in shadow, the lumpy ropes, the clunky scaffolding, the loose bricks, the saw, the mortar, the trowel, the entirety leaning, *is this. This whole chimney repair is what's not safe, especially with how the wind is unfettered on this high hill above a flat lake.* But, Siritas had resolved then, and resolves again, to turn off the part of his attorney brain that sees only risk and OSHA violations. He chooses to not get involved. He needs to focus on his appellate brief and nothing else.

✳✳✳

But, hearing wind voices, *her* voice, is not conducive to finalizing an appellate brief, and Siritas finds he's done nothing the entire day. He's mental toast.

Now, dinnertime, he walks down the third-floor hall, which serves the rooms in the original portion of Ten Stacks. He counts the paneled doors to guest rooms at eight; he counts the colorful oil paintings of fall leaves at seven; he counts his steps on the red runner to ten. *Eight doors, seven paintings, ten steps*, he says to himself, as if a reminder or an earworm, he's unsure. Upon the thought of these summarized counts, he stops in his tracks upon seeing the open window at the end of the hall. Wind rushes in, blowing green drapes which form the shape of a woman. When the wind stops, one panel falls flat. The other remains taut around the shoulder and hip of a woman, and her head moves forward to form a face in the panel. But then in a *poof*, the air or the entity or the total delusional nightmare deflates, and the panel falls flat.

Siritas doesn't have a second to blink or catch his breath from such a shocking vision, for cool air and an emptiness to his right forces him to turn his head. He notes the closest guest room's paneled door has opened, and curtains at the far end of the room blow in. A mirage of a woman materializes into something far more tangible than a taut curtain panel, but still not touchable flesh. Her undulating air-skin seems made of woven, moss-caked sticks. A woman of green, of moist moss and sticks. Her eyes are glowing emeralds. This apparition stands, or floats, in the center of the guestroom.

"Eight doors, seven paintings, ten steps, you remembered the sequence. Gather them after dinner," she says, and *slam*, the door shuts. The brass placard on her door reads "8,710 seconds = .00336 months," reminding Siritas of his own door's placard, "8710 = Spiritual Mentoring." Siritas recalls that, upon check-in, the front desk clerk explained how the inn owner's passion is numerology, and thus, each floor's doors are marked not by typical room numbers, but by interpretations of the same number. You found your room by the interpretation, not the number. With only eight doors on the third floor, it wasn't so hard. It is in the larger wings where interpretations have to be in some sort of logical order, but Siritas certainly isn't concerned with logical order right now.

The hall returns to empty, and Siritas grabs his chest. He staggers sideways, leans on the red-deer-patterned wallpaper. He looks around, behind, ahead, and down the curving grand stairwell catty-corner to where he leans on the pattern of red deer. All the paneled doors are closed, no guests. No valets. No maids or managers or maintenance. No ghosts or phantoms or vespers or hysterical delusions. No insanity.

I know I saw her. I know I heard her. Her.

He replays her words, which were actually his words that she claimed and then reformulated to her purpose: *Eight doors, seven paintings, ten steps, you remembered the sequence. Gather them after dinner.* In truth, Siritas might know what she meant by the sequence, but *gather them after dinner* is new.

Siritas blinks once and proceeds in a lean of a tripping gait down the stairs. As he does, with each tread and as his steps grow more definite and slower, he realizes that he is not panicked. He is oddly calm, entranced almost, to proceed to dinner with The Six Perpetuities. Even with the haunting vision of *her* and the total spectacle of a spectre of the past haunting him, perhaps deluding him, he feels in control. He also realizes he is not thinking a beat on the stress of his construction client and their important appellate brief. Whatever his intentions were when he set out to find working solitude at Ten Stacks has shifted. There is a new intention curling around in the back of his mind, forming into something more solid, it feels, but in a brewing stew that has not yet boiled. Siritas can't quite define this new intention yet.

Immediately upon entering Ten Stacks' main dining hall, Siritas is confronted by the triplets, Peter, Paul, and Pike Long. As a forward moving tripartite guard, they walk Siritas backwards into an old pine booth with a two-foot bench and a shelf with a rotary phone. Standing trapped within the booth, Siritas faces the triplets, who block the exit.

"Sir, we still have the same deal, right? You won't say a word on our secret, yeah?" Pike Long says, speaking for all three brothers. Siritas recalls how they started a firm, Long Brothers Law, LLC, an opulent, boutique firm, taking up three floors in a modern and expensive mid-rise in Boston's most toney part of town: Newbury Street, Back Bay.

Now, in the phone booth of Ten Stacks, Siritas considers the Long brothers' secret, something, frankly, he hadn't thought about since grabbing his Suffolk Law diploma and jetting off with his then fiancée, now wife, to Cape Cod for a weekend before the Canobie Lake post-graduation outing, which was meant to kick off everyone's summers to cram for the Bar. It would be a lonely exile studying for the Bar, for Siritas hadn't cultivated relationships in law school. He certainly wasn't a member of the power study group, The Seven Perpetuities. Siritas' free time was spent either with his long-time girlfriend (who was finishing an optometry residency and, who now, as Siritas' wife, is a practicing optometrist) or slinging plates to earn meager wages and slim tips, enough under-the-table cash to buy himself spaghetti and no-brand sauce. Unlike The Seven Perpetuities, Siritas had entered law school under a mountain of loans.

Remember, it's The Six Perpetuities, not Seven, the voice says, this time woven in as part of the instrumental end to a song playing out of an overhead speaker in the booth.

"Whoa, did you hear that?" Pike says, jumping back.

The two other brothers wear non-committal reactions. Not confirming, not denying.

Pike, startled, grows angry, likely due to fright and anxiety at the voice that Siritas definitely heard too. "Sir, did you hear that?" Pike says, stepping back in on Siritas and aggressively pointing, as if Siritas caused the voice.

Siritas holds up his palms in the gesture, *I'm not here to fight with you.* "Pike, you okay?" he says. "Not sure what you're talking about. But, hey, don't worry, I barely even remember whatever it is you don't want me to mention. Can we just go to dinner?"

Having calmed a number of bloat-brain meatheads on construction sites, Siritas says these words in a calm management, while walking slowly out of the booth and in a way that hypnotizes the three Longs to file away and make room for his exit. He's a ship, the Longs the water. Pike's body language calms, as do his brothers' noncommittal reactions, which reduce to blank faces and dead eyes.

They were never the brightest law students—hence, their secret.

You could predict such a cliché thing would happen, of course. Indeed, it was a running joke amongst their law school classmates that the Long triplets, identicals, would certainly run the ruse of pretending to be one of the others when sitting for tests on which one or the other might be strongest. The three Longs didn't help with this gossipy undercurrent in the way they always made sure to construct wholly different class schedules from each other. *Ha ha ha, whatever, real original,* they'd retort whenever this predictable accusation was flung their way.

But Siritas knew it was true in at least one situation, and it was all so simple, not even a major controversy compared to the massive corruption reported in the never-ending, 24-hour breaking news cycle in the wide world of corrupt governments and politicians and CEO's, genocide, bio-war, human rights' violations, decades of tax fraud by billionaires gone unprosecuted—the list, unfortunately, going on and on. To Siritas, the Longs' secret was banal compared to such a grander context of corruption.

Still, the Longs had lived a floor down from Siritas in an overpriced Beacon Hill brownstone, two blocks from Suffolk Law. On a day they had a Torts pre-exam (which was meant by the professor as prep for the real exam, but would count for 10% of the final grade), Siritas walked down to the Longs' apartment to drop a book he'd borrowed from Pike. Having walked to and from this same Torts class with Pike, and having lived in the same building with the brothers, unlike any of the other law students, Siritas knew Pike was the one who had a chip on his right fang tooth. Siritas knocked, expecting to hand the book back to Pike and walk with him to the Torts pre-exam. The door opened, and there stood Pike in an open robe and dirty boxers, his hair messed, dark circles under his eyes, and smelling of Jägermeister. In saying in a drowsy slur, "Sir Wretch in the flesh," his mouth opened enough for Siritas to confirm the chip in his tooth, marking him, without doubt, as Pike Long.

"Aren't you going to the Torts pre-exam, Pike? It starts in twenty minutes."

Pike, obviously still drunk from a long night drinking, or, in the least, seriously hung over, closed his eyes and wobbled his head. "What, man? Oh, yeah, sure. I'll be there."

Siritas wasn't so sure, but he didn't have time to waste with Pike. He needed to clinch a 100% on this Torts pre-exam, because that 10% bump was key. He needed all the help he could get. "Well, Pike, you better hurry then. I'm going ahead. See you there."

Five minutes later, when Siritas entered the classroom, a Long brother was already in Pike's seat, dressed in Pike's customary T-shirt of a hard rock band. This Long, either Peter or Paul, Siritas wasn't sure which of the two, certainly wasn't Pike. Siritas just left Pike in a robe and reeking of alcohol only minutes before. This Long was clean and bright eyed and already here. Siritas waved hello, and the brother said, "Sir Wretch in the flesh," with a smile wide enough to reveal no chip in his tooth.

Later that night, having come to his senses, Pike, joined by Peter and Paul, knocked on Siritas' apartment door. They groveled for his silence. "We've never done that and never will again, and it wasn't even the final, Sir. I had a rough night is all because my girl dumped me, and, damn, I needed my brothers to help me out, this one time. You understand, right?"

"Sure," Siritas said, wishing them to leave, for he'd only one minute before proposed to his then girlfriend-turned-fiancée, current wife. She was waiting for him to return to the couch and finish their toast to her thrilling *yes*. In Siritas' point of view, he couldn't care less in that moment about the Long brothers' ridiculous groveling and minor corruption that didn't impact him. *Whatever, leave.*

"Fine," Siritas had said. "Honestly, guys, I don't care. I need to get back to my fiancée, we're sort of busy, okay?"

"Cool, Sir. Thanks, Sir," they said.

And they, thereafter, like Jim and Maggie, once in a while checked in on Siritas' word to stay silent, chaining him to secrecy, while plying him with phony compliments and kindness.

Fine. Siritas simply didn't want to be involved in generating gossip and drama with the Longs or with anyone else in law school. He just wanted to plow through, secure his J.D., pass the Bar, and get married. He wanted to be left alone. To be uninvolved. Law school on massive loans and no money, confined to eating cheap carb-only meals with no protein, was hard enough. Siritas' parents were regular New Englanders who lived in a small Cape in Portsmouth, New Hampshire. They, like most, lived check to check. Sometimes they saved enough extra cash to re-paint the clapboard siding— peeling paint being a constant struggle in seaside towns such as Portsmouth, battered by the constant cold, salt air. Siritas didn't have the monetary luxury of gossip, which would take precious time away from study. He needed to achieve high grades in order to secure a rare, well-paying job in the restrictive law market of Boston. Afterall, Suffolk Law grads competed with Harvard Law grads, and only a handful of firms paid in the higher six figures. It was well known that the Long brothers simply had to graduate from law school to trigger a huge payout from a family trust, which they'd said would fund their own firm. They didn't have to battle it out for jobs. But, word of cheating would have spoiled their chances of securing instantly lucrative, for them, J.D.'s.

Now, Siritas leads the three Longs into Ten Stacks' dining room, and all four weave between the inn's two-tops and four-tops, with their white tablecloths adorned with crystal and patterned antique china place settings, to find Jim Graves, Maggie O'Deal, and Susan Red seated at an eight-top. Susan Red pats the empty seat beside her for Siritas to sit. He steps to the side to avoid colliding with a tuxedoed waiter, who just finished lighting the tables votive.

"Sir Wretch in the flesh," Susan says as he sits. "So good to see you." The others wave their hellos, but quickly draw attention to the waiter who is describing the drink specials. Susan takes their distraction as a chance to lean into Siritas' ear and whisper, "Sir, I know you won't say anything to the others about my little secret, yeah?" She leans back and winks. Siritas takes her in, meets her sparkling, blue eyes, recalling she was recently named a *Rising Star* trial attorney, which makes sense, for she can be convincing in her words and overall aura.

"Of course, Susan. Frankly, I barely even remember. It's no big deal, really."

She squeezes his arm and scrunches her nose. "You're a good egg, Sir Wretch."

The others are done with their drink orders, and a cough from the waiter pulls Susan and Sir's attention away from their minor stare down.

"Oh, sure, I'll have a glass of the pinot noir," Sir says.

"Same," says Susan.

"Shall I bring a bottle?"

"No," answers Sir, at the same time Susan says, "Yes."

"I'll bring a bottle then."

The dinner proceeds in the awful manner of others remembering group memories that Siritas has no connection to, mixed with intervals of forced small talk so as to include him in the group. It's tedious and agonizing and every second reminds Siritas why he prefers either total solitude or the company of his small family, and that is all. But, still, he's an attorney, and he's used to business development dinners and cocktails, the most unfortunate part of the job. So, he muddles through the courses and being overserved on wine, as he always does.

The hostess, a young woman in a green dress, much the same color as the moss-woman apparition Siritas encountered, walks toward their table. While watching her approach in her green dress, Siritas realizes he'd oddly forgotten his encounter on the third floor, as if he'd imagined it in a fleeting dream. But he did not imagine or dream her, and he recalls the vivid terror in seeing her. And it was *her*. The one long gone. Now, the hostess in that same moss green presents at the table. The group hushes.

"Pardon me," she says. "I have a message for a Siritas Wretch?"

The others point to Siritas, and Siritas holds up a hand. "That's me."

The moss-dress hostess walks to him and hands him a folded note.

Siritas doesn't know why he feels the need to hide what he's reading, but he cups his hands around the paper as he unfolds it.

Toast me, Sir. Say my name. -L

The paper is damp, and the ink forming the letter 'L' is bloated and warped from a water drop. A thumbprint of green marks a corner.

Siritas breathes in deep, folds and pockets the note.

326

"You look like you've seen a ghost," Susan Red says. "Everything okay, Sir?"

"Nothing. Just a message from a client, checking how I'm doing on an appellate brief."

"The law is a mistress, that's for sure," Jim Graves says. Maggie O'Deal meets his eyes on the word *mistress*, all of which is just so pathetically obvious to Siritas. *Is this as simple as a kink? This decade-long secretive affair, just a kink?* In studying the pair trying to hide their attraction, Siritas resolves it's as simple as that: a kink. He stifles the urge to roll his eyes.

He hears *her* voice in visualizing the damp note: *Toast me, Sir. Say my name. -L*

Siritas picks up his re-filled Pinot—he's on his third goblet. Raising it, he says, "A toast." The others raise their glasses. "To Lynn File," he says. He watches the others' faces freeze a moment, each one swallowing something phantom stuck in their throats, and how each avert Siritas' eyes. They recover quick enough though, each one alone in their own concern at the toast, for none look to another in these guarded and aversive reactions.

"To Lynn File," they each say, but not in unison, and not loud, and with some voices cracking, and an overall weak repetition of her name, someone who was once the group's seventh member. Their long-gone friend making up The Seven Perpetuities.

Susan Red stands. "Hey, Sir, why don't you take a walk with me to the porch. Maybe we can share a cocktail in those white rockers. Okay?"

"Sounds nice, Susan," Siritas says, rising to meet her. "Should I leave my card, or charge my portion to the room?" He says to the table.

"Don't worry about it, Sir. It's comped. My friend owns the inn," Maggie O'Deal says, not in her customary caustic tone. Rather, a distracted sort of answer. She continues to stare at the rug as she did when he'd mentioned Lynn File's name.

Out on the porch, Siritas sits in a rocker; Susan Red takes the one next to him. A green tuxedoed valet offers champagne from a tray, for this is a post-dinner custom on Ten Stacks' porch. Siritas clinks his glass with Susan's, as he looks out over the seven swings around the oak in the inn's side yard. The lake at the bottom of the hill is a bright navy bowl of light, for there are no clouds and the moon is full. Night boaters' lights of yellow and blue and red dot the surface. One boat holds a circular perimeter with glow-in-the-dark, floating flags. The local paper had explained that in the deep, stagnant end, night divers would be working the summer to mark finds, if any, of long-lost boats and even crashed cars, for debris had been dislodging from the depths of muck and washing up on beaches and causing dangers.

"So," Susan Red says. "Sir. Look, I can't help but feel you were goading me with that toast to Lynn File. I thought we were good with my secret, no?"

"Oh, no, Susan, wasn't goading at all. I just figured a toast was in order, right? You all were so close, and it was so tragic what happened with her. I mean, and pardon me for asking this. I mean, I am not in your circle, you Perpetuities. But, through that whole dinner, nobody mentioned Lynn at all. And, well, given how you all spent three years together, so close, at least from what I saw, and given how our dinner centered a lot on law school memories, isn't it strange that I was the first to mention her name?"

Susan Red turns her head, herself seeming to take in the vision of the seven swings around the oak. Wind ruffles her hair and then moves on to Siritas, at which point, Siritas hears a wind whisper: *Ask her about The Fellows.*

Susan turns back around with a practiced smile. "You got me, Sir. You're right. It is strange nobody mentioned Lynn's name. It's, well…I figured with my secret, you were goading me. But I believe you, if you weren't. I shouldn't be such a narcissist."

"Susan." Siritas smiles. "I remember your secret, of course. And I won't say anything."

"It was a crazy competitive time. Right? Any of us would have done anything to get that one available summer associate position at Stokes & Crane. I mean, sure, do I feel guilt? Of course. To a degree. But, to be honest, I'm not going to lie and say I wouldn't do it again. I'm almost partner, Sir. Named a *Rising Star.* Been there eight years. And Lynn…oh, Lynn. Gosh, I know she wanted that spot at Stokes & Crane so bad. Sure, yes, I do have guilt for her.

Mainly her. Everyone else can, sorry to be crass, but everyone else can go fuck themselves. Every man for him or herself. All is fair in love and law jobs."

Siritas nods, looking out over Suncook Lake at the bottom of the hill and to the night diver boat with its glow-in-the-dark flags. He looks to the swings around the oak and at the rockers on the porch, only a few seating other guests. He thinks on the afternoon when all the firms hiring for summer associates set up tables in the school's lobby. At the Stokes & Crane table, the firm attorney manning the table had asked Susan Red, then law student, to watch her bag, as she left the firm's table to use the restroom. Susan Red didn't know Siritas was watching when she took a sign-up sheet of students who wished to apply to Stokes & Crane and stuffed it in her pocket. What remained were blank sheets for sign-ups on a clipboard. Susan Red signed her name on the top and added all of her contact details. Siritas coughed behind her.

"Oh, Sir, Sir Wretch," Susan said. "You saw what I did, didn't you?"

"I don't want to be involved. I saw nothing."

There, in the law school lobby, Susan stared at Siritas, holding his gaze. She was, truly then and truly now, quite sure of herself and sure she could command people with her eyes, with her intentions. And so, Siritas nodded an affirmative at her that whatever mental trick she thought she was pulling, it worked. In truth, as with the other events of minor corruption, Siritas simply didn't want to be involved.

Tonight at Ten Stacks, he looks to Susan. "But since you raised it, your secret, in connection with Lynn File. You thinking I was goading you because I toasted her, and now, how you said you feel guilt because you knew Lynn wanted that spot at Stokes & Crane so bad, I take it you saw Lynn's name on that sign-up sheet, didn't you?"

"I did."

Ask her about The Fellows, the wind repeats, this time upon a gust that rolls up like a tsunami from the lake's surface, bending the canopies of trees along the way, and pushing Susan and Siritas back in their rockers. Another wave of wind brings a repetition of words: *Ask her about The Fellows.*

"What is this rumor I heard about The Fellows?"

For the first time ever, as far as Siritas knows of Susan Red, Susan cringes, shows fear. She bugs her eyes at Siritas, fully alarmed. "How do you know about that? You couldn't possibly know about that? I know the others would never say anything. Even we have never discussed it. Ever. Like ever. How would you know?" With each sentence, with each question, her tone grows in alarm, but not volume. Rather her tone grows fierce, angry, mixed with fright, as she leans in to Siritas and whispers her words through clenched teeth.

Siritas looks back at her, transfixed on her reaction and confused by his own utterance of the question, for he has no clue what's so important to ask about The Fellows. He's simply repeating what the wind said, what *her* voice said, what Lynn File directed him to say.

"Well, then," Susan Red says, her face in a scowl. She stands. "I'll get the others. I'm not going to play games with you, Siritas. We're all going to talk this out. Once and for all."

Meet me at the swings, the wind voice whispers.

"Meet me at the swings," Siritas says to Susan Red.

"Fine. We'll be there in ten minutes."

For the ten minutes that Siritas waits for The Six Perpetuities, he sits on one of the seven swings around the oak. He looks up to the leaning tenth chimney of Ten Stacks, considering again the rickety scaffolding and how the mason shouldn't have left his circular saw and mortar and loose bricks up high on a platform. The ends of the tarp flap in the wind.

It was the evening before law school graduation when Siritas found himself in the cafeteria with Lynn File. He'd been in her classes over the years, and they were good enough acquaintances to share a coffee, having found themselves both here, in the evening, finalizing last-minute details to close out their three years of law school. They hadn't planned on meeting up. They'd never been friends out of school, but were friendly enough.

"I've got nothing lined up," Lynn had said, sad in talking of her post-graduation prospects. Her limp hands around her coffee cup and her slumped posture spoke of mental exhaustion. "I've got no lover, no money, no job. Meanwhile, my friends all have these great relationships and money and jobs. The Seven Perpetuities, ha! More like The Six Perpetuities and a Loser." She made an L sign on her forehead, branding herself a loser. And then she broke down and cried real tears. Siritas, a good enough bloke, and one accustomed to listening to a smart woman, what with his optometry fiancée, didn't do that awful man thing and cringe upon a woman's tears and seek to escape. He also didn't like to talk down to people in distress, so he offered no trite platitudes or condescending soft talk, as if Lynn File were a child or older person, hard of hearing. He hated that. He hated to condescend to anyone, at any age, of any state, sane, insane, young, old, or infirm. He just wanted to talk straight. So, he tried that first.

"Lynn," he said. "Come on, look at me. You know full well you're not a loser. This shit is hard, I won't sugarcoat it. But you are, come on, Lynn, definitely not a loser."

"Easy for you to say. You have a fiancée and a job. I know you got that position with Lopez & Associates, doing construction claims."

"Yeah, well, I did. And yes, I am engaged. So what? Next week, who knows? Anything could happen. Life is a total roller coaster. The only thing I own is the past, and that is all."

But this did not soothe Lynn File. She cried harder. And Lynn was not the dramatic type. She truly was in a state of distress; she might be spiraling. They'd had some training on depression and addiction throughout their years at school. Wellness consultants and seminars peppered in with legal clinics and internships—the rates of depression and addiction amongst lawyers being of a considerable enough rate that the school wanted to be sure their grads were cognizant of the risks and could detect the signs in themselves and their colleagues. To get help. Something in the way Lynn File's eyes weighed heavy, and how she seemed to see no hope, alarmed Siritas. Still, he was no therapist. And he didn't think suggesting she talk with someone—a parent, another friend, a counselor—was appropriate in the moment. He worried it would make her think he himself did not want to help. He'd save that suggestion if his next attempt to calm her, assess her, didn't work, and if then his fear that she might be depressed in a dangerous way, seemed truer than his possible over-read of her sadness.

"You think your Seven Perpetuities are so perfect, ey?" he asked.

At this, he got Lynn's attention. She looked up, picking her head off the cafeteria table. Her mascara was smudged below her emerald eyes, which glowed wet from tears. "What?"

"I said, so you think your Seven Perpetuities are so perfect?"

"They aren't?"

Siritas couldn't believe he was going to do this. He'd done so well throughout law school staying out of everyone's business, and had done so well holding all these secrets. But he didn't like how Lynn File was led to believe she was a loser and her Perpetuity chums perfect in love and money and jobs. He needed to correct the record, because, when pushed, Siritas only likes truth. To be given it and to give it straight. So, he told Lynn everything, about Jim and Maggie's affair, and thus how their relationships weren't so crystal clean and perfect. How the triplets cheated at least once, but definitely more often, and so the trust that promised to pay out upon graduation would be fraudulently gained. And last, Susan Red, what she'd done with the Stokes & Crane sign-up sheet. Siritas could not then prove Lynn File's name had been on the sheet that Susan crumpled up in her pocket, but Lynn File sure believed that to be the case on hearing the story.

"I have higher grades than her," Lynn had said. "I never understood how she got an interview, and thus the position, and I got nothing. Not even an invitation to apply. And the others? What liars. Do you know how many times I've cried to Jim and Maggie about my failings to find anyone to date? And how many times they've told me to look out for someone with qualities as great as their partners? Oh, my, God, what assholes. And the triplets, for fucks sake. How nice to glide through life with all that money and still lie and cheat, and the rest of us scrape and scratch and claw and work our asses off. And we were all friends. They know how hard I work. How much I struggle on those damn dating sites. How much I wanted Stokes." For the next hour, Lynn went off on an epic bitch-rant tirade about every single member of The Seven Perpetuities. At times, Siritas snort-laughed; Lynn did too, given her darkly comedic takedowns of her now, her instant, *former* friends. In doing so, her posture returned, her resolve hardened. She was the regular Lynn

File that Siritas had come to know, but angry.

"You live in that same building as those fucking Longs, right?"

"Yes."

"Good. You're only a block from my place. Can you do me a favor, Sir Wretch?"

"Whatever you need, Lynn."

"Cool. I was thinking this anyway, but hearing all this shit, I'm going to take off for a month. Hike up north. Could you water my plants, maybe? Once a week?"

"Yeah, sure, no problem. You got a key?"

"It's one of those number locks. I'm at 22 Cartright. Press 8710, that's the sequence."

"Don't you mean 8710 is the code?"

"I prefer *sequence*. Who cares?"

Siritas laughed, for it was true that Lynn sometimes liked to use odd words where others were the norm. "Sequence it is," Siritas said, tipping his mug of coffee to Lynn.

The next day was graduation, and it was not until the Canobie Lake post-grad outing, three days later, that Siritas learned Lynn had never shown to receive her diploma. Siritas had not noticed, for he was immersed in watching his fiancée with his parents in the bleachers. And straight after, they set off for the weekend on the Cape.

Lynn File's body was never found. She was presumed missing. She was presumed to have offed herself in some hidden way, for a couple people had seen her crying the night before graduation. The rest of the Perpetuities reported how Lynn had met them at a bar called The Fellows that final night before graduation, after she'd left Siritas in the school's cafeteria. She was distraught, was all they reported to authorities. For his part, Siritas had reported her stated plan to hike up north and her request that he water her plants. No clues, no nothing, helped to resolve what had happened to Lynn File after all these years.

Here now, Siritas waits on The Six Perpetuities, sitting on one of the seven swings around the oak. Again, he thinks of DaVinci's Dream at Canobie Lake. That round-and-round nauseating feeling of danger, of being flung into the lake out of a bucket seat.

Or maybe the nauseating feeling of danger is the fact that a cold breath is breathing on the back of his neck. The hairs on his arms rise. "Turn around," her voice says.

Siritas turns his head, planting his feet on the ground beneath the swing so he doesn't move forward or backward. There, amongst the green shrubs beneath the green trees surrounding the oak, stands Lynn File, her skin made of moss-covered sticks. Her original emerald irises are transformed into large orbs of emeralds with no whites. The flowing gauze around her body is a dress made of moss. This time she undulates less, seems less transparent; yet, Siritas can see through her mossy chest to a boulder behind. She has no feet and floats above the green grass between the green shrubs.

"Sir Wretch."

Siritas chokes on his words, but is able to croak out a, "Lynn? Lynn File?"

When he says her name, her form becomes more solid, more human. And her words transform from watery, wavy wind, to something less strange and otherworldly. It seems to Siritas, that she appears and speaks now as if she never vanished. That she is here in the flesh. Her eyes reduce to emerald irises with whites. He doesn't dare look to see if she now has feet.

"Listen. They are murderers, and they don't even know. Their secrets led to the death of me, and it will lead to the death of them. That night," she stops, looking past Siritas to the inn's porch. The Six Perpetuities are still within the building and have not appeared on the porch on their way to the swings. "They'll be here any minute. I don't have much time. Listen, because I need you to know why."

"Why what?"

"Why I asked you to gather them. Why I'm going to do what I'm going to do."

Siritas shakes his head confused.

"That night, after talking with you, I did go and meet them at The Fellows. I confronted all of them, but I never revealed you were my source. I confronted the Longs at the table when the others were getting drinks. I told them I knew they'd been cheating because I saw them. I confronted Maggie and Jim at the dartboard and told them I saw them making out by the basement bathroom one night—a guess which proved true. I confronted Susan about Stokes & Crane when I went with her to buy shots for the table. I told her Risa Fischer saw her do it, and since Risa had died the week before when her car careened into a river, I figured I'd take my chance on damning the dead and inviting their games of irony."

Siritas blinks, hearing voices murmuring in argument up on the porch. Maggie O'Deal is the loudest. "Susan, this is ridiculous. I'm not going to stress about this after all these years."

"Look at me and listen," Lynn File says, her appearance fading back to undulating, back to transparency, a woman of gauzy moss in the bushes. She hurries to say the rest in a firm voice, but as she speaks, her voice wavers into wind, with long spaces between words. "At Fellows, after I confronted them separately about their sins, I said to them together, 'You each know I know secrets about you that the others don't know. I know they'd ruin your lives. Think on that any time you're smug to others, thinking you're so superior, acting like you have your shit together. Because you don't. I am not a Perpetuity. Go to hell.'"

Reduced again to being a phantom on the night air, and limited in words, Lynn points a moss-stick arm toward the lake. She commands, "Look."

Siritas looks over her shoulder to the end of the lake to see headlights moving along the road that snakes there, around the lake. Lynn points to a part in the bend of the road that is high atop a cliff, whose granite, jagged face lands in the water, fifty feet down.

"Look in my eyes," Lynn says, her voice blending with the watery navy, with the wind. Her eyes are back to being orbs of emerald, a total hypnotism.

Siritas stares on at Lynn; the summer air envelopes him in a cocoon, such that nothing else exists but for a collage of visions. He sees it all, as it was eight years ago. He sees Lynn coming around the road's corner and her front tire blow. A flash of another image appears, that of the Longs sneaking out of The Fellows, while the rest of the Perpetuities drank, and Pike jamming a nail in Lynn's tire, which led to a leak and the eventual blowout. Siritas watches Lynn's car careen over the cliff and into the water. He watches the vision of Jim Graves and Maggie O'Deal shoving dimes in Lynn's seatbelt lock, such that Lynn hadn't been able to buckle that night. He watches Lynn crash her head into the steering wheel, pass out, and awake submerged, fully underwater. He watches her try to find her metal safety hammer to smash open her electrical window to swim out, but another image flashes, that of Susan Red stealing the safety hammer, having snuck out of The Fellows when she'd made like she was going to the bathroom.

Lynn File says, "Their individual *mens rea* collectively killed me. Corruption is corruption, no matter how small. It all boils together to cause harm."

"Sir Wretch in the flesh," Jim Graves says, breaking Siritas' concentration on the bushes and the image of Lynn File as a transparent moss woman. Siritas blinks, and she's gone. He turns to find The Six Perpetuities each take one of the six remaining swings.

Before any of them launch into what would surely be an awkward conversation, yelling begins on the lake. Wind picks up on the surface of the flat water, rolling again like an endless series of wind tsunamis, up the hill, toward the swings. And still the yelling on the lake amplifies, the sound echoing in the bowl and to the inn. All of the night boats converge around the perimeter of the diving boat, which is the source of the yelling.

A wave of wind blows Siritas and The Six Perpetuities to twist on their swings.

"Holy shit," Maggie O'Deal says, her skirt flying up as high as her crotch.

A crack, a creak, the ropes twist, their anchoring boards strain. The wind grows even more forceful. Siritas looks up at the roof to the shoddy construction staging around the leaning chimney. Beyond the branches above him and the green canopy, it's hard to see the contraption in full, but he focuses, and through ample leaves, sees a green-dressed woman standing on the scaffolding. Her moss dress flies about her in the wind. With one pluck of her moss-stick finger to one of the ropes holding the tarp around the tenth stack, the rope snaps, which causes a cascade of catastrophic physics to follow. The leaning chimney falls one inch, which causes an edge to catch the rickety scaffolding, which then topples with the added force of a huge gust of wind in that precise moment, rocketing the circular saw to hurdle down and crush the skull of Jim Graves. In the very next second, the velocity of the falling trowel impales Maggie O'Deal through her gaping mouth and to her brain. In that same second, three loose bricks rocket into the backside of each Long brother, braining them instantly. They fall to the ground off their swings, dead. Dead, dead, dead. And last of all, the bungee cord that once held the loose bricks, hooks Susan Red's mouth like a fish, drawing her body up, for the other end of the cord hooks on the anchor board of her swing. In rising, rising, rising, her body twirls around one of her swing's ropes, such that it wraps around her neck. When finally, the bungee hook torque is too strained and snaps loose, Susan drops, but her neck, twisted in her swing's rope, cracks with the sudden drop. She is hanged sideways in the air, tangled in swing rope. In looking on, Siritas considers how strange her death matches the irrational fear he'd had in riding DaVinci's Dream, this exact series of mishaps, only with DaVinci's chains, not rope.

Siritas, spared, surveys the carnage. The bricks in brains. The skull-crushing saw. The troweled mouth. Susan hanged in swing rope. Everyone will blame the wind, and the mason.

Out on the lake, the night diving boat speeds to the inn's dock at the bottom of the hill. A woman in scuba gear, *sans* flippers, jumps off the boat, runs along the dock, and up toward the inn's porch. Siritas walks, haunted, toward her, knowing she is delivering news. Others are doing the same, eager to hear what the yelling was about, but others are also noticing the mass casualties from the chimney falling in the wind. Everyone's attention is divided between two, seemingly separate, emergencies. Someone catches Siritas' arm, "Pal, you okay? Hey, pal, you need to sit, you're in shock." This person guides Siritas to a granite bench by the circular drive.

The scuba woman is met by one of the green tuxedoed valets. "I've called 911. They say they're going to stage here, at the inn. We found a car at the bottom, the deepest part. A body inside. A woman. I saw her. She's been long gone, dead. It's stagnant there, the water. She's covered in moss or algae or milfoil, I don't know." Siritas tries to do his calming exercises, confined and not permitted to move from the granite bench. Someone is saying a paramedic needs to treat him. "You're in shock, breathe," voices say. No doubt they say he's in shock because part of his calming exercise prescribes that he smile to trick his brain. He breathes deep three times and says over and over in his mind a monotonous sequence of counts, *eight doors, seven paintings, ten steps. Eight doors, seven paintings, ten steps.* When the paramedics arrive and shine pen lights in his eyes, he counts more items to fit the sequence. He counts cop cars, *eight*. He counts news crews, *seven*. He counts the times a paramedic asks if he hears her, *ten*.

***

THE JOY
OF WRONG
NUMBERS

KELLEY ARMSTRONG

Gran was in the hospital, recovering from a stroke, when she discovered the joy of wrong numbers. She'd managed to convince my cousin to smuggle in her cell phone so she could call her bookie. Gran likes to play the ponies. Or that's what she says, but I must point out that her bookie is a silver fox with an Irish accent that makes Gran's voice trill up two octaves.

Gran's crush on her bookie is none of my business. Its only relevance here is that it launched her love of wrong numbers. With her right hand temporarily immobilized by the stroke, she dialed his number with her left, hit a couple of wrong digits and ended up spending a half-hour talking to a lovely young woman in Connecticut who shared her delicious recipe for apple tarts.

How does one go from "Whoops, wrong number" to a recipe exchange? Well, first, one needs to be my grandmother. Gramps claimed he was ready to propose ten minutes into their first conversation. Gran's verbal charms waned slightly as she reached middle age, only to roar back when she reached her senior years. No one wants to be rude to a sweet old lady, so they listen, and soon they find themselves chatting back because Gran isn't just charming; she's an excellent listener, and everyone needs a little more of that in their lives.

Soon Gran was "accidentally" dialing wrong numbers all the time. For her busy mind, those calls were like a telescope at her condo window. Glimpses into other lives, other worlds, satiating her curiosity while she was confined to that hospital bed.

When she'd recovered enough to come home, I left my college dorm to move in with her. I graduated last year, and I'm still with her. That would sting more if Gran didn't insist she still needs a live-in companion. It helps that I adore my grandmother. So while I juggle two part-time McJobs and keep applying for entry-level positions that won't pay a penny more, I'm living with Gran and kinda loving it.

As for the wrong numbers, she still does that when she needs a mood boost. Mostly, though, she's found a new source of social stimulation: being on the *receiving* end of wrong numbers. She seems to get a lot of them. As she says, the advantage to being the recipient is that she doesn't need to feel guilty about interrupting someone's day. Mix in the occasional chatty telemarketer, and Gran is in heaven.

That day, I get home from my barista shift to find Gran and her neighbor, Elsa, mixing cocktails at the kitchen counter.

I cast a pointed look at my watch. Gran lifts a middle finger, and Elsa laughs as she hoists a pink, frothy concoction.

"It's five o'clock somewhere," Elsa says.

"Are we celebrating something?" I ask, pulling up a stool to the kitchen island.

"We?" Gran says. "So you want one after shaming your old gran for a little day-drinking?" She pours me half a glass and passes it over. "Moonlight Over Manhattan came in at twenty-to-one odds. Your gran is five hundred bucks richer. I knew that old nag had it in her."

"You aren't that old," I say. "And not much of a nag."

She pantomimes throwing the pitcher of cocktails my way as Elsa chuckles. We all sip our drinks.

I gasp and sputter. "Do I even *want* to know what's in this?"

"Booze," Elsa says. "Lots of booze. Your gran is trying to get you liquored up before she drops the bomb."

I pause, glass halfway to my lips. "Bomb?"

"She set you up on a blind date. With one of her wrong numbers."

"*What?*"

"Lower your voice, Lily," Gran says. "At that pitch, you'll shatter my good crystal."

I lift the glass with "Carnival Cruises" emblazoned on the side. Gran only shakes her head.

"Tell her about the young man, Marie," Elsa says. "He called you, right? I will never understand how you get so many wrong numbers."

"Luck," Gran says. "And the fact that my number is apparently one digit off from a pizza takeout, one digit off from a library and two transposed digits from a travel agency. The last one is the best—people who travel are so interesting. Though I do get a lot of good book recommendations from the library patrons."

Gran tops up her glass before continuing, "This young man was calling his sister. He hit nine when he meant to hit eight. Poor boy was in such a state, one can hardly blame him. His tire blew on the highway, and he barely managed to control it over to the shoulder. Anyway, we got to talking—"

"Surprise, surprise," I mutter as Elsa snickers.

"—and I mentioned that my granddaughter went to college to be a legal assistant."

"And he's a lawyer with an entry-level opening?" I hold up two pairs of crossed fingers. "Please, *please* let those be your next words."

"He's not a lawyer, dear. He's a police officer."

"Who *knows* a lawyer with an entry-level opening?"

"You'll get a job soon enough. In the meantime, I appreciate everything you're doing to help me out here."

"Uh-huh. To show that appreciation, when you had the opportunity to set me up on a blind date with this cop, you restrained yourself."

"It's just coffee, Lily. All the way across town, too. For safety."

"So, if he turns out to be a serial killer, I'll have to run across the entire city to escape?"

Gran pulls a piece of paper from under the counter and passes it over. "His name is Colin. Thirty years old. Recently promoted to detective. Never married. No kids."

I look at the paper, where she's written all the pertinent data in jot-note form. "Did you get his annual salary, too?"

"For a new detective, it's about forty-five grand."

Elsa chuckles. "Your gran is thorough, Lily."

"I was married to a detective for sixty years. I know how to investigate." She looks at me. "Fifty grand is nothing to sneeze at. It comes with an excellent health plan, too."

I groan and thump my head down on the island counter.

"It's coffee," Gran says. "You haven't been on a date in months, and he seems like such a nice young man."

"Who is definitely not a serial killer?"

"I didn't ask," she says. "That would be rude. Also, they never tell the truth about things like that. Best to just play it safe and take your pocketknife."

As I approach the coffee shop, which is far too trendy for my tastes—thanks, Gran!—I can see the cop with the flat tire, better known as Colin. He sits at a window seat, anxiously scanning the sidewalk. His fingers drum against the scarred wooden tabletop. He looks straight out of central casting for "average cop." Short brown hair, clean shaven, nice build. Pleasant looking, as Gran would say. He falls just on the positive side of average, which is an excellent place to be.

He checks his phone. He'd texted two minutes ago to let me know where he was sitting and what he was wearing—gray chinos and a navy pullover. I'd sent back a thumbs-up. Now he's checking for another message; seeing none, he returns to anxious window gazing.

"Colin?" I say.

He looks over, and the relief on his face says I've passed the blind-date first-look test. Attractive enough that he doesn't regret agreeing to the meet-up, but not so attractive that he'd wonder why *I* was agreeing to blind dates.

"Lily," he says, rising with an outstretched hand. "Good to meet you."

I shake his hand. "Likewise. I'm just going to grab a coffee at the counter and—"

"No, I've got it." He scrambles up, hitting the table with his hip and setting his coffee sloshing. He makes a face. "Well, that was smooth."

"Sit," I say as I pull a wad of napkins from the dispenser. I hand them to him. "You look after that while I get myself a coffee."

I bring back a latte for me and a replacement coffee for him, which has him stammering more apologies. Kind of adorable, really.

I slide into my seat and ease into the conversation by asking whether he got that tire fixed. I may not have my gran's full allotment of conversational charm, but I inherited my share, and soon he's relaxed and talking.

We're about fifteen minutes in when he blurts, "About your grandmother."

I sigh and feign slumping in my seat. "Let me guess. She put you up to this. You guys got chatting, and the next thing you know, she's telling you all about her granddaughter, who happens to be single, and maybe you two could go to coffee sometime."

"No, no. It wasn't like that." He pauses. "Well, not exactly like that."

"Uh-huh." I lean my forearms on the table and meet his gaze. "Look, Colin. I appreciate that you were nice to her, but I know my gran can be a bit manipulative. Which is kind of like calling Svengali mildly persuasive."

He smiles. "True."

"I apologize if she put you on the spot. She's concerned because I haven't dated much lately. I've been juggling two jobs while helping Gran with her health issues."

"Health issues?"

I wave that off. "She's fine. The point is that I know you got roped into this. It's okay to admit it, and we'll finish our coffee, enjoy a few more minutes of conversation and then go our separate ways."

"No. I mean, that's not what I wanted to talk about. It's about your gran. She seems lonely."

I laugh. "She's not. Her social calendar is overflowing. If you mean she seems lonely because she spent twenty minutes chatting with a wrong number, she does that all the time. It's not a lack of outside contact. She just likes to talk."

"Okay. I get that. It's just...at her age..." He fingers his mug and then says, "She offered to call me a tow truck. At her expense."

I stiffen. "You asked her to get you a tow?"

"*No*," he says. "I didn't even suggest it. I said that I'd been calling my sister because I don't have AAA, and the next thing I know, she's offering to pay for my tow."

"She's generous with her money. Gramps left her plenty, and she likes to help people."

Colin goes quiet. He rubs one finger against his mug. Then he says, "Did she tell you I'm a detective?"

"A newly minted one. Congrats."

"Thank you. I just got promoted. Been in the job for a year now. I work mostly fraud."

His gaze lifts to mine, and he waits. When I don't react, he says, "Do you know what a sucker list is?"

"Mmm, no, but it doesn't sound good."

"A sucker list is a list of, well…suckers." He makes a face, half apologetic. "Basically, fraudsters will sell the names and contact information of people who've fallen for their schemes."

"Okay…"

"I have access to a few of the more popular ones. They're part of my current investigation. When your grandmother offered to pay for my tow, it set off alarm bells. Elderly woman, living on her own, seems lonely and eager to talk."

He raises a hand. "Yes, I know you said that isn't the case. She fit the markers, though. Including having a charitable streak. As you said, she's quick to offer help, even to strangers. That's very admirable. It's also…" He sucks in a breath. "Dangerous."

"She could be taken advantage of. Get onto one of those lists." I push aside my latte. "I know you're only trying to be helpful, Colin, but Gran isn't like that. She's shrewd and savvy. As far from a sucker as you could imagine. She'll never end up on a list like that."

"I found her phone number on two of them."

"That isn't possible."

"Is her name Marie Reid? Residing at 325 Marlowe Street, apartment 202?"

I stare at him.

"It's all on the lists, Lily."

"That's—that's not— There's some mistake. Gran isn't like that. She's nobody's fool."

"Being on those lists doesn't imply a lack of intelligence *or* common sense. I've seen doctors lose their retirement savings to fraudsters. The only thing the victims have in common is kindness.

They are good people, and the world preys on that, and it's not fair." He shakes his head. "Sorry for the rant. It just really pisses me off. My buddies joke that I went into fraud because I couldn't hack being in major crimes, that I'd get upset seeing people hurt. In fraud, I *am* seeing people hurt. Most of the victims wish they'd been roughed up instead. At least they'd recover from that. These thieves steal their life savings *and* their pride."

I sit there, staring into my half-finished latte.

"Talk to her," he says softly.

"I will."

"In the worst case, you may need to get power of attorney to help monitor her withdrawals."

"What? No. I wouldn't want that. Ever."

"Good." He passes me a wry smile. "I'd be a lot more concerned if you jumped at the suggestion. Hopefully, it won't come to that. Maybe it was a few slipups, and she's learned her lesson."

I nod.

He reaches out to lay a tentative hand on mine. "I'd like to help if I can, Lily. I'm kind of an expert on this." He gives me another wry smile. "You might even say that I didn't dial a wrong number. I dialed the right one—to someone I can help before it's too late."

"I hope so," I murmur.

"Let's talk, then. I'll give you a list of what to look for."

Two days have passed since I spoke to Colin. Two days of juggling his tasks in between my barista and retail shifts. I also score an interview. It's a junior receptionist post at a legal firm, which is not quite what I'm looking for, but it's a toe in the door. The door, as it turns out, opens into a low-rent high-churn law firm that specializes in defending domestic abusers.

I spend the entire interview mentally chanting "beggars can't be choosers" while wondering whether beggars should, perhaps, be a wee bit choosy after all. In the end, my moral compass doesn't need any jiggering. The guy interviewing me says that while my 4.0 GPA and three years of law-oriented volunteer work are very impressive, they've already filled the position. Seems the applicant before me was a thirty-seven-year-old lawyer who'd recently been downsized. Story of my life these days. Just when I feel as if I'm scraping the bottom of the barrel, there's someone with ten times my credentials scraping alongside me.

I do get a parting gift, though. Before I leave, my interviewer—the fifty-year-old HR manager who proudly told me he was one of the firm's success stories—asks me out for coffee. After all, it's not as if it'd be a conflict of interest if I know I'm not getting the job. At least I'm not scraping the bottom of *that* particular barrel yet. There's always Colin, the very sweet cop who's only interested in me because he's worried about my grandmother.

Speaking of Colin, he calls while I'm walking to my barista job, which is not coincidentally located next to the biggest law firm in the city. Someday, one of my carefully cultivated legal patrons will tell me about a job that just opened up, and I'll have my resume on HR's desk before they can post the position. So far, all I get are grumbles about how tough their jobs are and how much easier it must be to "just" pour coffee all day. The fact that I can commiserate without smacking them should earn me a job right there.

Colin is, sadly, not calling to tell me that he just heard about a new opening in the district attorney's office. Nope, he wants to talk about Gran.

"I tried speaking to her," I say. "It's not easy. You'd think it would be. The woman can talk the paint off the walls. But bring up something she doesn't want to discuss, and she suddenly has somewhere to go."

"She's avoiding the conversation?"

"Mmm. It's hard to tell. She always shuts me down if I want to talk about boring stuff like finances."

"She doesn't like to talk about money?"

"Who does? Anyway, like I said, she's got plenty of it. I did ask about the towing offer. She brushed it off. Said she was being nice and made it very clear that you hadn't asked for money."

I cross the road before continuing. "I honestly don't think she's doing more than giving out a bit here and there, which is her right. It's her money, and that's no different than donating to a stranger's GoFundMe, right?"

348

"Depends on if you're donating ten dollars or ten thousand."

"But if she has the ten thousand and feels like she's helping, maybe that's the important thing. That's what I keep telling myself. But still..."

"You're worried about your inheritance."

"What? No. Jesus. I'm living with my gran because she needed the help. I'm paying rent. Not much, but I pull my weight. I'm not a leech, and I'm certainly not thinking about my inheritance."

"I'm sorry, Lily. You wouldn't believe how many times I can only get the family involved by playing the I-card."

"Well, you don't need it with me. I care about my gran, not what she can do for me. If she's spending a few hundred bucks thinking she's helping strangers, I don't care. I only care if she's being ripped off to the extent that would damage her quality of life. Before Gramps died, the one thing he kept saying was that Gran would be fine. He'd made sure she had enough to be fine even if she lived to a hundred. That was important to him, and it's important to me."

"I understand, and I apologize for jumping to conclusions. You did suggest, though, that there's some reason you aren't dropping the matter."

I sigh and lean against a closed storefront a few doors from the coffee shop. "I want to trust Gran. This feels icky. It's treating her like a child or a senile old woman. We have an amazing relationship, and I'm afraid of her finding out that I'm talking to you about this. She'd be insulted. However, yes, I am concerned. When I talked about her offering to buy you a tow, she brushed it off, like I said. After that, twice I've walked in when she's on the phone, and she's taken the call into her bedroom. She never did that before."

"Guilt," he murmurs. "She knows she's been conned in the past, and she knows you're concerned. Like you said, she's a smart lady. While I could hope your warning might make her stop taking those calls, it seems to have just pushed them underground. They've become something she needs to hide."

"Great," I mutter.

"Were you able to find anything for me? Signs of financial distress? Unpaid bills? Creditor calls?"

"Nothing like that."

"Well, on the one hand, that's good. It means the situation isn't dire yet, and we can make sure it doesn't get there. We still need to know, though. If it's fifty bucks here, a hundred there, then that's her business. The fact she's on those lists suggests it's more serious."

"How do we find that out?"

"Get a look at her accounts. Look for unexplained withdrawals. At her age, she probably still gets physical copies of her statements. That'll make this easy. Minimal invasion of privacy. Here's what you need to do…"

A week has passed. Still no sign of a "real" job on my horizon, though I do receive daily e-mails from online universities promising that I just need a degree to jumpstart my new career. Yeah, got one of those, thanks, along with the debt to prove it. Me and the thousands of other millennials scrabbling for work. Along with the thousands of Gen Xers who've been downsized and the Boomers who want to "ease" into a slower-paced job preretirement.

On a more positive note, Colin asked me out for an actual meal today. Dinner. We spend half of it talking about Gran, and afterward, he insists on being a gentleman and walking me home, which I suspect is again more about Gran than me. I haven't been able to find what he's looking for. I've told him that I think Gran only gets virtual statements, but he doesn't seem to believe me no matter how much I insist my grandmother is twice as tech-savvy as my parents.

I open the door to the apartment, and I'm about to call hello, warning Gran that I'm bringing a guest, when I hear her on the phone. Colin motions for silence. We listen. She's…giggling? My brows shoot up, making Colin stifle a chuckle.

Gran continues giggling and, worse, simpering. Lots of "Oh, stop that" and "you sweet talker." I start to pull the door closed. If she's got herself a boyfriend, that is none of my business.

Colin stops me. Then, after a pause, he shuts the door himself and whispers, "This is not a good sign, Lily."

"Uh, yeah, it actually is. She hasn't been on a date since my grandfather passed five years ago."

"If that's what this is, then all the power to her. But the way she's talking, it's obvious that someone is buttering her up. Flattering her. Do you know what catfishing is?"

I give him a hard look. "I'm a twenty-five-year-old woman. Next, you'll be asking if I've ever received an unsolicited dick pic."

He flushes. "Uh, right. Well, you know what I mean then. The first step in catfishing is reaching out and making contact. The second stage is this." He gestures toward the door. "Flattery and sweet-talking. Nothing too over-the-top. Just lots of charm and pretty words. Especially if there's a lonely widow on the other end of the line."

He lifts a hand against my protest. "Yes, your gran isn't lonely, but it's a stereotype they play into. You did say she hasn't dated since you lost your grandfather."

"So, what do we do?"

"Walk in on her. Don't announce yourself. Pretend you didn't realize she was on the phone. She obviously didn't hear you come in. We'll walk in and see what she says."

I nod. Then I take a deep breath, open the door, and walk in. Without a word, we head straight for the kitchen, where Gran leans on the counter, deep in conversation, her cheeks pink.

"Hey, Gran," I say.

"Oh!" She nearly drops her cell phone.

"Sorry," I say. "I thought you heard us come in. This is Colin. We'll just head into the living room. You're obviously busy—"

"No, not at all. Just let me end this call."

Her cane tip-taps as she takes the phone into her bedroom. Colin and I exchange a look. A few moments later, she returns, still pink cheeked and bright eyed and sounding slightly out of breath.

"Sorry about that." She extends a hand. "Colin, it is so good to meet you. I hope you two had a lovely dinner. Where did you go again?"

"A new diner over on Petersburg. Kind of retro and funky. I liked it. The—"

"That sounds splendid. Just splendid. Now I hate to dash, but just before you came in, I realized we're out of milk."

"Oh," I say. "No problem. Let us run and grab it."

She lays a hand on mine. "No need, dear. I could use the fresh air, and it's right on the corner." She lifts her cane. "Even with this, I can manage."

Before I can say anything, she's trotting off, phone clutched in her hand. She barely pauses to grab her purse before she's gone.

"Should we follow her?" I whisper.

Colin shakes his head. "She's going to finish that call in private, and if she sees you, she'll cut it short again. It'll take a while for the guy to make his first move. Leave her to it for now. We need to find those bank statements."

"I really don't think she has any."

"Just show me where she keeps her records and then watch out the door for her return. I know exactly what to look for." He winks. "I'm kind of an expert."

Two days later, I'm coming back from lunch with my parents, which is always fun. I love my parents. They just try a little too hard these days. So many conversational landmines to avoid. Don't talk too much about Gran, or I think they're suggesting that I should move out on my own. Don't ask too much about my romantic life, or I might get the impression they're hinting for grandbabies. Don't even ask about my current jobs, or I might suspect they're judging my inability to get a real career.

I wouldn't think any of that because I know them, and they are awesome, supportive, understanding parents. But sometimes, being awesome and supportive and understanding means you can see all the landmines that your friends have stepped into with their kids, and you're constantly hopscotching to avoid them, which makes for very awkward lunches.

My one advantage is that I'm the youngest of three. My oldest sibling just finally landed a full-time job in her field, and my middle one just finally moved out of the house he's shared with five buddies since college. Until they're settled with careers and condos and kids, I have a nice window of time to ease into adulthood.

Speaking of time windows, I have exactly one hour between lunch and my volunteer gig at the women's shelter, where I help residents navigate the legal system. I'm back home and hurrying to Gran's condo when I see Elsa down the hall. She spots me and begins thumping her walker my way.

"Oh, Lily, thank God," she breathes. "Your gran isn't answering the door. We were supposed to meet up at one for cocktails. I was in my apartment having lunch, and I heard raised voices. I tapped on the wall and asked if everything was all right, and she said it was just a show."

I frown. "Gran doesn't watch TV."

Elsa wrings her hands. "I know. I thought of that afterward when she didn't answer her door. You have your key, don't you?"

I hold it up. "I'm sure everything's fine. Gran listens to podcasts on a speaker, and she sometimes calls them shows. That's probably what you heard."

I stride ahead to open the door. Then I hold it for Elsa as I call, "Gran?"

No answer. I walk into the living room and stop short.

"Oh my God," I whisper.

Gran is not the world's most particular housekeeper, but I can be a bit of a neat freak, and there is no way I left this morning with the living room looking like this. Books are pulled from the shelf. A plant is knocked over. One of the sofa cushions is half on the floor. A cup lies on its side, a stream of milky tea pooling on the floor below it.

Behind me, Elsa whimpers. "I knew something was wrong. I just knew it."

I turn to her. "Did Gran say she was having company over? You said you heard raised voices. Who else seemed to be in the room? A woman? A man?"

"A man. I heard a man's voice. She didn't say anything about having company, and she's so careful about letting anyone into the condo. The last plumber stomped off because she insisted on ID. Your grandpa taught her well." She looks around the room. "Something's happened."

"Don't worry," I say. "There's someone I can call."

A moment's pause. Then she says, "Oh! That young policeman you've been seeing. He's a detective, isn't he?"

I nod as I dial Colin's number. As Elsa frets loudly in the background, I tell him what I found. Then I say, "I figured you'd know what to do, being a police detective."

"Yes, well, this is exactly what I feared," he says. "It's gone beyond phone calls."

"What?" I say. "You think—you think she's been…" I look over at Elsa and lower my voice. "Kidnapped?"

His pause stretches on a little too long, and even when he says, "No, nothing like that," it's in the same tone Mom uses when reassuring me that my new haircut looks fine, just fine.

He continues, "It's more likely she's been lured out, possibly under some form of threat."

"What?" My voice rises to cracking, and Elsa starts up again, demanding to know what's going on.

"This person won't hurt her, Lily. There'd be no point in that. I suspect you were right. Your grandmother is a smart woman. She might happily give a stranger a hundred dollars for a tow truck, but she's nobody's fool. This person pushed too hard, and her purse snapped shut, and now he's said something that's changed her mind. They've probably gone to an ATM to take out money, and that's where we'll catch them."

"At an ATM? Oh, wait! You can catch them by having the bank notify me if her account is used."

"Well, no, they won't notify *you*. Not unless you have power of attorney, which we can talk about later. They will tell me, though. Which means I'm going to need to take a step I was really hoping to avoid. We couldn't find her bank statements. So, I need to ask you for her banking information, even if it means doing something that seems like a violation of her privacy."

"Anything. Right now, I don't care. Just tell me what you need."

I've barely gotten Colin what he needs when an exclamation sounds from the hall. I throw open the door to see Elsa hotfooting it toward the elevator as fast as her walker will move. Gran is stepping off it, holding a shopping bag.

"What's all this?" Gran says. "Did someone die? Don't tell me it was Frieda. We just put down the deposit on our cruise."

"Where were you?" Elsa says. "I was supposed to come over at one, and you weren't home, and then I remembered hearing shouting, and we found the living room ransacked."

"Ransacked? Did I forget to lock up?"

Gran hurries past us into the condo. Once she reaches the living room, she turns on her heel. "Ransacked? Really? I know you're a couple of neat freaks, but this is ridiculous, girls. I knocked over a few books looking for my reading glasses. I must not have noticed that one hit a plant. Then I dislodged a seat cushion when I got up, which apparently knocked over my teacup. I was in a hurry because I lost track of time reading and needed to grab mixer for our afternoon cocktails."

"And the shouting?"

"I was listening to a podcast, but no one was shouting."

"I definitely heard a man shouting."

Gran throws up her hands. "I don't know. The couple upstairs maybe? They're always going at it. The point is that I am fine, and my apartment isn't ransacked and—Lily? Where are you going?"

"The shelter. I'm late for my volunteer shift. Gotta run!"

I finish my volunteer shift early. I'll make it up later. Right now, I have something far more important.

I've tried calling Colin, but it was no surprise when I got a "not in service" message. That shifted me into sleuth mode. Gramps had been a cop once upon a time before he realized he could make more money as a private eye. Gran isn't the only one he taught the tools of the trade. At one time, I'd hoped to take over the business, but he'd soon convinced me legal work was more lucrative than peeping through windows. I'm no longer certain he was right.

The point is that I know what I'm doing, and an hour later, I'm standing outside Colin's station. Not a police station. A fire station.

He emerges from the side door, lunch pail in hand. I wait until he reaches the parking lot. He's moving fast and doesn't notice when I swing around in front of him. He reaches his car, glances up and stops short.

"Lily?" he says.

"Weird," I say. "This doesn't look like a police station at all. And that is *not* a detective's uniform."

"I can explain. I'm a volunteer firefighter and—"

"Save it. I know what you are and who you are, and it's not Colin Lawson, fraud detective. You did get the fraud part right, though."

He spots one of his colleagues coming out and waves at her while steering me across the lot. I let him lead me to a shaded spot under an old oak, which is much better for viewing photos and video anyway. That's what I give him. Screenshots of his real identity plus video of him rifling through Gran's financial records. Then I show him our texts, with him telling me exactly what he needed and confirming he was a police detective. Finally, a recording of our last call, where he'd reconfirmed he was a detective and instructed me on what I needed to get.

"The banking information I gave you is fake," I say. "I'd figured it out by then, which is why I recorded the call. As for the video, that was a lucky break. Gran suspected the cleaner was sneaking into her booze stash, and she's been trying to catch her at it."

His mouth opens and shuts; nothing comes out.

"You found Gran's name on those sucker lists," I say. "That's why you called the first time. Feeling out the situation. What a lucky break, her setting you up on a date with me."

"I—"

"You're a con artist, Connor Lake. All those things you said about people taking advantage of kind old ladies? You're one of those people. My gran offered you money for a tow. She set you up with me. I told you what an amazing person she was, and you *still* planned to take her for everything you could get."

"I—"

"You planned to ruin her life, so now I'm going to ruin yours. First, I'm talking to your boss. Then I'm speaking to the police. After that, I'll go to the press. I'm hoping that will make me feel better. It won't help Gran, though. How much money has she lost to people like you?"

I wrap my arms around my chest. "I lied when I said I couldn't find her statements. I've seen them. It's more than a hundred dollars here and there. She's fallen prey to bastards like you over and over. Ruining your life won't get her money back. I only hope it'll help someone else."

"I'm sorry, Lily. I really am. You're right, though. This won't help you get your gran's money back." He pauses. "What if we came to some arrangement?"

"Arrangement?" I snort. "Is that how you're going to get out of this? Toss me a few coins to keep quiet."

"More than a few coins. What do you say to five thousand dollars?"

I stare at him. Then I take a deep breath, meet his gaze, and say, "That better just be your opening offer."

I walk into the condo to find Gran reading in the living room. On the side table is a tablet, showing my location.

"Are you tracking me, Gran?" I say. "That is a grievous invasion of my privacy."

She snorts and swipes away the screen. "I wish you wouldn't insist on meeting with them on your own, Lily. It's not safe. Even with the tracker."

"And my knife," I say. "Never forget the power of my very small, very sharp knife." I squeeze her shoulder. "I can handle it, Gran. Daylight meeting. Public place. It's all good."

I open my purse and take out stacks of bills. "He paid promptly. They always do, don't they? It's as if they have stacks of cash on hand that they don't want to put in the bank. Weird."

I hand her half the cash. Then I take another roll and put it on the table. "Rent money."

She picks it up and presses it back into my hand as always. "I know you use your half to repay your school debt. Use this to buy yourself something special. You deserve it." She rises and kisses my cheek. "You're very good at this, Lily. Seems you take after your grandpa."

My gran *and* my gramps, to be exact. Gramps may have found private-eye work more lucrative than policing, but only because in private practice, he could cut ethical corners. He never conned anyone. Well, not anyone who didn't deserve it.

Gran had helped. Then, after her stroke, her love of wrong numbers led to some dubious incoming calls, and she realized she might not be quite ready to retire yet. Yes, Connor Lake had found her on those sucker lists. Because we put here there. One thing my gran is not? A sucker.

If Connor tries anything, he'll discover our numbers and names are fake, as is the apartment where he met Gran. We've already cleared out of that short-term rental.

"I say we go out to dinner and celebrate," Gran says. "We should invite poor Elsa, as compensation for that scare we gave her."

"Good idea."

We'd tried to keep that part of the con quick and painless, but I'd needed Elsa panicking in the background when I made that call to Connor. The fake kidnapping scare was just the thing to push him into slipping up on the phone, confirming he was masquerading as a cop and telling me in detail what banking information he needed.

Gran's about to call Elsa about dinner when her phone rings, and she glances down at it.

"Wrong number?"

She smiles. "The best kind."

I laugh and tell her I'll run down the hall to get Elsa.

***

UNDER PRESSURE

A *Thea Paris* Short Story

K.J. HOWE

Kidnap expert Thea Paris kicked her fins, the gentle whoosh of her regulator a stark contrast to the violent thumping of her heart. She was following her dive guide through a pitch-dark underwater tunnel system on Oman's coastline, near the Musandam Peninsula. Inside that narrow, winding tube of stone, sixty feet below the surface, a creeping sense of anxiety filled her. Her free hand brushed against the SIG Sauer hidden in her waterproof pouch for reassurance, but it was hard to imagine how it could be useful.

The reed-thin local diver, Juma Taber, needled the two of them deeper into the warren of tunnels, motioning "okay" with his flashlight at every challenging turn. She mirrored his latest signal, but she was far from fine. In forty-two minutes, the rising tide would flood a cave where a heavily armed kidnapper was holding three American missionaries prisoner. In exchange for the release of the hostages, the kidnapper—an Iran-allied Houthi named Kamran Moradi—had demanded the US government force the Saudis to withdraw from Yemen.

For three days of intense negotiation, the missionaries had been held captive inside a large, humid cavern at sea level, near the water line. The entrance to the cave had since flooded, trapping the kidnapper and hostages inside. Thea and her team had consulted the local pearl divers who frequented these waters, her new friend Juma among them. The father of two teenage boys had generously offered to act as a guide. Thanks to his previous explorations, Juma knew about an underwater access route, but he warned it would be difficult.

During his twenty-minute crash course, Juma had emphasized that cave diving was "penetration diving." In Arabic, he said, "If we have an emergency, we need to solve it together."

The thought of being separated from open water by countless tons of rock unsettled Thea. No free ascents if something went wrong, no help from above—they'd have to weave their way through the maze to escape.

"I promise to be a good dive buddy," Thea said.

"*Rafiq alghaws*; very important," he said with a smile, reinforcing their partnership was the most important piece of equipment they would bring with them.

She liked Juma's meticulous approach, the serious look in his eyes as he explained the cardinal rules of cave diving. He'd been a complete stranger to her yesterday, and now they'd need unshakable trust to safely navigate the labyrinth.

While Thea spoke with Juma, her colleague Rif Asker had surveyed the scant equipment Juma's sons had brought along. The two teenagers had grown up in these waters, becoming experienced cave divers. Their gear showed the wear-and-tear of countless dives, but everything seemed to be in good working order. Thea would use the eldest son's wetsuit and buoyancy control device—luckily, she and the teenager were more or less the same size.

On the first day, Thea and Rif had tried negotiating with Kamran through a fissure in the cavern's ceiling, but the kidnapper wouldn't budge on his demands. On day two, a cyclone hit the region, bringing with it an epic 243 millimeters of rain in under twenty-four hours, accelerating the timeline. Acutely aware of the danger posed by the rising groundwater, Thea and Rif had offered to stand down from their position on the rocky coastline and provide safe passage out for the kidnapper and hostages. But the volatile Iranian had insisted it was a trick, hustling the hostages into the farthest reaches of the cavern. Concerned the kidnapper might be suicidal, Thea and her team had no choice but to attempt a rescue mission.

There had been a debate in their mobile HQ about which team member should enter the underwater tunnel system with Juma. Rif was the only operative with cave diving experience, but Juma had insisted Rif's large frame wouldn't fit through a tight section inside the tunnel known as *Yadiq*—the Narrows—even with his scuba tanks in a slimming, side-mounted configuration. Only Thea was slender enough to move through the confined space. She'd only ever logged open-water dives, but what other option did they have?

Ahead of her, Juma followed the "gold lines," the yellowish

nylon ropes he had previously placed throughout the main cavern, including directional markers, creating a nonstop line to the exit. She followed closely, avoiding churning the silt on the floor with her fins by keeping her upper body lower than her legs. She'd memorized the route to the kidnapper's lair in case she and Juma became separated, but now that she was actually down here in the cold and dark, that exercise seemed hopelessly abstract.

A shiver zig-zagged down Thea's spine. Her diabetes heightened her sensitivity to hot and cold, and the cave's sun-deprived waters were frigid. Even with the protection of a wetsuit, hypothermia was a threat, especially as the dive progressed. She checked the diabetes app on her phone, relieved to see her blood sugar levels were stable. This was her first time using a "bionic pancreas," an automated biofeedback machine that added just the right amount of insulin to her bloodstream when her blood sugar level spiked. Given the intense stress on her body, this mission would put the system to the test. The device and her phone had been waterproofed using a small plastic camera case, attached to her wetsuit with an oversized safety pin.

With her left index finger and thumb circling the guideline, Thea followed Juma, the flashlight in her right hand highlighting the cavern's stalactites and stalagmites. The spiked protrusions contributed to the rugged beauty of the cave and suggested these caverns had been above sea level during the last ice age. A moray eel revealed its head from behind a spectacular rock formation before quickly disappearing again.

Thea checked her dive watch. Thirty-eight minutes before the western cave flooded.

Following Juma around another bend, she sensed movement to her right. She swept her light across the cavern, relieved to see it was just a snow-white crab skittering by, the lack of pigmentation an adaptation to living without light. She kicked her fins harder to keep up with her dive partner.

Three minutes later, they entered an even tighter tunnel and she experienced the first stirrings of the strong current Juma had warned her about. Because water is denser than air, the brisk flow in this section felt like a storm-level wind. Thea kept her face pointed directly into the current, as twisting her head to either side could flood or dislodge her mask.

Two more turns and they would reach the final tunnel before the underwater opening to the western cavern. The walls would constrict further as they approached *Yadiq*, the tightest squeeze of the journey.

Suddenly the flashlight in Juma's hand moved rapidly side-to-side, the prearranged signal to pay close attention. *What now?* Two seconds later, Juma's light tumbled out of his hand and he blew backwards, hurtling toward her.

She cocooned her body as he sped by, but one of his legs smashed into her right shoulder and sent a jolt of pain down her arm. A large and impossibly fast shadow propelled Juma through the water. She aimed her light upward, spotlighting the silvery skin of a white-tipped reef shark as it raced past, headed toward the exit. It must have been caught sleeping, frightened by their arrival.

She steadied her breathing and forced herself to remain calm. *Juma.* The encounter with the shark had stirred up silt, diminishing visibility to just a few feet. With one hand, she held her mask in place and turned her body, following the guideline backwards, tracing her dive partner's somersault in the ghostly haze.

Moving slowly, she searched for him with her flashlight. The current pushed her along, allowing her to retrace their earlier route. Amid the billowing clouds of silt she finally spotted him. Juma's arms were splayed outward, a stalagmite protruding from the right side of his torso, below the rib line, blood lightly swirling into the water. The shark had plowed him onto the spike in its haste to escape and now he was pinned to the cave floor.

She shone the light on Juma's mask. He was conscious, eyes wide, face contorted in pain, and the regulator was still firmly lodged in his mouth. Adrenaline jolted through her veins, as she considered her options. If she yanked him off the spike, its rough edges might do even more damage on the way out. Left in place, the stalagmite would serve as a make-shift tamponade. Either way, the risk of infection was high. She had no way to fully assess his injury while they were underwater. Keeping the stalagmite in place until she could get him medical attention was the only choice that made sense.

Thea freed her largest knife from its sheath and pantomimed to Juma her plan to cut through the stalagmite. The veteran cave diver nodded, remaining calm. He had warned her that panicking would just deplete the air supply, but she marveled at his composure.

Juma stabilized the tip of the spike with his hands while Thea used the knife to start chipping away at the base. Small bits of debris and white-capped barnacles floated away as she progressed. She struck at the spike over and over, attacking the soft mineral composite from different angles. Finally, she was able to break it off the cave floor, freeing Juma.

He righted himself, hovering in the water, holding onto the cave wall. She couldn't imagine the pain he was experiencing. The injury was low and on the right side, so it was unlikely it had punctured his heart or his lung. Still, the situation was grave. If one of the major blood vessels in his chest had been nicked, he could be bleeding internally. He required evacuation to a hospital immediately.

Should she head back with him or plunge on? Every safety regulation demanded she abort the dive. She had a severely injured dive partner, and they were inside a twisting labyrinth of caves deep below the surface, with no means of outside communication. The silt had reduced visibility to a few feet, and their precious air supply had been depleted by the extra activity.

But if she terminated the mission, the hostages would die.

Juma touched her forearm to get her attention, then pointed ahead, giving her the okay signal. He wanted to continue. The pearl diver was brave and experienced, but was he being rash? But continuing on might be the better option. They would have a shorter swim as they had already traveled well past the halfway point. Also, she might be able to get Juma evacuated and save the hostages. If they turned back now, they had a longer swim out—and it would mean certain death for the hostages and their kidnapper.

Wrestling with the decision, Thea shone her light on Juma's face and looked into his eyes. He gave her the "okay" sign again. They were going forward.

She released Juma and rifled in her mesh dive bag for her duct tape. The tape's rubber-based, water-resistant adhesive kept it sticky underwater. She used it to secure Juma's regulator on his mouth, so even if he passed out he'd still be able to breathe. She also wrapped duct tape around his mid-section, to minimize blood loss and keep the stalagmite from shifting around. A quick glance at both of their air gauges told her they should still be able to reach the western cave—barring any further mishaps, that is.

Thea threaded extra line through the D-ring on Juma's buoyancy-control vest so she could tow him in case he lost consciousness. Next, she checked to make sure his tanks were secure. She'd have to keep a close eye on his air consumption. Squeezing Juma's hand, she made him a silent promise to get him home alive.

Clinging to the guideline, she confronted the current again, Juma right behind her. She fluttered her short stiff fins, propelling them deeper into the cave. The shaft darkened and the walls closed in. If not for her flashlight, she wouldn't be able to see her hand in front of her face. Everything seemed more intimidating now that she was the lead diver. Thea took a few measured breaths, the bubbles from her regulator drifting upwards, then checked her watch again.

Twenty-two minutes before the kidnapper and the hostages would drown.

Moving through the cavern, they reached a fork. She visualized the map Juma had shown her during their pre-dive prep. Two lefts, then a right turn would lead them to the bottom of the spring that emerged in the western cave's floor. At least she hoped so. Turn the wrong way, and they could get trapped inside a blocked channel or lost in the maze.

The tunnel jutted downward, deeper into the stone. They'd reached *Yadiq*. Her tanks scraped the walls, metal grinding against stone. The tightest part of the route loomed ahead, the ceiling dropping dramatically. A small passageway, not much more than a crack, led to the rest of the tunnel system. Juma had told her they'd need to remove their tanks and push them through first. Claustrophobia clawed at her throat, but she forced down the rising alarm and turned to help Juma. She slipped off his buoyancy-control device and tanks, checking his gauges. With the injury, he was consuming a lot of air. He seemed less alert than he had been a few minutes ago. And it must be excruciating to move with that spike embedded in his torso.

Thea removed her own tanks, feeling naked without her air supply attached to her body. Edging the tanks ahead of her, she kept her teeth clamped down on the regulator before ducking through the crevice, the rough limestone ceiling grazing the back of her head and suit. She navigated another tight twist. Juma had been right about Rif not making it through.

She nudged her tanks ahead of her until the tunnel subtly widened, morphing into an underwater cavern. Out of the narrows, she turned and gently pulled Juma and his tanks along until he was fully through the cramped opening. She eased his buoyancy-control device back on, then strapped on her own. She shone her flashlight on his face—he was unconscious now, but his breathing was steady, the regulator still taped in place.

Thea linked her arm underneath Juma's and searched for landmarks. After a few moments the cave sloped upwards again. Could the opening above be the entrance to the spring? If so, she'd need to remove her tanks and surface in silence. A beam of light or a surge of air bubbles would announce her arrival and eliminate the element of surprise.

Pulling Juma along, she swam to a rock formation at the basin's left wall, where she removed her buoyancy-control device and tanks a second time. Securing Juma and her equipment to an outcropping of limestone, she wrapped the excess line around her hand, leaving plenty of slack. She couldn't risk taking him with her while searching for the opening—if he woke up and panicked, they'd be vulnerable to attack.

As she worked, Thea's regulator free-flowed for a few seconds. She fixed the issue quickly, but not before a barrage of bubbles floated upwards in the water. She removed and activated two ChemLights, attaching one to the tanks she had to leave behind and one to Juma's vest. The glowing sticks would help her find her way back once she located the opening. She kept her flashlight switched on for now, the loop snug around her wrist.

She took one last deep lungful of air, removed her regulator, and started the free ascent. As she rose, she carefully managed her exhale. She needed to let the air out quickly enough to avoid injuring her lungs, but slowly enough so that she had sufficient air to reach the surface. And she had to be careful to avoid the dreaded bends. Gently kicking her way up, one hand tracing the wall, she swam and swam, fighting to stay calm. Juma had advised her the spring was around fifty feet deep, with a twelve-foot-wide opening at the top, but the journey felt endless.

Time stretched, her lungs beginning to spasm. After what felt like an eternity she saw silvery bubbles moving along the surface. She turned off her flashlight. Finally, she felt the warm kiss of air on her forehead. She surfaced slowly, inhaling a deep, silent breath. Then she reached above her head. Her palm collided with rock just inches above the surface.

Dammit.

She flicked the flashlight on and shone it above her head. There was only ten inches of space between the water and a small ceiling of rock. Frustration and fear welled inside her. This was not the opening.

Thea's teeth chattered and her limbs seemed impossibly stiff. She sucked in another breath of the moldy air trapped in the air pocket. Maybe she could rouse Juma, get him to help. Then she remembered the silvery bubbles from her exhalation on the way up—they had all flowed in one direction, following the current. The opening had to be close by.

Inspired, she turned off her light, inhaled deeply, and dove back underwater, feeling her way along the roof as she moved in the direction the bubbles had been headed. Almost out of breath, her left arm finally surfaced.

At last.

She slowly raised her head out of the water to see threads of daylight filtering through the cracks in the cave's rocky ceiling. The cacophony of rushing water was deafening. She pushed her mask down around her neck so it wouldn't accidentally get knocked off and allowed her eyes to adjust to the hazy light. The main cavern was roughly circular with a rock-strewn floor. At the far end, there were two tunnels side-by-side—one large, the other small. In the distance, she could hear voices. The kidnapper and hostages must be somewhere deeper inside, through one of the tunnels. No doubt the missionaries would be dehydrated, exhausted, and hungry after three days in captivity.

Nineteen minutes to go before the water filled the cave system. She eased her mask back on and found a small outcropping of rock below water level, attaching another ChemLight to it so she could find her way back. After several deep inhales and exhales, she dove back down to retrieve Juma. The sooner he was out of the water, the better.

She felt a surge of relief when she found the pearl diver floating where she had left him. But he was still unconscious and breathing heavily, the bubbles rushing out of his regulator in large clouds.

After a quick inhale from her own regulator, she slipped her tanks back on. She untied Juma, looping her arm under his left shoulder and guiding him to the opening. Quietly resurfacing, she pushed her mask down around her neck again. She kicked off her fins and hoisted her dive partner onto the rocky floor. She listened for a moment, scanning the area, confirming no one knew they had arrived.

Two voices echoed in the left tunnel, one of which was Rif's. The former Delta Force operative was still trying to convince Kamran that leaving the cave was the only option to avoid drowning. But the strident tone of the Houthi's response offered little hope he had changed his mind.

Thea grabbed Juma by the shoulders and lugged him to the highest surface in the cave, the surge already at her knees. She removed his mask and the duct tape, gently pulling the regulator out of his mouth. The veins in his neck were bulging. His eyes flickered open and his nostrils flared. He was struggling to bring air into his lungs.

"We made it, Juma."

Thea checked his vitals. His pulse was faint and galloping, his lips tinged with blue. Even more disconcerting, his trachea had shifted slightly to the left. A gurgling noise bubbled from around the stalagmite, which must have clipped his lung.

Puncture wounds to the lung, like stabbings or gunshots, allowed air into the cavity between the lung and the chest wall. The pressure could build until the lung collapsed. The stalagmite must have punctured Juma's right lung, increasing the air pressure in his torso to the point where it was compressing his heart and blood vessels. With every inhale, a little more air was being trapped inside, squeezing his organs. Juma was restless, agitated, weakly flailing his arms. He was hurtling towards asphyxia unless she found a way to release the pressure.

Thea cut away the wetsuit around the injury and used both hands to gently spread the wound, hoping to create enough space for air to escape. No luck. She flashed on her combat-medic training, where she'd had to perform a needle thoracostomy—thrusting a hollow tube into the chest cavity to release the trapped air. But where the hell was she going to get a bore needle?

A loud crash caught her attention. A slab of rock had broken off the wall and smashed onto the cave floor, sending a large swell in their direction. The force of the incoming water was wreaking havoc.

Twelve minutes left.

She searched through the items in her kit—and Juma's—but found nothing even remotely workable. The ideal tool would be a tube around 2 mm in diameter and long enough to go through his chest and reach the air pocket. Her hand brushed against the waterproof case containing her insulin delivery device. An idea struck her. Part of the closed loop system was a stainless steel tube. It wasn't a needle, but it might work.

She disassembled the bionic pancreas and removed the tube. It wasn't quite three inches long, but it would have to do. Looking for the right spot, her index finger traced an imaginary line from Juma's right nipple up to his clavicle. She located the space between his second and third rib and placed one end of the tube against his skin before smacking it down, driving the tube into his chest. Juma grunted in pain.

A loud hiss sounded as the trapped air escaped. Juma inhaled once, then again. His breathing became softer, less labored, and the veins in his neck settled. The panic faded in his eyes and his lips changed from blue to a more natural pink. Good thing he was whipcord lean—if he had been a heavier-set man, the short cylinder would not have been long enough.

Two minutes later, she removed the tube, concerned about the bacteria she had just introduced into his thoracic cavity. She emptied the small sandwich baggie holding the gummy bears she carried to combat blood sugar dips and placed it over the lightly bleeding hole. Next, she duct-taped three sides of the plastic square to Juma's chest, creating a valve that would allow air to escape without letting any new air in. Finally, she inflated his buoyancy-control device and ditched his dive weights on the cave floor.

"Better?"

"Better," Juma croaked.

Thea created a lasso with her line and threw it upwards, looping it onto an outcropping of rock near the ceiling. She tied one end to Juma's wrist and then attached two more ChemLights to his dive vest. As the water level rose, he would float upwards until the surge completely filled the cavern. Then he could use whatever air was left in their tanks as he waited for her to return. Yet another ticking time bomb.

The rushing water was now above her knees. Kamran was still arguing with Rif. She tried to make out what they were saying, but there was too much background noise.

"Not that way," Juma panted, grabbing her hand and pointing to the left tunnel. "He'll see you. Use the right side...there is a small opening to the left one twenty paces in."

"Got it." She checked his pulse again. Steady. She passed him his regulator. "I'll be back as soon as I can."

"Just take care of my family," he said, breathing with effort. "If I don't make it."

"That's not the way this story ends." She gave him what she hoped was a confident smile. "Just keep yourself tethered to that rock so I can find you."

Nine minutes left.

After squeezing Juma's arm, Thea sloshed through the waist-high, churning water, one hand on the wall for support, the other one holding her SIG. When she reached the Y junction of the two tunnels, Thea edged forward, staying hidden behind the rock. The left tunnel was broad and oval-shaped with a narrow shelf of stone at the far end.

Three silhouettes trembled in the shadows. The hostages, two women and one man, were perched awkwardly on the ledge above the rising tide, their hands bound. Two battery-operated lanterns lit the scene. Barrel-chested and tall, Kamran was waist-deep in the rising water below them. The Houthi had an AK-47 slung over his left shoulder and a small, round object clutched in his right hand.

Kamran pivoted in her direction. She froze, nerves jangling, waiting to see if he'd spotted her in the gloom. After an endless moment, he faced the hostages again, shouting at them while waving the object in his right hand.

Thea brought up the SIG and lined up for a clear body shot, positioning the gun against a rock for support. A ray of sunlight stabbed through the cracks in the ceiling, spotlighting the kidnapper. Thea immediately lowered her gun. The bright light had illuminated the object in his hand—a grenade. And it looked like the pin had been removed. The kidnapper's fingers were closed around the safety lever. If she shot him, he would release the lever, killing them all. Insurance for him against being sniped from above.

She slipped the SIG back inside its waterproof pouch, adjusted her mask and dipped beneath the surface. She stretched her arms in front of her, cupped her hands, and pulled them down to her hips. Gliding underwater, she crossed the narrow space between the two tunnels, hidden from Kamran's gaze. One more powerful kick, and she stood up again, positioned in the mouth of the right tunnel. Trusting Juma's extensive knowledge of the cave system, she counted her steps, slowing as she reached twenty paces. And there it was—a narrow gap. If she hadn't known it was there, she never would have noticed it. She sidled into the tight space, making her way toward the hostages.

Several steps later, she crouched behind a mass of rocks in the larger tunnel. She risked a glance around the side. Kamran was waving the grenade around and speaking loudly, possibly to himself. Definitely no pin. Leaving only her head exposed, she slid down low in the water and moved toward the hostages.

One of the female hostages, a redhead, had blood running down the side of her face. Thea recognized her from the photos the US State Department had provided: Anna Whitmer. As if the woman could sense someone watching her, her gaze turned in Thea's direction. Anna's eyes widened slightly. Thea raised a finger to her lips.

Anna broke eye contact and immediately scurried towards the edge of the narrow platform where the hostages were huddled.

"Talk to that man outside. I want to get out of here!" Anna yelled at Kamran. Then she slipped off the shallow ledge and stumbled into the churning water, leaving the others behind. Thea silently thanked her for creating a distraction.

The kidnapper strode towards Anna, raising his fist and shouting at her. Thea powered through the water. Before Kamran could reach Anna, Thea lunged, snagging him in a choke hold with her left arm and grabbing his right hand in hers. She tightened her grip as the kidnapper bucked and twisted, trying to pry her off him. Her right hand clamped over his, maintaining his grip on the grenade's safety lever. But he was strong—much stronger than she was—and he would eventually break free.

Anna stumbled towards them.

"Keep his right hand closed!" Thea ordered.

Anna wrapped her bound hands around Thea's fingers, helping to compress the grenade's lever. As Kamran rocked back and forth like a bucking bronco, Thea tightened the vise around his neck. He fought hard, but she and Anna held fast. Finally, the kidnapper faltered. Staggering forward, he collapsed to his knees, then slumped unconscious, the two women splashing down into the water with him. Anna scrambled back up to the platform while Thea removed the grenade from his grip.

Thea undid the large safety pin attaching her bionic pancreas to her wetsuit. Straightening the pointy end, she carefully inserted it into the small holes on the grenade's safety lever. The explosive device had been neutralized. She tucked the weapon into her dive bag, grabbed two heavy zip-ties, and secured them around Kamran's hands and feet before dragging him to the platform. Anna and the others helped haul his unconscious body up with them.

Climbing onto the ledge, Thea used her dive knife to slice through the zip-ties on Anna's hands, then passed her the blade so she could free the other hostages.

"All clear!" Thea yelled up at the ceiling.

"Coming in!" Rif's baritone echoed from above.

Thea shivered, even colder now that she was out of the water.

Seconds later, natural light shone through the cave's roof, as the rescue team removed the final layer of rocks blocking access from above. Stone after stone was tossed aside until the hole was wide enough to accommodate a person. A rope with a harness attached dropped down. Rif rappelled down another rope, landing in the water with a loud splash.

"Get these people out!" she called to Rif above the din. "I'm going back for Juma."

"Wait—" Rif called to her, but she was already on her way.

Thea put her mask back on and slipped into the icy water. As she plowed against the crosscurrents created by the incoming floodwater, her body was pummeled from all sides. Turning her head for a quick breath, she inhaled a mouthful of briny water. She fought the urge to choke and powered forward.

Five minutes to go.

She lifted her head as she reached the entrance to the first cavern. Very little air space remained. Through the churning water, Thea caught a glimpse of the ChemLights she'd tied to her dive partner. A swell slammed her right hip into the wall of the cavern. Ignoring the pain, she coiled her legs and pushed off the wall, headed for the beacons of light.

When she reached Juma, he had his mask on, the regulator in his mouth. His eyes lit up as she approached. After sucking in another gasp of air, she cut the line anchoring him to the outcropping of rock and tied the loose end around her own waist, intertwining their fates. Her two tanks were empty. She checked the air gauge on his. Under 500psi, in the red zone.

Three minutes.

Waves crashed over them as she removed his fins and slipped them on her own feet. Juma was too weak to help, and she'd need every ounce of power to escape the cave. A wave smashed into her face. Water was everywhere, filling her ears, her mouth, covering her head. She spat out yet another mouthful of salty liquid, gagging.

Juma grabbed her hand, removed the regulator from his mouth and passed it to her. She sucked in a lungful of air and handed it right back. If they had any hope of escaping, they'd need to buddy breathe on the way out.

Linking her arm under his right, she swam in the direction of the left cave. Her legs burned as she kicked. She reached for the regulator only when she was desperate—Juma needed the oxygen more than she did. Every time their bodies crashed together she worried about aggravating his injury.

They finally reached the opening of the left tunnel. Thea's muscles were depleted, but she kicked and kicked until finally she resurfaced to find Rif securing Kamran into a harness. The kidnapper was now awake, struggling, but the ties held him fast.

One minute.

Treading water, Rif gripped the other rope that dangled from the hole above and moved closer to Thea and Juma. His eyes widened at the duct-taped stalagmite protruding from the pearl diver's chest. He shouted to the team above and another harness dropped into the water next to them. With Thea's help, Rif slipped Juma into the yoke and signaled to the team. They winched Juma upwards, away from the roiling water.

Rif held the rope out to Thea and she tried to grab it, but her frozen fingers struggled for purchase. Moving towards her, Rif wrapped one arm around her waist and yelled to the team above. The two of them rose into the air, slowly spinning as their feet left the water. As they exited the cavern, she shivered uncontrollably against the warmth of Rif's body.

Back on the surface, Thea gasped for breath, trying to recover. After a minute or two, she stumbled over to where a medic was working on Juma, preparing him to be airlifted to the nearest hospital. Juma's boys hovered anxiously a few feet away.

"How's the patient?"

"It's a serious injury, and he'll need immediate surgery, but your improvisation saved his life."

Juma glanced at his two sons, then turned towards her. "Thank you, Thea."

"I'm the one who should be thanking you—none of this would

have been possible without you."

Juma placed his hand on her forearm. "You are a good 'dive buddy.'"

"You're not so bad yourself." She smiled.

Juma's sons edged closer. They must be devastated at the sight of the large spike protruding from their father's chest.

"That's so cool," the eldest whispered.

"I'm going to keep it," the other boy said.

Thea almost laughed out loud. Only to be a teenager again.

Ten minutes later, a medevac chopper transported Juma and his boys to the local hospital, where an operating theater had been prepped for their arrival. Meanwhile, Thea and Rif's support team had examined the hostages, offered them hot beverages and a snack, shepherding them to safety. Kamran had been taken into custody by Omani officials.

Seated on a rock with a Mylar blanket wrapped around her shoulders, Thea yanked off her nylon hood, beyond grateful to be out of the cave.

"I'm relieved Juma will be okay," Rif said.

"Me, too. The company will cover his medical expenses, but I'd like to do something special for his family. He almost lost his life helping complete strangers."

"By the look of it I'd say you two aren't strangers anymore," Rif said. "Hey, do you need anything? Protein bar?"

"No, I'm fine. Just tired—and very cold."

"Blood sugar levels?"

She checked her app, relieved they were stable despite the intense physical and emotional stress. "All good."

"So, that bionic pancreas thing really worked," Rif said.

"The device is a real team player. It saved Juma's life." Thea paused. "Oh, and my life… And the hostages' lives."

"Looks like you were the right person for this operation, after all."

"One and done, my friend. Any future cave dives are all yours," she said, assessing his broad shoulders and muscled chest. "Better get started on that diet, stat."

***

ABOUT THE AUTHORS

New York Times and *USA Today* bestselling author DARYNDA JONES has won numerous awards for her work, including a prestigious RITA®, a Golden Heart®, and a Daphne du Maurier, and her books have been translated into 17 languages. As a born storyteller, she grew up spinning tales of dashing damsels and heroes in distress for any unfortunate soul who happened by. Darynda lives in the Land of Enchantment, also known as New Mexico, with her husband and two beautiful sons, the Mighty, Mighty Jones Boys.

SHEILA LOWE is a real-life forensic handwriting expert who testifies in court cases. In addition to writing nonfiction books about handwriting and personality, she is the author of the award-winning *Forensic Handwriting* suspense series and the *Beyond the Veil* paranormal suspense series. Her stories of psychological suspense put ordinary people into extraordinary circumstances.

SUSAN SANTANGELO is the author of the best-selling *Baby Boomer Mystery* series. She is a member of Sisters in Crime, International Thriller Writers, and the Cape Cod Writers Center, and also reviews mysteries for *Suspense Magazine*. She divides her time between Clearwater, Florida and Cape Cod, Massachusetts, and shares her life with her husband Joe and two very spoiled

English cocker spaniels, Boomer and Lilly, who also serve as models for the books' covers. Susan is also a proud, lucky two-time breast cancer survivor, and credits early detection by regular mammograms with saving her life twice.

J.T. ELLISON is the *New York Times* and *USA Today* bestselling author of more than 25 critically acclaimed novels, including *IT'S ONE OF US, HER DARK LIES, GOOD GIRLS LIE, TEAR ME APART, LIE TO ME,* and *ALL THE PRETTY GIRLS,* and coauthored the *A Brit in the FBI* series with #1 *New York Times* bestselling author Catherine Coulter. Ellison is also the EMMY® Award-winning co-host of the television series *A Word on Words.*

With millions of books in print, Ellison's work has been published in 28 countries and 16 languages. Her novel *THE COLD ROOM* won the ITW Thriller Award for Best Paperback Original. Her novels *FIELD OF GRAVES* and *WHERE ALL THE DEAD LIE* were each a RITA® nominee for Best Romantic Suspense. She is also the author of multiple short stories.

Ellison lives in Nashville with her husband and two unruly cats. Visit jtellison.com or @thrillerchick for more.

Agatha Award-winning and nationally bestselling author DARYL WOOD GERBER writes the popular *Aspen Adams* novels of suspense. In addition, Daryl writes standalone thrillers including *DAY OF SECRETS* and *GIRL ON THE RUN.* As a cozy mystery author, Daryl pens bestselling the *Cookbook Nook Mysteries* and *Fairy Garden Mysteries.* As Avery Aames, she wrote the *Cheese Shop Mysteries.* Fun Tidbit: as an actress, Daryl appeared in "Murder, She Wrote." She has also jumped out of a perfectly good airplane and hitchhiked around Ireland by herself. Make sure to visit her website to learn more: https://darylwoodgerber.com.

JAMIE FREVELETTI is the internationally bestselling author of seven novels and four short stories. Her *Emma Caldridge* series was awarded an International Thriller Writers Best First Novel award, a Barry award, and was a VOX media pick in Germany. In addition to her own novels she's written *THE JANUS REPRISAL* and *THE GENEVA STRATEGY* for Robert Ludlum's *Covert One* series. She's a contributor to the non-fiction anthology, *ANATOMY OF INNOCENCE, TESTIMONIES OF THE WRONGFULLY CONVICTED*, which was chosen by Literary Hub as one of the best True Crime books of 2017, as well as the Sherlock Holmes Anthology, *FOR THE SAKE OF THE GAME*. A former lawyer, avid distance runner and black belt in aikido, a Japanese martial art, she splits her time between Los Angeles and Chicago.

SUSAN WINGATE writes about big trouble in small towns. She lives with her husband on an island off the coast of Washington State where, against State laws, she feeds the wildlife because she *wants* them to follow her. Her ukulele playing is, "Coming along," as her Sitto used to say.

Susan's eight-time award-winning novel, *HOW THE DEER MOON HUNGERS* was chosen by *The International Pulpwood Queens and Timber Guys Book Club* as their October 2022 Official Book Selection of the Month. Susan has an insatiable appetite for online word games and puzzles. She thinks it might be obsessive-compulsive but is fine with that.

Susan's poetry, short stories, and essays have been published in journals such as the *Virginia Quarterly Review*, the *Superstition Review*, and *Suspense Magazine*, as well as several others. She is also a proud member of *PENAmerica, Int'l Thriller Writers, Mystery Writers of America*, and *Women's Fiction Writers Association*.

TOSCA LEE is the multi-award winning, *New York Times*, IndieBound, and Amazon bestselling author of eleven novels including *THE LINE BETWEEN, THE PROGENY, FIRSTBORN, THE LEGEND OF SHEBA, ISCARIOT*, and the *Books of Mortals* trilogy with *New York Times* bestseller Ted Dekker. Her work has been translated into seventeen languages and optioned for TV and film. A notorious night-owl, she loves movies, playing video games with her kids, and sending cheesy texts to her husband. She's also a big fan of her amazing readers.

New York Times and *USA Today* bestselling author ALLISON BRENNAN believes life is too short to be bored, so she had five children and writes three books a year. Reviewers have called her "a master of suspense" and RT Book Reviews said her books are "mesmerizing" and "complex." She's been nominated for multiple awards, including the Thriller, RWA's Best Romantic Suspense (five times), and twice won the Daphne du Maurier award. She lives in Arizona with her family and assorted pets.

Wall Street Journal bestselling author ISABELLA MALDONADO wore a gun and badge in real life before turning to crime writing. A graduate of the FBI National Academy in Quantico and the first Latina to attain the rank of captain in the Fairfax County Police Department just outside DC, she retired as the Commander of Special Investigations and Forensics. During more than two decades on the force, her assignments included hostage negotiator, department spokesperson, and precinct commander. She uses her law enforcement background to bring a realistic edge to her writing, which includes the bestselling *FBI Special Agent Nina Guerrera* series (soon to be a Netflix feature film starring Jennifer Lopez) and the award-winning *Detective Veranda Cruz* series. Her books have been translated into 20 languages. For more information, visit www.isabellamaldonado.com.

SHANNON KIRK is the multiple award-winning, international bestselling author of *METHOD 15/33*, which was optioned for film, sold in over 20 languages, and garnered critical acclaim, including three starred reviews and the coveted placement on School Library Journal's 2017 "Best Adult Books for Teens," as well as *VIEBURY GROVE, GRETCHEN, IN THE VINES*, and the award-winning *THE EXTRAORDINARY JOURNEY OF VIVIENNE MARSHALL*, which was given the Literary Classics Seal of Approval. Her most recent book is her first legal thriller, *TENKILL*. In addition to her short story in this anthology, Shannon has several in other anthologies. When not writing, Shannon is a lawyer. She lives in the Boston area with her husband and son. Find her online at shannonkirkbooks.com.

KELLEY ARMSTRONG is the author of the *Rip Through Time* and *Rockton* mystery series. Past works include the *Otherworld* urban fantasy series, the *Cainsville* gothic mystery series, the *Nadia Stafford* thriller trilogy, the *Darkest Powers & Darkness Rising* teen paranormal series, the *Age of Legends* teen fantasy series and the *Royal Guide to Monster Slaying* middle-grade fantasy series.

K.J. HOWE is the internationally bestselling author of *THE FREEDOM BROKER* and *SKYJACK*, and the Executive Director of the International Thriller Writers. Born in Toronto, Canada, she enjoyed a nomadic lifestyle during her early years, living in Africa, the Middle East, Europe, and the Caribbean, inspiring an insider's view into her kidnap and ransom thrillers. Learn more at: www. kjhowe.com.

CATHERINE COULTER is the *New York Times* bestselling author of 87 books. Her numerous historical romances established her as an icon in the genre and a must-read for readers world wide. Coulter's readership has also grown exponentially with her hugely popular "unputdownable" FBI thriller series, starring the husband and wife team FBI agents Savich and Sherlock. Her FBI thrillers have expanded to include a new international thriller series—*A Brit in the FBI*—co-written with popular thriller writer J.T. Ellison. This six-book series has also captured a dedicated readership with high-stakes, fast-paced international cases involving new characters Nicholas and Mike. Coulter has also added a new novella series, starring Grayson Sherbrooke (from the *Sherbrooke* historical romance series), titled *The Grayson Sherbrooke Otherworldly Adventures*. (The *Grayson* books are available only in ebook.)

Coulter lives in northern California with her thriller cat Eli and her thriller husband. She enjoys hearing from readers and posts on her Facebook page daily. Please visit her at her website www. catherinecoulter.com for more information.

SUSPENSE MAGAZINE was founded in 2007 on the premise that every author in the genre needed a platform to have a voice. From that original concept, Suspense Publishing was born in 2010 to publish high quality books in the suspense/mystery/horror/thriller genre. Suspense Publishing's goal is to be a leader in producing the highest quality books in the genre.

*

If you enjoyed *Infinity*, check out:
Nothing Good Happens After Midnight
A Suspense Magazine Anthology

The sun sets. The moon takes its place, illuminating the most evil corners of the planet. What twisted fear dwells in that blackness? What legends attach to those of sound mind and make them go crazy in the bright light of day? Only *Suspense Magazine* knows…

Teaming up with *New York Times* bestselling author Jeffery Deaver, *Suspense Magazine* offers up a nail-biting anthology titled: *Nothing Good Happens After Midnight*. This thrilling collection consists of thirteen original short stories representing the genres of suspense/thriller, mystery, sci-fi/fantasy, and more.

Readers' favorites come together to explore the mystery of midnight. The 'best of the best' presenting these memorable tales, include: Joseph Badal, Linwood Barclay, Rhys Bowen, Heather Graham, Alan Jacobson, Paul Kemprecos, Shannon Kirk, Jon Land, John Lescroart, D. P. Lyle, Kevin O'Brien, and Hank Phillippi Ryan.

Take their hands…walk into their worlds…but be prepared to leave the light on when you're through. After all, this incredible gathering of authors, who will delight fans of all genres, not only utilized their award-winning imaginations to answer that age-old question of why *Nothing Good Happens After Midnight*—they also made sure to pen stories that will leave you…speechless.

ACKNOWLEDGMENTS

We'd like to thank Catherine Coulter and Karen Evans for their exceptional guidance and encouragement in making *Infinity* a reality.

The creation of this book was filled with challenges and seeing everyone's efforts come to fruition was emotional. During the journey, we lost a priceless and irreplaceable member of the family, author and editor-extraordinaire, Amy Lignor. *Infinity* was her final project and she'd be so proud to see it come to print.

We couldn't have done this without the support of the contributors and readers of *Suspense Magazine*. Your support and love over the years has meant more to us than you'll ever know.

Thank you to our talented and patient friends, who sat down and penned these amazing tales. Shannon and I don't have words for how special you all are to us. It really is a dream come true.

~John and Shannon Raab

Ingram Content Group UK Ltd.
Milton Keynes UK
UKHW011808060423
419751UK00001B/13